About the author

Stephen Gordon Smith resides in North Yorkshire living a contented life with his adorable wife, four noisy children and four very furry cats, a grouchy old dog, two goats and an insufferable pony. Thankfully, around 08:15, Monday to Friday his wife loads the children into a beat-up SUV and delivers them to school. Watching the SUV disappear Stephen recites a short prayer in support of the children's teachers.

The house, now tranquil provides him the time to fight with his computer, in particular his use of the English language; the two find it difficult to agree.

Stephen's wife is the family's chauffeur trying to balance music, drama and dance classes, and rugby and hockey games. Stephen admires his wife's fortitude managing four children and their endless number of friends who move in for sleep-overs and tea parties.

Somehow, thanks to his family's support he finds the time necessary to write.

Phantasmagorias, the Journey Concludes

By

S. G. Smith

 New Generation Publishing

This second and concluding part of one man's search for love is dedicated to the many people that filled his life; those who shared his journey of discovery; those that flitted in and out and to those that together formed the cornerstone the man built his life upon. However, predominantly it is dedicated to women, their extraordinary beauty and their phenomenal sense of joy, the pain and fear they endure, and the wonderful love he experienced when in their company.

Prologue

Discovering you are in love once more is vital for satisfying the exigency of a journey beset with a perpetual pendulum gratifying one's heart on the upswing and blighting it in the downswing.

The discovery of a woman who is committed to love and is in love and who you love is when the pendulum realises its zenith. You hope and pray the perpetual motion ceases, fixing its position, but alas the downswing returns and your zenith is replaced with nadir.

Unable to fathom why life presented him with such joy only to snatch it away and replace it with deep sadness, he changes. He becomes a rogue; lovable, but indifferent. His warm personality and deference for humanity evaporates creating a self-absorbed, hedonistic and callous individual intent on self-gratification.

Eventually his chameleon existence once more changes; he realises the years lost to grief and self-gratification were in fact an irredeemable search for love, a painful journey to rediscover joy and happiness with one woman.

Inadvertently he achieves his desperate search, finding, at last, love, and it is love, a lasting love he shares and enjoys with one woman. He asks for nothing more.

"When a man finds the woman he really loves, the one he respects and wants to call wife, there is nothing on earth he won't do for her. No mountain he won't hike. No river he won't wade. No door he won't open. She is Eve and there's not a snake crawling that can keep them apart." **Yolanda Joe**

Phantasmagorias Love

Continuing his journey, embracing life's splendour, the anti-hero is initiated in love, inflicted with pain and immersed in unremitting sadness.

In advance of the final phase of his journey he encountered many situations, some pleasant some not, in his life he was forced to confront. Similarly he encountered many people, some wishing him harm, fortunately most wishing him well.

However, he does not waiver, remaining convinced he will fulfil his aspiration and realise everlasting love with one woman. In this book, the final instalment, he achieves his desire.

"I may not have gone where I intended to go, but I think I have ended up where I needed to be." **Douglas Adams**

Chapter 1

It was a completely different Sophie the next morning; she expressed cheerfulness, smiled and laughed at the smallest thing, radiating a fantastic mood. Her mood signified yesterday hadn't happened. We breakfasted on fried eggs on toast with liberal supplies of bacon. We were back to normal, kissing and hugging, jesting and teasing, and life felt wonderful.

Sophie, her lips very close to mine and her arms wrapped round my neck, looking into my eyes, very quietly whispered, "From this moment we will never mention the future we will live each day by day and see what happens, do you agree?" I nodded agreement. My reward, a tender, loving kiss.

In a few days I would commence a proper job working as an engineer. In the meantime Sophie was going from strength to strength in her work, and I gave serious thought towards planning our future. I needed to confirm our love, we needed to confirm our love, which could only be achieved if I proposed marriage appropriately and Sophie accepted. The problem, how and when, the solution, unbeknownst to Sophie and me was just days away.

Sophie decided Friday should be "clean-house" day. We started upstairs, dusting, scrubbing, vacuuming and polishing. If it didn't move we assaulted it with hot soapy water, or a dry duster or polish. High and low level we cleaned the house. Sophie insisted on holding the ladder while I cleaned the outside of the windows.

The house cleaned to Sophie's pernickety standard, we attacked the office and garage. The office, although dusty, took no time at all. However, the garage proved to be a headache, a disorganised mess needing rolled-up sleeves, a great deal of lifting, moving, re-stacking and storing, until a huge pile of rubbish decorated the garden path ready for the dustman.

The day's work completed we showered and dressed and walked to the Indian Palace for dinner and a couple glasses of wine. Sauntering home, we were in a cheery mood with our arms linked, animatedly discussing Saturday's rugby game.

We were both eager to be amidst the rugby fraternity, basking in the marvellous atmosphere rugby games generate and also to re-connect with friends. And to relish the added bonus of listening to the "experts" regaling of the game, the warm comradery and the thrill, when with glass in hand, larynx and tonsils are sorely tested, singing in accompaniment with like-minded supporters, knowing each and every individual is immersed in the excitement of the day.

When we arrived home we packed ready for the following morning. Sophie expressed her excitement, looking forward to reliving the fun she had so much enjoyed previously.

Chapter 2 - England versus Scotland – The Proposal

Suddenly it is Saturday 20th March and once more we were heading for Twickenham to watch a rugby game; this time it would be England playing Scotland. We were only staying one night, Saturday. Hugo besides making all the arrangements to gain entry to his box had also managed to arrange a room in the same hotel as our last visit.

We arrived at the hotel shortly after eleven, checked in and went to the bar. There were several people we recognised and said hello. I scanned the bar, no sign of Hugo but the same barmaid worked behind the bar. Sophie remembered her name, Miriam. We ordered our drinks, Sophie opting for gin and tonic, expressing forcefully she would not become so intoxicated this time. I saw the barmaid's eyes suddenly sparkle; turning, I saw Hugo with three guys, including Bret and Casper, enter.

Hugo, ignoring me made a bee-line for Sophie. Hugging her he said, "So, young lady you are still with this good for nothing." He added, smiling, "What news, anything planned for the future?" He ordered four bottles of champagne saying, "You never know, one day we may be able to toast a special occasion." Sophie searched my face for a clue that would indicate what Hugo referred to. I shrugged my shoulders.

The day's routine would be the same as the French game, board the coach at one returning to the hotel after the game. Pulling Hugo to one side, knowing Sophie was watching I told him keep his big mouth shut and cease with the innuendos.

He looked at me and repeated his words from the previous month. "You're a fucking idiot." Changing the subject I thanked him for the invite and for arranging the hotel room. The champagne disappeared as quickly as it arrived, without touching the sides. During the guzzling we were introduced to fellow passengers. Names, never a strong point, flashed by; I caught Dorothy and Geraldine, and Chris but missed the rest. Sharp at one we were shepherded from the hotel to board the coach.

Sophie and I were sat together as the coach travelled towards the stadium. She wanted to know what Hugo had referred to and why I pulled him aside. I didn't want to lie but on this occasion I didn't have an option. I said, "He thinks I should move to Richmond, bringing you with me to work with him for his father's company, or rather one of his father's companies."

Sophie, not to be put off, pushed me for the type of company, what type of work, wanting to know the ins and outs of whatever we had discussed. I made the responses up as I went along digging a hole I doubted I would ever climb out of if she ever unearthed that my responses were pure fabrication. Eventually, thankfully, she stopped pushing.

Sophie wanted to search the stalls and soak up the atmosphere before going to the box. We said we would follow on. We were wearing the scarves Sophie had purchased during her first visit. This time she bought two Saint George decorated hats.

Noticing the Scots wearing traditional kilts she couldn't get over the sight. The Hugo thing forgotten, she completely immersed herself in the goings-on. I knew I had to forewarn Hugo of the coach conversation I had had with Sophie.

The box buzzed the mood full of merriment, everyone confident we would beat the Scots. The view from the box, although good did not generate the atmospheric sense of comradeship we had thrilled in watching the French game. Sophie quietly commented on this.

Two young ladies, the one from the coach and a colleague, ensured people's glasses were maintained with their chosen tipple. The buffet, proved to be an excellent presentation including caviar and champagne. Sophie hadn't tasted caviar before, however she made-up for lost-time relishing bread with caviar at regular intervals.

The game started, initially a pretty dour affair with much scrummaging and limited free-running rugby. Nonetheless England held a nine-five halftime lead thanks to the boot of Bob Hiller the full back. Brown for Scotland scored the only try of the half.

Half time was devoted to discussing the mistakes the English had made, particular attention being applied to the soft try the Scots scored. During those conversations I managed, unnoticed by Sophie, to put Hugo in the picture asking for his support. He shook his great head giving me a look. Quite clearly he thought me a poor excuse for a man.

The second half, also a dour forty minutes with one healthy positive, England had an emerging star in Fran Cotton who put himself about in a self-destruct manner, caring little for his opponents. If a player wore a blue shirt, he signalled open season to Cotton. He bulldozed his way through and over rucks determined to secure ball. Sophie admired his courage, openly stating it was a shame some of his team-mates didn't apply the same fire.

England lost by one lousy point. The dissatisfaction of the box, particularly palpable after the final whistle when heads dropped into hands and unfocused eyes stared down on to the chewed-up turf, became evident during the after-match summation.

One question was repeated: "How the hell could we lose to the Scots, especially at Twickenham." We had lost, which demanded some stiff drinks. Sophie, Hugo and I measured our intake. The alcohol won through as the box's inhabitants began to cheer up.

Dorothy, inebriated became very amorous, pulling Bret into the loo for some hanky-panky. Dorothy, a clerk who worked in one of Hugo's offices, was one of the girls, usually the attractive ones from his office, he invited to rugby games, to "add colour" by mixing the sexes. Hugo believed fervently that all male functions lacked the gaiety the company of woman enthused.

Coincidentally the same two Twickenham security chaps I had opened the box door to few weeks earlier again asked for the box to be emptied and the stadium cleared, which we did, boarding the coach for the return journey to the hotel.

Sophie although quite happy, enjoying the day, albeit not as enthralled as the previous visit to Twickenham, stridently stated, "We lost. We tied with the French after leading now we have lost to the Scots after leading. If you ask me the will to win is missing." Her vociferous deliberation raised a cheer. Hugo booming, yelled, "That's it Sophie my girl, you've hit the nail on the head."

The hotel bar, although there were thirty-plus customers, had the atmosphere of a morgue. The normal arguments about this player and that player, the questions, often the cause of debate asking, why did that happen? Why did he do that? Why did they select him?

We were in the company of supporters expecting to return to the bar and celebrate a glorious win, singing song after song and drinking pint after pint. Instead they were in mourning for their beloved England rugby team.

By mid-evening the ambience had improved considerably, the supporter's discussions returning to their clubs and the club's games due to played out before the end of season heralding discussions embracing the changing from shorts and shirts to white flannels and white shirts to play cricket.

Hugo, Casper and I were closeted together having our own discussion, Bret having disappeared with Dorothy. Sophie gestured, expounding her disappointment to two chaps from the box, both of whom were more interested in her than the rugby.

Hugo suddenly veered away from discussing rugby saying, "Now is a good time" Looking at him quizzically I said "Good time for what?"

"A good time to propose you idiot, Do it now and she will be yours. She will feel so special, the Queen of Sheba."

Casper, catching on agreed wholeheartedly saying, "Bloody hell, now, Richard and she will be mesmerised. She will look into your eyes and say "I do'." I realised a sense of mockery in his words, nonetheless I thought why not. Hugo, determined there may be a chance I could be persuaded, attacked me with verbalized romance describing the scene.

He could clearly see me on one knee, he explicated, Sophie looking at me in amazement when I propose. She will be overwhelmed. He wouldn't stop so he with Casper's support egged me on. I said, "Are you still prepared for the best man thing?"

He took my hand shaking and squeezing saying, "I would be honoured and proud to be your best man." His sincerity sparkled in his eyes.

Their bullying combined with alcohol, albeit not inebriated, convinced me they were right. I said, "Okay it's now or never."

He looked at me asking, "Are you sure?" I nodded. Hugo, his voice booming, called for hush, demanding absolute silence. All eyes, including Sophie's turned to face him. Some people edged forward.

"Sophie," I stammered, Hugo again signalled and called for hush. "I have a question for you, a very important question." She looked at me quizzically.

"Well, what is it?" she asked looking around the bar trying to understand why the sudden quietness. I dropped to my knee, the bar's crowd pushed forward realising what they were about to witness.

Ignoring my surrounds I looked up at Sophie into her beautiful face, she expressed utter confusion and said *"Life offers many challenges. I know we can meet and beat them if you will agree, no honour me, by becoming my wife forever and forever, for the rest of my life?"*

A pin could have dropped in that bar and it would have shattered the silence. Sophie's expression changed from confused to utter delight; she screeched, and yelled "Yes" and dived on top of me repeating, "Yes, yes, yes, yes". The bar went crazy.

Hugo's shovel-sized hands grabbed Sophie and lifted her above his head before lowering her to hug and kiss her. I lay on the floor, receiving hand-shakes and back-slapping. Sophie surrounded by a throng, sobbing uncontrollably and laughing, not knowing what to do, her eyes were darting everywhere searching for me. I managed to stand, seeing me she jumped into my arms kissing and kissing me. She couldn't stop sobbing, sobbing with immense joy.

The rugby game dead and buried, the rugby fans who love to party and sing had been presented with the perfect excuse. For the next hour or more the officially engaged couple became the centre of attraction as a series of wedding songs resonated around the bar.

Later in the evening, Sophie never leaving my side, the bar emptying, the supporters heading home or to meet with friends, some moving on to other pubs effected an eerie quietness. Hugo, Sophie, Casper, Miriam the barmaid and I clustered towards one end of the bar debating the effectiveness of Fran Cotton on his debut, when I sensed Miriam and Hugo, also sensed by Sophie, were more than just barmaid and customer.

Sophie, never one to hold back, still beaming and flushed with delight following my proposal, asked if they were courting. The Honourable Hugo for the first time in my company blushed. Sophie squealed, hugging Hugo.

During the next ten minutes we learnt that Hugo's father's business head offices were housed on the prestigious Richmond Green. Miriam, a late errant, studied at Richmond College. They had been courting for eighteen months. Sophie ordered a bottle of champagne to celebrate their courtship and our "official engagement".

Hugo told Sophie I had proposed to him before her. Sophie, her eyes on me asked, "What do you mean he proposed to you?"

Hugo, laughing, replied, "He didn't exactly get down on one knee but he did ask me a few weeks ago and once more this evening seeking confirmation I would honour him as his best man."

Sophie and Miriam now pouring the champagne were laughing while Casper, slightly the worse for drink, expressed an inane smile. Hugo continued, "You have to give him credit to get down on one knee in front of a crowd of drunken rugby players and supporters to propose. Actually if you think about it, a very romantic gesture, don't you think."

Sophie glowing said, "The most romantic moment of our whole time together. He has always been a romantic at heart and God bless him, we have had some magical romantic times but he has never, never made me as happy as I am this evening, never."

Sophie whispered in my ear that she wanted to be alone with me, asking if we could retire to our room, plus could we order sandwiches because she could feel hunger pangs. I nodded. I took Hugo's enormous paw in both my hands and thanked him for spurring me to propose. He grasped my hand saying, "Just tell me when and where and keep in touch to arrange the stag-night."

We asked Miriam if she could arrange sandwiches, she agreed she would. We said goodnight to Hugo and Casper, receiving a ragged cheer from the few remaining customers as we headed for the door hearing some wag singing, *"If he was the marrying kind, the kind of girl he would marry would be a rugby forward....."*

In the room we were pleasantly surprised to find an ice bucket complete with champagne, compliments of the hotel management and staff. I didn't think I could consume any more alcohol. I called to Sophie who by now had gone through to the bedroom, lying on the bed, she declined.

She signalled for me to lie beside her, which after kicking off my shoes and undoing the zip and pulling off her boots I flopped beside her. She nestled herself into my arms.

Sighing she said, "I have been worried you would never ask me. I had, nearly, concluded we would live in sin forever. And you sod, what a proposal, suddenly I became confused, flabbergasted and completely overcome, all within a matter of seconds, but my darling, the moment, oh the moment, so wonderful. Richard Chambers, I love you and love you and yes I will be your loving wife."

A knock on the door signalled the sandwiches, Miriam entered with a plate of sandwiches and a bowl of salad. She kissed me and hugged Sophie, who on hearing the knock joined me in the living room, wishing hearty congratulations.

Leaving the room she said, "By the way a bloke took some photographs, I have his contact details and will chase him for the negatives." Sophie, ecstatic knowing there would be photographs depicting the proposal hugged and thanked Miriam.

Sophie obviously starving, attacked the sandwiches as if there wouldn't be a tomorrow. In between mouthfuls she murmured, "I think the champagne would be appropriate for two, what is it your father calls us, oh I know, two star-struck lovers." I managed to salvage half a sandwich.

While I popped the champagne Sophie said, "When you dropped onto your knee, the fact you were going to propose didn't enter my mind, and when you said those beautiful words. I wanted to scream, overcome, yes, completely overcome. I know I screeched and then I dived on top of you on the floor. My mind scrambled, I couldn't stop saying yes. What did I look like?"

I smiled saying, "I have no idea-- I had a demented woman on top of me smothering me in kisses yelling yes, yes."

Sophie suddenly serious said, "You have been the most loving, the most attentive and the most beautiful man a woman could ever ask for. You discharge happiness throughout my mind and throughout my body. I never know what wonderful surprise, or what wonderful words are coming next."

Her voicing breaking she continued, "Living with and loving you for the rest of our lives, will always be the most extraordinarily wondrous experience any woman could ask for, and I am the lucky one because I have you, I am so…, so amazingly ecstatic I can't articulate exactly the feelings I am being subjected to, and I doubt I ever will."

Sophie's beautiful green eyes fast becoming tearful held my hand very tightly, in a whisper she added, "Thank you, Richard Chambers for loving me."

Becoming emotional I squeezed her hand. "Sophie," I responded, "There isn't a man on this planet, or indeed any other planet who couldn't love you. Nor is there a man who wouldn't see and feel the love and goodness in your heart. Who couldn't fail to realise that you are a woman who loves with total commitment, a commitment that necessitates, nay demands, a positive and robust love in return."

I hesitated for a moment. "But most of all it is the pleasure I feel loving you, just being with you. My feelings and the love I have for you is immeasurable beyond the limits of life itself."

We, slowly and solemnly, melted into each other's arms very content with life, very content to be in love and very content to be in a deeply satisfying embrace.

Sophie's embrace I felt a surge of relief and I could feel extreme contentment after finally beating my demons, I had actually proposed, a warmth spread through my body.

I owed The Honourable Hugo the utmost respect and appreciation for making me see beyond my nose, and for making me realise I had a woman who loved me with a love so rare yet so beautiful, yes I owed Hugo.

I opened my eyes three wall lights were shining as were the two beside lights. I could feel the cold the coldness had woken me up. I couldn't move my left arm, it was under and holding Sophie. I had to move.

We were still in our clothes, Sophie with her two sweaters and jeans and I wearing jeans and shirt. Where had I put my Guernsey? Glancing down towards Sophie I marvelled at her serenity, the little laughter lines, and her beauty. She slept, at peace with the world.

I kissed her purposefully, waking her. Her eyes flickered open she smiled a bright and loving smile whispering, "My man, my loving lovely man." She closed her eyes. I eased my arm from underneath her warm body.

Off the bed I wandered into the bathroom and relieved myself, washing my hands I checked the time, six-ten. I walked through the bedroom, pulling the bed cover over Sophie and turned the lights off as I passed into the living room. I sat in one of the easy chairs looking over the room, trying to remember the events of a very memorable day. I noticed the champagne bottle upside down in the ice-bucket but I couldn't remember drinking the fizz, nor could I remember how we ended-up fully clothed on the bed.

Rugby songs and Hiller's first try for England were prominent in my thinking before the whole day began to unfurl before me. My proposal, how did I do that in front of thirty or forty strangers? The songs, which started with the first verse of *"Daisy, Daisy"*, quickly followed by *"Love and Marriage"* and the inevitable *"If he was the marrying kind"*. I recalled the well-wishing from strangers and all the hugging and hand-shaking.

Most of all I remembered the brief conversation with Hugo, he with his arm round my shoulders chastising me for being an idiot if I didn't propose and propose quickly. He could see much more than I; he acknowledged without qualms that Sophie and I belonged together.

I remembered the decision I made as Sophie turned to look towards Hugo wanting to know why he called for hush. I remembered her green eyes and then I was on one knee, the bar hushed. God I would never forget that moment.

I remembered how the despondency of the rugby supporters caused by the game's result had changed they had been given something to celebrate, to become full of merriment with jokes and laughter flying here and there.

I could see very clearly Sophie's happiness with the day, remembering her marvelling how rugby supporters were so boisterous and so full of song. I recalled how she loved the atmosphere generated within the stadium, the game, which she had thought magnificent but also sad because we had lost. I sat, thinking I too am at peace with the world.

I wondered where Hugo and Miriam were, hoping they could feel, if they wanted to, the love for each other Sophie and I had. I thought of Sophie's parents, my parents and Tina and all matters pertinent to Sophie and me.

Sophie, sliding onto my lap and kissing me awake, startled me for a moment. Opening my eyes I looked upwards to be greeted by the most radiant smile and a face aglow with happiness. My Sophie hugging her man, her fiancé, and she could feel I loved her back with all my might. I hoped and silently prayed the "sea" would be pushed to the back of her mind, probably still there but dissolving, freeing her of worry.

Sophie sitting upright on my knee said, "What happened? I remember the sandwiches and the opening of the champagne, I remember we toasted our love but afterwards, for the life of me, I cannot recall what happened. Why did I wake-up fully dressed? Darling Fiancé."

"My darling," I smilingly said, "I haven't a clue. I too remember the toast and also, admittedly vaguely, pouring a second glass of champagne. I awakened cold, went to relieve myself and wandered in here to recollect the day's events. Obviously I fell asleep because you have just wakened me."

I checked my watch; we were too late for breakfast. I suggested we hit the road stopping off for lunch on the way home. Once we had cleared London Sophie closed her eyes and slept. I drove steadily, not wanting to disturb her.

We were south of Crawley when she awakened asking where we were. Sitting upright, after I told her roughly where, she asked me to slow down. She said, "There's a pub off to the right, if you haven't passed the turning, mum and dad have dined at, on occasion. I can't remember its name." Silence as she searched the road for the appropriate turn off, then, "Yes I can it's the Chequers."

We passed close to a village called Handcross, which sparked her memory. "Take the next right. I am sure it's down there somewhere."

"Somewhere, could you be a little more scientific?" I smilingly asked. I took the next right.

Less than a mile and I pulled into a car-park in front of The Chequers Inn. I went to exit the car, intending to open Sophie's door. However, she held me back pulling me close to kiss me. The kiss lingered, I enjoyed the attention.

Sophie whispered, "I will never know how you came to propose in a bar full of strangers but I will tell you this, an unbelievably romantic moment. There isn't a woman in the world who could ever expect to receive such a loving proposal, a wondrous moment I will cherish all my life, and yours too."

Sophie once more kissed me, another loving, lingering kiss saying, nay demanding I repeated the words I had proposed to her with. I had to remember; satisfied, I whispered, *Life offers many challenges. I know we can meet and beat them if you will honour me, by becoming my wife forever and forever, for the rest of our lives?* I missed out the word "agree", purposefully also changing "my life" for "our lives".

I wasn't sure whether I couldn't remember exactly what I had proposed or whether my sub-conscious implemented the alterations. It didn't matter to Sophie she held on to me and silently wept. After a while she asked me to have the words printed professionally and framed ready for when we married and for our own home.

Sophie, her tummy demanding food, finally uttered her favourite phrase "I am starving" and laughed. We entered the Chequers enjoying roast beef with all the trimmings accompanied with a glass of red wine, a jolly good lunch in a pleasant ambience.

After using the facilities and paying we departed for home looking for a garage with a service shop to purchase limited groceries. We managed to purchase milk and a sliced loaf. With relief I pulled into the home straight the familiar sight of Sophie's Mini heralding we were home.

We unpacked, loaded the washing machine and sat in the kitchen enjoying mugs of tea. Sophie recalled the match day events, expressing her sorrow that England had lost. And asking when we could go to all the other Five Nation team's grounds I had mentioned. I suggested we place the names in a hat and choose which one we would visit first, second and so on. Pleased with my suggestion Sophie leaned closer and kissed me on the nose.

Reaching behind, Sophie tugged a calendar magnetised to the fridge door and said, "Are you absolutely certain we met on the 7th August?"

I confirmed, emphasising absolutely, adding it would be impossible to forget. Abruptly she excitedly yelled, "Richard, Richard the 7th is a Saturday can we be married on that day it is so important, so symbolic. Please say yes."

I said, "Yes".

In less than six months we would be married, married on 7th August 1971. Sophie sighed full of happiness. I felt the same happiness. She placed her arms across my shoulders saying, "We will beat the sea, we will."

Sophie wanted to inform her parents, she checked the time deciding we would go to the Bear. Before leaving she made me telephone mother first followed by my father.

Mother was pleased and after speaking to Sophie the receiver back with me she told me I had a wonderful girl and to look after her. Father, quite simply said, "About time," and wished us well, adding him and Tina expected a visit.

In the Bear Sophie's mother cried and cried. Ken yelled and dished out free drinks. The pub's customers proffered congratulations. Sophie cried and hugged and kissed anyone and everyone.

Chapter 3 - Life Histories and the Celebration Weekend

We arranged the following weekend to celebrate our intended wedding and new career at the Eastbourne hotel using the reservation I had given Sophie for Christmas, which now seemed a life-time away. We collected the arranged Tuxedo and popped into the Bear.

Irene, Ken and Joe were pleased to see us. Sophie, in particularly good form, happily expressed how she couldn't wait for the weekend, looking forward to being with the love of her life.

We straddled stools, saying hello to regulars and some of the irregulars we recognised. The bar being busy emanated a lively atmosphere, it seemed very happy. One or two, probably more came over to speak to either Sophie or I asking where we had been, what we were up to, and some proffering congratulations. We laughed off the constant joshing and settled to enjoy a delightful hour pending the pub closing.

We helped clean the bar and prepare for the evening session. We learnt Josie, now full-time working five lunchtimes and evenings, would be opening with her mother Gwynne, one or the other going home at eight-thirty when Joe or Ken or both provided relief.

The biggest surprise was that Irene and Ken were flying to Newcastle for an extra-long weekend to meet with Tina and father. Joe had organised a friend of his to drive Irene and Ken to Heathrow and also collect on the return journey. Father would organise transport in Newcastle. Both were excited.

We released the news regarding the job I had landed, explaining a reasonably good position in Southampton, which raised eyebrows (not the job but Southampton). Bombarded with questions relative to my position with Maybury, I answered the best I could but I didn't admit the full title of my position, Trainee Marine Engineer-- well I did, accidentally-on-purpose forgetting the word Trainee.

We chatted, generally enjoying a comfortable aura, relaxed and happy. Sophie said we should to go home, pack and drive to Eastbourne. The goodbyes, hugs and see-you-soon comments dispelled we departed.

Once home we finalised packing for the weekend leaving for Eastbourne observing a watery sun, slowly diminishing over the horizon. We briefly debated whether we should take the A27 or the coast road, and the coast road won.

In under an hour we were registering as Mr and Mrs Gladstone, at which time we reserved a table for dinner.

We were directed to a junior suite with a clear view of the English Channel. The suite, lavishly decorated, comfortable had the biggest bed I had ever seen. After the porter departed Sophie climbed onto the bed utilising it as a trampoline. I laughed shouting "Careful, don't forget you are a helephant," which encouraged Sophie to spring higher.

Actually the bed wasn't springy enough to project Sophie too high. She reached out with her hand, which I interpreted as a signal to help her climb down from the bed when in fact she gave a terrific tug, further strengthened when she fell backwards onto the bed. On the bed she began to tenderly kiss my eyes, neck, cheek and lips. I responded with ardour, which ignited a frenzy of kissing and hugging as we simultaneously stripped, wrestling naked.

Out of breath, naked and laughing Sophie insisted I stood upright on the bed. I did her bidding thinking, "what is she up to?" Sophie climbed off the bed so I went to lower myself. Jolly Roger stirred.

Sophie ardently insisted I remain standing. Walking round the bed she declared, "Richard Chambers you have no idea what a wonderful male specimen you are, do you?" Before I could respond she went on, "Your height, what is it, six-two," I nodded, "Is impeccably balanced by your breadth of your upper body with its flat stomach, your long muscular legs."

I began to feel embarrassed; however, Sophie wasn't finished. "You walk like a god, you are passionate and sensitive, and you make love as only a god can. And I know and I feel your love for me. You are a prize catch and I caught you." Jolly Roger during her inspection wrinkled-up and went to sleep. "Lie down," she commanded.

Sophie lay down beside me, her arm laying across my chest her lips nibbling me ears. Jolly Roger began to rouse himself. Sophie caressed my torso, my legs and kissed my feet before running her tongue up my legs tickling my inner thighs, taking a fully aroused penis into her mouth.

Her mouth was extraordinarily gentle she utilised her tongue until I shivered and moaned. Satisfied she climbed aboard, gradually lowering herself. I shivered as sensation after sensation shot up Jolly Roger's shaft. Sophie moaned saying, "You also have a penis, Jolly Roger, most women would kill for." She pushed hard down. I responded arching my back and pelvis to thrust upwards.

Together we raced towards fulfilling the intuitive sexual demands we both craved. I could feel my sperm ready to explode. Sophie's vagina muscles were tightening, relaxing, and tightening signifying she also neared eruption, and we did, in sensational harmony bonded together wholly committed to pleasuring each other. Sophie squealed, not her usual loud scream but a never-ending squeal that mingled in with my whistling sigh, harmony in love.

Laying on the bed with Sophie's leg casually laying over my penis, her warm thigh offering protection I started singing an old Cliff Richard song;

"Once in every lifetime, comes a love like this.
I need you and you need me.
Oh my darling can't you see."

Sophie intervened, "At long last the message has finally reached the man's brain, glory halleluiah." We remained clasped in each other's arms, occasionally kissing, gently caressing and saying very little, very content.

Although we had reserved a table for eight o'clock, my watch registered twenty past before we sat down to dine. Sophie wearing a white dress, I am absolutely certain the dress designer's intention, his, or her vision envisaged a portrayal of innocence.

The long sleeved dress, its length extending a few inches below the knees, trimmed with pale yellow lace, Sophie wore emanated exquisite loveliness. The designer obviously hadn't taken into account the affect a beautiful dazzling woman with cascading auburn locks would have on the dress.

Sophie looked amazing, the dress elaborated every curve of her beautiful body, further it enhanced the colour of her hair, the brightness of her green eyes and exaggerated the length of her legs. An enchantress, her arm linked to mine, entered the dining room.

I looked to the diners knowing as we entered I escorted a flawless and stunning woman upon my arm. People, especially the males stopped eating to look, a hush descended over the room. Those diners with their back towards Sophie swivelled to see what their partners were admiring.

Earlier in our suite I had experienced a similar awe the diners were now experiencing.

When I told her how beautiful she looked, typical of Sophie, I received a big smile accompanied with the words, "Don't be silly Richard, I am beautiful to you because you love me-- not all men love me."

I thought to myself at the time, "My girl, your innocence is refreshing, your beauty is sensuous, but you would be shocked, possibly upset if you had the slightest inkling what passes through men's minds when they see you."

For some reason we both decided on dine on fish and crustaceans. Sophie selected a prawn cocktail followed by haddock broiled in butter while I chose half a dozen oysters accompanied by Dover sole grilled, also in butter.

With the crustaceans starters we opted for a glass each of Prosecco and for the main course a glass of Chardonnay, a delightful fruity wine. We skipped desserts, preferring to hold hands and whisper loving endearments, after which we retired to the bar for coffee and cognac. The evening, loving and warm, romantic and interlaced with tenderness, will always be remembered.

In bed Sophie persisted and persisted until I agreed to clarify with more detail the story of my life I originally glossed over in the Bugle Inn, Southampton.

For a long while I reminisced, remembering the good and the bad albeit the good times far out-numbered the bad. I told of starting life in Southsea, living in Osterley and Southampton. Schools close to relatives and of travelling through life attempting to understand the trials and tribulations one encountered during childhood and the teenage years.

I recalled, not all, unhappy times; I extolled my enjoyment of school and college. I mentioned Freda, Stan the landlord, both my grandparents, aunts and uncles, and talked endlessly of the periods I spent with Grandma Jean and Granddad George in Silverdale. I proudly exclaimed of my prowess at rugby and cricket and how I would swim and jog to keep fit. I ended my reminiscence exclaiming how lucky I had been when I walked into a pub called the Bear in Hove to observe the most beautiful woman to walk upon God's earth.

Sophie for whatever reason presented a coquettish smile, becoming very flirtatious. "Okay," I said, "I have finished-- your turn to regale me with your life and I promise not to laugh."

"No it's not," she said. "You haven't told all."

"Yes I have, unless you are insistent upon hearing nonsense or irrelevant episodes," I replied.

Sophie smiling, her eyes glistening said, "No, I accept you have drawn a pretty accurate picture but my darling, now I want to hear all there is to tell about your sex life. I want to know who taught you to be such an accomplished and experienced lover. I want to know how and why you are so sexually sensitive."

"Sophie," I said with exasperation, "That is totally unfair and unreasonable, and why for goodness sake would you want to know who they were."

"Aha," she shrilled, "There was more than one, you said they."

"Probably."

Not satisfied, Sophie climbed over me, her face close to mine saying, "I want to know who, where and when."

"Why for goodness sake, be reasonable sweetheart. It would be an act of betrayal," I cried.

"You know all there is to know regarding my sexual activities, so why can't I know yours," she demanded.

"Fine," I retorted, "I will reveal the basics but that is all you are getting, okay?"

"No, I want to know who the number one tutor and the older woman were, who taught you anal sex, oral sex and the sensitivity you express during our love-making," she responded in her schoolgirl voice.

"Why for heaven's sake," I retorted my voice tinged with an edge.

"At last," she said, "You want to know why. I will tell you why my darling man, so I can write to her or is it them, and thank her or those, responsible for sending the most wonderful loving lover in the world for me to enjoy." Her piece said, my darling Sophie went into hysterics rolling back and forth laughing madly, laughing so much she had to rush to the bathroom.

Coming back into the bedroom she climbed into bed, snuggling close. Once comfortable she said, "There is no need for detail, just tell me "the basics" as you called it." I rushed through my memory bank, mentioning the loss of my virginity to a girl three years older than I, the few girls during my first year in college, Cheryl, Suzy and Sandra without mentioning names and one or two others, and Ruth, again without mentioning names and finally Jocelyn who I referred to as an older woman.

I emphasised that since we had met she was the only woman I had loved or had made love to. Sophie kissed my cheek saying, "Three words, eight letters, spell I LOVE YOU," closed her eyes and went to sleep. I thought, "Bloody hell I will never understand women," and I too went to sleep.

I heard knocking on the bedroom door and I heard the word breakfast. I jumped out of bed grabbing a bath robe and answered. I had completely forgotten we had ordered breakfast in the room.

The waiter entered, observing Sophie, who sat up in bed with a sheet providing modesty, laid the table sited by the window saying, "Looks as if today will be quite nice Sir, Madam." I picked-up the loose change I had deposited on the bedside table passing him fifty or sixty pence.

Sophie rose gracefully to stand on the bed allowing the sheet to tantalisingly slide down her body, she reached high with both arms lifting her nipple hard breasts then collapsed, falling in a heap kicking her legs high in the sky, commencing to move her legs in a cycling motion. For some reason her display caused Jolly Roger to react.

Breakfast disregarded, I moved to the bed, opened Sophie's legs and drove Jolly Roger home. Sophie moaned saying, "I hoped you would." She forced her legs round my head making sure I went deep into her. We were riding a rollercoaster together, our love full of promise, our connectivity sincere, we loved being in love.

Sophie tried to stifle her screams. Climaxing stifling, normally, would be the last thing on Sophie's mind, and it transpired this time wasn't any different, she did scream expressing her pleasure. I swiftly followed firing my sperm up against her cervix. She cried with pleasure, "I love it so much when I feel your sperm, it's such a thrilling feeling. And I love you so much it hurts, do not ever, forget, I love you so much it hurts, do not forget those words."

Slightly perplexed I stayed silent lying in Sophie's arms. "Bath time," she shouted, pushing me from her body. "Then, my super fit man we are jogging. I'll go first." I queried "Together?"

"No," she loudly exclaimed displaying a mischievous smile, "You have ravished me, filled me with your sperm and now you want to bathe with me. Absolutely not, I need solace." Dancing into the bathroom she closed and locked the door.

I remained motionless thinking back to the past few weeks after we had made the decision to regain fitness. The three weekly sessions in the gym, which had initially been one hell of a challenge we had overcome. The two games of squash we played each week, which started as one game.

And the Saturday morning five-hundred yard swims at the swimming baths plus the twice-weekly jogs along the promenade sometimes as late as ten o'clock at night. Even our food intake had altered-- bacon and sausage sandwiches were history, and instead Sophie expected me to enjoy pieces of rolled up cardboard, commonly known as Muesli, every morning saturated in disgusting soya milk. Ugh!

Sophie had argued we should pack our jogging kits and jog at least once over the weekend or the hard yards in the gym we were putting in would be wasted. My view simply aspired to a weekend in a posh hotel with a gorgeous woman translated into two nights of decadence and two days intertwined with decadence. Hey-ho, Sophie made sure I would enjoy both jogging and decadence.

After all the years we have been together I still couldn't get over Sophie's complete ignorance of her beautiful body; she displayed it quite shamelessly, especially at that moment, delving into her suitcase to unpack her jogging gear displaying her delicious bottom, her vagina and anus vividly exposed. Wearily exhaling a loud sigh, I moped my way into the bathroom.

Leaving an untouched breakfast we ran down the broad staircase, Sophie, in the lead called back that we should grab something light to eat washed down with black tea and fruit juice. At the bottom of the staircase she trotted on the spot, calling to the slow coach to get a move on.

The reception staff and the guests reading Sunday papers in the adjacent lounge were all watching and hearing Sophie. I arrived bowed towards the lounge before tailing behind Sophie into the breakfast room.

The head waiter raised his eyebrows rushing over he said, "Madam, Sir, the breakfast, is there something wrong?" Obviously aware we had ordered breakfast to be served in our room, he politely requested whether the breakfast had fallen below the hotel's high standards.

18

Sophie flippantly replied, "By the time we were ready it had gone cold." Hovering he asked what we would like. Sophie ordered for two, two scrambled eggs with grilled tomatoes, pot of tea and not to bother with the milk and sugar and two glasses of fresh fruit juice, emphasising that the flavour was unimportant but that it must be freshly squeezed fruit.

Looking at me as he scribbled the order I could read his brain clicking over and over thinking, "She may be beautiful but by golly she's got you under her thumb." He did not know my Sophie.

While waiting, Sophie dispatched me to the concierge for a map displaying walks. Spreading the map we decided we would jog to Beachy Head and back, approximately six miles if we switched between coastal path and South Downs Way.

Afterwards we would utilise the hotel's swimming pool and sauna. A waiter delivered two orange juices to the table in half-pint glasses. Sophie tasting the content expressed her pleasure to the waiter. "Well done, very good."

The lumpy, tasty juice had obviously required the kitchen staff to squeeze several fresh oranges to fulfil Sophie's specific demand. The scrambled eggs and tomatoes consumed, we took our time drinking the tea to ensure the food digested sufficiently not to impede jogging. Breakfast over we exited the hotel walked towards the main road and crossed over onto South Downs Way.

Sophie considered me to be the family's expert jogger. On the other hand, Sophie, without doubt, represented the family in the swimming pool, much stronger than me. In fact on those Saturday mornings I would religiously swim ten fifty-yard lengths; by the time I completed the five-hundred yards, Sophie would be sitting pool-side at the opposite end of the pool. I would swim an extra fifty yards to be with her.

The final fifty yards, using the breaststroke as opposed to freestyle encouraged Sophie, when I reached her, to jump on me playfully followed by five or more minutes frolicking and play-wrestling. Those few minutes more than compensated for the five hundred and fifty yard toil.

When we reached the path we would follow to Beachy Head, I lazily set off with Sophie tagging five yards behind, gradually easing our bodies into cohesion without causing any strains. Once into the rhythm I would slowly, not on purpose, extend the distance leaving Sophie thirty-plus yards behind.

Often I would run on past the objective of the jog for fifty yards, turning to reach the objective simultaneously with Sophie. We didn't rest but turned and re-traced the jog's route. When the Grand's entrance came into view I slowed to affect a cooling down routine.

Sophie caught up with me. Together in full view we undertook stretching exercises coupled with controlled breathing to gently return the body back to normal. Satisfied, we crossed the road returning to our room.

In the room we showered and put on swimming costumes and the hotel's bath robes, making our way to the pool. The pool thankfully wasn't fifty yards in length, probably ten. A guy swimming lengths heading towards Sophie suddenly stopped. For an instance I thought he could be in trouble, before I realised Sophie had kicked off her slippers and removed her robe, standing resplendent in her "itsy-bitsy" bikini.

We identified the deep end and dived in, hearing a whistle when we surfaced, a life guard shaking his head indicated a huge sign stating "NO DIVING". We acknowledged his signalling.

We started swimming. I raced Sophie for the first few lengths, holding my own. Thereafter I ended up following in her wake. We hadn't been swimming for long when, unfortunately, the pool began to fill with guests, in my experience an unusual occurrence. The numbers curbed our exercise putting a stop to swimming lengths. Sophie hauled herself out standing to her full height pool-side.

It then dawned on me that all the swimmers were male and they had come to ogle. I winked at Sophie and we both displayed very, very broad smiles before she slipped into the pool, gracefully swimming two strokes to reach me. Show time, similar to New Year's Eve, the time had come to give the voyeurs something to write home about.

She grabbed my head, climbed all over me, planting one of her all-encompassing kisses. Display over we climbed out of the pool, attired ourselves with the bath robes and ended our swim.

Dressing in the room Sophie innocently asked, "Why are men such pricks?"

"Sophie, you swore," I said grinning ear to ear.

"Did I, oh well." I honestly believe she hadn't realised. Continuing she added, "If they want to ogle there are plenty of girlie magazines, I have seen them in the newsagents."

"I am sorry my darling, you have two overriding advantages a nude or partially nude girl in a magazine does not have," I said with a chuckle.

"Have I? What are they?" she responded, losing interest.

Still chuckling loving her innocence I told her that girls in magazines were not as beautiful as she, nor could they hold a light to her poise and intelligence. Further, I told her that those men came to see her, yes because of her beauty but also because she stood before them in the flesh, almost within touching distance.

I laughed coarsely saying, "I bet they are all in their respective bathrooms relieving themselves." Sophie grunted, not amused.

Changing tack, she asked the time. "Coming up to midday," I answered. Mournfully, still upset by the ogling and maybe my coarseness she said, "What shall we do for the rest of the day?"

I replied with a bow, "Sir Galahad is at your service your Ladyship, he will, being ever resourceful run down to reception and ask." I managed to squeeze a smile from her.

Returning I said, "Rye looks interesting. It is a medieval town built on a mound once surrounded by the sea. Now it offers the chance to meander through its ancient streets, explore its alleyways and if we are lucky a tearoom may be open. Besides it is sunny and reasonably warm so it could be enjoyable."

"Where is Rye, is it far?" she asked.

"The concierge reckons roughly an hour's drive if we by-pass Hastings," I informed her. With resignation Sophie retorted, "Okay, okay Mr Tourist Guide, let's go to Rye."

Conceivably it could have been the sunshine or perhaps because Rye is a pretty town, even in early spring. Nevertheless, we had fun. We made the journey in fifty minutes in time to have a drink in a 15th century inn, which had a terrific atmosphere, although when Sophie entered all eyes were on her until I walked in behind.

The inn, extremely busy, did not deter Sophie, sweetly smiling repeating, "Excuse me, excuse me," she pushed her way close to the bar; magically we were afforded space. Sophie opted for half a shandy and I ordered a pint of ginger-beer shandy. We supped the beer, recognising the quaintness of the pub. Sophie chatting away expressed how she looked forward to this's evenings dancing.

Shandies consumed, we commenced touring Rye. Sophie peered into shop windows, particularly the antique shops. We studied the various landmarks. We played hide and seek in amongst alleyways and streets, thoroughly enjoying ourselves. Sophie hiding her eyes to count to twenty, called aloud one, ten, twenty, I am coming. I had no chance.

We ambled around the fishing boat harbour and expressed joy when spotting one of the many interesting houses or an unusual design. Rye thoroughly explored we strolled back to the car returning to Eastbourne. Sophie noticed a road sign indicating Battle and said, "Could we have a look at Battle?"

I drove round the streets of the town, which contained some beautiful Georgian homes, which Sophie thought splendid. We found the abbey Norman the Conqueror built, supposedly resting the abbey's altar upon the area where King Harold had died. In the vicinity of the abbey, an array of cottages and houses clustered close provided a picturesque setting. The cottages looked inviting.

Leaving Battle behind, closing on Eastbourne Sophie quietly asked, "How do you do it Richard Chambers?"

"Do what my love?" I queried.

"Find interesting, often pretty places to charm me, or if you prefer to entertain me. You always manage to find something, somewhere I enjoy seeing or visiting, so I repeat my question, how do you do it?"

Yet again I found myself flummoxed-- why did Sophie, as she so often did, have this knack of putting me on the spot. "Sophie, I asked the hotel's concierge a couple of questions relative to local places of interest. He passed me the information. I glanced through it suspecting Rye would be worth a visit."

"Exactly, exactly my point, you glanced through a brochure suspecting, your word, Rye would be worth a visit. No, Richard Chambers what you did, as you always do, you studied several brochures or whatever, you then considered me, before deciding what I would be happiest with. Isn't that the truth?" she exclaimed, turning to stare at my profile.

"Sophie, have I upset you?" I quietly asked. "You sound angry."

"Damn right I am angry not with you but with me. You think of nothing else but me. You are not happy unless I am happy." I kept quiet.

Returning her eyes to the road she said, "I love you so very much that I am unable to express exactly how much I love you. Remember the languages and dictionaries I once mentioned wouldn't be capable of expressing the words I wanted to express. Well nothing has changed I cannot express, proclaim, shout or expound the level of my love. Saying I love you is insufficient and ineffective in so many ways."

In a whisper she continued, "Richard do you realise my love for you is higher than the highest mountain, deeper than the deepest ocean, stronger than the strongest element known to mankind, my love is eternal, my love is beyond the moon, the sun, beyond everything." Sophie's next words were a very loud command. "For Christ's sake stop the bloody car I want a hug."

I pulled into a farm gate entrance. "Not here, somewhere private I am wet, very wet I need you inside me."

Three or four hundred yards further on I noticed a farm track on my left leading towards what looked like derelict buildings and without indication I turned onto the track. A blast of a horn and a threatening fist and the car bounced along a bumpy unmade road.

I pulled up alongside two buildings, quite clearly in need of attention, I searched the area. "Richard, can you see anyone? Are we alone?"

"Yes my little angel, we are alone," I replied.

The next moment Sophie dragged me from the car heading towards the smaller of the two dilapidated buildings. Entering the dust-filled outbuilding, Sophie daintily removed her cream-coloured panties.

Leaning against a wall supporting her body with her arms, her body bent I pulled up her skirt displaying her beautiful bottom, she quietly whispered, "Richard I need you now." I unbuckled my belt easing Levis down my legs.

Jolly Roger, less than half way into her, when she started to scream and scream. "Oh my God, Jesus, I wanted you so badly, I thought I would die." Sophie came, spasm after spasm.

Jolly Roger, albeit hard and proud, waited, unsure what to do. Sophie resolved the situation she said, "Push in Richard, push." I pushed deeper. Sophie went into ecstasy twice more heralding orgasms. Bewildered by her rapid orgasms I pushed hard. "Stop" she cried, "No more"

I withdrew my penis, puzzled and mystified I pulled by Levis up and re-buckled my belt. The extent of my involvement, a big fat zero, yes, Jolly Roger had penetrated her vagina. Yes I pushed him in deeper, but no more than that. I didn't move in and out, thrust or pummel, there hadn't been the need, or the time.

I held Sophie's hand helping her to balance as she, unusually unladylike used her panties to clean my penis and wipe between her legs, discarding the panties into a corner. Sophie, smiling coyly took my hand and pulled me close kissing me, a touch embarrassed by her antics.

Returning to the car, she asked for music, I pushed a Four Tops compilation into the cassette player. She listened for some moments, reached over reducing the volume. She twisted in her seat, took my right hand in both of hers, facing me she said, "I am sorry for my disturbing behaviour. I couldn't help it. I needed you, desperate to have you inside, to feel you, I literally experienced pain in my chest and my head spun. I could sense wetness seeping from my vagina, which at first I didn't understand, then I realised the wetness reinforced the need for you." I gently pulled her into my arms.

Uncomfortable we stayed huddled together watching the evening close around. I whispered into her hair, "If you want to dance tonight my lovely, we need to return to the hotel, if not, no problem, we will remain here." She moved her head to look at me. "Yes my man, my very own man I would like to dance, dance secure in your arms."

I started the car turning to return to the main road.

Dressed in the tuxedo, ready to descend to the ballroom I sat watching Sophie drying her hair. Her hair had always fascinated me. Within minutes she would wash, dry and brush, and bang, it faultlessly cascaded onto her shoulders. Her hair, naturally luxuriant, the auburn colour resplendent, with an eye-catching sheen, always looked perfect. Looking at me through the dressing-table mirror she blew a kiss saying, "You are an incredibly handsome man."

Satisfied with her hair Sophie stood, naively modelling the briefest of panties, suspenders and stockings stoking memories of the wonderful New Year party just three months previous. She crossed gracefully to the wardrobe affording an opportunity to feast upon her unquestionable loveliness.

Stepping into the blue gown she turned her back so I could complete the zipping and secure the clasp. I gently ran my hands up her body stopping at her breasts, which I affectionately grasped.

Sophie pushed her head back under my chin whispering, "I love you Richard."

"And I love you my Sophie," I huskily responded. "And my darling you look absolutely stunning. You are a naturally beautiful woman, naturally radiating warmth and an amazing fragrance. What is the fragrance, it is incredible?"

My last words momentarily muted the moment. Sophie rescued the situation, turning to rest against me she quietly whispered, "Guerlain Shalimar, a perfume representing a love story, which could be our love story." She gently brushed my lips with hers. I looked into her green eyes responding to her brushing of the lips with ardour. Tenderly she pushed clear lifting her clutch bag to replace the lipstick I had just removed.

Descending the imperial staircase with Sophie's arm elegantly draped round my shoulders signalling I belonged to her. We walked towards the ballroom following the sound of music, elegance personified; we were two beautiful people.

An attractive young lady waiting at the entrance wearing a sleek gold gown, she too looked good. "Good evening Madam, Sir; Mr and Mrs Gladstone?" she asked.

I responded, "Good evening and yes." She took the lead asking we followed her. I could feel a hundred eyes or more. Looking ahead I could only see one empty table, which annoyingly, was set bang smack in the centre of the room, providing open season for oglers.

I asked for another table but Sophie placing her hand on my arm smiling said, "No Richard, we will give them something to write home about, remember?" Still standing she lightly kissed me, holding me close with a hand gently pulling on my neck. I thought, "strike one" we are going to have a fun night.

Fun we certainly had. If either Sophie or I caught a set of eyes upon us, or noticed whispering with glances in our direction we would kiss and stare into each other's eyes. Our action acquired the desired result, the ogling increased so we increased our performance, constantly stifling laughter bubbling within.

I am not sure if the oglers stopped ogling or if, our kisses becoming more demanding, we gave up before we acted inappropriately. Our fellow

24

diners, a mix on young, twenties and thirties, and middle aged, forties and fifties, judging by the happy atmosphere were enjoying the evening. The younger element probably accounted for sixty percent, pleasing because the music would, I presumed, be directed to the more adventuresses, those who would utilise the dance floor often.

A sextet of musicians played light music, a sound balanced between classical and popular music, quite often associated with radio and television programmes. I recognised the tunes but no-way could I name one. Nonetheless, it proved pleasant to listen to.

I am convinced Sophie and I, the last to take our seats, held-up proceedings that evening. We had just received our welcoming cocktails when the sextet stopped playing placing their instruments safely into instrument cases before leaving the stage. They were making way for a DJ.

The DJ opened his repertoire with "Delilah" by Tom Jones. Eight bars hadn't played when Sophie tugged me onto the dance floor. She melted into my arms where she stayed until Tom Jones faded out to be replaced by Vanity Fair's "Hitchin' a Ride".

We danced the popular hitch-hike where we used the hitchhiker's gesture, waving our stuck-out thumbs. We, keeping step, moved right three times right thumb to the right over the shoulder, clapped our hands, moved three times left thumb to the left over the shoulder, clap hands.

During the stepping we were constantly shimmying, displaying body ripples. Sophie was putting on one hell of a show and I was giving it my best shot, but wow when Sophie shimmied, she shimmied, sending shock waves through the audience. Surprisingly we did receive a ripple of applause.

"Leaving on a jet plane" sung by Peter, Paul and Mary, the next record, inspired Sophie, radiating a huge smile brighter than the sun to fall into my arms. Our mini-exhibition encouraged other people onto the dance floor. I silently thanked God. I am not comfortable exhibiting myself.

After a couple more songs I could see a waiter hovering by our table. I assumed not only were we the last to arrive but we would be the last to place our order. I whispered to Sophie we had to return to the table to order dinner and wine. We squeezed in between the tables receiving glances and looks, revealing unexpected appraisal. I felt good but there again who wouldn't with Sophie on his arm.

We had finished ordering when a suave young man, probably nineteen or twenty came to the table, he said, "Excuse me Sir, could I ask your delightful wife for a dance?" I glanced at Sophie, she smiled answering, "Yes you can" the young man taken aback said, "Madam may I have the pleasure of the next dance."

Sophie barely disguising the laughter in her voice "If my husband will allow it I shall willingly dance with you." I couldn't say what I would have liked to, "eff-off", so I graciously gave my assent. The young man, obviously well-schooled in etiquette offered his hand, Sophie bowing her head to control her giggles accepted before standing. The young man stood to one side to allow Sophie the lead to the dance floor.

Under my unwavering eyes they danced for two tunes appropriately without any attempted hanky-panky from the young man. After the second song I noticed Sophie gesture towards me indicating she had to return to her husband. He escorted her to the table, politely thanking me.

No sooner had she seated when another guy turned-up, late twenties I guessed also requesting a dance but directing his request direct at Sophie, ignoring me. Big mistake, I answered with a sharp "no". The cheeky so n' so turned, apologising for interrupting.

Through the course of the evening he tried another twice, I twitched the second time. Sophie, ready to break out in schoolgirl giggles touched my arm saying, "Just one darling." She elegantly stood then with exaggerated swaying of her hips she led him to the dance floor.

Following two dances, Sophie seated said, "He's harmless, darling and he's nervous of you. He said while we were dancing "your feller's a big guy." I told him you played rugby and boxed. He never said another word." We laughed and Sophie added, "You, my darling are my guardian angel I will always be safe with you."

Waiters started to appear delivering the first courses to the tables, which signalled the music to change moods playing light music similar to the sextet's choices. Towards the end of dinner a piano appeared being pushed onto the stage resting close to where the musician's instruments were stowed. The musicians followed beginning to re-tune their various instruments.

A waiter busy removing our dessert plates jumped when Sophie squealed, "Oh my goodness that's Gertie." Completely in the dark, my eyes darted here, there and everywhere except the stage. Finally looking at the stage, Sophie was now fast approaching, I witnessed a very attractive lady, her hair piled high wearing a close fitting evening gown, turn, raise her arms in the air and yell, "Sophie".

Sophie, forgetting herself, hitched the skirt of her gown, turned her back towards the stage and pulled herself up and into the arms of Gertie in one very swift exercise. In fact, she demonstrated a very impressive display of agility. The ladies' yells silenced the ballroom for a moment, all eyes were on the two women as they embraced, gestured and happily smiled. The musicians stood bewildered, not sure what to do.

Sophie and Gertie exited the stage, animatedly conversing. Conversation returned and a buzz resonated throughout the ballroom. I thought, Well guys, that's it, the night's entertainment is postponed for an indefinite period.

In a short time Sophie re-appeared from the right of the stage and Gertie re-entranced onto the stage. Taken the microphone placed above the piano, she faced the diners saying, "Ladies and Gentlemen, fellow musicians, I apologise for my unseemly behaviour, Sophie, the lady crossing the floor is a very long-time friend, we haven't met for some time, and we schooled and attended the same university together." Sophie, amidst stares returned to the table very pleased with herself.

Before sitting she, with a little help, forced her chair close to mine, once seated she took my hand and squeezed. Quite excitedly she whispered, "We were at school together, there were three of us Gertie, me and Jessica. We were great friends."

The sextet lead introduced Gertrude Bigelow and the musicians, whom called themselves "Palm Court". He then proclaimed the forthcoming music would be a mixture to suit all tastes.

The music played proved to be lively and entertaining but not easy to dance to albeit many other couples managed. We did try until Sophie, exasperated with my efforts to foxtrot and quickstep said, "Enough, enough, you have three left feet, not two." I assumed Sophie had told me I couldn't dance for toffee.

However, there were several males who did offer to dance with her. I watched her, a very capable dancer. Holding her head high exhibiting gay poise she managed to accommodate the dance steps favoured by the music, whether it a waltz, a quickstep, or foxtrot, my Sophie could oblige.

I looked on intrigued, unaware of her dancing ability. I didn't count the number of dances but I would hazard a guess it she swirled around the floor for seventy percent of the musician's playing time. It thrilled me to observe her enjoying herself so much.

When the final waltz, I think the Danube, completed I couldn't help myself-- I stood, applauded and cheered, which encouraged the majority of the diners to do likewise. Gertrude flushed and the musicians expressing huge smiles accepted the applause with great aplomb. Sophie left her dance partner with a curtsy, disappearing backstage. A few minutes later she re-appeared, tugging Gertie with her aiming towards our table.

When they reached the table I stood waiting to take Sophie into my arms, which I did, exclaiming how wonderful she had danced. Sophie glowing and, excited, introduced Gertie. Up close, Gertie an attractive woman closely matched Sophie, in the looks and figure department, a good-looking woman and she knew it.

She looked into my eyes, her dark hazel eyes sending a signal I couldn't fathom. After polite hand-shakes and hello murmurings we sat at the table. I called a waiter asking Gertie her favourite tipple. She plumped for whisky and soda, Sophie followed suit, so I ordered three.

After a while the two ladies deep in conversation realised my presence; feeling guilty, Sophie kissed my cheek. "What do think of my Lionheart, my very own man? The man who will be my husband very soon?" she asked Gertie. Gertie shrilled, "You're getting married?" Sophie excited, replied, "Yes, and you and Jessica must be my Maids of Honour, the "terrible threesome", you will won't you." Gertie looking first at me and then at Sophie said, "Of course, I would love to."

Talk of dates and venues consumed time before Sophie pushed for an answer to her earlier question regarding Gertie's thoughts of me. Gertie focused her dark hazel eyes into my eyes. She answered, "Dashing and incredibly sexy. He has sensuous take-me-to bed eyes."

Sophie, shocked, cried, "Gertie behave." Sophie focused on my eyes, searching for whatever Gertie had seen. Unsure what to do I winked. Sophie smiled a weak smile. I could see plainly she felt threatened by Gertie, Gertie noticed too. Gertie not wanting to be intrusive or upset Sophie excused herself, reminding Sophie to telephone her.

Alone, Sophie hugged and kissed me. I noticed Gertie's backward glance, towards me.

Her composure regained Sophie wanted to dance, particularly because the DJ now back on stage opened his repertoire with a popular Tamla Motown track. We danced, shimmied and smooched. Other dancers came and went but Sophie ensured we were going nowhere. She held her man tightly with no intention of letting him go.

The dancing encouraged Sophie to relax, to forget Gertie and return to a normal, albeit slightly brazen, mood. Midnight eclipsed the ballroom, overhead lights flashed on and the evening officially closed. Polite applause echoed within the ballroom.

An announcement came over the speakers advising the bar would remain open for residents and their guests. Sophie with a very sexy smile and non-too quietly said, "I think, my man, we have had enough alcohol, it's time for love-making." I noted she achieved the desired effect trumpeting to all within hearing range, she and I were going to bed to make love. How dare Gertie say Sophie's man has "sensuous take-me-to bed eyes"?

In the bedroom Sophie removed her dress and panties, nothing else. She paraded knowing how I loved suspenders and stockings. Twirling and pirouetting, she removed an article of my clothing with every twirl, finally achieving her goal of a naked Richard with a very hard and erect Jolly Roger waiting and wanting to satisfy her needs.

Standing facing each other, very close but not touching Sophie taking my hand placed it over a very hot and wet vagina. "Feel how wet I am, wet for you my love," she throatily whispered. She pushed her vagina against my hand my fingers slipped inside her. She took my hand to her mouth sucking each finger.

Moving into my arms she steered me into a chair. With her back to me she straddled my penis using her hand she guided it exactly where she wanted, then with all her might pushed hard down emitting a squeal. Her juices were gushing. I couldn't fail to notice her wetness when reaching round to locate her clitoris. Sophie began squirming thrashing her head side-to-side. Driving hard down and for the first time she used the "f" word yelling, "Fuck me Richard, fuck me."

We made love on the floor, on the chair, over and in the bed and finally in the shower. Every orifice thoroughly explored and overpowered, I realised it wasn't my Sophie. An irrational female just happened to be in the same room.

The sex over and in bed, Sophie asleep, I reflected upon Sophie, upon the last hour and more, accepting with heavy heart we had not made love, we had sex. Sophie had been driven by an inner-self I didn't recognise, demonstrably erotic, arguably lewd, wanting to prove no other woman alive could satisfy her man, only she could. The episode, in which I had played a major part, brought with it, confusion.

Yes Gertie, without doubt, certainly a very attractive woman, even sexy but I would never betray Sophie. I made a point as I drifted off to sleep to tell Sophie in the morning intending to alleviate her concerns.

I awoke feeling Sophie's presence, or to be more precise the intense scrutiny I witnessed in her troubled green eyes that had caused the evaporation of my sleep pattern. She lay close without touching.

Sophie spoke first "Hello sleepyhead."

"Hello you," I said leaning forward to kiss her forehead. "You look troubled," I continued. "Is everything alright?"

"No I have been awake for hours fretting" she replied. "Fretting about what?" I asked. "Us" she murmured.

I instantly thought, "oh no" not another grievance centred upon the Sea. No, her thoughts were directed towards Gertie. She continued, "I only realised yesterday evening when Gertie mentioned your sexiness and sexy eyes that I will have my work cut-out to keep you by my side."

I sat upright forcing a pillow behind my back saying, "Sophie do not be daft, you are my fiancée, you are my lady, nobody will come between you and I."

"I am not daft Richard, I am aware. Over the years, as I have told you on many occasion I have observed women looking at you, knowing they wanted you in bed. Gertie, being Gertie said what she thought, the first one to voice the words."

I tried to interrupt, however Sophie wanted her say. "Gertie never slow, always forthright, even at school and college, basically said she wanted to take you to bed, if you didn't get her inference, more fool you."

I remembered my thoughts last night prior to falling asleep. "Sophie, stop it," I said. "Who do you think I am, Don Juan? I would never betray you with another woman, I love you too much."

Sophie with unhappiness in every word retorted, "You say those words now, but what of tomorrow, the next day?"

I could feel anger simmering below the surface. "For crying out loud Sophie, last week it was the sea that would break our relationship, this week it is other women. When will you rid yourself of the insecurity swirling around in your brain? I am going to work tomorrow, starting a new job, a joint decision between you and me. The job, we both agreed, is the foundation for our future. Now my darling, will you, for goodness sake stop it, please?"

Sophie didn't respond in words she responded by laying her head in my lap and encircling me with her arms. Time passed, desperate to relieve myself but I held. I didn't want to mar her sanctuary. Sophie held me tight and didn't want to let go, not just yet. I tenderly stroked her hair and her shoulders.

Her poise realised she lifted her head eager to share her thoughts saying "I am daft aren't I? We have been together for all these years and not once, and I am sure you have had opportunity, have you betrayed me. I am a fool. I am sorry."

Sophie grasped me tighter, irritating my bladder. "Sophie darling, I do need to go to the bathroom," I pleaded. Sophie looked at me and smiled, the crisis had abated, so she freed herself allowing me to answer nature's call.

The plans for the day ahead undecided, we agreed to discuss them over breakfast. Quickly showering, me shaving, we descended to the breakfast room, we were just in time. The room busy with people discussing their own agendas for the day or in some cases, I presumed, yesterday evening's dinner and dance.

Following a waitress to a table we acknowledged nods and smiles and the odd "good morning". I ordered a full English breakfast whilst Sophie chose haddock, insisting on brown bread as opposed to toast.

During breakfast we decided after we had checked out and deposited the luggage in the car we would walk along Royal Parade taking in Eastbourne's frontage onto the sea, walking until we had seen enough before re-tracing our steps back to the hotel.

Once in the car we would drive to Wilmington, north of Eastbourne to take a look of the Long Man engraved in a chalky hillside. Sophie recalled seeing it as a child. Thereafter we would return home, perhaps, but doubtful because of the recent breakfast, having lunch on the way.

Needless to say we departed from the Long Man heading for the Bear where we would join Sophie's parents for their usual late Sunday lunch. I ensured Sophie telephoned to pre-warn of our intended arrival. Sophie reported back her mother would be pleased and we were most welcome. The weekend ended as it started, on a happy note.

Chapter 4 – New Job and Jessica

Early, very early attired in a new grey suit with accompanying blue shirt and dark blue tie, I finished the last of my black tea washing down the muesli as Sophie hovered all around me. She made me stand in the hall for a final inspection, with her approval, and now satisfied she kissed me lovingly, wishing good luck.

Not yet six on a dark, dreary Monday morning, a mere hour since Sophie pushed, shoved and kicked me out of bed to get ready for my first day in a new job I started the car and reversed out of the garage. Sophie stood at the living room window waving good-bye; I waved back blowing a kiss, and started the drive towards Southampton.

The trouble with driving a long distance is the time one has to think, even with the radio playing the mind explores the past and present. However, I also realised the thoughts and the recollections I experienced during the drive revolved around the many discussions and conversations with Sophie, particularly her concerns. Specifically her conviction I would sail off into the sunset, and now "other women". I interpreted her concerns to be a high level of insecurity, which I couldn't come to terms with.

I considered her work, where I know she is highly efficient and effective in her role, gaining immense satisfaction. I also knew she is highly favoured by her bosses with the likelihood of a promotion before too long. Therefore I confidently assumed the insecurity she felt did not relate to work.

I considered my position, whereas I had broken away from R J Construction, admittedly an uninteresting job, and although it had been hard work, and quite often it demanded long hours, there had at times been a level of job satisfaction.

Selfishly, I further considered the financial element. I had chucked in sixty pounds per week plus expenses for a miserly eleven pounds fifty without expenses. I wondered what a psychiatrist would make of a guy who suddenly decided to cut his weekly income by seventy-five per cent. I could feel the straight jacket.

I realised entering Southampton's suburbs that the time taken for the drive had flown by. Recalling the interview visits and the last visit to Southampton with Sophie, I found the office without much trouble. I pulled into an empty car-park noticing the only other vehicle to be a dark blue Bedford Dormobile van with the Royal Navy insignia imprinted on a side panel. I correctly reasoned no cars equated to unoccupied offices. I remained in the car.

I dozed off being awakened by urgent knocking on the car window. Opening my eyes a smiling Mr Maybury indicating me to open the window stood by the car. He asked, "How long have you been here Chambers? It is Chambers isn't it?"

Looking at my watch I answered, "Yes, Mr Maybury I am Richard Chambers. I have been here thirty-five minutes." I climbed out of the car gathering my jacket from the hanger and the new brief case Sophie had presented to me a few days earlier. "Remind me, where do you live?"

"Hove," I replied.

"Ah yes I remember." Still smiling he added, "First impression is important and you have made a good start. What time did you get up?"

"Four-thirty" I responded.

"Good grief man," he exclaimed. "You need to learn time management."

He unlocked the car-park office door allowing me to enter first. I took the stairs on the run taking two steps at a time. I respectfully waited by the locked reception door for his arrival. "You're fit as well, another good impression," he said.

I followed him into the main office area, an area I had not seen before due to the two interviews I had attended being conducted in a small meeting room off of the reception area. He told me to follow him. We walked down a corridor with glazed partitioning to the left and perimeter offices to the right. Each of the perimeter offices had the name and position of the occupant, or on occasion occupants.

He unlocked his office door and pointed to a chair. During the few minutes I waited for his return I studied the office. Certainly large with a small meeting table to the left, fully carpeted and with walls adorned with various ships and dockyard locations. He returned with two coffees.

He pulled a pipe and a tobacco tin decorated with a large oil tanker from a desk draw starting to prepare for a smoke. "Do you smoke?" he asked.

"No sir," I answered.

"Good, we have too many smokers." He continued, "I enjoy my pipe in the morning, once more at lunchtime and when I arrive home." I remained silent.

With his pipe alight he said, "Right, the first month is induction month when you will be assigned to specific engineers who will run through each department's responsibilities."

He thought for a moment saying, "How old are you?"

"Twenty-three, twenty-four in August," I replied.

"Bit old for a trainee," he said, adding, "I wonder why we employed you."

He answered his own question. "Yes, yes I remember, you have management experience and a good degree, correct?"

"Yes I managed several contracts for a small to medium construction company," I answered.

His interest waned, wanting someone else to arrive so he could unload me. A voice penetrated his office. "Morning Mr Maybury."

"Ah Tommo, take young Chambers here and show him his desk." After introductions I followed Tommo to an area with four desks sited close to the reception interconnecting door.

Tommo said, "This one is yours, make yourself comfortable; your team leader Jock Inglis will be here soon." Left alone sitting at an empty desk in an empty office, I thought, "Great start."

During the next twenty minutes the office filled with "good morning"; "good weekend"; "Saints won again" comments flying around but no Jock Inglis. Although a young chap did arrive quizzically looking me over before taking the desk to my right. "You must be the new bloke," he said. I stood to shake hands.

"Richard Chambers," I said. Without standing he proffered his hand, giving his name. "Gary." I shook hands with a wet fish.

He started taking documents from various draws spreading them in some kind of order on his desk. His task completed he said, "Come on I'll show you the kitchen, although during the next few weeks you will get sick of the sight of it."

I retorted, "Why will I be sick of it?"

He presented a half sneer, half smile. "Because my friend, you are the new bloke which means you are automatically assigned as tea boy."

I didn't like the sound of that nor did I like him very much, the type of guy who constantly worked at being superior.

The first week crawled by. I sat around waiting for my name to be called by this person or that person. And true to Gary's word I near lived in the kitchen making tea or coffee. I recalled Maybury and his "first impression" comments. My first impression of Maybury Marine Engineers did not correlate with his.

However, each evening I reported back to an anxious Sophie explaining the work very low key until I proved myself, expressing how interesting I found the job.

Within two weeks utter disbelief and complete discontentment had set in, I began to despise working for Maybury. I had made a mistake; I wasn't cut out to be treated like a second-class citizen. Nor did I gain any job satisfaction.

I had always suspected working in an office I would be treated as a go-for. A major irritation evolved from the treatment I received from the senior engineers, especially Jock Inglis, my team leader who considered me a buffoon.

During the forty-five minute lunch-break, whatever the weather I wandered off seeking solitude. Inevitably I passed the Royal Navy recruitment centre, flanked by Royal Air Force and Army recruitment centres. The more often I passed, the more often I looked towards it. Each time I fought an inner battle against going back on my word to Sophie.

A huge relief, Easter weekend arrived, a welcome break from being Maybury's number one tea boy. I had been looking forward to the weekend, a "forget all your worries" weekend with Sophie. We were driving to Minehead to stay a couple of nights with Jessica, the mysterious third member of the "Terrible Threesome" the name Sophie, Jessica and Gertie had been tagged with during their boarding days at school and later during college.

I actually sneaked off from work two hours early, a spur of the moment decision, which came about because Mr Maybury did not turn in on the Thursday. Hence other directors and all the senior engineers, imparting varying excuses left the offices at lunchtime with no intention of returning. By mid-afternoon the middle and junior engineers had also deserted, so I thought why not me, and at three-thirty I departed to drive home.

Sitting in father's chair with a can of beer listening to The Moody Blues I heard the front door slam and in a trice Sophie covered my eyes with her hands. "Guess who?"

"My urban economic princess," I replied, which for some reason had her giggling.

"I love you Richard Chambers."

"I love you too Sophie McKendrick," I whispered, adding a loving kiss.

Pulling her dress over her head exposing her gorgeous body sexily adorned in bra, panties and tights, "Shall we make love?"

"If you insist," I responded kicking my shoes off.

Love-making recently due to my early mornings and late evenings had been severely curtailed. Keen to ensure we enjoyed the whole experience I decided we should be in bed. I guided Sophie up the stairs my eyes glued to her delightful bottom. In the bedroom we disrobed.

In bed Sophie demanded immediate action. I refused; I wanted to enjoy Sophie because I loved her. I also wanted Sophie to enjoy because she loved me.

For hour after hour including periods of inactivity we kissed, cuddled and explored making love unhurriedly and tenderly teasing each other with intimate discoveries. I would enter her, withdraw and re-enter, withdraw dropping to lick, suck and kiss her vagina, re-enter, move in and out, suck and nibble her nipples.

Penetrating deeply or just holding my penis between her warm labia lips, keeping still forcing Sophie to wriggle towards me to force deeper penetration we revelled. She sucked and licked Jolly Roger at times gorging herself on its length.

We loved and loved, never too frantic, never rushing. The orgasms came, more followed and still we loved. She whimpered, I sighed, we moaned together. We ran our tongues over each other's bodies immersed in love, every action a powerful signal amplifying our love.

I sucked her toes, her fingers and nibbled her bottom. She ran her tongue and fingers over my back. We didn't stop we kept going on and on, wonderful, wonderful exquisite sensations tickled through our bodies.

Very happy, full of love, we went to sleep, sated and deeply in love.

We awoke together in the middle of the night Sophie turned her back pushing her bottom towards me. I entered her still moist vagina once more. We remained tender not wanting to change anything slowly moving together, synchronised and totally connected. We climaxed, my penis, nature's own connection, ensured we shared tremors and electrical spasms together, glorious feelings warmed our love.

I came awake feeling Sophie's kisses gently falling on my face. I opened my eyes. "Richard, what a wonderful night of love, so beautiful, so fulfilling, such love and tenderness, my darling a night of absolute loving, a never to be forgotten loving experience." With a huge smile and with glistening green eyes she said, "Can we do it again?"

"We will my darling, we will," I lovingly replied.

Forcing ourselves from bed we showered, packed a single holdall, not including evening or overly smart clothes knowing from Sophie's expectation of the impending visit to Jessica we would probably walk a great deal, perhaps pop into Minehead for a pub lunch but that would be it. Jessica lived in a cottage on her parent's farm.

At ten o'clock armed with atlas, an array of cassettes, a couple of magazines, ham sandwiches and a flask of tea and the holdall in the boot we set off for Minehead. Sophie expected the journey would take five hours. I expected longer.

The journey to Jessica's parent's farm located close to a village called Woodcombe, surprisingly lasted only four hours. I surmised because we were travelling east to west whilst the majority of the Easter weekend's traffic headed south to north or vice versa.

We observed when crossing over main trunk roads they were congested. We did become entangled in traffic crossing the A303 near to Salisbury, otherwise we did extremely well.

We located, with comparative ease thanks to Jessica's hand written instructions, her parent's farm a little after four-fifteen. Jessica lived two hundred yards down a farm track to the right of the farm entrance.

We pulled up outside. Jessica I presumed must have espied the car because she stood in her cottage's small front garden waiting for us.

Sophie jumped out running to meet her old friend who left the garden to rush towards Sophie. Embraces and kisses and garbled speech were eventually replaced by my introduction to Jessica.

She immediately hugged me and congratulated my wise choice in selecting Sophie to be my wife. She gave a stern warning that I had to care and love her forever. Just like Gertie, this girl proved to be yet another beauty; did Sophie's old school specialise in breeding only beautiful girls?

The cottage, decorated rustically with warm colours provided a warm welcome. I thought I could live here quite happily. We were to be billeted, Jessica's word, in the right wing, reached up a very narrow set of stairs into an open bedroom with bathroom. I delivered the holdall to our billet.

The room with an old bedstead fitted with brass railings a yard or so high for the head board, and a foot or so for the opposite end felt comfortable. Everything within the cottage I had seen so far generated warmth and comfort. Holdall delivered, I returned to Sophie and Jessica.

Sophie stood beside Jessica making cooing noises. I saw why-- Jessica playfully wrestled with a toddler. Sophie had neglected to inform me of this aspect of the visit unless, I thought, perhaps Jessica could be baby-sitting for a friend. But no, James belonged to Jessica.

Two-year-old James and I were introduced. Mental arithmetic, knowing Sophie and Jessica were of a similar age helped me to determine Jessica had given birth to James when twenty-one.

James had now transferred from Jessica into Sophie's arms and Sophie I could see became bewitched with the toddler's charm. She nuzzled her head into James's chest making him laugh and giggle, she swung him above her head down between her legs and up again. James giggled and giggled having a great time. I stood quietly on the side-line.

Jessica asked me to help her in the kitchen where she had prepared food. She asked me to choose and open a bottle of wine. Following her into the kitchen I entered a perfect setting complete with Aga, an aged pine dining table with four matching carvers.

To the right there rested a cabinet, half-storage and half-wine rack, containing three bottles of red wine. Opposite a large American fridge-freezer, which were becoming popular, took up half the wall.

Jessica smiling said, "I have baked a pheasant and black-pudding pie, which I will serve with Jersey Royals and carrot and swede in black pepper and butter." It sounded delicious. She continued, "I prefer white so I suggest you open a white and a red. The white is in the door of the fridge."

I checked the reds choosing a Merlot. Jessica said, "The corkscrew is in the drawer." I opened a draw immediately above the wine rack locating the implement. She then instructed me to lay the table directing me to where table cloth, cutlery, glasses and place mats could be found.

I could hear Sophie chuckling as she entertained James. One minute she pretended to be a train, toot, tooting, next a jet plane blasting across the skies. James continued to have a great time.

"You don't say much do you?" queried Jessica.

"Sorry," I said wondering why I should apologise. I continued, "The only information I had was that I would meet Jessica, an old and dear friend who completed the "terrible threesome" from Sophie's school and college days."

Jessica controlling the vegetable cooking said, "Aha, the "terrible threesome". I heard from Sophie you met Gertie who apparently made a play for you, which looking at you and knowing Gertie doesn't surprise me one little bit. Although I am surprised by Sophie's reaction and how upset Sophie sounded when she telephoned."

"When the three of us were at college you were the mysterious Richard. Sophie didn't even have a photograph although recently she did send one of the two of you dancing, very erotically, at a New Year do in Brighton." Photograph, what bloody photograph, more news. "Yes, the mysterious Richard handsome, loving and so much loved by Sophie," she said, sounding aggrieved. "All she could think and talk of revolved around holidays and occasional weekend assignations with you."

Jessica gaily laughed, "She worried, terrified you would fall in love with a girl at college." I kept quiet, happy to let Jessica ramble on. "I did have photographs galore of my Charles, the dashing Guards officer. James's father, by the way, ditched me when I told him I had fallen pregnant, the bastard." She spit out the word bastard.

Saved by the bell or rather James's chuckling when he toddled through the door closely followed by Sophie. He had come to find his mother. Jessica announced the food nearly ready. I opened the wine.

Jessica directed me through a door leading from the kitchen to locate a high chair, the other side of the door. I placed it alongside where I guessed Jessica would sit.

The pie and vegetables were served. Sophie offered a toast to Jessica and James, we all drank the wine, white for Jessica and red for Sophie and me.

The pheasant and black-pudding pie tasted superb, in fact the whole meal proved very satisfying. I ate in silence listening to the two ladies re-live school and college days. I did laugh when I heard the story when the "terrible threesome", each with two mice secreted them into "old Mary's residence; "Old Mary" being the deputy head and a lesbian to boot at their school. The whole school guessed who instigated the dastardly act and who to blame but fortunately lack of proof meant the "terrible threesome" escaped punishment.

Sophie and Jessica discussed how understanding Jessica's parents had been through the dark period when her dashing Guard's office abandoned her in pregnancy. Her father felt particularly aggrieved because prior to the pregnancy news he had expected to plan a wedding for his daughter with a man he liked and respected.

We were due to meet the parents the next day for a light lunch at the main farmhouse.

Supper finished during which time James had been an angel throughout, Sophie and I shared the chores while Jessica readied the toddler for bed reading a story until he fell asleep in her arms, sound asleep Jessica transferred him into a cot in her bedroom.

In her absence I raised by eyebrows saying to Sophie, "Well?" She knew exactly what I referred to. She whispered urgently, "I didn't mention James because I thought you may baulk at the idea of the visit." I thought, umm, probably correct.

Jessica returned and speaking normally she said, "He's sound asleep; he will sleep now until five in the morning." Looking at the coffee table nestling between a sofa and two armchairs she said, "Where's the wine? I'll get it." Coming back into the cosy room she said, "I am impressed you certainly know how to leave a kitchen clean and tidy."

For the rest of the evening the conversation flowed back and forth. Sophie's work discussed in depth and my new job explored. Jessica admitted envy regarding Sophie's work and the involvement it demanded.

She didn't hide the jealousy of the period we had remained together. Although she expressed her happiness and thought we were very lucky, especially a house to share without paying a penny. Eventually, the wine talking, Jessica quizzed Sophie over the Gertie incident. Sophie didn't exactly bristle but I could sense her unhappiness.

After Sophie had finished both the telling of the evening and defending herself, Jessica admitted she often conversed with Gertie via telephone. Gertie, in fairness to her had relayed a similar report admitting she had fancied Sophie's man, but valued Sophie's friendship over and above a roll in the hay.

Sophie, smiling said she would telephone and apologise. Sophie did add she had asked Gertie to be a maid of honour and also hoped Jessica would be also. Jessica squealed happily that she would.

Jessica emptied her glass saying goodnight, advising more wine could be found in the kitchen. Winking at Sophie and laughing gaily she said, "And no acrobatic love-making, keep the noise down remember James and his poor deprived mother." Sophie, who surprised me, thought the comment funny promising to keep the noise to a minimum.

Jessica disappeared, closing the door behind, up the stairs to her bedroom. I assumed it mirrored the one we were sleeping in. Sophie collected the glasses together taking them into the kitchen I followed with the two empty bottles. We washed and dried the glasses and retired to bed. We didn't make love.

We heard James crying; I thought "shit", six-thirty. We forced ourselves from the bed washed and clambered down the narrow stairs. I hit my head when I went to duck under the door at the bottom of the stairs, which did nothing to improve my resentment.

James, quite happy sitting in his high chair, busied himself using his fingers to eat his breakfast, in between he deposited food onto the floor, which he considered hilarious.

Jessica expressed a grand mood, smiling and chatting commenting how nice to have friends visiting. She quickly made bacon door-steps with enough bacon to feed the five-thousand. She also produced coffee from an Italian type coffee machine, the coffee tasted wonderful.

Jessica apologised for waking the household so early but with a smile and shrug she said, "What can I say?" She did, however say it would be a good time to go for a walk. The sun had commenced its climb from the horizon. She added, "We could walk up to Culver Cliff Woods, from there the view overlooking Minehead and the bay is quite exhilarating.

Jessica emphasised the walk with James wanting in, then out of his buggy would take approximately an hour there and an hour back. Sophie and I agreed it would be a worthwhile walk.

The buggy loaded with James and necessary toddler paraphernalia we set off. I became chief buggy driver leaving Sophie and Jessica to reminisce. They were following behind while I played racing cars, for the benefit of James, with the buggy. He gurgled and chortled having a gay old time. When he walked, he, after initial shyness took my hand. On occasion I would lift him onto my shoulders. He and I were getting on like a house on fire.

Once at Culver Cliff we stared out to sea and studied Minehead from up high. We could make out the Butlin's Holiday Camp on the opposite side of the town. I said to Sophie the town looked pleasant and that we should make the effort to have a look round.

The walk back, because James slept most of the way, proved to be quite quick. I retained my position as chief buggy driver, carefully manoeuvring the buggy watching for obstructions or ruts in the path working hard not to wake him. Sophie and Jessica continued to converse albeit I couldn't understand what else they could talk about, they had hardly stopped since departing the cottage.

James, suddenly awake demanded Number twos; Jessica grabbing a bag took him into the bushes. 'Number twos' over, we completed the walk returning to the cottage. Once in the warmth of the kitchen we enjoyed tea and cake. The cake, orangey flavoured, Jessica had baked, melted in the mouth, very tasty.

On arrival and during the evening before I had been a wee bit unsure regarding Jessica but I became impressed with her efficiency and permanent, happy personality. She obviously loved James dearly. I realised her outpouring in the kitchen the previous evening had to be said, she felt, by way of an explanation to a near stranger. I decided I liked Jessica, an okay girl.

Sharp at twelve forty-five we set off to walk to the farmhouse, a fifteen-minute walk. I followed the two ladies. As we walked I watched Jessica in her jeans. She walked assuredly with purpose, her shapely hips, in particular her bottom swaying quite nicely.

She had long blonde hair reaching half way down her back, which because she had worn it up previously I hadn't noticed. Following behind I assessed she stood a good three inches shorter than Sophie. Yes, I thought, certainly curvaceous, and very attractive, although her choice of clothes left much to be desired.

Her parents were wonderful people. Her father Graham inherited the farm from his father who had inherited it from his. Her mother, also named Jessica, an extremely attractive woman who also had blonde hair depicted a very self-assured lady. I liked her straight off, very much the farmer's wife who would work the farm dawn to dusk.

They knew Sophie of old. They also knew she had a long-term boyfriend known to Jessica and themselves as "mysterious Richard". They were glad they could put a face to "mysterious Richard".

The farm, dairy and arable, had a dairy herd of seventy Friesian, a dozen sows and a boar purely for producing regular litters and farmed over one hundred and twenty acres of arable fields

They served a typical ploughman's lunch of chunky ham, pate, cheese, salad and wonderful bread still hot from the Aga. Jessica senior produced a bottle of wine she had fermented herself, a jolly good wine.

During the lunch I listened intently to the difficulties inherent in nineteen seventies farming. I told of my adventures as a child visiting an uncle and auntie's farm in Lancashire explaining they were mainly dairy farmers.

Graham explained that the day-to-day problems today's farmer faced were relentless and unforgiving. Milk quotas were, he declared nothing more than a ministerial "balls-up" causing heartache to dairy farmers the length and breadth of the country. He exclaimed passionately if farmers were left to farm and the Whitehall Mandarins and politicians concentrated on governing, opposed to interfering, the country would be much better off.

While I sat absorbed, listening to Graham, the ladies were engaged in remembering Sophie and Jessica's school and college days. The visits to each other's homes, their first dates with boys and laughed at the antics the "terrible threesome" instigated during both school and college terms. James jumped from knee to knee and enjoyed all the fussing he received. He also worried the two cats and a black Labrador until they retreated from the kitchen.

Jessica junior had pre-warned earlier we should respect her parents had to work the farm, therefore we should be aware we couldn't take up too much of their time. Although we were warned regarding time the afternoon rolled on until late-afternoon before we thanked them for their warm hospitality and departed. James cried because he didn't want to leave his Grandma and Granddad.

The stroll returning to Jessica's cottage with the sun shining brightly gave rise to James and I playing a toddler's version of hide 'n seek while Sophie and Jessica were walking arm-in-arm, talking. For the life of me I couldn't even begin to imagine how two women could resort to so much conversation, it was beyond my comprehension.

Back at the cottage a chap sat waiting behind the wheel of an aging sports car, an MGB, with its roof down. Jessica broke into a trot, evidently pleased to see him. With James seated on my shoulders calling words in toddler language, sounding like "Uncle Simon", I increased my pace.

Sophie and I were introduced to Simon Goodfellow, a tenant farmer with a few beasts, as he called his cattle and forty-seven acres, of which twenty-nine were arable.

Simon, an affable chap, a few years older than Jessica, with a ready smile and cheerful disposition seemed a really good guy. Both Sophie and I liked him. He and Jessica certainly appeared to be very fond of each other. James also displayed great affection for him.

He wasn't staying too long, only calling in to remind Jessica we were lunching in a country inn the next day, stating he had arranged a table for twelve-thirty. He did have time for a cup of tea and slice of cake. Shortly afterwards he left a disappointed little boy and mother to return to his farming responsibilities.

James showed signs of tiredness prompting Jessica to put him in his cot with toys and pictures until he fell asleep, a tried and tested resolution for when he became fractious and tired.

Sitting in the kitchen nursing cups of tea Jessica, straight to the point, asked Sophie when we were to be married. Sophie answered saying, "Goodness Jessica, I'm sorry I should have said. The big day is 7th August." Jessica clapped her hands saying, "Fabulous, a warm summer wedding, why 7th August?" Sophie described our first meeting in the Bear.

The rest of the day consisted of an early supper followed by a walk to a local hostelry where Jessica, a regular with her father gained access for James and a couple of drinks before retiring to bed.

In bed Sophie expressed her keenness to discuss the weekend thus far. She wanted my opinion of Simon, who had been dating Jessica for ages without once becoming over-familiar, an issue worrying Jessica. Smiling she wanted to know whether I considered myself the fatherly type, although having observed James and me playing she decided I had the necessary attributes to become a good father.

However, Jessica and Simon were to the forefront of her questioning. Simon, according to Sophie, seven years Jessica's senior had admitted to a four-year relationship during his college days, when in his teens and early twenties. Apparently, the limited information available regarding his previous love-life worried Jessica.

Sophie stressed Jessica's fondness for Simon but she had a further two issues, the first being his reticence to go beyond a kiss and a hug, worried he may be homosexual or perhaps just not interested in the sexual aspects of a relationship.

The second issue regarded his suggestion to give up the tenancy to find permanent work, which being a farmer's daughter, she knew would not be easy, nor did farm work pay particularly well.

Sophie, tired of discussing Jessica's problems began kissing me, seeking out Jolly Roger who she found to be receptive. Giggling she turned her back, over her shoulder she whispered, "No moaning and groaning, we are making love not starring in a pop concert."

Sophie still giggled when guiding my penis into her moist vagina. Sophie moaned and groaned intermingled with giggling. I pushed long and deep, withdrew before tenderly pushing into her once more, and again, and again.

We weren't seeking earth-shattering orgasms. We were making love because we were in love. Inevitably I climaxed, slowly releasing my sperm into the depths of Sophie's vagina, she relaxed her vice gripping vagina muscles, quietly enjoying her own climax.

The morning brought forth Easter Sunday and Easter eggs and cute little fluffy chicks. I played with James using the soft fluffy chicks to tickle him. He gurgled and giggled, his naturally sunburnt colour turning crimson and his eyes bright with childish pleasure.

Coffee and Easter egg chocolate replaced breakfast, not as a preference but because we were under James's orders.

We bathed and dressed, and of course I shaved. Shortly before Simon arrived Sophie asked me to talk with him in attempt to judge his character. I asked, "How?"

"I don't know, do I? Discuss manly things or something." she retorted.

"I know, I'll talk about sex and women," I said with a smile, unseen by Sophie.

"Don't you dare Richard," she abruptly responded before continuing, "Just instigate a conversation and see where it goes. You have enough information to question him subtly." I laughed saying, "Yes boss-lady."

Simon pulled-up at the cottage in a beat-up Landrover a little after twelve. I noted a child's seat fitted in the back. Sophie and I followed the Landrover through country lanes arriving at Porlock Weir, a pretty village complete with a choice of two dining venues.

Simon had reserved a table in an Inn. The inn gave Simon and Jessica a friendly welcome, we now knew one of their courting destinations. The landlady, taking James in her arms tickled his tummy with her head making him giggle. Sophie and I were introduced as long-time friends of Jessica visiting for the weekend.

We were shown to a table and issued with menus. We ordered drinks. I opted for tomato juice with Worcester sauce knowing within three or four hours I would be driving back to Hove. Sophie and Jessica decided, after what seemed an age to share a bottle of white wine.

Simon ordered lemonade for James and a ginger-beer shandy for himself, when hearing his order I came to close to changing my mind. I did enjoy a ginger-beer shandy.

The menu, because of Easter was comprised mainly chicken dishes. Food ordered, besides keeping James happy, we talked about Portlock Weir and the nearby Watchet Harbour a picturesque village the other side of Minehead.

Complying with the orders issued earlier by Sophie I broached the subject of Jessica and Simon's friendship, asking simple questions such as how they met, how long they had known each other, how often they went out together, were they actually courting or the relationship platonic, which triggered dagger looks from Sophie and Jessica and a great laugh from Simon.

Simon answered in three sentences stating, "We met when Jessica was driving too fast rounded a bend as I trekked my beasts between fields, gosh that happened twenty months ago. After the initial "getting to know you" six months, which is how long it took to receive an acceptance to my constant requests for a date, we have been dating regularly trying to involve James, as much as possible. And yes to the best of my knowledge we are courting."

Sophie smiled, indicating Simon had answered perfectly. Jessica although only proffering a weak smile did look relieved but also reserved as if she had wanted to hear a tad more commitment. I smiled broadly satisfied I had achieved an answer fitting to the company.

The lunch proved to be a delight. Sophie and I selected chicken Kiev, which was delicious. The inner butter, garlic and pepper sauce probably the best I had tasted, which led me to assume they were home-made. When we were leaving I asked the landlady who self-effacingly admitted she prepared the Kiev.

Jessica chose chicken breasts wrapped in bacon stating they were very appetising. Simon selected roasted half chicken with all the trimmings. The food piled high on his plate suggested we could have organised a hill-walking event. For dessert James, Simon and I shared several ice-cream flavours served with wafers and chocolate sauce. Sophie and Jessica shared a huge serving of cheese and biscuits.

Simon and I left the ladies to finish their bottle of wine going for a walk to entertain James. I could feel Simon wanted to either ask a question or comment regarding he and Jessica. I blathered on and on exclaiming the lushness and greenness of Somerset.

I returned to the earlier conversation when Watchet Harbour had been mentioned expressing I had sailed in a Post Boat from the harbour when young. My constant blathering finally achieved a reaction.

He said, "Richard do you mind if we talk I need to get something off my chest?"

"Not at all," I replied.

"When at college in Hertfordshire studying agriculture I had a long-term relationship with a young girl working in the kitchens. The relationship lasted four years."

While Simon talked I held tightly onto James, eager to get down and explore the harbour walls, which I couldn't allow. Simon continued, "When we met we were both virgins. We lost our virginity after six months courtship. We were not ardent lovers, more occasional because of the circumstances. She lived in Wheathampstead with her parents and I lived in college sharing a room."

Sighing he resumed, "One summer I collected her from Taunton coach station. I had booked a week in Butlins. When I collected her from the bus station she had two suitcases. The fact didn't register. Anyway after two days in Butlins she told me she had run away from home, accusing her father of being a drunk and her mother of infidelity. However, she startled me when she said she expected to marry me."

During the walk we diverted away from the harbour so I could put a fractious James down onto terra firma. Simon took James's hand and I the other to keep him under control.

Realising the ladies would soon finish their wine and come looking I said, "Simon without wishing to sound rude, what is the point of your story." He gave me an angry glare. I quickly countered, "Simon I am sorry to say this but you are telling me this for an alternative reason, either to advise you or to ensure the story gets back to Jessica"

He looked at me long and hard finally saying, "You're not a bad bloke are you."

What could I say, I answered, "I suppose not."

"Okay I will cut to the chase. I told her there and then that I would take her home, not because she had run away or because she wanted to marry, but because I knew nothing of her family or her home circumstances."

He kicked a few stones saying, "Marriage wouldn't have been a problem, I suspect we could have made a go of it. However, because I hadn't met her family I explained we should return to Wheathampstead to meet her parents, keeping our relationship above board."

We were a good distance from the Inn when I spotted Jessica and Sophie waving. I told Simon saying we should ignore them so he could finish his story. He continued, "I forced her into the car, an old Ford Poplar and returned. She wouldn't tell me where she lived. We were driving around the town when I noticed the police station. I parked the car and frog-marched her in. I blurted the whole sorry story out and the duty officer looked at me, deciding I must have a screw loose."

Simon shook his head. "She started yelling rape, the consequence of which they arrested me for suspected abduction."

"Nice lady," I said asking, "Did you get off?"

"Yes although it took four months to finalise all the legal bullshit."

Looking over his shoulder he continued, "I eventually met her parents who were quite normal. I wanted to apologise, the solicitor arranged a face-to face meeting. They would not accept the apology arguing one wasn't necessary and that Sara, the girl's name, confessed the truth to a solicitor therefore they accepted my innocence."

The ladies were closing fast behind, calling our names. James hearing his mother tried to change direction to meet them. I quickly said, "Tell all, and hold nothing back. Jessica is an intelligent woman, she will understand. Once in the open you can both get on with your lives, hopefully together if that is what you both want."

We shook hands seconds before Sophie and Jessica, both flushed with a mixture of unexpected exercise and anger because we ignored their hollering were upon us. Sophie looked at me. I winked and she smiled back at me.

Later in the afternoon we departed Jessica's lovely cottage to drive home. Jessica and Sophie were in tears and little James crying because his mother cried. Hugs all round before Simon and I shook hands one final time. He whispered, "You never know one day I may be looking for a best man." Waving goodbyes, we headed for home.

Out of sight of the cottage Sophie wanted chapter and verse relative to Simon's troubled past. I expressed most emphatically he didn't have a troubled past only a period when younger he became entangled with a young woman confused with life.

After completing the telling of Simon's past experience with Sara, Sophie leaned across kissing my cheek saying, "My clever man I love you." Clear of Taunton, Sophie laid her seat back and went to sleep.

Four and a half hours later, near to nine o'clock I drove the car into the garage. I unloaded the car, including the milk and sandwiches purchased at a petrol station, put the kettle on and gently kissed Sophie awake.

Sophie naturally put her arms round my neck and kissed back with fervour. She said, "I am home aren't I?"

"Yes my darling you are home," I answered.

"Do you know I dreamt of the evening you walked into the Bear," she exclaimed.

I automatically answered, "Monday, 7th August 1967."

Sophie still lying back in the reclined car seat, struggled to force herself upright. I helped her up and out of the car. Sophie replaced her arms round my neck and looked intently into my eyes. Her eyes never straying from mine continued, "Richard my mother once told me that if a woman ever wanted to know her man loved her she only has to ask the date of the day they met. You know the day and the date."

She kissed me hard pressing her lips forcing her tongue into my mouth. "Christ," she said. "My God I love you." Kissing me again she said, "I can't walk you will have to carry me." I carried Sophie into the living room and dropped her onto the sofa. She bounced straight back up jumping into my arms, fortunately knowing Sophie I half-expected her leap, hugging and kissing like a woman possessed. I loved her so very much.

Easter Monday we volunteered, or rather Sophie volunteered our services for the lunchtime shift before lunching with Irene and Ken. In the evening the four, parents, daughter and fiancée were going to the cinema leaving Joe in charge with Gwynne and Josie.

The selected film, "Get Carter", starring Michael Caine, a film we all wanted to see everybody was talking about it saying what a great film.

Chapter 5 – Work and Boredom and Dissatisfaction

Tuesday morning, in a bad mood I struggled out of bed. Sophie followed to prepare my muesli and black tea. Easter weekend over and muesli, rolled pieces of cardboard were once more being served for breakfast. Could it be the muesli why I had woken in a bad mood? Partly, I thought, the major contribution to my bad mood, not the drive, which I quite enjoyed. No, I despised working at Maybury more and more each day.

After the fifth week I requested a meeting with Mr Maybury; he granted my request for five-thirty Wednesday evening. My assigned team leader, Jock Inglis, who, metaphorically speaking had smoke escaping from his ears, muttered not too quietly I should be shot, a turncoat and not fit to be in his team.

Come five-thirty waiting outside Mr Maybury's office knowing Inglis had been in with Maybury for fifteen minutes, probably slating me beyond redemption, I realised my immediate boss, Inglis only gave support to those who pandered to his self-esteem.

Inglis could take a run and jump; I had requested the meeting for me, not him. I needed to express dissatisfaction to the top man. Jock Inglis finally exited. Mr Maybury called my name. He indicated the meeting table.

He studied me before asking why I had requested the meeting. I wasn't going to hang back. Mr Maybury, when he asked the question, unfortunately turned the tap on.

Working to keep emotion under control and intent on being objective I explained to Mr Maybury I had applied and accepted the position to work for Maybury as an engineer not a tea boy, or a go-for or the butt for a string of invasive comments from my team leader.

I firmly stated without any compunction if the company needed a permanent tea maker then they should employ one, not insult people's intelligence with bullshit tradition.

Unwavering I told him I had a bloody good degree, excellent work experience, albeit I did admit the experience gained was not in engineering. Nonetheless I emphasised I had managed profit and loss, attended meetings with senior representatives of business and local government institutions, designed and implemented an inventory system to control costs. Managed payroll and suppliers, and reconciled the company's business banking.

He now looked at me in a different light not sure what to do or say. However, the moment dissipated, Inglis knocked on the door and walked in.

I continued, "Mr Maybury I received offers for several positions before opting for Maybury. I chose Maybury because I believed it to be an engineering company seeking determined and dedicated engineers. Since my first day, with the exception of the poor excuse of an induction I have not undertaken one single engineering task. No one has asked my opinion. No one has questioned my past experience. No one has asked why I wanted to work for Maybury. In fact I spend all day carrying documents from one desk to another, making tea and coffee, running to the shop for cigarettes or sitting at my desk utterly bored." Finished I sat waiting for a response.

I could feel Jock Inglis stiffening, wanting desperately to say his piece. However, he had to wait until invited. Mr Maybury looked at me as if I had just landed from outer space.

Finally Mr Maybury spoke, "I remember your first day we had coffee together here in this office." I felt Inglis stiffen again, he didn't know this. "I also recall mentioning your punctuality and fitness. Nevertheless," he said, "You cannot become a competent engineer overnight; one is expected to learn the ropes. However, I do agree following a period of five weeks you should have progressed further than tea-making and being a messenger boy."

He looked towards Inglis, the bastard squirmed, and I could feel it. "Mr Maybury," he began, "Maybury has a tradition where trainee engineers are expected to undertake menial tasks. When I started seventeen years ago I went through exactly, if not worse, than Chambers is going through now. We were expected to respect our superiors."

Mr Maybury stopped him; he was waffling, embarrassing himself and his boss stopped him before he made a complete fool of himself. He wasn't contributing to the meeting.

"Maybe so Jock, but do you know of this man's history? Do you know of his previous experience? Have you read his application, his CV? No, you haven't Jock. He is not a run-of-the mill trainee."

Looking at me he said, "I have heard you and I understand your concern. Jock and I will discuss it further, come and to my office same time tomorrow in the meantime get yourself home, Hove isn't it?

"Yes Mr Maybury Hove it is, and thank you for your time." I departed leaving the two of them to consider my future; maybe I didn't have a future.

Driving home I re-lived the meeting. I considered Maybury a good guy, hoping he would tear a strip off high and mighty Jock Inglis. I actually believed I could build a worthwhile career with Maybury. I believed I could become an excellent professional engineer.

When bored in the office I had researched the company's history. In particular, the fact Maybury engineering works were national and international, not limited to Southampton but serviced all shipping. The available information I unearthed described engineering activities globally where Maybury were appointed as the specialist engineers as far afield as Hong Kong, Cape Town, Buenos Aires, and most of the major docking facilities throughout the UK and continental Europe.

I had read reports where Maybury engineers would be delivered with test equipment and tools to repair ships at sea. I turned into the garage convinced if given a fair crack of the whip, Maybury's would benefit, Sophie and I would benefit and life's little problems would be erased.

I sat in the car for a few minutes, thinking if the evening's meeting produces positive results I would knuckle down to ensure swift promotion, deciding the quicker I climbed the slippery pole, the better for Sophie.

Plus the added advantage that Sophie and I could seriously consider Southampton as a base for the future. A sudden bang on the car's bonnet alerted me to Sophie's presence. I alighted and hugged my darling Sophie, feeling very pleased.

Arms round each other's waists we followed the corridor past father's old office into the kitchen. I took Sophie into my arms kissing her ardently. "Why Mr Chambers, what is with you this evening?"

I thought before answering, broadly smiling I said, "A better than normal day at the office" "Oh Richard I am pleased," she replied.

"What about you young lady, did you have a good day?" Sophie in response went to the fridge producing a bottle of champagne and two chilled flutes.

"Darling man open and I will tell all," she retorted with a wonderful smile, she added. "And don't you dare say a word."

I poured a touch too fast, producing two glasses of overflowing bubbles. Sophie lifted her half glass and chinking my glass saying, "Mr Chambers meet Sophie McKendrick, the newly appointed head of a new but her own department entitled Urban and Environmental Economics Planning Department."

I said laughingly, "Your door will not be large enough to fit all those words, however my darling congratulations you deserve every success."

We sipped the champagne before I refilled the flutes. Flute in hand I pulled Sophie close, kissing her thick luxuriant hair murmuring my love for her and my happiness for her promotion, especially because she will be managing her very own department.

Smiling, her eyes sparkling Sophie added, "I am the youngest department head by a good few years ever, how about that?" Still holding her close I said, "You are terrific, my lovely lady, bloody marvellous, a beautiful rose climbing the framework to success. I am very proud of you, my darling you deserve every success."

"To celebrate I have reserved a table for the Bath Arms for dinner Friday evening, just you and me. I have also booked a taxi for seven-thirty, so do not be late," she said smiling and smiling.

In response I said, "The evening will be a double celebration. First for your wonderful promotion and secondly because the Bath Arms is where I fell in love with the cleverest, most loving and most beautiful woman in the world."

I prepared myself for the inevitable and I wasn't disappointed as Sophie launched herself into my arms. With kisses raining down on me and Sophie shouting and laughing, "You remembered, my lovely man, you remembered."

The excitement receded, working side-by-side we set about our shared household responsibilities. Each time we were within touching distance we touched fingers or on occasion tenderly kissed.

Wednesday evening, normally a gym night, had been overshadowed by Sophie's fantastic news and her obvious delight, and the champagne automatically cancelled out the thought of any exercising. Subsequently we prepared a light supper of baked beans on toast and went to bed early.

Our ablutions completed, we were lying in bed with Sophie explaining the day's events at work when she had been called into Personnel and informed of the news. She expounded with delight how she had remained demure, remembering distinctly the disbelieving look on the Personnel Director's face.

Afterwards she received an invitation to the boardroom for tea and biscuits with the Chief Executive Officer, Gordon Wilson and other department heads to cement her promotion. Ending her explanation, she solemnly declared Gordon Wilson who she quite liked and who had always supported her had now become her ex-boss.

Snuggled close Sophie suddenly remembered I had come home in a better mood than normal. She wanted to know why. During the past weeks, with regards Maybury Marine Engineers, I had not been fully honest with Sophie, never letting her know my new career included an apprenticeship in tea and coffee making.

Therefore, I couldn't tell the truth that evening. I simply told her I had attended a meeting with Mr Maybury to discuss progress, an assessment of my work to date, which would be clarified in a second meeting tomorrow afternoon. Pleased with what she had heard Sophie decided we should make love.

Driving to work the following morning, deep in thought, I attempted to envisage the many scenarios the scheduled meeting with Mr Maybury could, or would develop into. Consequently I focused solely on the meeting not paying attention to the road ahead.

I pulled out to overtake a lorry however, I hadn't noticed, hidden in front of the lorry, an old van. I didn't have a choice I had to overtake both vehicles. Ahead there lay a bend, which I knew to be blind. I floored the accelerator to pass as quickly as possible.

The sudden surge of the Cortina succeeded in getting the car past the lorry and abreast of the van. However, the surge of speed also careered the car into the path of a previously unseen oncoming line of traffic exiting the blind bend with a petrol tanker in the lead.

With a cacophony of horns blaring, head-lights flashing on and off, and vehicles swerving to evade the Cortina's path, I crashed the gear box into third gear to gain an instant increase of speed. I cut in front of the old van, managing by the smallest of margins to avoid causing a very serious accident.

Embarrassed and angry I maintained speed wanting to put my carelessness behind me, once clear I slowed keeping to the speed limit. I berated myself. Thereafter I concentrated on driving working through Southampton's suburbia navigating the traffic dodging the queues by using the back-roads I had found more by accident than design. I drove into the company's car park.

Jack Inglis, alighting from his aging Ford Anglia noticed the Cortina. His contorted face expressed anger and jealousy as he watched a mere trainee pull into the car park in a new top-of-the-range Cortina. I climbed out of the car wished him good morning, which he ignored. I reasoned today wasn't going to be a fun day.

At the top of the stairs Inglis waited; he said in a friendly voice unable to hide his cold eyes, "Why don't you make yourself a coffee and join me in my office for a chat?" "Certainly Jock," I answered knowing he would seethe because I had not called him Mr Inglis.

I made him and me a coffee although while waiting for the kettle to boil I tried to anticipate his next move. I entered his office saying, "I wasn't sure you wanted a coffee however, I made one anyway." He thanked me with a nod. "Take a seat we have a few things to discuss," he retorted.

"Yesterday evening I read your CV and your application. I admit it is a very good piece of theatre." I ignored his jibe. Resuming he said, "Why would a twenty-three-year-old give up four times the wage he was earning by changing jobs. I thought about it deciding your CV is pure fantasy and goodness knows who you bribed to write your references."

I stayed quiet, very relaxed, which he did not expect; he wanted a reaction. Frustrated he continued, "Alright Chambers why did you leave your last post as a regional manager to become a trainee engineer with Maybury." I didn't respond quickly enough. "Well, I am waiting?"

I continued to consider my response. He drank his coffee. I watched him carefully, trying to gauge his thoughts. Finally I said, "The answer is simple-- I want to become a very good professional engineer."

"Is that it? You want to be an engineer," He retorted.

"No, Jock I want to become a very good professional engineer," I emphasised the words "good" and "professional". "Why?" he demanded.

"Why at the age of twenty-three suddenly decide you want to be an engineer?"

Once more I purposefully paused before answering, "The answer remains the same, and I do want to become a very good professional engineer."

He was flabbergasted and definitely flummoxed by the coolness I projected. On reflection that was the moment he realised I was a cut above the norm. Unable to continue, his little game disintegrating, he gave up saying in a hushed voice, "Get out Chambers, get out."

I deliberately moved at a snail's pace, carefully replacing the chair I had been sitting on, lifting my coffee mug I said, "Could I get you another coffee Jock." An unsettled man looked at me and shook his head. However, he did have the last word. "You think yourself so clever Chambers but you will get your comeuppance, you will."

Exiting his office I felt my days with Maybury Marine Engineers could be numbered. Mr Maybury would not be the instigator. I had strong conviction he had earmarked me for a promising career. No, Inglis would without doubt circulate disinformation.

In time Inglis would gather support to worsen my situation, hell-bent on making my life unbearable. The malice I had seen on his face would be gradually interwoven into the minds of his peers.

On the surface, for the benefit of Mr Maybury and the other partners, I would be treated fairly. Below the surface lies would circulate to disparage my character. In terms of work delivery I would be kicked from pillar to post by his colleagues determined to break my spirit, to drive me out.

I received a message from reception informing me to report to Mr Maybury. I looked at my watch, three hours early, good or bad I speculated. Leaving my work area I noticed Inglis leaving his office. I followed him. Inglis knocked and entered, I tailed in behind.

Besides Mr Maybury, another chap I hadn't seen before sat at the meeting table. Mr Maybury indicated the empty chairs. Before I could sit the unknown man stood putting out his hand saying, "Doug Robertson". I shook his proffered hand, receiving a firm handshake.

Mr Maybury looking at his watch said, "We have twenty minutes before Doug and I will be departing to attend an important meeting. Jock, did you read Chamber's CV and application plus Personnel's comments?"

"I read the CV and application. I didn't have a copy of Personnel's comments," replied Inglis.

"Never mind, your comments?"

"Impressive Mr Maybury I didn't realise although I find it hard to understand why he gave up such a high wage."

I interrupted, "Excuse me," I said, "Mr Inglis I explained this morning, when you called me into your office for a chat. I'll repeat what I said at the time, I want to achieve a successful career by becoming a very good professional engineer with Maybury." Silence reigned as I watched Inglis go red.

Mr Maybury said, "Jock I told you yesterday evening no contact until this meeting, why the meeting?"

Squirming Inglis responded, "Mending bridges, Mr Maybury especially after reading Chamber's information I thought I owed him an explanation."

I kept quiet knowing I could have wiped the floor with him there and then.

Mr Maybury waved his hand in the air cutting the tense atmosphere saying, "No matter. Well, Chambers you will be pleased to know I took your advice subsequently two tea ladies working two shifts are being sourced by Personnel." I looked at Inglis; if looks could kill.

Mr Maybury continuing said, "Following yesterday's discussion I have called on Doug to help. Doug, in case you are not aware manages an office of specialist engineers based in Millbrook with two smaller operations, one in Liverpool and one in Immingham. His team responds to emergency requests both nationally and internationally. They also travel internationally to undertake certain works on ships in dry dock or laid up for some reason or another."

My heart leaped into my mouth. Inwardly I shouted yes, yes. Resuming he said, "I have asked him to take you under his wing for two weeks to assess your potential. Afterwards you will return to this office while we decide whether you have the makings to be a good engineer, fair enough?"

"Excellent Mr Maybury, thank you," I happily replied.

"Good that's settled. Jock any comment?"

Inglis asked, "Only whether Chambers will be returning to my team."

"Don't know, he may have uses elsewhere. We will wait for Doug's assessment." He stood saying to Doug, "Have a chat with Chambers while I collect the paperwork together for the meeting."

Inglis left the office in a dark, very dark mood. Mr Maybury busied himself, placing documents into a brief case. Doug said, "I too have read your CV, application and I did have a copy of Personnel's comments. I found the information interesting and informative. You obviously put a great deal of work in putting the CV together."

I nodded, "A combined effort orchestrated by my fiancée. She is a clever lady."

"Aha, I thought it had an interesting angle whereas the information expressed strong ambition linked with an admission that the finished article; i.e., you, would need work to achieve the polished finish. Very good approach, we'll talk next week. Ask reception for a map to the office.

54

Meet you eighty-thirty on Monday morning." We shook hands before he trotted off behind his boss.

I decided to pull a fast one. I knocked and entered Inglis's office. "Jock," feeling his toes curl I said, "I am, as instructed going to locate the Millbrook office. Is there anything I can do before I go?"

He looked at his watch saying, "No get off, no need to come back here, go home."

On my way out I collected a map with directions for Doug's office, willingly accepting Inglis's instruction to go home. In the car I played Black Sabbath and Moody Blue's music full volume as I drove home in record time. Nearing Hove, I slowed looking for a florist. I spotted a garden centre where I purchased a huge mixed bunch of flowers and a pretty congratulations card, I wrote;

"My darling Sophie, Any achievement you have attained is indeed the success you more than deserved. I wish that you may encounter more honour in the near future. Well done my darling. Your loving and extremely proud other half. Xxx"

The timing was perfect; we converged on our home from opposite directions. We flashed our lights. I pulled into the garage whilst Sophie parked in the street. Entering through separate doors we once more converged, this time in the hall where I presented the flowers.

Sophie accepted the flowers, read the card and threw her free arm round my neck pulling me down to meet her lips. Letting go Sophie went off in search of a vase calling over her shoulder she had promised to be at the Bear by seven-thirty.

This was not unexpected-- her parents would, quite rightly, be waiting for the full story regarding Sophie's promotion. Halfway up the stairs I heard, "Uncle Don's coming over to have a celebratory drink, picking up his lady-friend on the way."

I shouted back "Lady-friend? What lady-friend?"

Sophie carrying the vase said, "I thought I told you. He's being going with the same lady for over three months, for Uncle Don that my darling is a record."

I quickly showered throwing on Levis and a polo-shirt. Sophie came in the room kissed me and stripped. I watched her. Realising my eyes were focused on her said, "Don't get any funny ideas."

"What funny ideas? Can't a man admire his woman?"

"Yes but no touching. I read you like a book Richard Chambers."

Her gaze travelled towards Jolly Roger imprisoned by the Levis. "I knew it, look at him he wants out." She laughingly squealed.

I laughed "He doesn't want out, he wants in."

I smiled as I pulled the Levis's zip down, unbuckled the belt and dropping Levis and underpants.

"You are so romantic," she yelled as she lay on the bed. "I have been swept off my feet yet again. Come on hurry up." She cried in between giggles and laughter.

I pulled her into position lifted her legs and gently guided my penis into her rapidly moisturising vagina. "Yes," she said, "Yes my man, nice and easy."

A whimpering sound, half moan, half sigh exhaled from her throat. "Yes Richard, now harder push harder," she exclaimed.

I thrust my hips forward driving Jolly Roger to his full length deep into Sophie. "Oh Richard I love you. I love Jolly Roger."

Squealing she pushed towards me to meet my thrusts. We both thrust hard thrilling in the connecting of our love, our bodies. I could feel tingling in my loins closing my eyes I climaxed and I shuddered calling her name over and over.

Sophie lying on the bed expressed a loving satisfied smile, her cheeks the colour of roses. Her auburn hair spread on the lemon yellow counterpane capturing her wondrous features reminded me just how beautiful she was. I leaned forward and kissed her tummy running my lips up to her nipples.

"No," she screeched. "Stop right now. I have to shower and dress and you need to wash your privates."

I watched mesmerised as Sophie, within minutes, converted her wet hair into glorious tresses cascading down onto her shoulders, her only tools a hair-dryer and brush. She put on a cream dress with the Petticoat Market leather jacket. As usual she looked as if she had just walked off a film set.

We dashed down the stairs deciding to walk to the Bear. As we walked Sophie complained we were failing to commit to the keep-fit regime we had set ourselves stating with strong emphasis we had to re-commit. Her oration ended as we entered the Bear's side door.

We were twenty minutes late when we walked into the bar. Don and Ken were enjoying a beer in the far left corner. I could see there were two ladies seated in chairs behind them, whom I assumed were Irene and Don's lady-friend. Ken noticed Sophie and waved. Heading closer we apologised explaining I had been late leaving Southampton. I would have enjoyed telling the truth.

Don fussed over Sophie re-christening her with names, such as "miracle lady and super Sophie". The two ladies stood to meet our arrival. Irene hugged me, introducing Christine Don's lady-friend. Don hugged me telling me he was pleased I had chosen a proper career. Ken behind the bar leaned across to receive a peck on the cheek from his daughter.

Thereafter three or four regulars came forth to proffer their congratulations. Ken announced we would be going to the Indian Palace for eight-thirty explaining Joe and Josie would hold the fort.

Sophie and I declined alcohol, opting for tomato juices with Worcester sauce blaming the pressure of work plus, as Sophie eloquently explained, the laxity creeping into our keep-fit routine. Entering the Indian Palace, I was startled to observe the change since my last visit, the evening Jocelyn and I sharing a Biryani and half a dozen side dishes three plus years previously.

The Palace had expanded considerably in size enveloping an adjacent book shop. The row of booths formerly running alongside the right-hand wall where Jocelyn and I had sat was long gone. The original Indian gaudiness had been replaced with a much more subdued expression of Indian culture, which included a subtle lighting design. The restaurant, especially considering it was mid-week was very busy. We were shown to a large round table.

Don and Ken were in great form, reminding me of the days when father, Don and Ken would josh and jest. I had no idea the three were so close. Suddenly I thought of the "the terrible threesome", Sophie's school and college gang.

I considered father, Ken and Don together, deciding whatever Sophie's gang may or may have not been involved in, the thought of an alternative terrible threesome made me smile.

Nevertheless, it was Don and Ken who between them and with help from Akram the elderly owner who decided upon an array of dishes, jugs of cold water and two bottles of wine.

Much of the conversation centred on Sophie and her promotion, particularly several enquiring questions posed by Don as he tried to understand what exactly Urban Economics entailed. Sophie in her element, enjoying the attention, would have sermonised all night given the chance however, Irene, fortunately, quietly said, "Sophie we are very proud and pleased for you but do we need to sit here all night discussing whatever it is you do." Sophie gaily laughing retorted, "Of course we do, I have to seize the moment." We all laughed with her.

Don briefly questioned me with regards my work, which I explained away with words such as "challenging" and "interesting" without divulging, or hinting that for several weeks I had been working as a glorified messenger come tea boy.

Ken expressed how Irene's catering expertise had increased the Bear's turnover, especially the lunchtime trade. The pubs revenue increased month on month.

The Blue Indigo, now called the Sapphire Club had been extended into the car-park to include an intimate restaurant becoming a much vaunted venue for the punters with money as Uncle Don succinctly explained. The disco element continued to be packed Thursday, Friday and Saturdays. He closed on Sunday and Mondays but could be certain of a good turnout on Tuesday and Wednesdays.

Throughout the dinner Don and Ken kept the company amused, reminiscing their childhood and early teens with anecdote after anecdote. I did, when my mouth wasn't busy devouring the superb food, say a few words, expounding how I loved the McKendrick clan especially the auburn-haired wonder I had become engaged to.

With belts loosened and shirt buttons straining, the food, thank goodness, stopped coming. Sophie at this stage decided it was time we were tucked-up in bed. She used my early morning drive to Southampton as an excuse, announcing we were going home pointing out to her parents it was near to pub closing time.

Her father with a grin said "You may be the youngest head of a government department but your mother and I remain the bosses of the Bear." Smiling, we said goodnight and walked home.

The evening had passed quickly. We were preparing for bed when I thought only a few minutes ago we were making love here in this room. In bed with the alarm clock set, two bloated, one more than the other, lovers were quickly asleep. A few hours later I declined Muesli and gulped down a coffee before commencing the drive to Southampton.

During that morning's journey I noticed at regular intervals being overtaken by motorcycles. I had dabbled with riding motorcycles during my younger days. I had even taken a test and passed. With that in mind I started to think I could with a motorcycle probably reduce the journey time by fifteen or more minutes. I associated the improving weather with the steady influx of motorcycles.

The more I considered the more the idea became a reality whereas I considered a motorcycle could be fun for Sophie and I. I also considered finances, realising the Mini could be used to provide fiscal support. I would pass the Cortina onto Sophie, which I am sure she would be happy with, paving the way for a purchase.

Negotiating the rush-hour traffic the day-dreaming vaporised, until in the company's car-park when a gleaming chrome motorcycle arrived. The rider passed to my left disappearing beyond one of the door entrances jutting from the central part of the building close to where the three armed forces recruitment centres were located.

I jumped out of the car jogging to where the bike and its rider had disappeared. I soon discovered the bike but no sign of the rider. Studying the machine, a Triumph T100R Daytona, I decided to seek out the owner at lunchtime.

In the office all was quiet, most of the senior guys were out, and even my nemesis was absent. With very little happening I wandered off informing the girls in reception I would be back shortly. I departed the office via the front entrance leading onto the High Street, turned left, walked less than one hundred yards before entering the Royal Air Force centre. They were helpful advising the motorcycle rider was one of the navy chaps.

Shortly after thanking the RAF guys I was in the car-park with the Triumph's owner discussing motorcycles. The young man, a Sub-Lieutenant clearly very proud of his recently purchased Daytona motor cycle explained its power output, engine design and the effectiveness of the gear change.

Digressing away from his bike we briefly discussed, or rather he spent time expounding life at sea. He had recently returned from seven months serving aboard a frigate based in Malta.

Thinking of Sophie and feeling guilty I returned the conversation to his pride and joy. It transpired he lived in Farnham, Surrey. The journey to Southampton driving a car took on average sixty-five minutes, therefore being a bike fan, he decided to sell the car, and purchase the Triumph.

His journey home to office had been reduced to forty minutes plus, he exclaimed the journey had the added factor of fun. I thanked him for his time. Shaking his hand he said, "If you have twenty or so minutes to spare during my official lunch break, an hour from twelve-thirty I'll give you a pillion ride." He dashed into the centre returning with a brochure detailing telephone numbers.

Back in the office I collected an assortment of documents and secreted myself away in a meeting room off reception. After first spreading the documents to portray work I borrowed a telephone directory from reception. I telephoned several garages to identify a fair price for the Mini. Thereafter I called the Triumph dealer to price a Triumph T100R Daytona. Satisfied with my subterfuge I returned to my desk.

From four onwards, a general departure from the office, most sneaking off early swiftly emptied Maybury's offices. Dave Armstrong, one of the few decent chaps in the office wandered by my desk saying, "when the cat's away, the mice will play". Dave Armstrong's comment generated a desire to drive home.

Prior to my departure I called Keith Henley explaining I would be on temporary secondment to another office for the following two weeks, asking if I could arrange a ride when I returned, which he heartily agreed to. After fighting my way through busy streets for twenty minutes to clear Southampton my mind was made up.

Chapter 6 – Sophie's Party and Going Greek

Arriving home well after six, the lateness caused by an accident, I expected Sophie to be at home. I entered the house noting a message on the answering machine, one message from Sophie ordering me to meet her at the Blackbird pub in Brighton. I called for a taxi, the dispatcher said, "fifteen minutes mate".

The telephone rang. Sophie immediately wanted to know where I was. I explained the taxi delay and Sophie hung-up. I thought wow what is going on, she had never hung-up before. I opened a beer to wait for the taxi.

Entering the Blackbird I walked in on a group of thirty or more people with Sophie immersed near to the centre. Voices were raised fighting the juke-box and losing, bedlam reigned. I decided to keep a low-profile, I edged left of the group working my way into the furthermost corner opposite to Sophie's group.

The barmaid served the requested pint of bitter. A chap approached, putting out his hand saying "Richard isn't it?" shaking his hand "Yes how did you know?" "Sophie has a huge photograph of you on her desk and another of the two of you mounted on her office wall."

I must have looked perplexed. He laughed saying, "I'm Gordon Wilson, Sophie's ex-boss." "Oh hello Gordon, Sophie speaks highly of you," I replied. "What's going on?"

"Sophie's promotion party, the staff heard for the first time yesterday, her popularity instigated a whip round to buy a card and present."

Gordon continued "Thereafter quickly circulated by Sylvie the girl who stood by her during the unpleasant affair….."

I interrupted, "Yes, her old boss."

"A celebratory drink seemed natural. Anyhow the staff with Sylvie using a ruse to persuade Sophie to have a quick drink before home… well as you can see it worked."

"She looks very happy," I said adding, "and I know she is immensely grateful for the recognition."

Gordon smiled "She deserved it, she is fast becoming nationally acknowledged as an innovative specialist in her field."

"I didn't know," I croaked.

"I am surprised," he retorted, "It is difficult to hold a conversation with Sophie without your name cropping-up."

Sophie's voice pierced the momentary silence of the juke-box. "Gordon that's my lovely man." Suddenly I became the new attraction, heads turned and eyes appraised me. Gordon smiling paternally whispered, "That's your Sophie."

He stood aside as Sophie the tornado bared down. Not caring her arms wrapped round my neck and we kissed. The inevitable cheer resounded round the pub. Next I was being dragged into the throng of Sophie's co-workers, doing my best to remember the machine-gun speed delivery of names, some I remembered from previous meetings, responding to hugs and handshakes.

The juke-box blasting out the hit records of the day was abruptly silenced. Sylvie moved clear of the throng calling for attention. When quiet she said, "Sophie, I have the honour of presenting to you this gift to celebrate your promotion and what a promotion. Not only do you have the best looking guy in Brighton (all eyes on me again)," she paused for laughter, continuing, "But to be a departmental head at twenty-three is unheard of." Cheers and applause rubber stamped Sylvie's words, resuming she said "Sophie McKendrick all your friends, some whom couldn't be here this evening, wish you every success. And oh yes everyone wants to know when you and Richard are going to tie the knot."

Louder cheers rang round the Red Lion. Sophie in tears accepted the gift and with the words "speech, speech" ringing in her ears Sophie said, "Thank you for being so kind, thank you for being my colleagues and most of all thank you for being my friends."

Smiling broadly and looking directly at me she added, "Richard proposed to me in a pub in Richmond, which was full of rugby fanatics after the England, Scotland game. He went down on one knee and proposed I was stunned and oh so happy. It was romantic and loving so my friends the date is set for 7th August and you are all invited."

Cheers and applause. The music re-started. We were hugged and congratulated by Sophie's co-workers. Gordon Wilson shook my hand saying, "You are a very lucky man." I nodded and agreed.

Sophie very much overwhelmed mingled with her colleagues thanking them, each receiving a hug and pecks on the cheek. With tears running down her cheeks she looked utterly overwhelmed and extremely happy. I wanted to rescue her but waited patiently.

Eventually she reached me melting into my arms and said with tears running down her cheeks, "I love you Richard Chambers, don't you dare leave me." Wiping away the tears with a handkerchief one of her co-workers passed her, Sophie, instantly reverted to the happy smiling Sophie everyone loved, especially me. I loved her and had no intention of leaving her.

Family and friend demand began to thin the throng, people started to drift away leaving Sophie, Sylvie and three other ladies. Following a second introduction I repeated their names over and over in my mind promising not to forget.

Sophie said, "I'm starving." Thinking Sophie code to invite the ladies for dinner I said "Sylvie, Helen, June, Deborah and darling Sophie, why don't we find somewhere to eat and make a night of it." In reply I received a choused agreement. I noted Sophie kept quiet.

Deborah explained she knew a great Greek restaurant with music and dancing, which became the venue we headed for. During the walk Sophie and I lagged behind, she whispered, "I wanted to go home."

I replied, "You should have said so not state you were starving. We all misunderstood."

"Yes I know a stupid thing to say in front of everyone." She laughed, "You should have realised I was hinting I was hungry for you not food." Sophie squeezed my arm and smiled accepting we would soon be sitting in a Greek restaurant.

We were welcomed into a near full restaurant, because many of the diners were new arrivals, we had to queue waiting to be shown to a table. The ladies left their coats in the cloakroom. I swiftly removed jacket and tie.

Once seated, the ladies decided to have a cocktail. The attentive sommelier recommended two Greek classics. A raspberry flavoured, vodka-based one called Mount Olympus, the other a Santorini, a pear and vodka concoction. Sophie and Sylvie selected the Santorini, Deborah who had obviously dined before chose the Mount Olympus, which Helen and June echoed. I plumped for a dry white wine.

The ladies decided we should order two Meze each and share. When asked for a choice I responded asking for them to select on my behalf. I am not sure how it worked out but we ended with more than twelve dishes on the table. I remember Spankopita, Xoumas, Tzatziki, Melanzanosalata, Pita chips, Dolmades, Keftedakia and Kolokithakia after those I lost count. Two bottles of white wine were also ordered.

By the time the cocktails were consumed and the wine delivered to the table a group dressed in National Greek Costume were tuning their instruments. The food, at Sylvie's insistence, would be served in two batches, each batch to be liberally accompanied with Pita bread.

The restaurant filled rapidly, reiterating Deborah's assertion that the Pathos Temple would be a great night out. The group now fully tuned were playing melodic music to encourage conversation and eating, creating a cheerful atmosphere.

The first Meze dishes were served quelling the lively dialogue we were enjoying, eating took over. Someone ordered a third bottle of wine. The Greek musicians were playing good music as well as providing humour with the various antics they included into their repertoire, enticing a regular flow of dancers onto the floor. At our table the Meze and wine disappeared fast, encouraging the second Meze batch to be served and yet another bottle of wine arrived.

The five ladies whom had started drinking much earlier were in a very lively mood. The cocktails and wine completely loosened their inhibitions with comments suggesting if Sophie became fed-up with me they would be available. Sophie enjoyed their innuendos.

The second Meze serving adorned the table untouched, being replaced by dancing. Helen, June and Sylvie danced together, shimmering out of control. They remained on the floor for a second tune encouraging Deborah and Sophie, Sophie trying to drag me with her. The five were excellent dancers; they soon abandon all bashfulness, dancing with complete lack of inhibition, which in turn attracted other woman onto the floor to join the fun.

I resisted all coercion and attempt to force me onto the floor, until Sophie ordered me to dance with her, to a slow number. Thereafter, it was open season. I had no choice but to dance with her colleagues, not once but two or three or more times.

Sophie loved the fuss being imposed upon me, laughing merrily as her colleagues either dragged me from the table or I they enforced me to remain dancing whilst consistently alternating, regularly excusing one another.

The night progressed becoming livelier and livelier shouting and squeals resonated, the diners possessed by the dancing. Goodness knows how it came about but I ended up as a pivotal member of Greek Folk Dances.

Following a swift tutorage I became embedded into virtually every dance. Mercifully thankful for the recent keep-fit regime Sophie had demanded, in particular the strength in my legs.

The demand by the Greeks for my dancing skills emerged because I had put so much effort in, when dancing with Sophie's and her colleagues. The Greeks elevated me from pivotal dancer to star performer.

The Greek guys coached dance step after dance step, refusing to allow any rest. The sweat poured from every pore in my body. One I remember vividly, called The Hasapiko, started nice and easy, gradually increasing tempo, until legs were flying up and away, squatting and jumping and kicking legs became a way of life. I matched the Greek guys kick for kick, squat for squat but it was bloody hard, until with a sudden bang the music stopped leaving me bemused trying to kick. The diners roared and cheered.

However, the killer dance, name not known heralded in the end of the evening. The Greek musician who had initiated my earlier tutoring tried to pull me on to the floor, when I resisted he immediately looked to Sophie, who aided by the ladies forced me onto the floor.

Of course, the exhibition of force encouraged raucous cheering. I gave up and allowed myself to become, yet again, the centre of attraction, or the consummate fool.

The dance necessitated a swift lesson where I followed the steps of my tutor plus two of his cohorts. Once the Greek musicians, watching from the stage were satisfied I had mastered the basics of the dance, involving a series of accentuated dance steps in time with a beat, which was fine, they, the musicians, gradually increased the tempo. Initially keeping to the beat isn't a problem but when the dance transposed from sedate to wild, keeping in tune demanded excessive exertion.

The Greek waiters and chefs joined the melee, throwing plate after plate beneath our feet. This of course encouraged the diners, who too began to throw their plates, instigating exaggerated dance steps one could only imagine necessary when scrambling over the moon's surface.

The dance quartet, embodying three Greek guys and a crazy Englishman were throwing every last ounce of energy into a riotous demonstration, which had the whole restaurant clapping to the beat and cheering wildly. By the time the musicians realised the summit of their musical output I was utterly stuffed, knackered beyond knackered.

I have never been as relieved when the music finally ceased. My clothes, every stitch, were saturated. Sophie and her colleagues were all over me, kissing and hugging with Sophie glued to my lips.

I collapsed on a chair, absolutely shattered. The Greek guys inundated me with congratulations as if I had just won Olympic Gold for the marathon. Some of the diners encircled our table applauding madly. Sophie sat on my knee hugging me like crazy. I wanted a drink.

Fortunately one of the waiters read my mind delivering a stein of beer, which I gulped down. After a few minutes of chaos people began to drift away. My socks, underpants, shirt and trousers were sopping wet. Sophie whispered in my ear, "My star, you are amazing and I love you."

We fell from the restaurant in very high spirits as did many of the other diners. The evening had been fantastic one of the best. Sophie in an amazingly light-hearted mood constantly commended my dance prowess. For the next twenty yards or so a dozen or more of the diners who had witnessed my exhibition also proffered praise. One lady, much to Sophie's annoyance, forced herself close to kiss me.

Finally, free of well-wishers, we six, walked arm-in arm spread across the pavement giggling and laughing recalling the evening, in particular my dancing, of course, why not. We reached West Street, time to seek out taxis. Each of the girls wanted big hugs and proper kisses, which I obliged once Sophie with an imperceptible nod gave her assent.

Sylvie and Helen would share as would Deborah and June leaving Sophie and I. I insisted the girls took the first taxis. Sophie gripping my arm tightly said, "We have just had an amazing evening. Thank you my darling for being such a great sport. You succeeded in becoming a champion Hellenic dancer and shared yourself magnanimously with five women, although I always knew you were mine."

I hugged her close saying, "Darling as long as you had a great night celebrating your well-earned promotion that is all that matters." She assured me the evening had been great and she had loved every minute. I reminded her to thank Deborah for her recommendation and her other friends for being great fun.

At last a cruising taxi came into view we flagged madly managing to secure it. In the back of the taxi Sophie still holding firmly onto my arm and looking into my eyes whispered, "You know and I know you know that all four of my colleagues would jump into bed with you in a flash." I pretended to be aghast with her statement, which earned a playful squeeze of my private parts.

A moment later she added, "This evening, Monday morning, will circulate the office within minutes and by the time my colleagues have expounded your wonderful qualities, and Mr Hellenic man's energetic Greek dancing, you my darling will be mounted on a pedestal."

The taxi dropped Sophie and me off at the house entering we headed straight upstairs. Sophie overcome by the evening was smiling and giggling so much it took two attempts to hang her work skirt and jacket in the wardrobe. She then discarded her tights, bra and panties in a heap on the floor.

Not as affected by events as Sophie I stowed my work suit and placed shirt and underpants and socks in the laundry receptacle before having a much needed shower. By the time Sophie climbed under the sheets I had nodded off.

Chapter 7 – Sophie and Breakfast Mayhem

Saturday morning, what was left of it proved to be a chaotic forty minutes during which Sophie burnt the toast, used coffee granules in the tea-pot and broke a coffee mug. Not satisfied with her initial burst of enthusiasm, throwing her arms towards the ceiling in despair she knocked a glass pasta jar off of a shelf scattering shattered glass.

Half asleep, I heard the scream. I jumped from bed and ran downstairs. Sophie shouted, "Don't come in the kitchen, there's shattered glass on the floor."

I surveyed the scene; registering the situation, I quietly told her to stand motionless and not to move her feet. The pasta jar was not important, Sophie's bare feet were important. Searching the floor as I tip-toed, I carefully negotiated the breakfast bar to reach the cupboard housing the dustpan and brush.

On my hands and knees using my hands to check the floor for glass I manoeuvred around the kitchen sweeping pasta jar shards into the dustpan. Sophie giggled and giggled unable to stop, watching me, naked, systematically sweep the floor. Satisfied the glass had been cleared from the floor I stood. Sophie still giggling said, "Today we buy a camera."

Standing with dustpan and brush in hand dressed in my birthday suit Sophie, still conscious there may be a stray shard, giggled her way over to me. "Richard, if I live to be a hundred your house-keeping expertise, naked, will remain with me forever."

I evaluated the kitchen; besides the odour of burnt toast and the remains of the broken mug placed on the draining board, the sink was full of burnt toast crumbs and the room a shambles. "Sophie my darling what on earth have you been doing?" Giggling her reply she managed to say, "Making my darling man breakfast."

"Your darling man thinks his darling woman should have a cold shower, dress for shopping and report down here in fifteen minutes, okay?" Sophie still giggling saluted and ran up the stairs. I followed her to our room grabbing tracksuit bottoms I returned to the kitchen to clean the mess.

Sophie dressed in jeans and sweater her thick hair dropping onto her shoulders reappeared displaying a huge smile. "Master I await your bidding," she said in her little girl lost voice. I responded also smiling, "Your master bids you to pour the coffee that is if we have any mugs left."

Sophie grabbed me round the neck and kissed hard. "I cannot begin to imagine life without you," she said, continuing she added, "Nor can you without me, can you?"

"No, I admit I can't therefore we remain as one until hell freezes over."
I was rewarded with another hug and kiss although the kiss much more fervent the second time.

Drinking coffee Sophie smiling said, "A camera, we must buy a camera. Watching you sweep the floor, naked, demanded photographs. Believe it or not, you were beautiful, the most beautiful sight I have seen for a long time. You were magnificent exhibiting every aspect of your manly body, not realising I had a birds-eye view of every inch." I smiled with her, kissing her forehead before dashing to have a shower and dress.

Dressed similarly in jeans and sweaters, Sophie with a scarf wrapped around her neck we headed into Brighton to purchase a camera to be followed by traipsing the aisles of Safeway's supermarket for the weekly shop. I was surprised how difficult purchasing a camera proved to be. Two specialist shops bamboozled Sophie and me with jargon neither of us really understood.

Armed with brochures we retired to a café for a light lunch in an attempt to decipher the content. We returned to the first shop we visited, generally because the assistant serving seemed quite knowledgeable. We purchased a Zorki 4, 35mm rangefinder and three rolls of film. The assistant loaded a film and also provided an on the spot lesson, which Sophie picked up on much quicker than I.

Camera in hand we headed for the beach to take photographs, of each other and also the sights of Brighton. The film quickly expired. We were nervous with regards to removing it and installing a replacement. Subsequently we returned to the shop for a second lesson, this time I listened carefully.

During the course of the weekend we used the other two rolls of film depositing all three in the chemist for development. Washing-up after lunch on Sunday I remembered to ask Sophie whether she had any photographs of her and me or any individual ones. She didn't answer immediately trying to decide if I was aware. Nodding she said "Yes I have six or seven." "Really," I said. "I can't recall posing with you for a photograph."

Sophie knew I had caught her out. "You didn't. I wanted natural photographs of you and me depicting our love." she replied.

"How did you manage to achieve your photographs?" I asked.

"When we were away for weekends or at an event where there a freelance photographer operated I would, when you were occupied, ask the photographer to take a picture."

"Could I see these photographs?" I requested. "Of course but you will have to wait until tomorrow evening, they are in my office under lock and key," she sheepishly responded.

Chapter 8 – Testing Times

Monday morning, sitting in a traffic queue on the outskirts of Southampton I reflected upon the weekend. We had fun, which we always seemed to do. Friday had been an unexpected night out, which turned out to be a fantastic fun evening. Saturday had certainly had its moments following Sophie's misadventures in the kitchen and we had enjoyed becoming photographers.

However, Sunday had been a day of disconnection. I decided this was because I had discovered, due to information received from Jessica and Gordon Wilson, Sophie had photographs taken without my knowledge, which struck me as strange.

After querying if photographs existed followed by Sophie's admission the Sunday after lunch was a mute affair. We read the Sunday papers, listened to music on the radio and watched a crappy film on television. In bed we cuddled but didn't make love.

Entering the car park of Maybury offices, Millbrook I pushed the weekend to the back of my mind. I entered a small reception, asking for Doug. The girl asked my identity. I followed the girl's directions towards his office. I knocked and entered.

Doug came round his desk to shake my hand. "Let's walk I'll introduce you to the gang." The office buzzed, a hive of activity, telephones constantly trilled, and engineers huddled together studying drawings, typewriters hammered away but the most interesting aspect, his team all seemed happy extending a warm welcome. The atmosphere the office emitted completely opposed the head office. This office was alive.

Back in Doug's office he explained how he would assess my capability. For the next two weeks he would assign me to work three challenges. The first challenge would be with the design engineers where I would be required to study and understand a specific design. I would be required to measure and count the engineering components within a drawing, listing each item. When satisfied I would return to him with the drawing or drawings, with the list.

Thereafter, I would explain to him the design and the design's objective. Therefore I needed to comprehend clearly the engineering disciplines whether electrical, mechanical, steam or diesel, or hydraulic. He asked if I fully understood his expectation, I confirmed I did, he passed me to Peter Jackson, head of design.

Peter on the surface was a studious guy, but with a wicked sense of humour, which came to my notice on several occasions during the two weeks I would work with Doug's team. He immediately set me to work providing a set of six drawings depicting the workings of a ship's engine room. Not having room in the overcrowded office he placed me in a meeting room.

For the next two days I arrived early in the morning and left late into the night. I fully committed myself to understanding every nut and bolt, every switch and device and every function of every machine. An overriding factor of those couple of days, I realised I thoroughly enjoyed the solitude and the challenge.

Monday evening, the evening Sophie was due to show me the photographs I arrived home at ten past ten. I had called from the office informing her I would be running late albeit I had said I would be home by eight-thirty to nine. She heard the garage-to-house interconnecting door close rushing to meet me, obviously upset and concerned. I apologised for being late hugging her tight deciding to explain to her what had happened at work.

I missed out the confrontations with Inglis and also decided not to tell of the meetings with Mr Maybury. Sophie said, "Isn't that a good thing?"

"Yes my lovely it is but I have to finish the two weeks completing the assessment with flying colours. If not I will have to take the slow route, which is mundane and uninteresting," I answered.

Taking my hand she led me into the kitchen. "I'll cook you some supper." I declined, asking for a cup of tea.

On the breakfast bar sat a large buff envelope. Sophie filling the kettle said, "Open it." Lifting the flap I withdrew seven large photographs consisting of four of Sophie and I, two of me and an individual one of Sophie. I spread them across the bar. I studied each one however one jumped up and slapped me round the face.

It portrayed Sophie and I up-close, dancing, Sophie in the blue evening gown me jacketless with one hand on her bottom the other in the small of her back. Our pelvis connectivity spoke volumes and we were also locked in a deep kiss. Obviously it had been taken during the New Year's dinner and dance.

A second photograph taken the same evening depicted Sophie sat on my knee embracing and kissing me. Both were superb photographs capturing exactly what she had asked for from the photographer.

Laughing I selected the up-close one saying, "I could sell this to a girlie magazine and make a few bob." She lightly clipped me round the ear. The individual one of Sophie taken in London, the evening at the Marquee when Genesis were the star attraction, displayed Sophie in an amazing pose.

Wearing the figure-hugging cocktail dress with the ultra-short skirt, her hair reflecting the club's lighting strobes and her eyes were amazing, green, green, and green, she looked magnificent. The photographer had also captured her beautiful face in half-profile displaying her white teeth as she laughed. Sophie looked ravishing, stunning and very, very beautiful. The photograph portrayed a beautiful woman at ease and very happy.

As I studied the remaining photographs I, for the life of me, could not remember any roving photographers. A third photograph of Sophie and I depicted a close up, holding hands and looking into each other's eyes displaying obvious love, our faces no more than three inches apart albeit we appeared to be slightly younger.

In the background a very blue sea reflected dancing diamonds. I didn't recognise the venue. Sophie supplied the information. We were in Rimini, Italy sitting at a balcony table enjoying a cool drink before venturing out for dinner. It was a wonderful romantic photograph. Sophie, confirming Gordon Wilson, explained the photograph hung from her office wall.

The fourth one of Sophie and me, the most recent one taken during the weekend in Eastbourne again pictured Sophie and I dancing but this time we were shimmering side by side, the photographer somehow managed to take the picture as our hips touched, which made for an excellent photograph.

The two individual photographs were also very good. One was taken during my college days when I was playing rugby during a tour which perchance encompassed Brighton. I recognised the picture showing a guy tackling me from behind and the sheer determination in my face to press on regardless.

I asked Sophie how she came to have the photograph. She expounded how she worried the photographer, who worked for the local newspaper, to death until he provided her with a copy. I remembered where I had seen it before, in the College magazine.

The second photograph showed a man in bathing trunks, winking with a sexy smile. I appeared to be looking straight at the camera. I studied the background, sand and sea, but I couldn't place where we were. "Okay my love where are we this time?" I asked.

"Monte Gordo, Portugal," she replied. My mind skipped back a couple of years recalling the beach.

I said, "I am absolutely positive there weren't any freelancers on the beach."

Laughing Sophie agreed saying "But there were two young girls in bikinis who fancied you, one of which had a camera who took the picture when you were skylarking with them." I could vaguely recollect the girls, probably fifteen or sixteen. However, I couldn't recall a photograph being taken.

"So Sherlock, how did you track this one down?" I smilingly queried.

"Do you remember the night you decided to stay-on in the casino and gamble and I went to bed?" she asked.

"Yes, just," I replied.

"The following morning I left you in bed going down to breakfast. The girls were at breakfast. They came over to my table to show the photograph of you. There and then we did a deal, which gave me access to the negative, I had it enlarged and there it is."

"Is this the one in your office?" I queried.

"Yes, how did you know?" her face a frowning question mark.

"Aha a little birdy." I rose from the bar and encircled Sophie in my arms kissing her passionately. Still holding her I asked two sixty-four million questions. "Why keep them a secret from me? Why didn't you share the photographs with me?"

Tears welled into her lovely green eyes, which pained me. I said, "Forget it you do not need to answer."

"I wanted photographs of you, of you and me in love, for me. I need something to remember you, remember us by."

"Whoa lady, do you know something I do not? Are my days as your Lionheart, your man due to end? Are my days on earth finished? Explain Sophie," I said light-heartedly. Controlling emotion she said, "It's not a joke Richard. You will leave me. I keep telling you but you will not listen. You hear my words dismissing them. But you will, you will leave me."

Her eyes flooded pouring uncontrollable tears down her cheeks. She pushed me away running into the hall and up the stairs. I followed.

She lie front down on the bed sobbing her hands gripping the counterpane. I sat beside her and stroked her hair. I said very quietly, "Sophie darling look at me." No reaction came from her. "Sophie please darling look at me." Once more Sophie refused to look at me.

I had no choice but to speak to her back. "Sophie we have had this conversation a hundred times. I am not going anywhere. I am with you today and forever." Sophie remained silent. I continued, "Darling, give me one good reason, and for goodness sake do not say the sea, why I will leave you? Why in God's name would I want to? Come on, Sophie answer me."

She rolled over to her back and sat up leaning into my chest. I put my arms round her. "Richard, it is the sea. I wake up at night knowing you are out there sailing somewhere thousands of miles away from me. It's not a dream it's a reoccurring nightmare. I try so hard to dismiss it but it comes back. Sometimes not for days, then it's with me night after night."

"Sophie," I whispered into her hair. "I am going to make a success of this job. We will be together come hell or high-water. Nothing will break you and me, nothing."

"Richard I believe you because you believe it to be true. I know you will not accept what I say. But please, please hear me. The nightmare is as vivid as you and I sitting here at this moment. I even see the ship, a red and grey ship with black funnels. The vividness of the nightmare is torturing me."

She started crying. I attempted to reassure her. I whispered my love for her. I kissed her hair and her cheeks. I cuddled and cuddled her but to no avail.

Although awake she was non compos mentis, not in the true sense but very, very fragile. I gently undressed her pulling the bedclothes back to manoeuvre her into bed. I lay on the bed continuing to whisper and hold her. She fell into a deep exhaustive sleep. I quietly prepared what I needed for the morning and climbed in beside her.

Someway I responded positively to the alarm. I collected my belongings entering father's room to shower and shave. In the kitchen I put pen to paper producing the most loving letter I could:

My dearest darling Sophie,

You mean the world to me and I care about you so deeply that it hurts for the short time that we are not together each day. My every thought and breath, I draw from you. I truly do love you.

I love you and you are my world. You are the sweetest, most precious of all women. I will love you forever - don't' ever doubt that. I will never want anyone else's love but yours. You make me feel like I am the only man in the world. And as far as I am concerned you are the only woman. You are my heart and soul. I feel and know we were destined to be together, that we have been brought together by our creator.

You are my soul-mate, I see it every time I look into your eyes and I feel it when you are in my arms. Sophie, my sweet Sophie, I love you.

Sophie, do you remember the dictionaries and languages you once mentioned? I do, and like you I know there are no words to express how I feel about you. I constantly search for the words, and they all seem less than I truly feel. You are my life, my heart, and my soul. You are my best friend. You are my one true love today and the future.

I love you with all that I am, all that I was, and all that I ever will be. Love always, Richard

I left the letter prominently displayed, propped up in the centre of the breakfast bar.

The drive into work proved a shocker not because of traffic or road conditions but because of the sorrow for Sophie. I recalled the time I considered psychiatric treatment, deciding we had to find a cure for her nightmares. The fixation she had that I would leave her for the sea. There has to be a cure, a solution.

I arrived very early the office in darkness. I sat in the car, waiting and thinking. I knew it imperative I concentrated on the tasks Doug had set me but I also knew Sophie needed my love and my attention. I thought of Sophie how distraught she had been.

A car came into view, thankfully it was Peter. I alighted from the car walking with him towards the office. He said, "Good morning Richard, what's this? The early bird catches the worm?".

"Hello Peter," I replied, "No not really I am eager to achieve a great assessment. Your office is so different from HQ. Here I feel commitment, there I feel complacency."

"I know what you mean. I worked there for twenty-three years until Doug gained promotion. Luckily he chose me to help build this end of the business," he laughingly answered.

Inside the office I didn't bother with tea or coffee I went straight to work. I took my wrist watch off placing it in plain view to remind me to telephone home at seven-thirty when Sophie would be up and about. I continued on from the night before studying the design objectives. I made copious notes. I kept a wary eye on the watch.

At seven forty-five after three attempts Sophie answered, "Oh Richard, thank you darling, thank you for loving me, and thank you for the love-letter. I don't deserve you or your love. I am going to drive you away with my neuroses."

I smiled, "No chance you are stuck with me." I quietly asked how she was feeling. Whispering she said, "I am fine Richard, perhaps a wee bit tired, but fully revived from last night's defeatism."

Lightening the mood of the conversation I said, "Good, don't forget you are the boss-lady so chin-up when you enter the office and give them what for. And remember I love you."

I could hear the relief in her voice, "I will darling I will but now I have to get ready or I'll be late, which would not set a good example would it?" I mentioned I would probably be late again before reiterating my love for her. We said our goodbyes.

The next ten hours surpassed me so quickly I did not stop except two visits to the toilet. I was reading through my notes when Doug came in seating himself across from me. "Well, young man what is obvious is your determination. I doubt whether you have had lunch or even a cup of tea. Peter tells me you were first in this morning."

I nodded. "Yes, I suppose I was."

"When will you be ready?" he asked "I have a meeting in the morning and will not be in the office until midday."

"Midday will be fine," I said.

"Good, I'll see you then. I'll come in here with Peter; okay?"

"Okay," I replied.

I arrived home at eleven o'clock. I had called Sophie three times delaying my arrival. I refused to leave the office until wholly satisfied, except for a couple of hours work in the morning, I was ready for the Part

One test of my competence. Sophie looked a picture, fast asleep in father's chair.

I gently wakened her with little kisses. She opened her eyes and for what seemed the millionth time her arms encircled my neck. We kissed for a moment before I took her hand leading her to bed.

In the morning I awoke before the alarm. I quietly re-set it for Sophie and once more used father's bathroom to wash, shave and dress for work. I quietly slipped out of the house and leisurely drove to work. With the car interior light on, sitting in the car-park I read and reread my notes ensuring I would be prepared. Peter and Doug arrived simultaneously.

After the usual morning greetings I made a coffee and set to work to complete the final notes relative to the objective of the design, which entailed establishing the design requirements a task I had mostly performed during the design feasibility analysis.

I concentrated on ensuring the notes I had compiled fulfilled all aspects of the challenge I had been set. I ticked off the elements necessary to fully understand the design objective, including operating parameters, operating and non-operating environmental motivations, test requirements, dimensions, maintenance and testability provisions, materials, reliability requirements and design life. Satisfied, all I had to do was wait for Doug to return.

During the waiting time I carefully laid out the drawings, which were littered with inscribed notes and also made sure the notes, all forty pages were properly titled and numbered, and in order. At five past twelve Peter and Doug entered the meeting room. My palms were sweaty.

They nodded their greetings before, without touching the drawings and notes, carefully scanned my work. Peter whispered something to Doug, which I didn't hear. Doug said, "Okay Richard where are you going to start?"

"First," I said, "Here is the relevant information with regards all the data contained within the design, which includes where appropriate a paragraph or two explaining the reason it or they are included. I will go through the pages one by one."

"How many pages?" asked Doug.

"Seventeen, they are all titled and also have page numbers." Peter took the pages from me and moved to a chair at the top of the table.

Doug queried what the other notes consisted of. I explained how I had defined the design objective into ten sections, each section containing a breakdown, defining the engineering issue, including expected solutions and why specific design parameters and / or design ideas had been generated. He gave me a positive look of approval. He queried and named my university; I confirmed yes.

He took the other twenty-three pages and moved to the chair opposite Peter. For the next hour I fretted. At one stage Doug told me to bugger off and get a sandwich and drink.

When I returned they were still pouring over my notes. I stood looking from the window watching a huge bulk carrier move clear of the dockside into clear water to start its departure from Southampton. I heard Doug say, "Do you want to explain the drawings and the inscribed notes?" I turned; they were both standing by the drawings.

I began my explanation carefully describing every element, the reason for it and every component and also its need. The whole exercise lasted ninety minutes. Doug, satisfied, told me to go for a walk and return in half an hour. It was a very nervous Richard Chambers who walked aimlessly seeing nothing, nor hearing anything, except for the watch I constantly checked.

When I re-entered the office the receptionist directed me to Doug's office. I knocked, Peter opened the door. Doug indicated a chair.

I waited for someone to speak, finally Doug said, "Richard your work is exceptional, both Peter and I are astonished by the detail, the knowledge and your obvious competence. Confidentially I would say, and I am sure Peter would agree, there isn't a junior engineer in head office who could have produced this standard of engineering understanding. In fact I can think of one or two senior engineers who would also fall short."

I didn't know whether I had to respond. Peter saved me when he said, "Richard I will admit I doubt, until five or six years ago, whether I could have prepared a better report, especially the attention to detail, where did you gain the experience?"

I turned to face him saying, "I haven't any industrial experience everything you have witnessed is from my college days."

Doug intervened, "Do you have a special interest?"

"Not particularly," I said. "But I do have a retentive memory and a fundamental need to understand, especially if I come across something, anything really, I want to fully comprehend. An example is when a schoolboy I became extremely interested in steam locomotives so I studied intently until I convinced myself I had identified exactly how they worked."

"Well," Doug said, "You have convinced Peter and me. We suspect you will become the good professional engineer you emphasise so strongly. However, I want you to go home, take tomorrow off, and be here Friday to start Part two of your competency programme, okay?"

I was overwhelmed, stammering, "Yes sir and thank you."

"Doug, my name is Doug I haven't knelt before the Queen, yet." he laughingly responded. I shook their hands and very nearly let a delighted yippee escape from my happiness.

I returned to the meeting room, collected together all my work to take home to show Sophie. I couldn't wait to talk to her. Before leaving, three times I tried to telephone her being told she was in a meeting and couldn't be disturbed. I left a message saying I would be home early.

I left the office and drove home in an extremely happy mood listening and singing along at the top of my voice to the Moody Blues.

Sophie obviously received my message her car was parked outside the house. I pulled into the garage where she came to meet me. "Sophie," I yelled, "I have just received praise beyond all my dreams. They loved the first phase of the competency programme. You will never believe what they said to me. Oh Sophie I love you."

I hugged and kissed her completely swamping her with my loving attack. "Calm down Richard," she cried.

"Oh darling you have no idea how I feel," I retorted.

"Well my lovely man you had better take a deep breath and tell me all about it."

Grabbing the drawings and notes I followed her into the kitchen. In the kitchen I cleared the breakfast bar hastily sorting the drawings and notes into order. I briefly explained the task I had been set. After which I quickly described, using the drawings as props, how I had prepared my solution in response to the task. Watching her face I could see the pleasure, she was so happy for me. Thereafter, trying to recall what was said verbatim, I told Sophie what Doug and Peter had expressed.

"My darling Richard, my man, I am so proud of you. I knew, just knew, if given the chance you would shine and you have." It was her turn to hug and swamp me with kisses. Breathless we stood embracing until I said, "Sophie I want you and me to walk to Fish Bone for a fish supper remembering the first time, the night you and I walked down from the Bear, when we first hugged, can we?"

I sounded like a little boy. Sophie, tears welling said, "I remember and we will my darling, we will." We both wept with joy, with happiness and with deep, deep love.

I changed out of my work suit putting on jeans, sweater and my faithful Musto. Sophie wrapped herself ready for Antarctica. Hand in hand eclipsed with many kisses we sauntered to the fish shop, reminiscing over a similar walk of long ago. We ordered our preferences and sauntered back. I did walk a low wall and leap between two brick gate pillars, which made Sophie smile. Once home I opened our penultimate bottle of wine, with which we toasted love and success.

We retired to bed chatting, actually it was a one-way conversation whereas I extolled my own attributes. My enthusiasm brimming over I talked endlessly with regards gaining success with Maybury and our future together, whether in Hove, Southampton or a nearby village perhaps in the New Forest.

Sophie, cuddling close, permitted the constant rambling, sharing and enjoying my happiness. I so much wanted her to be happy for both of us. In the back of my mind I was praying the news I had brought home would go some way towards allaying her fears of the sea and I. I dearly hoped so. I left the alarm clock set for Sophie's call to work. She had fallen asleep before I had the chance to tell her I had the day off.

I awakened early, the inbuilt alarm clock waking me at my usual time. I decided to jog. I silently dressed in tracksuit and set off to pound the promenade. I forced exertion to clear head and work muscles. Exercised and feeling pretty good I returned home before Sophie stirred. I searched the fridge to prepare a breakfast in bed surprise.

Scrambling eggs, toasting bread and percolating coffee took longer than expected. I turned with the tray to face Sophie with a beautiful smile leaning against the door architrave watching me express my culinary skills. She took the tray placing it on the breakfast bar before giving me an exquisite loving kiss making me feel on top of the world.

Sitting enjoying her surprise breakfast she said, "It abated a little bit last night." Perplexed I asked what she was referring to. "The sea silly, I actually dreamt, well I think I did, because when I awakened we were together, not you on a ship God knows where."

I went behind her and kissed the top of her head saying, "I told you so." Suddenly realising I was still at home and not in Southampton she exclaimed, "Richard why aren't you at work?" I told her the story of my unexpected day off.

She said, "Don't be late tomorrow we have a dinner date."

I responded, "I know darling you and I together celebrating your career and our first date."

Smiling she said, "I thought we lived our first date last night when you romanced me all the way to the Fish Bone and back."

Sophie at work and being alone in an empty house proved too depressing. I jogged to the gym and worked out for an hour followed by a steam room session. I jogged back followed by a shower. Switched the television on, switched the television off.

I had been wrestling with a dinner menu for the evening for ages struggling to come-up with a surprise recipe. I went to the kitchen looking for the two recipe books Tina had left behind and the one Sophie purchased.

Flicking through, I noticed Knickerbocker Glory. That was it, Welsh Rarebit followed by Sophie's sweet tooth weakness. I listed the ingredients for the Knickerbocker Glory realising I would need the appropriate glasses and checked whether we needed cheese. I also checked for Worcester sauce and Tabasco for the Welsh Rarebit.

Whilst in Safeway's shopping, I unexpectedly noticed Jocelyn, hoping she hadn't spotted me I dodged down an aisle leading to the butchery. Bad mistake, once I reached the butchery there was only one way out, turn and head back down the same aisle.

I killed time sifting through packaged meats. A voice instantly recognisable as Jocelyn said, "Hello Richard, no need to hide I am not going to repeat my action of the last time we met." Looking-up, Jocelyn, looking absolutely stunning, her blonde hair probably two or three inches longer stood smiling.

If anything she looked younger than she did three and a half years ago, I replied, "Oh hello Jocelyn, how are you?"

"I am fine but I could be much better, perhaps when you have bought me a coffee," she said still smiling.

I smiled back saying, "Ah Jocelyn what a great idea, unfortunately I am duty chef tonight, you know how it is."

She laughed, quite loudly attracting stares saying, "So the male species of the perfect couple is under the thumb, cooking for his better half."

"Yes, you could say that however, we share all household responsibilities. In fact I am a dab hand with an iron and a hoover," I responded with a huge smile.

I said "Good to see you, take care," continuing to seek out the ingredients I needed. Jocelyn followed as I referred to the list gathering together the shopping including a bottle of champagne until, with the exception of the ice-cream, she finally spoke saying, "Sophie obviously has a sweet-tooth."

Feeling inadequate and a tad angry I said, "No, tonight I am spoiling her."

"Why?" she retorted.

"Why? Because I love her, that's why," I replied a touch too stridently, which attracted more stares.

Continuing in an angry whisper, "Look Jocelyn I apologised and you whacked me. It was years ago, so could you please leave me alone."

However she persisted, "Buy me a coffee and I'll leave you alone."

"Alright, alright for goodness sake, I'll buy you a coffee, where?"

"There's a tea room next door." She indicated with her head.

"Okay I'll pay for my shopping and meet you in there," I exclaimed

She shook her head. "I don't think so, do you? I'll keep you company at the check-out."

Standing, ordering two coffees I remembered the special glasses. I cursed Jocelyn. I joined her at the table, a table slap bang in the centre of the window. I sat down facing inwards, fingers crossed no one Sophie or I were acquainted with would notice me with an attractive blonde.

She pulled my face round so she could look into my eyes saying, "You still have those sexy, take-me -to bed eyes."

"*Oh shit,*" I thought not another one. "Have I? I don't recall you mentioning it before."

Displaying a crooked smile she said "Richard don't worry I am not trying to seduce you, why would I? I wouldn't stand a chance. What, the perfect couple splitting-up over a long-lost love. I don't think so, do you?"

Trying to be pleasant I asked her how she was. Whether she still worked at the Swan, and if anything exciting had happened these past years. She thought for a moment before saying, "It took me a while to get over you. I have never stopped thinking of you, not full on, you understand, but from time to time you do become an annoyance."

"Jocelyn what is it you exactly want?" I asked.

"Nothing, just a coffee with an old friend. You can go now and prepare your wondrous Sophie's supper."

I looked at her, stood, picked-up the shopping bag and rushed from the tea room, tail between my legs. I heard her laughter as I pushed by incoming customers to reach the street.

Somehow I located the special glasses. Nevertheless, I needed to return to Safeway's to purchase three or four different flavoured ice-creams. Holding my breath I rapidly walked past the tea room window ducking into the supermarket.

Shortly afterwards safe at home I unpacked the shopping, putting the ice-cream in the freezer section and the champagne into the fridge door. With my hands resting on the breakfast bar I slowly collected my thoughts; "what the fuck was that all about?"

I had just placed the Knickerbocker Glories in the fridge when Sophie walked into the kitchen saying, "Hello handsome, you owe me five hundred kisses, one for every minute we have been apart," and laughed. I loved Sophie laughing.

"Okay, go and take you clothes off, and lay prostrate on the bed and I'll be up in a minute to administer five hundred and one kisses," I said trying to make my vocal chords sound sexy. "What's the extra one for?" she asked, "That one my darling Sophie is the one that makes you tingle all over as I transmit through your body a powerful "I love you" message."

Smiling she walked round the breakfast bar and held me her head pressed into my chest. I kissed the top of her head asking, "Hungry?"

Nuzzling my chest "Yes, I think I am. What has the master chef prepared?"

"It is for the chef to know and the gannet to wait in anticipation," I retorted.

She broke the embrace. "Gannet, who's a gannet?"

"You my darling or you will be very soon," I answered.

"Have I time to change?" she queried

"You have, there is no rush," I replied.

Running up the stairs I heard her call, "What's happened to keep-fit? Another session cancelled."

I called back, "I had a lengthy session this morning." I heard an exclamation.

Wearing a sloppy top and shorts Sophie reappeared and said, "It smells suspiciously like cheese on toast is the chef's culinary offering."

"The gannet is wrong. The chef is preparing a very special supper to challenge the cuisine of a certain restaurant somewhere in London," I responded laughingly. "In the meantime please make yourself comfortable at the breakfast bar and the chef will serve a pre-dinner drink, champagne madam?"

Popping the cork I filled two flutes. Seconds later I was grabbing the Welsh Rarebit before it burnt. I was just in time the cheese on toast with Tabasco on one slice and Worcester sauce on the other I, with great ceremony laid the two slices on Sophie's plate.

We chinked glasses and tucked in. Actually the two sauces had enhanced the cheese on toast greatly. I removed the plates to the sink. Opening the fridge and with much ceremony I produced the Knickerbocker Glories. Sophie laughed hugging and kissing me. Sophie dispatched her Glory in double quick time, kissing me once more.

Chapter 9 – Work Assessments and Success

The following morning, Friday, I was once more the first to arrive at the Maybury office. Doug arrived a few minutes later. After morning greetings he led the way to the meeting room. Sitting opposite he explained my next challenge, programmed for the day and Monday. He explained he wanted me to audit the procurement and stores processes and prepare a report of my findings and add any recommendations, which could or would improve the existing systems.

I wasn't sure whether he was aware of previous experience I had gained working with R J Construction. In fact, my retentive memory failing, I couldn't remember if the information was included in my CV.

He left the room returning minutes later with a bunch of keys indicating I should follow him. I followed until we parked next to an ugly black building. He unlocked the door entering what looked like a very well organised warehouse with numbered rows, lettered shelves, each shelf accompanied with a list of the shelf's contents.

It looked impressive. I followed him to three offices. They were for goods in and goods out, national and international shipping and the largest, a room shelved floor-to-roof, stacked with hundreds of hard backed files clearly numbered with suffixes and prefixes. He asked me what I thought. I told him it looked very impressive.

Taking a seat in the shipping office he explained the warehouse manager, Casey, an experienced stores and knowledgeable materials manager, had for months been demanding a specialist to objectively audit the warehouse's operations.

Casey was convinced there were improvements to be made; however because of the persistent non-stop movement of goods the staff consisting of Casey, three warehousemen and a clerk, Casey's daughter, did not have the time or the inclination to investigate. He said, "Therefore Mr Chambers you are my specialist." He left the warehouse saying, "Casey will be here soon. He is expecting you. Good luck."

I watched two cars traversing the concrete road towards the warehouse. Casey and daughter were in the first car, two guys in the second car before a motorcycle pulled in with a younger guy astride.

Casey strode across introducing his team and himself. He said, "Okay let's get to it. I understand you have today and Monday, yes?" I affirmed. I followed him into the shipping office. "Candy will give you two hours, less I hope, for you understand how the system works. Clive, the dark-haired guy will walk the warehouse explaining the goods in, goods out operation. Clive junior, not his son, the biker will demonstrate the shipping procedure and Sandy the filing system. I'll be around for questions. Got it?" I assured him I had.

During the morning I witnessed vehicles in and out, stores arriving and shipments leaving. As instructed I spent the allocated time with the team during in which I took copious notes. I locked away in my brain that I needed a Dictaphone. By the time they closed the huge chain operated doors, closing for lunch-break I was pretty much up to speed.

While they lunched I interrogated the filing system and a rather complex index card system. Satisfied, I undertook random stocktakes of shelves checking shelf contents against shelf lists. I found a quiet corner perched on a packing case and studied my notes and findings. I decided with the exception of the card index system the stores operation appeared quite effective.

I had to test efficiency, but how. I was racking my brain trying to figure out how to approach the test when the penny dropped. Realising it would take dedicated hours to complete, I asked Casey, if I could have keys because I would be staying late. He grumbled but found a set of keys and demonstrated the security system.

The longest task would be comparing goods status for movement types against the warehouse's general ledger paying specific attention to the methodology employed to log goods and how shipping was programmed. The second task also a long one required checking inventory back posting to previous periods ensuring they were correctly recorded, this would simplify the card index system.

The final task, which if the first two produced the information expected, would be a cross-check exercise to create goods in and goods out reservation with authorization checks from recipients tied into delivery inspection.

First I prepared a plan of attack, which would decide actions developed to lessen double handling followed by warehouse re-arrangement and index card system re-configuration and pre-proscribed delivery inspection cross-checking.

Satisfied, I started the work. I called Sophie explaining what I was doing and I would be late, probably very late and not to wait up. I apologised profusely for ruining her planned celebration dinner at the Bath Arms. She sarcastically asked if I found another woman. I laughingly replied "Yes, she is big, ugly and full of nuts and bolts."

I left the warehouse at eleven arriving home at just before twelve-forty. I crept into bed kissed Sophie's hair and fell asleep. The next morning Saturday, I was on the road at five-thirty, knowing I would be on my own all day.

I left Sophie a loving note promising to be home by six o'clock. By mid-afternoon I had completed the first two phases. I checked and re-checked to ensure I had captured all relevant information. Pleased with progress I telephoned Sophie and told her I loved her and would be home between five and six.

I would dedicate the remaining hours of the weekend to Sophie. Saturday evening we enjoyed an Italian pasta dinner lovingly prepared by Sophie, her first attempt at a pork and mushroom cream sauce, excellent. We shared a bottle of white wine, listened to music and talked of our impending wedding.

Sunday, we drove out to the Fox to have roast beef, Yorkshire pudding, roast potatoes, cauliflower and broccoli. In the afternoon ignoring the rain we walked Hove promenade. In the evening we made love very tenderly, well into the night.

Monday morning Casey and his team turned in for work to discover me busily working. Casey asked what I had achieved. I provided a brief synopsis. He appeared impressed, informing me that Doug and Rod the chief accountant would be coming to the warehouse late afternoon for a meeting. He and Candy would also attend the meeting.

Candy helped me to organise all the notes and after an explanation understood the changes I thought necessary to the card index system, which she liked. It was closing on four when Doug and Rod walked through the door. Casey and I were sitting at his desk completely hidden by the paperwork.

Doug looked at the paperwork and laughed saying, "What did I tell you Rod, he is intent on drowning us in paper." In my jacket pocket I had written a little note to pass to Doug when he asked after his inquisition the question I knew he would.

Leaving the inquisitors to check my work I called Sophie to inform her not to expect me until eight o'clock. She laughed, pleased, recognising my determination to prove a success with Maybury.

I walked in a light drizzle along the dockside killing time. Clive junior obviously irritated tracked me down. I entered the shipping office Casey, Candy, Rod and Doug were waiting.

Doug, reading from some notes, asked a series of questions, which I answered. Rod asked for an explanation on two or three points within the notes, particularly relative to the warehouse re-organisation and what savings were envisaged.

Candy spoke up on my behalf, describing the proposed changes to the index card system would eliminate two other cross checking actions. Doug's voiced the expected question. I handed him the paper I had prepared. He read it passed it to Rod who passed it onto Casey. Casey leaning against the wall simply said, "Proves my point."

The note said, "Guaranteed savings of seven per cent within two months with the potential to realise twenty per cent within six or seven months." Rod, nodding his head slowly agreed but did accentuate there would be a cost to implement the proposals I had put forward.

In a serious tone I said, "Probably seven thousand with payback during the first two months, which I have included in the seven per cent."

Doug looked at me saying, "Go home Richard, my office ten in the morning not a minute earlier." He shook my hand and gave a wonderful smile. I thought, "Chambers you done good."

I rushed through the front door into the kitchen slamming the door, lifted Sophie high and kissed her hard, very hard. Sophie squealed kissing me back. "My man has done it again, my wonderful man." She calmed me demanding the full story. It took time but I got there. Sophie was so pleased for me, so very pleased.

The following morning I knocked on Doug's office door as ordered. He stood and shook my hand. "Richard you are something else, how the hell did you come up with all that." I explained how the penny had dropped thereafter it was all about time and re-checking processes. "I hear you worked all day Saturday." I nodded.

He continued, "Rod and Casey are well pleased with your work and so am I. I have already informed the old man (Mr Maybury). He is looking forward to meeting you sometime towards the end of next week however, now for your final challenge."

He told me to sit. He took a drawing from a drawing cabinet. "If," he said, "If I asked you to go and get dirty, roll up your sleeves and demonstrate your practical knowledge how would you feel." I smiled, "Bloody marvellous"

He too smiled. "I thought so, well first things first. Prepare a maintenance schedule for a diesel generator then bring it to me." I left Doug's office walking on a cloud. Within an hour and a half I returned with a twelve-point plan. He studied it.

After a while he said, "You need overalls, safety equipment and tools. A chap called Dan Keyper will accompany you and report on your work. He will be waiting for you after lunch. Casey has left tools, overalls and safety equipment in reception. You'll need this drawing." I thanked him leaving his office on cloud number two.

I waited in reception for Dan. He entered, asked if I was Richard, I confirmed. He helped me with the gear loading it into the back of a Maybury van. During the drive to our destination he questioned my experience and practical knowledge. I told him the truth. He laughed. "You're kidding, your first?"

We boarded a freighter docked towards the far end of the dock. He helped me unload the gear. We manhandled the equipment down into the engine room. Pointing to a diesel generator he said, "The baby's all yours--

I am here to observe however, if you head off in a wrong direction I will get you back on course, okay?" I affirmed and thanked him.

I was laying the drawing out when he said, "Tomorrow, you start work tomorrow. I'll drop you back at the office." In the van he said, "Do you think you will be able to find the ship in the morning? She's called Trojan Three." I confirmed I could. "Okay, eight-thirty." He dropped me off.

Doug was talking to Peter the design boss when he noticed me. He shouted, "Go home Richard, read-up on your challenge tomorrow." Couple of the guys looked at me and laughed.

At home while waiting for Sophie the telephone rang. I heard my mother's voice. She had decided to visit the week after next staying with us. She also wanted to meet Sophie's parents. We discussed her travel arrangements. I decided Sophie and I would meet her in London. Pleased with my offer she passed her love to Sophie and ended the call saying she would call again nearer the time with travel details.

Sophie walked in as I was replacing the receiver. Immediately she asked who was calling. I smiled saying, "Just one of my admirers. Who else?" I explained mother's call and the agreement to meet her in London.

Sophie first questioned why I was home so early. Secondly why wasn't dinner ready and thirdly she wanted to know how my warehouse lover was. Finally she asked if I still loved her. A simple response, without doubt, I loved her with all my heart. My reward, a hug and a kiss, miss dinner, and go to bed instead. We made fantastic glorious love until we were too tired to love anymore.

Driving towards Southampton and Trojan Three I kept kicking myself for not boffin-up on diesel generators. I did bring an appropriate book with me but would I be allowed to read it under Dan's beady eye. Time would tell.

Dan was already onboard. I showed my temporary pass and descended to the engine room. Dan was reading the sports pages on a daily. He greeted and I returned the greeting. "Ready?" he asked. "As much as I ever will be," I replied. Pointing at the generator he said, "All yours."

Sitting studying the drawing Doug had issued I asked Dan if I could get a coffee. Of course, he confirmed, volunteering to find the ship's mess room. The moment he departed I pulled the book out and quickly scanned the relevant pages.

A long way from being confident, I knew I had to make a start. I hid the book in a hole below the generator and started the routine. Dan was gone quite a while.

He returned passing some comment about a football team his team had beat if a cup game. I could hear his voice however my only interest at that moment was generators.

Suddenly everything fell into place, I knew what to do and for the best part how to do it. I managed the odd glimpse at the book, which helped and directed the routine. I continued with the work until late afternoon. Covered in sweat, oil and grease I felt great, having a wonderful time.

Dan called across from his position, "Time to knock-off."

I called back, "Twenty minutes." Finished for the day I climbed up to the gantry saying, "Another three maybe four hours and we can run her up for testing."

I cleaned my hands and arms with Swarfiga to remove the oil and grease, peeled of the overalls and went in search of the heads (washroom) where I scrubbed down and washed my oily face. I felt alive.

I asked Dan how I was doing. He stayed tight-lipped rubbing a finger down his nose. "You'll know soon enough, see you in the morning." He climbed into the firm's van and drove away. I looked back at the ship smiling, pleased with my day's work and what I had achieved. I drove home.

Sophie was in the kitchen. Hearing me she turned coming towards me then stopped. "Goodness Richard what on earth have you been doing? You look filthy, your jeans are smudged, with what, is it grease? Your hair needs a good wash and no doubt so does the rest of you. I'll go and run your father's bath."

Nonetheless Sophie wanted a hug and a kiss, which we enjoyed for a moment. Pushing me back she said, "You smell, what is that smell, it's like exhaust fumes or oil, or something." I laughingly replied, "It's the smell of a man, your man, who has been working as an engineer knee deep in oil and grease."

She hugged me again saying, "I'll run the bath."

Bathed and dressed in shorts and T-shirt I returned to the kitchen to be greeted by, "Did you clean the bath?" Sophie armed with a nail brush was trying to scrub the grease from my jeans. I put my arms around her nuzzling her neck.

Sophie repeating her earlier question wanted to know what I had being doing. I explained my final challenge expressing how much I enjoyed working on the generator. Adding I would be finished tomorrow, all assessments complete leaving the powers to be to decide my next stage of development. Sophie keen to know when I would be privy to their decision asked when. I said, "Probably Thursday or Friday next week."

After dinner and the washing-up we helped ourselves to brandy and soda, sitting on the sofa we talked about Sophie's new challenges. She had received invitations to speak at colleges and conferences extolling the importance of Urban Economics, which would involve travelling but she doubted if she would need to stay overnight. Her bosses and peers were very happy for her to fulfil the engagements recognising the kudos associated with such invites. We went to bed falling asleep in each other's arms.

Sophie decided, while I readied for work to prepare poached eggs on toast, allowing me to forsake the tasteless Muesli, explaining physical work needed and demanded energy. She apologised for not having sausages or bacon. I kissed and told Sophie I loved her, and set off for Trojan Three.

Once in the engine room with no sign of Dan. I scanned the book to check I had completed all the tasks demanded by the routine. I heard footsteps descending the ladder-- quickly hiding the book I looked up to see Doug's smiling face. "Good morning young Richard, I guessed you would be here." I returned his greeting. "Right," he said "Explain where you are and what's left to do."

I quickly run through the fuel systems, the checking of fuel, pipes, filters and injection equipment. I mentioned the battery maintenance, the coolant mixture, and all the filters I had cleaned and the ones I had replaced. I expounded the work to be completed, which included the electrical panel and electrical connectivity and ensuring the torque settings were correct adding that I hadn't completed corrosion inspections of ancillary equipment.

Doug after making himself comfortable on the gantry sat in silence observing my work. I tightened the last bolts in the casing saying, "I think that is it."

He smiled. "Is it fuelled?" I affirmed. "Okay, show me the starting procedure and run the bloody thing." I did as told. I run-up the generator undertaking final inspections, checking temperatures and fail-safe equipment.

Satisfied I signalled above the noise I would shut down. Doug nodded his agreement. I smiled, finished, all assessment tasks completed. Now it was a waiting game. Doug said, "Let's get the gear and tools out and returned to Casey and you can bugger off." I asked where I had to report on Monday.

He thought for a moment. "Come to the office I will call Mr Maybury and tell him I've set you to work and we'll see what happens after that." I thanked him.

At the dockyard gate I stopped at a telephone kiosk and called Sophie saying, "Hello light of my life, I've finished and heading home. I should make it by five, okay?" Sophie asked how the day had gone. I told her to wait until we were together at home.

On the way home I stopped at a small florist and purchased a huge bunch of flowers and a card. On the card I wrote *Darling Sophie, Thank you for loving me and thank you for supporting me through these past weeks. I love you.*

In the off-license I picked-up a bottle of good wine, a Pouilly Fuissé to accompany dinner. My next port of call, the supermarket to purchase mussels, shallots, parsley, basil and garlic and a cheap white wine to prepare dinner. I had seen a recipe days earlier when flicking through one of Sophie's recipe books.

At the time I thought it would be a nice treat for us both. In the house I left the flowers on the hall-stand in full view. In the kitchen I prepared the dinner. Sophie arrived home at six-thirty. She kissed me and told me the flowers were beautiful and she loved her darling man, but why was I cooking. I remembered she had re-scheduled dinner at the Bath Arms. I said, "No problem, tomorrow's dinner is ready," and smiled.

The Bath Arms was busy but not too busy where we were seated. We enjoyed pastas. Sophie selected Penne and Creamy Asparagus while I chose Spaghetti Bolognese. For wine we agreed upon a Rose. We recollected upon our first date but most of all we discussed Sophie's challenges. In particular the expansion of her department in to regional economics, supported by the county, and generating national interest.

I was so proud of my girl and I made sure she was aware of just how proud. I held her hand and looking into her eyes I said, "You make me feel so happy, so content. I am an extremely fortunate chap to be blessed with your love. Your astounding success in work warms my heart."

After a moment I said, "Do you recall our first date here when you expressed how you wanted to make a difference, and now darling Sophie you are making a difference. I am so very proud of you and so delighted for the accomplishments you are realising. I love you my darling Sophie, I love you."

Sophie squeezed my hand leaned forward and kissed me. Her face very serious she said, "You, my man, will also be a success and I now know the Sea has lost and I have won." A tear or two slowly rolled down her flushed cheeks. In return I gently squeezed her hand mouthing, "I love you".

The weekend, the first for a while when we were not absorbed in work, we dedicated to Sophie and Richard. We returned to the gym, we jogged and we enjoyed each other. Saturday evening we popped into the Bear to warn them of my mother's arrival the following week and enjoyed the company of the regulars.

Monday morning I reported to Doug. He passed me to Peter. Peter set me to work assessing a Request for Proposal for a job in Genoa, Italy. Mid-afternoon Doug called me to his office we were going to meet Mr Maybury.

An hour later an ecstatic marine engineer called Richard Chambers shook Doug's hand and thanked him with all his heart. The word trainee had disappeared and I could call myself an engineer and a member of

Doug's team, which came with three pounds a week pay-rise. I called Sophie she yelled her delight, so happy for me.

Chapter 10 – Wedding Plans

15th May, the wedding less than three months away, we were sitting at the kitchen bar preparing to catch a train into London to meet mother. We were also checking through Sophie's speaker invitations which would entail a good deal of driving.

Looking at her list of engagements I said, "Next weekend I am going to sell the Mini and buy a motorcycle you will then have the Cortina to fulfil your engagements, which will provide safer and more comfort travel for the longer journeys."

Sophie's head swung round, and for a very rare moment speechless before saying with strong conviction. "A motorcycle, what do you mean a motorcycle?" I explained how I had been given the opportunity, not mentioning the Royal Navy guy to try a bike, I had loved it and thought it a great idea, especially as my journey time would be reduced by a good twenty minutes.

Sophie standing, her finger firmly pointing very sternly said, "Richard Chambers there is absolutely no way I am going to let you lose on the roads riding a bloody motorcycle you will injure yourself, worse have a fatal accident, absolutely no, no, no, do you hear me, NO."

I laughed. "I won't injure or kill myself. I have driven carefully and sensibly these past months, which I will continue to do, whether riding a bike or driving a car. Plus there will be a huge saving on fuel costs."

Sophie would not discuss my suggestion any further; her decision final, I would not be purchasing a motorcycle. She decided for her long drives I could have the Mini and she would take the Cortina.

She said with finality, "Richard that is it, no further discussion, you are not having a motorcycle, now get that into your thick scull, no motorcycle, end of, that is my final word."

I smiled and kissed her saying, "Okay mother." Sophie smiled.

Mother's train arrived five minutes early, a British Rail miracle. We had wandered down the platform to where the ticket guy had said the first class carriages would stop. Mother, looking younger everyday emerged with a young guy in tow carrying her case.

She thanked the guy before ordering me to get the other case indicating where she had been sitting. Sophie and mother wandered off leaving the pack-mule to struggle with the cases.

In the taxi to Victoria Sophie and mother talked and talked, and talked. I watched the London landscape pass by. The journey to Brighton passed quickly while I listened to their discussions, based on Sophie's success at work, the wedding and a short reference to my work albeit Sophie did express her pride for my achievement.

Because mother would be accommodated in father's room, Sophie and I had thoroughly cleaned and scrubbed both the bed and bath rooms. The curtains had been dried cleaned and the net-curtains washed. Sophie purchased roses to decorate the room.

The pack-mule lugged the luggage upstairs, my services expended I left the two ladies to unpack. I opened a can of beer and switched the television on.

Finally, all smiles, they joined me. Both had changed and both were wearing blue and both had auburn hair. I could have been looking at mother and daughter. Mother looked stunning standing next to my stunning fiancée. My mother did look good, her slim body enhanced by her height, and the cut of an obviously expensive blue dress, made a typical mother "look at me" statement. Speaking to Sophie she said, "I think we should go and meet your parents."

We climbed into the Cortina, Sophie driving, mother in the passenger seat and I stuffed in the back, we parked outside the side-door. Sophie opened the door ushering mother in leaving the door to nearly close. I managed to catch it and tail behind up the stairs Sophie calling a warning we had arrived. Irene appeared at the top of the stairs. Mother meet mother introductions were followed by hugs before Ken arrived and also hugged mother.

Sophie, mother and Irene were immediately into the wedding and flowers, and bridesmaid's dress colours and receptions, and services and choices of music. Next item on the agenda was how many church wedding guests and how many to attend the reception discussion went on forever. My only thought: "roll-on 7th August and get this over with." Ken sat in his chair reading the newspaper oblivious to the goings-on. I nudged him, indicating a beer.

Josie and Gwynne had just opened and there were seven customers. Ken leading, we gathered in the regular's corner. Ken ordered two pints. I asked if he had stocked up with Canadian Club and Canada Dry, mother's regular tipple. He nodded he had.

Ken laughingly said, "The great thing about weddings is men become superfluous. You and I could walk out, get drunk, come back and go to bed and they wouldn't notice. No Richard while your mother is here and for the next few weeks you are superfluous to requirements."

The next two weeks proved Ken to be spot on. I went to work, come home and went to work. On occasion someone would notice me and acknowledged my presence. Sophie disappeared Monday and Tuesday travelling by train to speak at some conference in Manchester. Irene and mother also disappeared God knows where and I thanked heaven for the Fish Bone.

Sophie took Thursday and Friday off while the three went off to consider bride's dresses and bridesmaid's colour schemes. Towards the end of the second week we did manage dinner one evening at a French Restaurant and a farewell drink attended by Don, minus lady friend. Sophie left it to me to escort mother to London to catch her train to home.

During several very fast weeks Mother had visited and returned to Freckleton, father and Ken had enjoyed their Channel island cruise, refusing to relay any information regarding their escapade. Irene and Tina had a great time in Majorca spending time to regale funny moments, especially recalling amorous young Spaniards, which they thought very flattering.

Sophie did find time to give me some news regarding the wedding. Uncle Don had secured the use of The Queen of Clubs for our reception with band and DJ. And for Saturday 5th June Sophie had arranged a meeting with the Reverend Michael Jefferson for the first discussion regarding the actual wedding.

Purely by chance I learnt that Jessica, Simon, James and Gertie were arriving on the 11th June for a long weekend. The following weekend we would be off on our long awaited holiday of romance to enjoy my Christmas present.

I arrived home Friday evening the 11th, to find Sophie sitting on the floor in the hall with the telephone receiver glued to her ear. She giggled. Gertie had arrived, calling from a telephone kiosk to ask final directions. Sophie, her giggles subsiding, identified Gertie's location, dispatching me to locate her.

Gertie was sitting in her car, a sleek MGB. We hugged and said hello. She followed me to the house. We arrived to see Sophie on the pavement embracing Jessica, Simon and James. Simon entertained James and the pack-mule unloaded the car including a cot.

I have to admit the reunion of the "Terrible Threesome" were a sight to behold, three gorgeous girls very thrilled to be reunited. They screeched and jumped, and hugged before locking themselves away in father's room, the room Jessica, James and Simon would be utilising.

During the excitement a bemused Simon sat reading to James while I transferred luggage and cot to the landing. The excitement finally abated the girls emerged from the room. Sophie announced she had utilised the Bear's kitchen preparing a platter of cold meats, cheeses, canapés, salad and fresh bread. I thought in a few weeks we will be married and immediately on the bread-line. Money flowed freely from bank and building society accounts.

We walked to the Bear. We arrived at a very busy pub, the norm for Friday evenings. We entered the side door working our way round the bar, which stood two deep. The wolf whistles started, a Bear phenomenon, whenever pretty girls walked in. Suddenly there were three, a brunette, a blonde and Sophie's auburn hair, with short skirts long legs and bodies to die for. Simon, an obvious country boy, looked startled by the welcome.

We managed to squeeze into the corner Ken had worked hard to reserve. Gwynne came over with a bottle of red and a white in an ice-bucket plus an orange squash for James.

James, looking around found he was the centre of attraction hoisted onto a stool in a central position. He loved the attention, enhanced when he was given a small packet of sweets. Gwynne rushed off to serve one of the customers, leaving me to become the barman and pour the drinks. Sophie held onto my arm, which made it slightly difficult but with Simon's help I managed.

Irene came in working her way round to our side of the bar, the customers clearing a path. She obviously knew Gertie and Jessica from school and college days. After a great deal of hugging and squealing she was introduced to Simon. She said, "I heard the whistling and cat-calls and I assumed you three had walked in." she laughed.

Finally she pulled my head down and kissed me asking, "How is my gorgeous son-in-law to be?" I hugged her back.

"He is fine and desperate to get the wedding over and back to normal."

Irene beaming retorted, "Weddings are very important for ladies; it is the ultimate day, full of pageantry and ceremony, and your wedding is going to be one of the best. The Three Musketeers have made sure of that."

"The Three Musketeers?" I queried.

Still beaming she winked. "Ken, Don and your father."

Irene, Sophie and I talked over the flying visit by father and Tina when they all met up for their two holidays, the ladies to Majorca and the two reprobates on their mini-cruise, and my mother's visit. Irene thought my mother a very elegant lady, which Sophie endorsed. Irene turned her attention to Gertie and Jessica; they laughed and remembered.

Simon happy to keep James entertained allowed Sophie and I to have a few minutes for each other. She kissed my cheek. "Isn't life wonderful?" she asked. "Just listen, the atmosphere, the smiling faces, I love it. Life I mean."

I laughed and brushed her lips with mine. Her arms went round my neck and we were kissing until we heard Ken's voice calling for decorum, halting our moment. Ken said "Where are the other two?" I looked at Sophie questionably. She replied, "They'll be here soon." I thought Uncle Don and his lady friend.

I heard a voice. "Jesus a giant." Instantly I knew. I turned and there he was, The Honourable Hugo Theobald Garton-Maugham. In a trice I was in his huge arms shaking his hand and hugging Miriam. He grabbed Sophie and lifted her high above his head showing all, protected by her panties, to the world.

Sophie screeched with happiness. Miriam laughed and laughed, Gertie and Jessica just stared, and Ken's face a wonderful picture. Irene looked horrified. Hugo lowered Sophie and she jumped into his arms. Down once more, she and Miriam were hugging.

The pub's customers, all eyes on our gathering, were dumfounded. A space had cleared Hugo went straight to James and said, "Hello little fellow, who are you?" James with a delightful but surprised smile gurgled, "James."

Introductions took ages. Ken still gaping shook Hugo and Miriam's hands. Irene found herself lifted and each cheek kissed, she blushed, making Sophie laugh.

Gertie jumped into Hugo's arms and being Gertie her arms went round his neck, he reached for Jessica lifting and hugging her. Simon had his hand shook. Miriam following in Hugo's' wake received hug after hug Sophie and me greeted her enthusiastically. Suddenly James found himself on Hugo's shoulders.

My best man had arrived and didn't we know it. Gwynne and Josie stood looking not sure what to make of the situation. Hugo ever the gentlemen asked their names and kissed their hands. Josie went red and giggled.

Hugo boomed, "Landlord six of your best champagne if you please."

Ken, startled, said, "Yes sir." The pub over the initial shock went into uproar laughter and shouting filling the bar. Drinks were being ordered quicker than Gwynne, Josie and Joe could respond. Sophie and I went behind the bar to help. For fifteen minutes we worked hard to satisfy demands.

Party time had arrived all instigated by Hugo, his natural good humour warmed one and all. The initial demand diminishing Sophie and I returned to our friends. In the passage behind the bar I demanded to know how she had arranged all this. She laughed, hugged and kissed me. "Forgive me my master I forgot to mention." I kissed her back.

We guzzled the champagne and gossiped our happiness and humour spreading an exemplary ambiance throughout the pub. James fell asleep in Simon's arms. Jessica and Simon took James upstairs to settle him on the settee wrapped in blankets. We took turns to creep up to check on him.

It took ages to clear the pub, no one wanted to go home. Finally we succeeded thereafter the bar received a cursory clean. Josie and Gwynne worked hard to wash and dry the glasses and re-stock the beers and mixers Joe has carried in from the store earlier. Josie and Gwynne were invited to stay on for the cold platter, assured there would be plenty for all. They gleefully accepted.

The cold platter, very quietly, not to disturb James, was swiftly transferred from the living quarters to tables in the bar. Bottles of wine appeared Hugo and I working to open them. Glasses were lined along the bar, all were filled.

The terrible threesome with Miriam had settled in a corner howls of laughter ringing loud and clear. Hugo and me were re-living our college days. Simon and Ken were in conversation. Gwynne, Josie and Irene were conversing, the topic, judging by the hilarity, had something to do with her recent Majorca holiday, perhaps the young Spaniards.

Hugo asked whatever happened to Ruth. I told him last I heard, years ago, she had disappeared to a Kibbutz. He said, "Lovely girl, good looker too, but a very single minded lady, actually we were surprised she walked out on you, everyone was, we all thought you two would tie the knot."

I laughed saying, "So did I," adding, "God moves in mysterious ways for which I am grateful." I asked him about Hannah. He laughed out loud. "Little Hannah, she wanted too much, she wanted what I wasn't willing to give up."

"And?" I asked.

"Marriage, a house full of kids, and limitations on my rugby, anyway I had told her right at the beginning we didn't have a future that is why I refused to let her move in, which really irked her."

I asked what plans he and Miriam had. His voice dropped. "We've have talked marriage, agreeing we will, but not until Miriam is self-sufficient, her demand not mine. She is open and honest as the day. I love her, but that is between you me and Miriam, maybe Sophie but that's it." I congratulated him and he slapped my back and laughed.

Music played quietly in the background adding to the pleasing atmosphere. We stayed talking, moving from group to group well into the night. Gwynne and Josie departed at midnight overjoyed they had been part of an impromptu party.

Gwynne in a great mood kissed all the men and hugged all the women. Josie joined in not wishing her mother to have all the fun. I opened the side door for Gwynne and Josie offering to walk them home, they declined.

James somehow slept through all the activity. When he was gently lifted by Jessica he first cried then wanted to play. We gave our goodnights to Hugo and Miriam who were billeted in Sophie's old bedroom, which I knew to be out of hearing range of Irene and Ken's room. I did warn Hugo that jumping off wardrobes shouting Geronimo may not be a good idea.

The residents of father's house slowly walked home allowing James to charge around, secretly hoping he would tire himself.

Sophie, Gertie and Jessica in between keeping James entertained, were talking through the future when Sophie heard of Jessica and Simon's unofficial engagement adding that we were invited to the official bash on the 24th July being held in her parent's farm in a barn that was in the process of being cleaned and prepared for the engagement party.

Meanwhile Simon talked me through his plans for the future, which also included an invite for Sophie and I to attend the official engagement party. He described how he and Jessica's father had come to an arrangement. Simon would work towards taking over the running of the farm. In the meantime he would continue to work his own farm until the tenancy expired.

He made me aware of the long hours he worked, stressing that in due course all the effort would pay-off. He suspected Graham, Jessica's father would eventually slow down, giving him the chance to prove his worth. They had mentioned a world cruise leaving Simon with full responsibility, but not until his tenancy had expired.

I made coffee and went in to join the girls. James had been put to bed in a strange room, in a strange cot without his colourful mobile. Nonetheless, he soon fell asleep. Gertie asked for a brandy, an hour later a three-quarter bottle of brandy had disappeared, thanks to the 'terrible threesome'.

Finally three very merry girls, taking note of my persistence that tomorrow they had a big day, agreed to go to bed.

In bed Sophie cuddled me and told me she loved me and she was very happy. I returned her cuddle seeking romance and hoping to make love with my fiancée. No such luck, Sophie soon fell asleep.

The next day after a very late breakfast Simon and I were detailed to look after James. The girls went to meet Miriam and Irene all five visiting the wedding dress shop where they would meet Sylvie. Thereafter they were going to meet the appointed caterers, associates of Uncle Don, for the wedding reception. They would be lunching in Brighton.

Simon and I strolled to the Bear to meet Hugo. James with two new Uncles and a new dad on the way was royally entertained he had a fantastic time. We played on the beach and he had rides on small carousels. We took him to the aquarium which thrilled him. He had ice-cream and sweets. Heading back he slept nestled in Simon's arms. We walked the promenade talking about careers and the future, reaching home after the girls.

They, minus Sylvie and Irene were in the kitchen drinking yet more alcohol, another bottle of wine disappearing. Simon, Hugo and I learnt we were baby-sitting, they, the terrible threesome, with Miriam and Sylvie would for the evening be the "fab five" were going out.

Once James had settled Simon, Hugo and me opened a couple of beers and watched television. We were exhausted after a hard day's work entertaining a toddler. They asked about my work, which I proudly expounded remarking how I had at first attempt worked successfully on a diesel generator. I realised they and generators were not an ideal marry.

They asked about the wedding. I had to admit with the exception I and Hugo had to be at the church waiting for Sophie at eleven I had no idea what had being planned. I explained that in the past weeks everyone including a man and his dog had been to Hove to discuss the wedding.

However, the groom had not been invited to participate. I told them what Ken had said regarding "superfluous" They laughed. In fact they laughed throughout my whimsical telling of those hectic weeks. At ten Hugo and I walked to the Bear for a final beer leaving Simon in charge of his adopted son.

Dead to the world, I didn't hear a thing until Jessica appeared with a coffee to shake me. Suddenly Gertie and Sophie were in the room, all three girls sitting on the bed. They openly discussed me, good and bad points, my nose, my eyes, my muscular shoulders, as if I wasn't in the room.

They were laughing and joking, Sophie poked my biceps, Jessica rubbed her hand over my two-day stubble and Gertie tickled my feet. They had me twitching, especially Gertie's attack on my feet. I tried to hide under the covers. As suddenly they had arrived they departed laughing all the way down the stairs and into the kitchen. What a way to be woken up. I closed the door and showered, not forgetting to shave.

I joined the group in the living room, James giggling and squealing and Simon were pretend wrestling on the floor. The girls were discussing the bridesmaid outfits and I thought "superfluous". I once more wished the wedding over and we were back to normal.

I was in the kitchen making a second cup of coffee when Sophie came in and hugged me, asking after her man. I said her man was looking towards next weekend when he would have his woman all to himself.

"Oh my God, Richard," Sophie loudly exclaimed, "I have changed the dates to our honeymoon. I am so sorry with everything going on I completely forgot. Oh my darling." she hugged me hard kissing me. Gertie and Jessica rushed in. Sophie explained her exclamation, they just laughed. I sulked. Sophie shooed them out of the kitchen, closing the door.

Sophie put her arms round my neck and kissed me properly for the first time in ages. "Richard I am so sorry, I know it was your present and I should have talked to you but I have been carried away with the wedding. Oh my darling, please forgive me." I smiled saying, "You're forgiven, good idea honeymooning in an isolated bungalow, what then, shall we do instead?"

Another exclamation, "Oh Richard, I haven't discussed anything with you have I, just charged off doing my own thing. Please forgive me once more, I cancelled my leave."

I was angry and it showed. Sophie wrapped her arms round me and apologised profusely explaining that the past six weeks had completely taken her life over. She kept kissing me, hugging hard until a little tear rolled down her cheek. "I have been so selfish ignoring your existence. Darling, darling Richard I will not make another decision without discussing it with you first, I promise."

I kissed her tear. "I am so happy we are getting married and I am going to be Mrs Chambers I have completely lost track of reality. Please believe me you are the last person in the world I would want to hurt, please don't be angry."

Brightly smiling I said, "Go off and join our guests, they'll think we're rowing."

"I don't want to I want to stay here with you for a little while," she quietly responded. "I want to make sure you know I am the happiest woman in the world. I need you to know you are the most wonderful man I could have ever wished to love me, to make love to me. I am yours today and for every day, completely and utterly yours. I love you very, very much."

Her eyes firmly fixed on mine Sophie resumed, "I am proud of you, your work and what you have achieved. I know it hasn't been easy and I guessed they were treating you shabbily until you revolted, which I am sure you did. I know you Richard, quiet and unassuming but by golly if you're riled, you are riled. I watched you forcing yourself to work all those hours, reading books to prove your worth and you did, you showed them, that is one of the many, many reasons why I love and adore you, you will always look after me, look after us."

I gently kissed Sophie, a long lingering loving kiss. I pushed clear of her arms saying, "I love and adore you too my lovely lady." Smiling I added, "However, I know where there are three people and a toddler, and parents and good friends, and an uncle waiting patiently for Miss Beautiful to show her face, a face without tears." I kissed Sophie once more before guiding her towards the door. She hugged and kissed me whispering she loved me, opened the door and re-joined our guests.

Irene and Ken had organised Sunday lunch at the Bear. We were due on parade at twelve-thirty to catch-up with Miriam and Hugo, and Sylvie who would be bringing her man. Simon and I went ahead to have a swift pint.

In the Bear I received congratulations for our impending marriage. While we were waiting for Josie to pull the beer Hugo and Miriam, who looked gorgeous wandered through. I added their drinks to the order. A few minutes later I added Sylvie and her man, Ryan to the order.

Suddenly there was uproar we turned and along with forty pairs of eyes we witnessed Sophie, Jessica and Gertie walking in through the pub's main entrance, provocatively dressed, very provocatively; they had reverted to being the "Terrible Threesome" out for some fun. Not only were their dresses provocative but their accentuated walk designed to exaggerate provocation throughout the Bear raised bedlam.

They had on the shortest of skirts. I noticed Jessica wearing one of Sophie's, stockings obvious to all, tight tops and not much else. The cat-calls, the wolf-whistling and cheering bounced from wall to wall. Hugo collapsed in stitches.

Simon without having experienced Jessica in such a frolicsome mood stared, his mouth wide open. The girls curtsied and skipped to the bar. Hugo lost, could not stop, his thunderous laughter ricocheting off the bar's roof and back up again. Sylvie looking at her boss double-taking to make sure it was her boss squealed. Goodness knows what Ryan thought albeit his eyes were firmly focused on the girls.

Some of the regulars presented their stools. The girls, their backs to the bar clambered onto the stools in what could only have been a choreographed movement they must have perfected during their college days. For their final act they crossed their legs. The bar went potty. Ken rushed in thinking trouble. He spotted his daughter being a naughty girl and joined in the laughter. I thought of their college days and then of St Trinians, no wonder they were dubbed the "Terrible Threesome".

The entertainment over the three girls vacated the bar, returning in much more modest clothing their faces full of smiles, their eyes bright and looking very mischievous obviously having enjoyed their trip down memory lane. Their return registered booing and jeering, which they laughed off. I thought what hell the boys at their university must have gone through with those three.

Simon, shell-shocked managed to hold on to his faculties, asking after James. Jessica laughing up a storm pointed to Irene walking in holding James. Irene had obviously been in on the prank, not bothering to inform Ken.

Shortly after the "Terrible Threesomes'" little exhibition we were clearing the bar before setting to, preparing for lunch.

Miriam and Sylvie were pushing Sophie, Jessica and Gertie for information regarding their antics whilst at college. Simon listened hoping to learn. Hugo his beaming smile lighting up the room extolled his praise. Ken seeking sympathy expressed what he had had to put up with during Sophie's college days.

The "Terrible Threesome" were in their element regaling story after story. Simon at last began to realise he had landed a great girl full of fun and mischief, which could only enhance their marriage. I wandered where the "dashing officer" could be. Could he be missing Jessica, probably, I doubted he realised what a wonderful girl he had given up, so full of spirit, all three were.

James jumped from one knee to the next, utilising adults as a giant climbing frame. Meanwhile the story telling had ceased and I found myself sitting next to Gertie. Asking her what she was doing I learnt her musical career had gathered momentum.

She received regular session work and from time to time the odd television work. What I hadn't realise previously until she described her work how multitalented she was, able to play several instruments to a reasonable standard and she also sang backing for radio recordings and records. Whilst we talked she whispered, "You still have those take-me-to-bed eyes." We both laughed, knowing our friendship would remain a friendship, no more.

Although we enjoyed a great lunch and we had great fun I was glad to leave and go home albeit Hugo and Miriam, Ryan and Sylvie plus our house guests did rather dampen any thought of a couple hours sleep.

Nevertheless we had a very pleasant evening spread around the living room telling tales of school and college, and funny incidents we had all endured during our childhoods. However, the frivolity really started when someone suggested charades. The game proved a huge success. Laughter and tears became the order of the day.

Although it was midnight before Sophie and I climbed into bed, the following morning started at seven-thirty. I climbed out of bed and went jogging returning to the house before anyone had stirred. I thought of Sophie throughout the whole run.

I quietly showered, threw on shorts and polo shirt descended the stairs to prepare breakfast. I had a long wait, even James slept. Simon and James were the first to show. I poured James fresh orange juice and gave him a chocolate biscuit. He happily charged around the living room and explored the garage.

At ten I telephoned the office asking for Doug, explaining I had a major problem. He called back fifteen minutes later to check the problem. Fingers crossed I gave an elaborate description of an absent-minded fiancée who had arranged a holiday and mixed the dates, therefore the holiday started this coming week and not the one after. He thought the whole situation hilarious, adding his blessing for an enjoyable holiday.

Gertie appeared, she looked astonishingly well. She kissed my and Simon's cheek demanding coffee. Wearing a short dressing gown displaying her long legs, not caring who had access she casually hitched herself up onto a stool. Next Jessica, Simon and I once more benefitting from kisses on the cheek. She too displayed half her body.

I busied myself readying to cook. Sophie appeared carrying James, she too only half dressed. James had found his way into our room calling "Aunty Sophie". I started cooking.

Sophie's failure to keep me abreast of the wedding plans had proved detrimental in terms of the day ahead which she had organised for the bridesmaids, the best man and the bride to explore the church, meet the officiating Reverend, visit the reception venue, collect the wedding rings and have final fittings for the wedding day dresses, but not including the groom and best man's morning suit.

To say she was mortified would be an understatement. When she realised she had failed to explain her plans she burst into tears. It took a combined effort for all present to console her distress.

Hugo and Miriam arrived while I telephoned the dress shop regarding a fitting for the morning suit, which they swiftly accepted. Their acceptance helped Sophie over her guilt. The church where we were meeting Sylvie and Ryan would be the first port of call.

The Reverend Michael Jefferson gave a short lecture on the wedding process asking if we had any particular preferences with regards the vows, which we didn't. He accepted the list of hymns stating the selection very fitting. He asked if we would like to walk through the process, we agreed we should.

Two attempts later he thought we would be fine. He was quite a humorous chap, reciting moments of past weddings he had conducted, which had ended in fiasco for one reason or another. As we were leaving he said, "I do not believe I have had the pleasure of so many beautiful and handsome people attending a practice run before. I am sure the wedding will be a wonderful success."

The Queen of Clubs, an impressive venue, was greatly admired. The manager explained the table plan he had received from Ken, father and Don, which pleased Sophie because it differed from the norm. There wouldn't be a top-table, instead a central circular table fed into by three separate lines of other circular tables leaving space for intermingling had been meticulously planned. We were all impressed.

Thereafter we split up. The girls disappearing off to the dress shop whilst Hugo and I visited the men's outfitter. Simon with James and Ryan sat in the garden of a pub until we were finished. Satisfied with the fitting we collected the wedding rings from the jewellers, meeting Simon and Ryan, and little James.

The girls, their fitting having been a success, were in the bistro where we had agreed to meet, complete with a bottle of wine. Sophie immediately took control of the wedding rings and their unreadable inscriptions unless someone happened to have a magnifying glass to hand. However she knew the words, she had composed them.

They were both similarly inscribed with "Mon cœur est a vous", French for "My heart is yours". Gertie asked why French. Sophie exclaimed her love for the French language and how beautiful it sounded, adding there is something sexy when listening to a French man sing about love.

After lunch, less Sylvie and Ryan, we returned to the house. Hugo and Miriam would be leaving around six to drive back to Richmond. Jessica, James and Simon were departing the following morning.

Gertie asked if she could stay on for a couple of days to look up some old friends, promising not to interfere with our routine. I noticed Sophie's look. Sophie was due back at work and I had the week off. Sophie obviously remembered Gertie's comment regarding my "take-me-to-bed" eyes during the weekend in Eastbourne. Gertie also noticed.

Gertie said, "Fuis le plaisir qui amène repentir." Sophie laughed and hugged Gertie. Mystified I asked what was going on. Sophie translated Gertie's words, "Avoid the pleasure which will bite tomorrow". I needed further explanation but I was told not to worry, it was their business.

Not forgetting we would all be together weekend 23rd to 25th July for Jessica and Simon's engagement party, we waved Hugo and Miriam off, making them promise to telephone once they were home.

In the morning Sophie said good bye to Jessica, Simon and James giving James a huge cuddly dog, which he decided would be a terrific wrestling partner, and went off to work. Gertie just managed to come down in time to say goodbye before they departed.

Gertie and I chatted over a coffee before she readied herself, used the telephone and she too disappeared. I cleaned the house, changed the bed in father's room and spent the afternoon improving my ironing technique. I decided ironing was for the mindless, what a boring job. Nevertheless I persevered.

A couple of days later, Wednesday, Gertie loaded her MGB and she was off back to Hammersmith. At last, Sophie and I had our house back.

Sophie unexpectedly arrived home mid-afternoon gripped my hand and tugging me upstairs to bed said, "You, my man have your work cut out to make-up for the past week."

We stayed in bed except for tea and sandwiches until the next morning, discussing the wedding, our fantastic friends, and our wonderful families and making love at regular intervals.

The wedding plans were in hand and I had, at last, been allowed to see the wedding guest's lists, put together by Sophie and our families. There would be ninety attending church and three hundred the reception. I didn't know ninety people never mind three hundred.

Chapter 11 – The Black Hole

The weeks thereafter shot by. Sophie travelled here, there and everywhere attending conferences and speaker engagements. Usually the travels ensured she would make it home, although sometimes it could be past midnight, when she arrived. I always waited for her sitting reading one book or another relative to engineering principles or how to do this or that.

I was happy at work being given more and more responsibility. I actually went to sea for a day, which I loved, wanting more. Doug confirmed that in time I would get my fair share of sea-time. The driving back and forth, on occasion, did become tedious I took to purchasing audio tapes released by the BBC, plays and comedy became my favourites.

The weekend we were due in Minehead, was closing rapidly, when Sophie explained she would be attending a conference in South Wales on the Thursday so we agreed she would take the Cortina and drive direct to Jessica, leaving Swansea Friday mid-afternoon, using the spare time to purchase an engagement gift.

We estimated Sophie's journey time would be approximately three and a half hours. I would drive the Mini from Southampton, which would take three hours. Hugo and Miriam were also departing from Richmond mid-afternoon, picking Gertie up on their way through Hammersmith. Their journey expected to take near to four hours. Ryan and Sylvie had the longest drive from Brighton so they were leaving at lunchtime.

On the Friday Sophie called the office at lunchtime; I wasn't available. She left a message with reception, which the girl had recorded. "Terrific present, see you in a few hours, love you." I smiled. I left Southampton at two-twenty.

I drove fast, taking the odd chance, singing my head off to the Beatles. I hit frustrating traffic in and around Taunton thereafter, a quick drive. When I arrived Ryan and Sylvie were sitting in Jessica's kitchen drinking tea.

Jessica had received a call from Sophie at lunchtime saying she expected to arrive at six-thirty to seven. Hugo, Miriam and Gertie arrived at seven-fifteen. Jessica opened a bottle of wine. We were joshing remembering the wedding plans weekend when Simon arrived to be welcomed by James.

I looked at my watch seven forty-five, where was Sophie. Traffic, an accident, perhaps a puncture or had she been unexpectedly held-up were good intent excuses being proffered by my friends. At eight-forty the telephone trilled. Jessica answered. I saw her face drop, she called me over. It was Ken. I felt my heart sink, I felt pain, and I instantly knew there was an accident, Sophie was in hospital.

Ken sounded choked as if crying. I said, "Ken."

His voice breaking he said "Richard, Sophie," he stuttered, "Sophie is dead." I dropped the phone and screamed. I fell to my knees and beat the floor. I yelled and I screamed. I was shouting "No, no, no, no, no." I wanted to know where, how, I wanted to see her. I wanted my Sophie. Hugo lifted me from the floor. I collapsed into his arms and cried and cried.

He rocked me in his arms. My crying a continuous sob, I gasped for air. I must have fainted; I came round sitting in an armchair. Jessica and Gertie had replaced Hugo.

I talked nonsense. I knew it but couldn't stop. I apologised to Jessica for spoiling their engagement. Eventually I called Ken and Irene. Joe told me they had left for Chepstow. I thanked him he offered condolences. I returned condolences knowing how much he loved his niece. Replacing the receiver I said, "I am going to Chepstow, where the fuck is Chepstow?" and laughed, a release. I knew Chepstow, I had played rugby there. Hugo would drive.

Hugo floored the accelerator, reaching Chepstow in ninety minutes. He found the police station and asked where Sophie's body was. The police man on the desk exited a door. He seemed to have been gone for ages. She was in the hospital morgue. Hugo asked for and received directions to the hospital.

In the car park I saw Ken's Austin Cambridge with Jed leaning against it smoking. He stamped his cigarette out coming across to offer his condolences. I thanked him.

Sometime later we were actually shown to the morgue, the fact we weren't relatives causing a delay. Hugo very patiently explained the situation. Sitting outside the morgue doors were Irene and Ken. They were distraught, Ken holding Irene in his arms. We embraced, we were all weeping. I asked if they had seen Sophie, they had. I pushed the door and walked in. Hugo had to placate the attendant and hold me back.

Sophie lay on a steel table covered by a sheet. I wanted and didn't want to see her. I was in a hell of a state. Hugo shepherded the attendant away. I lifted the sheet and screamed, cried, and cried. I lie across Sophie quietly calling her name telling her I loved her. Reminding her we would soon be married. Hugo lifted me into his arms and carried me to the door before steering me into the waiting area.

Sitting with Irene and Ken I pulled myself together. We talked in hush tones remembering Sophie. Hugo stood by the door. I asked if I could travel back to Hove with them.

Ken convinced me I would be better off with my friends. Hugo reinforced his argument. We returned to the cars.

Ken needed to make arrangements to have Sophie transferred to Hove. We embraced. Ken holding my hand said, "Don't mope, remember Sophie as a fun girl, a generous loving girl. Hold a party, the wake will come soon enough." Irene and I embraced for a long time.

Hugo headed back to Minehead driving much more sedately. I watched the world pass by. I had a hole, a Black Hole where my heart should be. I had left my heart in the morgue with Sophie; it would always be with Sophie.

Pinned to Jessica's door was a note saying they were at the main farm. Hugo drove up to the farm. All my friends, Sophie's wonderful friends came out to meet us. I hugged and kissed every one of them over and over. Sophie and I were very lucky to have such fantastic and caring friends.

I sobbed for a while, not too long. I held onto Jessica and Gertie. Jessica senior and Graham hugged me giving me their condolences. Abruptly I said, "Ken said we should have a party to remember Sophie. Remember her as she was and not to mope."

The following day lasted forever, it wouldn't end. Jessica and Simon's official engagement party wasn't due to start until 7:00 p.m. People were quiet, and they fussed over me, trying to lighten my heartbreak. I worked hard to lessen the impact Sophie's passing would have on Jessica's special day and the evening's celebratory party. There was talk of postponing but I argued forcefully that the engagement should proceed. I wanted my friends, Sophie's friends to enjoy their day.

That evening we did party and we did celebrate Jessica and Simon's engagement. I made a speech on behalf of Sophie and me. I danced with Sylvie, Miriam, Gertie and Jessica and a couple of ladies all night long remembering my Sophie.

I didn't hug them or touch their bottoms as I would have with Sophie, but that didn't matter, Sophie would know I was dancing with her. We all worked hard to make sure the engagement party went well. Jessica and Simon were not all smiles but they were happy.

The next morning around four I left a note and set off for Hove to be at home with Sophie in our home, sad but not weepy. I wanted to be alone with her things, smell her and lie on our bed with her.

Chapter 12 – Celebrating Sophie

I hated the next two weeks. First I contacted the Reverend asking for an urgent meeting, which he agreed to. Before meeting him I asked Irene and Ken if they would mind if I insisted on Sophie's funeral to be held on our wedding day.

I convinced them but more I convinced myself that we should contact all the guests and inform them that the wedding and reception would be a funeral and wake to celebrate Sophie's life, to celebrate a wonderful woman. The Reverend understood and agreed. For him I suppose it was a case of swopping one reserved slot for another.

After the Reverend I telephoned mother then father. They both arrived the next day, which although grateful I didn't really want to see them, not just yet. I wanted a few more days with Sophie. In the afternoon I wrote a letter:

Dear...........

The Passing of Sophie McKendrick

We write to inform you of the sad news that our wonderful and lovely daughter and Richard's loving fiancée, Sophie, died unexpectedly on Friday afternoon. She was driving between Swansea and Minehead when she had an accident crossing the Severn Bridge. Sophie's car crashed over the safety barrier into the river. We believe she died before the car entered the water.

Sophie and Richard's wedding date, 7th August 1971 will be the day we lay Sophie to rest. The funeral will be held at the same church at the same time as the planned wedding.

We extend an invitation to you to attend the funeral and the wake thereafter, which will replace the planned wedding reception, which is intended to be a celebration of Sophie, of her life and of her dreams.

Please be advised the wake will be a remembrance memorial. There will be music and dancing. We have chosen to proceed in this manner simply because Sophie was, still is a humorous loving person who would have expected a celebration to remember her life.

Please do not be offended by the family's wishes. The family will understand if you choose not to attend. However, we ask for flowers, we ask for colour and we ask for a beautiful, wonderful girl to be remembered for being Sophie, there is only one Sophie.

Kind Regards

RSVP

I showed the letter to Irene and Ken they signed it and I had sufficient copies made and posted the letters. Within six days we had a response from every invitee. They would all attend. I was overjoyed for Sophie, so many people wanted to be a part of a celebration of her life.

Chapter 13 – Sophie's Funeral

The Three Musketeers, no expense spared, ensured the funeral would be extra-special, a celebration. They ensured the wedding's planned entertainment including Cloud Sixty-Nine the group Sophie and I had danced so rapturously to eight month's previously would be maintained albeit they were given an option to pull out.

Several hearses carried Sophie and flowers, thousands upon thousands of flowers. I was permitted to walk ahead of Irene and Ken following my Sophie, desperate to keep the perfect couple together. People came out of shops and houses to show their respect. The following entourage consisted of at least fifty people, who included all Sophie and my friends, our families, and the family's friends, many of Sophie's work colleagues and my boss, Doug.

In the church, awash with flowers the Reverend Michael Jefferson regaled the practice run for the wedding. He repeated his words of that day expressing he had not had the pleasure of so many beautiful people at one time. He told the congregation of the good he could feel emanating from Sophie. We prayed and we sang hymns.

Ken with Irene by his side, tears cascading down their sad faces spoke of the love their wonderful daughter had given to each and every one she encountered. How she could so easily forgive and forget. He expounded the love Sophie and I shared. He remembered Sophie's school and college days. He exclaimed the trouble caused when Jessica, Gertie and Sophie were together. He emphasised her love of life and of her need to do good. He told the story of an irate parent standing on his doorstep, berating Sophie for smacking a fellow pupil, a boy, the irate parent's son. He closed the door on the lady. Sophie had smacked the boy for pulling the wings off of a butterfly.

Gertie and Jessica delivered their eulogy, sharing in the telling. In many ways their rendering was humorous as they recalled the pranks, the mischief and the havoc the threesome would cause. They related the story of the deputy headmistress and the mice. With enthusiasm, first Jessica and then Gertie, both smiling told the congregation of their latest prank, of the mini-skirts and stockings parading before a packed pub. Other stories emerged, some I had heard and others I hadn't.

Holding hands and openly crying they announced the next hymn, "All things Bright and Beautiful" saying in unison, "For our Sophie."

Gordon Wilson, Sophie's ex-boss before her promotion described an exceptionally intelligent and talented lady who could only give, expressing Sophie's will to work hard and her determination to better the lives of others.

I could feel people looking towards me expecting a eulogy. I would deliver my eulogy later to all Sophie's guests.

At the graveside Reverend Michael Jefferson spoke of beautiful people expressing the beauty of Sophie in both her body and soul. Ken and Irene said goodbye to their daughter. My mother tears streaming down her cheeks expounded how life could be so unfair. I watched, an observer, amidst a hundred or more, I would say what I had to say from the lectern at the Queen of Clubs.

When we arrived at the club all the guests were waiting. They applauded when we entered. Many had tears, some smiled in an odd way demonstrating sadness. Charlie met me with a small box. We hugged. I asked for drinks and food to be served.

I asked for music, pop music, and Sophie's favourite songs. I asked Jessica and Gertie and Sylvie and Miriam to dance with me. They did. People danced, my mother and father led the way, Irene and Ken, Uncle Don and Christine, his lady friend all danced. I started to smile; I smiled for my Sophie.

My cue started to play, Deeper and Deeper by Freda Payne, I walked to the lectern, lifted the microphone and with a hoarse voice I sang with Freda;

Deeper and deeper, I'm falling in love with you
My life grows sweeter every day
There must be something in the things you do
That makes me love you in a helpless way
You're my joy, my all and all
A fountain of love that keeps me falling

Deeper and deeper in love with you
Each day gets sweeter and sweeter just being with you
I'm so in love with you

Stronger and stronger, my heart beats for you
You give me a feeling I can't explain
And every day you prove your love is true
You give me comfort like no other can
You're my dream, my one desire
You're the hope that lifts me higher

Deeper and deeper in love with you
Each day gets sweeter and sweeter just being with you

Freda and I finished our duet everyone was seated and I started talking.

"Hello, I hope you are patient people. Deeper and Deeper, the song I just tried, I emphasise the word tried, to sing to you is a song Sophie once sung to me, we were dancing at the time, actually we were smooching. Today it was my turn; I sang it for Sophie, my Sophie."

From my jacket pocket I removed a small pile of index cards. *"These cards contain prompts for my tribute to Sophie, a tribute I have memorised."*

From my inside pocket I extracted several sheets of paper. Waving them above my head *"These papers are the tribute. I am not going to tear them up nor am I going to read them. I don't need a written tribute everything I have to say will come from within."* I allowed my gaze to sweep the room. The congregation looked serious.

"Sophie and I met on this day four years ago. We were in love within four days, yes four days. Sophie always maintained she fell in love with me on the 7th. I think it took me to the 11th to fall in love with Sophie, but fall in love I did.

The day it happened, realising I was in love, was when Sophie unexpectedly asked me to drive to a village called Small Dole a few miles north of here. Just outside the village there is a Scout and Guides camp called Hillside. There is a wonderful meadow full of wild flowers. We sat amidst the flowers and talked, and watched the sun setting, blazing an orange tinge across the meadow. That is when I realised I was in love with Sophie.

The following day after being untruthful to Irene and Ken we took off for a weekend in London, a subterfuge helped by my mother and father although they didn't know it was a subterfuge. We did, or rather Sophie did admit the subterfuge to her parents.

In London we had cocktails at the Savoy, we watched the Changing of the Guard, and we walked London. We were in love. We had fun travelling on the underground we explored and explored and we made love, such beautiful love. We kissed and hugged, we were the only people in the world. We also fell out for the first time simply because we were immature; more probable I was immature. Fortunately we made up and became deeper in love.

After London for a few weeks we were inseparable until we had to return to our respective universities. The universities were at opposite ends of the country but somehow we still managed to meet regularly. We spoke on the telephone for hours. We wrote love letters daily. Eventually university was over. Goodness knows how but we secured good degrees, Sophie's much better than mine. We talked of love we talked of life together. We never stopped talking of Sophie and Richard.

Sophie started her career for which she excelled becoming an expert at a very young age. She travelled the country speaking at conferences and at colleges and schools. I, thanks to my father, had a regular job with a good wage but it wasn't my future. Eventually supported by my parents and Sophie's parents but most of all by Sophie I found my calling. My boss is here today.

One night just before Christmas Day 1970 I was involved in a fight. I was drunk; I learnt the next day I had spent the evening chatting up girls. I was dancing with a girl when her boyfriend head-butted me. I was dragged off of him. Sophie heard what had happened. We fell out. We made up once more never to fall out again. Our love strengthened.

We became engaged Christmas Day 1970 a memorable day thanks to our parents, a lady called Tina and Sophie's uncle Joe. What will surprise you is that I proposed to Sophie in a pub full of intoxicated rugby players in Richmond after the England, Scotland game. My dearest and best friend Hugo and his pal Casper instigated my proposal.

Imagine this, I went down on one knee and said these words: "Life offers many challenges. I know we can meet and beat them if you will agree, no honour me, by becoming my wife forever and forever, for the rest of my life?" The pub, thanks to the commanding presence of a certain gentleman called Hugo, was silent as I spoke those words.

My Sophie went berserk she jumped on me shouting yes over and over. Hugo lifted her above his head and hugged her. Hugo and Casper and thirty or forty rugby players started singing. It was amazing. Sophie was so happy. I was so happy.

Sophie realised the day we met today's date would be this Saturday so we planned the wedding for today. The Three Musketeers, Irene's name for Ken, my father and Sophie's Uncle Don have provided astonishing support lovingly and financially. My mother, the lady called Tina and Irene never failed to support whatever we asked for. We were incredibly lucky.

Through the years we have travelled Europe, visiting Italy, Portugal, Spain, France and Greece. Wherever we visited we made friends. However there are friends here today, many friends, and in particular two young ladies two beautiful young ladies I might add. Jessica and Gertie were Sophie's close friends through school and college. They with Sophie were dubbed the "Terrible Threesome" the antics they involved themselves in would make your toes curl. They were shockers, but three beautiful, intelligent and high-spirited shockers who I love very much.

A quick word regarding Hugo, Hugo and I were at school and college together we played rugby, on occasion we got drunk but mostly we studied. Hugo is a giant of a man not in body alone but in his heart.

Sylvie, a work colleague, is also a close friend of Sophie's who stood by her side throughout a very unsavoury experience involving a demented man who harassed and eventually tried to assault Sophie.

An off duty policeman prevented the assault. He is here today and I thank him for his presence on that terrible day.

Miriam, the gorgeous Miriam, Hugo's better half also became a friend of Sophie's, which generated and expanded in recent months.

I mustn't forget two gentlemen and a little boy called James. Simon is Jessica's fiancé and Ryan is Sylvie's man. These people, these wonderful people somehow through Sophie became a group of friends sharing the ups and downs of life, our lives. Their contribution to Sophie and my happiness is immeasurable.

I would like to finish but I can't, my Black Hole will not let me, therefore for my Sophie I have these words to say. Probably, best described as my eulogy for Sophie:

Sophie lived a hectic busy life; to her family, her friends and other people around her she gave much, but asked for very little in return.

The deep love and sincere affection for Sophie is undeniable, I stand before you and I feel the love and affection, I am therefore safe in the knowledge there is not a single phrase or word I could say, which would express any better the feelings and sentiments shared here today.

Sophie is a very special lady who became a sincere friend to all. Compared to some here today I have only known Sophie for a few short years. However she had a huge influence on my life and I came to love her very deeply, not today or yesterday but way back when at the Hillside camp, a love that never stopped growing.

There wasn't any pretence with Sophie she was the woman people chanced upon and she was the same woman thereafter. Sophie had a magical way, she smiled, the world smiled, she was sad, the world was sad. Sophie was sincere always, unpretentious definitely, authentic without doubt. However what she really was, was a woman full of humanity and in love with life, she trusted people.

Sophie's beliefs were simple, so simple; she believed and lived by them. Her philosophies were humble, she was never judgemental and loved people for what they were. Sophie could read a situation within seconds, she could understand people and she never criticised.

Sophie could be and was extravagant not necessarily for Sophie but for me, for you, for friends and for family. Sophie loved the finer things in life but she never expected to have them. At times Sophie wanted the best but wouldn't forsake what she had to have the best.

She loved people, she adored Irene and Ken, her parents, she loved Uncles Joe and Don, she loved all the friends I have mentioned and many more I haven't. She loved her work colleagues, she loved the milkman. To

Sophie all these people were tangible, her day-to-day people. The people she built her love of life upon, the people who represented the people of the world.

If you knew Sophie you know she wasn't one to make a fuss, but she was always there for you and me and anyone else who just happened to pop into her life. She loved to be with people. Sophie embraced all of you and a thousand other people. Sophie was Sophie, loving people, loving life.

When at the tender age of twenty-three she was promoted, unheard of for a girl, or boy so young, to become the head of a department, she was at first shocked. Later, a few days, perhaps a week after the promotion she became immensely proud of her achievement.

Sophie and I and a bottle of champagne celebrated her promotion. I loved Sophie and I was so hugely proud of her. After the champagne we made love, amazing love, love, which far exceeded realism, far exceeded existence, a love we experienced together that travelled beyond the stars, beyond our galaxy. We reinforced our love.

For months, colleges, schools, other government entities and many people from academia have called upon her to speak, to attend conferences, to share her principles with the world. Sophie, my Sophie responded willingly. She would not decline. Her duty, Sophie's duty, her want, was to investigate and resolve issues, which would improve life for people.

I have no idea how a person becomes a Saint, or who decides who should be a Saint but what I do know is that Sophie is my Saint. I love her and will always love her, my Sophie.

When I heard the heart wrenching news that Sophie had died, my dear friend Hugo instantly knew I had to see Sophie. He, my friend, decided I was incapable of walking never mind driving; he loaded me into his car and delivered me to a hospital morgue in Chepstow.

When I walked out of that Morgue I left my heart with Sophie, for Sophie to know my love for her is with her and will never die. Here where you see my hand is a Black Hole, a Black Hole, which will remain a Black Hole until the day I am with Sophie once more, which will happen. Sophie and I cannot be parted forever, only for the time permitted by our creator."

I stopped and looked at the congregation I saw smiles, I saw tears and I saw love. I continued, *"I understand there are three hundred-plus people before me. I say to those three hundred people there was Sophie, here, now at this very moment there is Sophie and for my remaining life there will always be Sophie.*

I say to you all remember Sophie, love Sophie and most of all know Sophie loved you."

Tears were streaming down my cheeks. My voice had diminished to a whisper I wanted to say much more but couldn't. I was too emotional, too drained.

I took the small box Charlie had given me and opened it. I could feel every one watching. Inside there was a crystal bride and groom statuette.

I lifted the statuette high and shouted, *"For now and for the future we have a responsibility to Sophie to celebrate who she was and what she still is."*

I yelled *"Get happy, enjoy a drink or two, dance and be merry. Enjoy the memory of Sophie, enjoy your own memories."* I walked to where Charlie was standing and hugged her with all my might.

The DJ and the band, Cloud Sixty-Nine played happy music, there were no dirges, no laments only cheery music. People danced, laughter could be heard. Memories were being shared. I quietly slipped away. I walked the long walk, content to be alone, to Sophie and my home. I lay on our bed and for the very last time I cried.

A Dispassionate Objective Life, Until!

When you have lost the reason for living, when you have lost the wonder of your life, numbness for a while takes over offering protection against painful emotions. To survive the pain I suffered I immersed myself in work. Many days passed, days I couldn't remember.

The numbness diminishes freeing the emotions to initiate anger, anxiety and confusion. During sleepless nights a hand automatically reaches out, searching. Body and soul yearn, seeking relief from pain. To survive I worked, worked and worked. Work was my salvation.

Anguish gradually replaces the painful emotions. Anger dissipates and anxiety lessens, only confusion remains. I disengaged from people, people who wanted to help beat the pain. The intensity of my emotions slowly weakened.

Normality slowly, very slowly returns, confusion dissolves and recovery begins. I began to smile, I re-engaged with people and I was able to come to terms with my loss. Grief remained and would always remain.

However, sad memories melted away to be replaced with happy memories. I began to visit family and friends. Work was pivotal to my recovery, a substitute to hold onto to beat the pain and the grief.

I remained true to and loved family and friends but inside I was a changed man. I realised the change but many didn't. I concealed the change in self-confidence and in cheeriness.

Time passed and memories faded, dreams were vanquished and I was soulless. Life was work or it was a chore, each day, controlled by the sun and the moon started and ended, I didn't notice.

One day I did notice, she was a porcelain beauty, an English rose, elegant and intelligent, bright and cheery, and once more I gave my soul and my heart to a woman. The English rose accepted my heart and returned hers, I was overwhelmed and once more deeply in love.

The decision to love once more was absolute, ending a despairing and painful episode in my life. I rediscovered joy and happiness, and love with one woman, a lasting love, a long, lasting love.

"The best love is the kind that awakens the soul and makes us reach for more, that plants a fire in our hearts and brings peace to our minds. And that's what you've given me. That's what I'd hoped to give you forever."

Nicholas Sparks

Chapter 14 – Sophie for the Last Time

After the funeral, I moved into digs (bed and breakfast) close to my place of work. Father and Ken cleared Sophie's belonging from the house and the house sold. Father very kindly, from the house sale proceeds, purchased a one-bedroom ground floor flat for my use in Southampton. I salvaged a few of father's effects to furnish it and make it comfortable.

I visited Irene and Ken once a month. I engaged with all the regulars in the Bear and re-lived some of the fun we had enjoyed. From time to time Sophie's name cropped up and quiet voices remembered her cheerfulness and her open arms, sometimes words such as "terrific lady" or "gorgeous girl" were mentioned, more importantly her inclusion into conversation proved significant helping Sophie's parents, her Uncle Joe and me to fight grief.

I replaced the Mini with a motorcycle, which I would ride for miles into the New Forest. On occasion I also used it to visit mother, particularly after she moved. She sold her large house on the outskirts of Freckleton and purchased a house facing the sea in Lytham St Anne's. Grandma Jean now in her late seventies and who had become quite frail, decided to sell her bungalow and move in with mother. I don't think mother liked the decision but lived with it.

Father and Tina because they were regular visitors to Hove eliminated the need to ride to the north east. I would meet them every two or three months.

For fifteen months I worked hard, bloody hard, gaining promotion to lead a small team of engineers repairing and testing, and inspecting ships. The team proved to be very profitable, earning good bonuses. Consequently I would often meet the guys for a beer and play the odd game of darts. Eventually I did return to rugby, training hard. The club appointed me as captain of the first team January 1972.

Every evening I said goodnight to Sophie and every morning I said good morning to her, a ritual of dependency I did not want to lose. In those fifteen months I did not approach women. I met them here and there, especially after rugby games or when meeting the guys for a beer but I did not go beyond saying hello, how are you.

Although I didn't realise it at the time sub-consciously I was protecting myself from any chance of repeating the pain and confusion when Ruth walked out, but much more I was protecting myself from the absolute pain, anger and anxiety I suffered when I lost Sophie.

Grief is remorseless, it does not go away. However, inside I had changed I had become calculating and cold, indifferent to my surrounds. Subsequently one Saturday morning I cancelled an arranged trip to visit

Irene and Ken, and instead embarked on a journey of rediscovery searching for sex, not love, I didn't want love, I wanted sex.

From the gossip at work I identified the bars and clubs where women congregated. The very first bar I entered, just after nine o'clock, reminded me of the time I met Sally in Windsor. The bar had exactly the same type of clientele, late teens to late twenties. Girls, or women, were grouped sitting at tables, standing by the bar and they outnumbered the males two to one.

I allowed my gaze to slowly travel the bar looking for a target. I spotted three girls, two blondes and a brunette standing in a corner of the bar. I took a fancy to the brunette. I walked to the corner, excused myself to get closer and ordered a beer.

Once served, I turned leaning my back against the bar and looked directly at the brunette. She sensed my eyes and stared back. She whispered to her friends who turned, trying to be discreet but failing miserably, to look at me.

I said, "Hello ladies," the taller of the two blondes answered, "Hello stranger, haven't seen you in here before" Smiling I replied, "Probably because I haven't been here before."

They huddled together whispering. The same blonde, the appointed spokesperson asked my name. Without answering I asked their names. In turn they answered, Carol, Anne and Diana. Carol the brunette.

Purposefully I turned away, intent on getting a reaction. A reaction and there would be interest, no reaction and I would look elsewhere. Carol spoke, "You didn't say what your name is." I turned back to them and apologised giving my name. The ice broken we started talking.

In a very short time I had extracted their ages, their jobs and their expectation for the night. Their expectation involved night-clubbing, they intended to move on to a club called the Moonlight. They questioned what I did and where. They learnt that I worked as an engineer and travelled a great deal.

Carol, a partner in a hairdressing business shared a flat with her partner, Sheila, who was out with her boyfriend. The shorter blonde asked my age and whether I had a girlfriend. I said with a broad smile, "Twenty-five and still searching." They laughed. The taller blonde, Diana edged closer, touching my arm. I looked at her thinking, if Carol blows me out you will do.

Anne ordered refills asking if she could buy me a beer. I declined, stating I did not drink too often, just the occasional beer. I noticed Carol's expression; the comment impressed her. The pub became louder and busier; the juke-box couldn't be heard. I allowed myself to be pushed closer to the three girls, which suited Diana. She rested her body against mine.

Carol too edged closer leaving Anne slightly isolated. I concentrated on talking to Anne, once more looking for a reaction, particularly from Carol. Anne worked with animals, a veterinary nurse. I asked how she had chosen such a caring job. Diana and Carol were reacting exactly as I wanted, looking to be involved in the conversation. Anne explained her love for animals which had started at an early age so quite naturally she worked with animals.

A guy behind knocked into me. I turned swiftly; the guy apologised and moved away. I stepped back, regaining ground. The three girls foolishly moved with me. I told them to take their space and hold onto it I would hold back the people clamouring at the bar.

I noted all three now looked at me with expectation. I smiled, looked at my watch saying, "Too busy here, I think I'll make a move. I hear the Golden Fleece is a good pub, I'll pop in there for a while, bye." There faces were terrific, shocked looks. I turned to walk out. Carol said, "I'll come with you." She left her drink and followed.

Outside, looking at the pub door I said, "Where are your friends?" She turned and looked at the door waiting to see if they had followed. "They're not coming," she said. With a smile I said, "It's just you and me, coming?" I started to walk towards the Golden Fleece some two hundred yards further down the street. I heard her chase after me.

The pub, compared to the last one was quiet. I bought Carol a gin and tonic and grapefruit juice for me. She looked at me funnily. Obviously not used to a guy who prefers soft drinks to beer, nor used to a guy who treated her off-handily. We moved to a table, it was time to study her. She was tall, perhaps five-five, figure looked good, legs were long and her dark hair cascaded down hanging just above her shoulders. Her features were attractive, particularly her eyes.

She said, "Why did you walk away?"

"The pub was too noisy and too crowded, I like quiet pubs where you can hear yourself think," I replied.

Carol studied me for a moment saying, "You're strange, you chat to three girls, the girls respond and you walk away, explain."

I laughed. "Explain what?"

"Explain why you walked away and don't tell me because the pub was too crowded."

I thought, intelligence, the girl thinks and asks questions. I considered my response. "Okay, I was attracted to you. However, I realised you were out with your friends and I didn't want to be with your friends, only you. I noticed your interest while we were talking went from zero to three, to five hitting seven. I gambled you would follow, if not I knew Diana would, which would have had me running down the road." For the first time she laughed.

Carol lifted her glass chinked my grapefruit saying, "Cheers and hello Richard." I lifted my glass returned the chink and said, "Hello Carol." We both laughed.

She said, "What happens now?" I checked my watch.

"You tell me, I'm the stranger in town."

She gave a puzzled look. "Are you really a stranger?"

I chuckled, "I certainly am." Maintaining her puzzled look she asked how long I had worked in Southampton. I thought what the hell, tell all.

I explained I had worked in Southampton since March 1971, but originally I had lived in Hove, near Brighton driving back and forth until October when I, no mention of father, purchased a small flat.

She interrupted. "October last year?" she queried. I nodded. "You have lived in Southampton for nearly a year?" she asked

"Correct," I replied.

"Tonight is your first night on the town?" she queried once more.

I laughed, "It is."

"I don't believe you," she firmly stated.

"Neither here nor there but it is the truth," I responded with a broad smile.

Carol shook her head. "What have you been doing?" I returned to my explanation emphasising how work kept me very busy, expanding on the traveling. I explained I hadn't had the chance to explore Southampton. I told her my nights out were dedicated to Rugby training and that sometimes I would meet the guys I work with for a beer. "My goodness" she said "You are strange, definitely different and rugby. You are big aren't you?"

"Big?" I queried with a smile. Carol smiled "I don't mean big, big, I mean tall and broad. I saw that man at the bar when you turned to him he saw how big you were and backed off." "The size comes with the training." She openly laughed her teeth white and even.

Carol abruptly changed the subject. "There is a new club called the Midnight Hour. It is below the Bargate. I would like to go there."

I had seen the club just round the corner from my flat, a definite plus sign. "Okay. Do you want to walk or should I hail a taxi?"

"We'll walk and we can talk. I need to know more about the tall strange-- not dark, you hair is light brown-- but definitely handsome man."

During the walk I learnt that Carol and the other two girls plus her flatmate went to school together. I also discovered Carol's parents lived in Park Gate a few miles outside Southampton and that Diana worked as a physiotherapist at Southampton General Hospital and she and her flatmate, Sheila owned two successful lady's hairdressers.

We passed the end of my street I pointed saying, "My flat is just up there." She smiled. "Why didn't you say?"

118

"You never asked," I laughingly replied.

We managed to gain entrance to the club but only after I had borrowed a tie from a collection at reception. Carol was laughing, constantly laughing. "I've have not, ever, been out with a guy like you. You are so distinct and you are so laid back, so horizontal."

We skirted the busy dance floor heading towards the bar. She ordered a pineapple juice and I ordered a glass of red wine. She looked at me and laughed. "You are a so 'n so," she cried. I took her glass and steered her towards the dance floor.

The drinks forgotten we danced and danced, the music romantic. We danced close enjoying the touching of our bodies.

When the band took a break to be replaced by a DJ, we returned to the bar to retrieve our drinks. I purloined a stool, which I helped Carol onto. Smiling she said, "You are the gentleman aren't you." Sipping her pineapple juice she said, "I would like a glass of wine."

I refilled mine and purchased one for Carol. She said, "Tell me about your flat." I enjoyed her company, easy to be with.

"My flat has one bedroom, one bathroom, a dinky little kitchen and a living room. I have a record and cassette player and a television, which is rarely on. I tend to listen to music." Suddenly she startled me. "Take me there and show me."

I looked at her quizzically. "You are showing me a flat, which doesn't mean I am going to sleep with you."

Smiling I said, "If you are not going to sleep with me there is no point in showing you the flat."

"Show me the damned flat," she cried.

We walked the few hundred yards to the flat. I opened the main door leading into a lobby. I unlocked my door and opened it for Carol to enter. I switched the lights on. Carol said, "It's warm, but not much else, quite stark really."

I dimmed the lights crossed to the cassette player and played a Cat Stevens album. Carol melted into my arms saying, "I am going to sleep with you aren't I?"

"I hope so," I smilingly replied. We started kissing my hands went to her bottom I squeezed pulling her into my loins. Jolly Roger for the first time in a very long time stirred.

Holding her hand I walked towards the bedroom. Indicating the bathroom. I said "In the cupboard below the sink I think there is a spare toothbrush."

She giggled. "Were you expecting me?" I laughed.

"No from my mother I caught the habit of always having a spare, which could include anything from a bottle of disinfectant to a toothbrush." Carol giggled once more.

In the bedroom I stripped down to my boxers waiting my turn for the bathroom. Carol entered the bedroom noticing Jolly Roger who by this time had come out of hibernation. I passed by kissing her cheek. Re-entering the bedroom Carol lay in bed. I noted her panties on the small chair by the bed. I removed my boxer shorts and climbed in.

I said "I have not slept with a woman since July 1971."

Carol laughed. "I haven't slept with a man for six or more months. We will have to practice." I pulled her to me and leaning across started kissing her. Her arms went round my neck.

I did and I didn't want to explore her body. I tenderly kissed her throat and her ears. A very low moan escaped from her lips. I touched her breasts so very gently. I squeezed her nipples. I lowered my head taking her nipple into my mouth. I sucked and flicked it with my tongue. She moaned once more. My hand found her vagina placing it over the entrance protecting her womanhood.

Carol's hand found Jolly Roger, hard an erect. She took a deep breath. I caressed her body stroking under her breasts and on her breasts. My mouth moved further down kissing her flat tummy. She writhed. I nibbled her navel. Her legs opened inviting me lower. I fastened my mouth onto her vagina.

She said something I didn't catch. I heard her say "yes, oh yes." I very tenderly eased her clitoris between my lips applying pressure. The clitoris slipped from my lips. Carol drove her hips towards my mouth. I moved my tongue to lick and kiss her clitoris. She strained to push up. I concentrated on her clitoris, my hands roaming over her firm body.

She started bucking up and down to meet my tongue. I could feel her searching for Jolly Roger, I slowly turned my body. Her lips fastened onto him. I felt him slip into her mouth. She started to suck moving her mouth up and down the shaft and I concentrated on her warm wet vagina.

Her love juices were flowing freely she bucked hard, bucked hard again. She squealed and squeezed my head between her thighs. She climaxed not noisily but with a gentle squeal and a long sigh, her body relaxed. I carried on licking her clitoris.

She eased my head away pushing my body above her so I could easily access her open vagina. I hovered above her. I directed with her help Jolly Roger towards the opening of her vagina. I gradually eased into her. Carol leaned towards me kissing my nipples. Her legs wrapped round my waist. I drove all the way in. She cried out. I withdrew to the entrance of her vagina and drove hard. She cried out once more.

From the bedside light I could see the whites of her eyes, she was trembling, she rammed upwards. I rammed down. Her arms were round my neck, her legs securely wrapped round my waist and she was driving up and down urging me to move with her. I started driving, thrusting harder and harder she returned my thrusts driving her body upwards.

She began to moan Jolly Roger let go, my sperm jettisoned into her. She lifted her torso clear her head and shoulders taking her weight and began to breath hard, gasping. I moved my arm beneath, sharing her body weight.

She wanted the release and it wouldn't come. I kept driving. Carol shrieked. Her legs tightened, and her body started trembling. I slowed to a stop. Her legs slackened their hold, her body still trembled. She gripped my upper arms waiting for the trembling to cease. The trembling stopped her body went limp she sighed and crumpled onto the bed forcing me with her. I withdrew Jolly Roger, a very satisfied Jolly Roger.

I eased her arms from my shoulders and rolled onto my back pulling Carol with me so she was lying across my upper body. I nibbled her nipple, she squealed and then laughed. She stretched her body alongside and kissed my cheek leaning forward she kissed my lips. She was still slightly out of breath.

She stopped kissing me resting her head on my chest. We lay in silence gently caressing each other. She moved onto her side looking at me. I kissed her, she kissed me back.

I awakened. The bedside lights were still on. I could hear Carol snore a very quiet snore, her mouth slightly open. I kissed her, pushing my tongue into her mouth. She shrieked and jumped up. She looked terrified. I cuddled her. "I forgot where I was, I didn't know what had happened then I remembered you made love to me. You didn't push my legs open and grind away you actually made love. I find it hard to believe you haven't had a woman for so long, why?"

I didn't answer. I could feel Sophie looking at me, smiling, pleased I had broken my celibacy. I told Sophie, mouthing the words that I loved her. I closed my eyes. Carol wanted more, for the moment I wasn't interested.

During the metamorphosis from Richard Chambers, loving fiancé into Richard Chambers, indifferent workaholic I shed many of my good points, the most noticeable being my lack of interest in long protracted courtships or words of love. I wasn't capable of falling in love, not anymore.

I left the sleeping Carol and donned my running shorts and shoes and went jogging. I left a note. I jogged for ninety minutes maintaining a set pace, not varying. I followed the road passing parked cars and into a park following the parks' perimeter until satisfied with my exertions, I jogged back to the flat.

Carol stood in the kitchen, wearing my short kimono making coffee. She turned when I walked in casually moved into my arms, she smelled fresh. I cuddled her for a moment saying I needed to shower, after the shower I accepted the coffee sitting on the sofa. Carol seated herself close to me. I prepared myself to tell her that last night was a one off and I wouldn't be seeing her again. I told her bracing myself for a slap or a tirade of damning words. Neither happened, she simply said, "I know." I turned to look at her.

She smiled. "Someone somewhere has hurt you, hurt you very much, too much, breaking your heart." Her smile fading she said, "I realised in bed you were making love not having sex, which was wonderful. I also realised you weren't making love to me, to Carol, you were in fact making love to a woman in your mind, a woman who is going to haunt you all your life."

Her smile returned, a pretty smile. "You are going to break many hearts but inside you can't help that, it is the way you are, the way the pain has changed you."

Carol left me on the sofa, dressed, kissed the top of my head and said, "Goodbye Richard, take care," and walked out of the flat.

Chapter 15 – Stabilisation or was it?

I stopped visiting Hove utilising the telephone to keep contact giving work and non-stop travelling as an excuse. I did agree to visit mother for Christmas and father for the New Year.

I journeyed to Minehead to see Jessica and Simon and little James every three or four months and visited Hugo every five or six weeks.

After Carol, there followed more girls. I became selective, I never chose a girl with auburn-coloured hair. I bumped into Carol once or twice when we would have a drink and talk. She would ask, "How many." I would shrug and laugh.

I was fond of Carol, she, though she didn't realise it had helped me tremendously to beat the self-sacrifice I had lived with for so long. My chosen lifestyle became fully focused on work, rugby and girls.

The team I managed had built a robust business, much of it repeat. We had a tremendous reputation for good work and always on programme. A very pleased Doug added three more engineers to my team. I also attended the senior team monthly meetings at head office, which pissed Inglis off having to sit and listen how well the team was doing and how financially viable it had become.

We did get four days in Genoa to re-work a competitor's dismal work. I remembered reading the tender documents at the bid stage. While there I met Isabella, she worked as a receptionist in the hotel the company had booked me into. The second night I was wandering around the city looking for a restaurant, while the team watched a football match on television when I heard a female voice call, Signore Chambers.

Surprised I looked towards the voice to see Isabella with two friends. I walked over and joined their company. Following introductions to Ceri and Leora I bought a drink and chatted with the girls. Their use of the English language impressed me apparently they all studied the language at school. They explained the many sites of Genoa I should see before returning to England, volunteering to be my guides.

I agreed, saying once the work had been completed I would stay on for the weekend. Friday evening after the team caught their flights back to England I met the girls in a small restaurant for dinner. They selected the food and I ate it, enjoying a wonderful relaxing evening. We consumed carafe after carafe of wine served from a barrel, the girls kept me amused with humorous stories of Italian boys they had dated. Towards the end of the evening Ceri and Leora suddenly said good night and wandered off.

Isabella asked if I knew my way back to the hotel; expecting her to leave, I confirmed I did. She didn't leave but reached for my hand asking if I had a wife or girlfriend. I responded my asking if she had a husband.

She laughed saying, "You first." I admitted I didn't. She admitted the same.

We talked about my work and how often I travelled and she told me of her travelling experiences during which time she decided that the following day we should visit Boccadasse a nearby fishing village. We said goodnight and I set off towards the hotel. I heard rushing footsteps behind me. Isabella caught me and said in her wonderful accented English, "I have a nice flat do you want to see it we could have coffee."

Indeed her flat was nice, full of colour adorning the white walls and the wooden floor. She made coffee and we sat talking about relationships and love, her thoughts revolved around finding a romantic man who would love and care for her. She emphatically stated that Italian men are romantic for a while but once the woman gives in the romance disappears explaining that because they think they are the best lovers in the world, which they are not, and that once the woman has succumbed she is theirs forever.

I smiled and told her that some Englishmen, including me were the same. She asked if I was a good lover I quietly replied, "I try but I would never boast I am the best only that I try." She took my hand leading me through a small door into a bedroom.

She said "Try and be the best lover in the world."

I laughed saying, "Okay I will try."

We made love, sometimes tender and sometimes roughly, we both experienced pleasure reaching exciting orgasms. I did try to be the best lover in the world. I smothered her in little bites, I gently caressed her body my fingers tantalising her spine, her legs and her beautiful proud breasts. I nibbled her bottom and run my tongue up and down her inner thighs and onto caress her vagina.

Very gently I inserted my penis into her welcoming vagina and tenderly moved without any thrusting until she demanded more, she didn't yell or scream just whimpered and quietly wailed, the longer I held off coming the more she demanded until I had to start pummelling, ramming as hard as I could forcing Jolly Roger deep into her. I would then slow down returning to a steady rhythm she responded expertly locking into my motion moving her hips to meet my long slow thrusts until once more she demanded more and I would ram hard. We loved for hour after hour, I exploded into her four times, the sun started to shine through her flimsy curtains before I finally tired and slept.

When I awakened the first awareness I had was the rich aroma of sex, it filled the bedroom. Isabella lay on her side still sleeping I leaned toward her kissing her eyes. Startled she opened her big brown eyes and smiled her arms reached out for me clasping my shoulders levering her body above me. She deftly felt for Jolly Roger gently running her nails across his head until he responded standing erect she eased herself onto him and began to wiggle her hips. Her face sparkled, and her eyes shone bright and she lightly laughed.

She pushed down hard once more whimpering using my leg muscles I thrust my hips up to meet her demands, we pounded in to each other her light laughter exploded in to a deep throaty roar before she suddenly tensed and collapsed onto me. I encircled her waist with my arms and she whispered, "Maybe you are you certainly try," and kissed me.

It was mid-afternoon before showered and dressed and in need of a shave we wandered off for my tour. Isabella decided it was too late to travel to Boccadasse. Instead she acted as my tour-guide. We enjoyed coffee and cake watching a beautiful fountain spraying its water in the centre of Piazza de Ferrari. I gazed around at the wonderful historical buildings that formed the square's perimeter.

Isabella pointed out the splendour of Palace of the Doges and explained the Teatro Carlo Felice famous for opera and ballet. After coffee we walked to see the birthplace of the great explorer Christopher Columbus. We walked along Via Garibaldi admiring the many Baroque Palaces.

Our final destination was an amazing medieval labyrinth of alleyways locally known as Caruggi. I have to admit I became enchanted with Genoa, eternally thankful to Isabella for showing the city to me.

I needing a change of clothes so I returned to the hotel, alone to check out. Remembering Isabella's directions I found the café where I had encountered her with Ceri and Leora. When I arrived both girls were sitting with Isabella. She stood to meet me linking her arm with mine and kissing my cheek. Isabella ordered a carafe of wine, which we shared while Isabella described our day site-seeing.

The girls were very keen to know my opinion of Genoa I simply said, "A beautiful city that blossoms with the beauty of its women." At first they didn't quite understand my analogy, they smiled expressing puzzlement, Isabella said something in Italian, all three erupted laughing gaily.

The evening, I was informed, we were all dining together in a restaurant overlooking the port. Ceri would drive. The restaurant specialised in sea food, the girls ordered the largest Fruits de Mer or as it is called in Italy Frutti di Mare, I have ever seen, to say huge would be an understatement.

They ordered a local white wine called Cinque Terre, in fact through the evening they ordered three bottles. We fought for hours trying to beat the Frutti di Mare, eventually, very merry and laughing freely we yielded, we agreed Ceri and Leora should take it home for the following evening. Three gorgeous Italian girls and an English man departed a jolly good restaurant to be driven home in Ceri's little car.

Isabella and I arrived at her delightful flat with my luggage. Upstairs we sat and talked drinking coffee and grappa recalling a fantastic day. I hadn't enjoyed myself so much for a long time. We were holding hands when with a mischievous smile Isabella said, "Richard will you try again?" I did try that night and again Sunday night after we returned from Boccadasse, a lovely fishing village, a vision of pink and yellow buildings where we enjoyed a light lunch.

I caught the first flight out Monday morning taking with me wonderful memories of a marvellous weekend. Isabella held onto me while we waited for the taxi she had arranged for me. With my luggage, I kissed her goodbye and thanked her for terrific hospitality especially the tour and the enjoyment we had shared. She whispered, "Keep trying."

The following weekend back in Southampton I met a sexy Sandra look-alike who was a few years older with her own house in Portswood, a suburb of Southampton. We dated for a three weeks, which worked out fine because we both wanted sex and we were not interested beyond.

The routine never changed. I would meet her Friday night in The Clarence where we would have a drink or two. I steadfastly stuck to soft drinks or a couple of glasses of wine. Jenny would drink whisky and ginger ale. She loved to dance, which meant we would end up at the Midnight Hour, the Fallen Star or Cabaret City, three night clubs where the age group ranged a few years above discos. I wasn't taken with discos all that jumping and shouting didn't do anything for me.

Around one in the morning we would jump a taxi returning to her house. There weren't any preliminaries as such, unless one considered Jenny's skirt lifted and her panties off and me riding her doggy style across a chair in the living room, or I had her on the dining table her legs on my shoulders, before we made it to bed, and then yes there were preliminaries.

Sexually we just did what we wanted and how we wanted. Jenny loved vaginal sex, no caressing, cunnilingus, nibbling nipples or too much kissing, just get it in and do it. She would only suck Jolly Roger when she wanted to make him erect, or keep him erect. The sex, which included most of Saturday, after a while, became monotonous we agreed to move on, no hard feelings it had been fun.

After Jenny there a many other girls, Verity, Susan and Rebecca to name a few before I met an American, on secondment from Pittsburgh working for a subsidiary company owned by an international group. I wasn't quite sure what she did albeit it had something to do with pharmaceuticals.

We met when I literally knocked into her entering a mini-market to replenish stocks at home. I pushed the door open and moved to let a lady exit and walked into Stephanie, Steph for short. I apologised, she said, "No problem." In the shop we kept bumping into each other until she said, "Buy me a coffee."

I smiled. "Why not."

I checked the time, six-thirty, before saying I would be heading down to a hotel opposite Southampton's main dockyard gate where I could get a great steak, would she like to join me. She smiled and said yes.

The walk to the hotel encouraged conversation. She had been in Southampton for seven months due to return to Pittsburgh the week before Christmas, which she looked forward to being home with her folks. She was twenty-eight, single and not ready for a permanent relationship. She had too much to do before she would consider settling down. I presented a similar story.

The hotel served up its usual big steak cooked exactly how ordered with all the trimmings. Steph ordered a bottle of red wine. The plates cleared away we remained at the table talking and drinking the wine.

She explored my work and I hers although I couldn't figure whether she worked as a chemist, scientist or manager. I think manager because she studied time and motion against output. On the other hand she did express herself in terms relative to scientific research and laboratory work. Did it matter, not really so I didn't push for a definitive explanation?

After the early dinner I walked her back to her car, parked round the corner from the mini-market where I had knocked into her. At the car she said, "Thanks for dinner," and I said, "Thanks for the wine?"

I started to walk away. She called, "Do you live far?"

I turned saying, "No not far a five minute walk."

"Let me give you a lift?" she asked.

"Okay, but it's not far," I smilingly replied.

I climbed into her Mini. I told her I had once owned a Mini but had swapped it for a motorcycle. She loved motorcycles and wanted a ride, nattering non-stop about riding bikes across deserts and over mountains.

I directed Steph to the rear of my flat hopped out of the car telling her to wait. I trotted down the interconnecting alley and entered the flat. I picked-up two crash-helmets and my cold-weather kit, my faithful Musto, and the bike keys and climbed out through the living room window. The washing machine blocked the back door.

I removed the tarpaulin from the bike, opened the back gate and pushed it into the alley and out onto the street where Steph had parked. She immediately fell in love with my Triumph Bonneville, the glistening blue and shiny chrome.

I handed her a crash-helmet and the winter kit warning her it would be bloody cold. I climbed astride and started the bike. Steph after struggling and then disappearing into the winter kit climbed on behind.

I carefully steered the bike out towards Totton and the New Forest. On the dual-carriage way, a short stretch leading to the open road into the Forest I shouted hold-on. I felt her arms clasp tighter and I let rip. She screamed.

I roared on through Ashurst gathering speed heading for Lyndhurst. Steph whooped and yelled. I dodged through the traffic in Lyndhurst turning onto a windy road that provided a circular route through the forest to Ringwood. Although dark I had no concerns, I knew the road particularly well.

I gunned the Bonneville leaning into bends and out again. Steph was having a fabulous time. Very quickly we entered Ringwood from the direction of Bournemouth. Through Ringwood I joined the A31 and hammered the bike toward Cadnam before turning towards Totton, over the River Test Bridge working my way back to the flat. I pulled in behind Steph's Mini.

She dismounted asking, "Do you live here?" I nodded.

"Who with? she asked.

"With me," I replied. She laughed.

"Can I use your washroom?"

"Of course but you will need to climb through the window or walk down the alley to the front of the house." Laughing once more she said, "The window will be fine."

She held the gate and helped with the tarpaulin. After she had stripped the winter kit off I helped her through the window, my eyes firmly fixed on her legs and white panties. Steph saw me looking and smiled. I clambered in behind her and directed her to the bathroom.

When she exited the bathroom I asked if she wanted tea or coffee or something stronger. She opted for black tea. Standing in the dinky kitchen asking if she wanted sugar, I heard her move behind me, she put her arms round my waist. She said "Are you hetero or homo?"

I turned and laughed, "That is a very weird question especially as you espied me studying your legs and beyond. Why the question?"

"A lot of the guys in the states with big bikes are homosexual," she casually answered. I stated firmly, "I assure you I am not a homosexual."

She laughed. "I didn't think so, where's the bedroom?"

"The door to the left of the bathroom." I replied. Tugging my arm she said, "Forget the tea come to bed."

We were two weeks away from Steph's flight home. During those two weeks she moved in, not completely but near enough. Sex morning and night and for lunch on weekends became the norm.

The evening after the first bike ride lying in bed she said, "I'm a butt girl"

"What the hell is a butt girl?" I asked.

128

"I like it up the butt, in my ass." I roared with laughter.

"Why are you laughing?" she demanded. I kissed her.

"My sex mentor, an older woman who introduced me to sex in a big way loved anal sex." "Well do it then fuck my ass," she retorted. Steph wasn't over keen on oral sex but she loved vaginal and "ass" sex. I think we had more anal sex than vaginal sex. She loved Jolly Roger's size and said so many times.

Steph moved out on the 18th December driving to Heathrow to return her rented car and catch a flight home. I enjoyed Steph and she me. She loved the many bike rides we took into the New Forest astride the Bonneville.

When I returned from my round trip over Christmas and New Year a card waited inviting me to America or if I visited to let her know.

Chapter 16 – The Week before Christmas 1972

The final week before Christmas with Maybury is a series of lunch time meals entertaining important customers. The alcohol flows freely and the food is piled mountain high. Every morning and every evening when I arrived home I would jog.

We had an emergency team on call-out to cover any unforeseen eventualities, therefore I was normally home by four and jogging soon after. Rugby training continued until the 21st, which wasn't a full-on session but more a beer and song session. We had a good evening boozing and singing and full of comradery. I would miss two games, the 30th league game and the Boxing Day charity game.

Post, the very little I received, usually waited on top of the lobby radiator left by my upstairs neighbours who I rarely encountered. I knocked on their door when I moved in and introduced myself. They were Mr and Mrs Featherstone. He was a dockyard crane driver and she worked in the docks as a clerk with a shipping company.

The evening of the 20th December I had a stack of post, cards from friends and family. I also received a hand delivered one. Quite surprised, I opened it first, finding a card from Carol depicting Father Christmas and Rudolph. Inside the card there was a note asking what I would be doing over Christmas and a number to telephone.

I opened all the other cards, one from Miriam and Hugo, another from Irene, Joe and Ken, even one from Uncle Don. There was an extra-large one from Jessica and Simon, with scribbling in red ink, James's attempt at writing. The surprise one came from Gertie with a pleasant chatty letter enclosed asking how I was and if in London to give her a call for lunch or a drink. Her telephone number was included beneath *"Best Wishes, Gertie"*.

I completed a short jog, no more than three miles, returning to shower and laze around listening to music. I was also reading a bloody good book by Michael Crichton called The Terminal Man.

I made a cup of tea, put the "Fog on the Tyne" album by Lindisfarne on the record player and found my page in the book. I started to read but my thoughts were consistently interrupted by the card from Carol and to a lesser extent the card from Gertie.

In the end I called Carol. We talked niceties for a few minutes before she said, "I have two choices for Christmas, which are to give my body to you for your enjoyment and mine too or go home to my parents. I would prefer to give my body to you, what do you say." I explained my plans to visit divorced parents living in remote areas of England, well remote to Southampton.

She laughed, "Alright then ravish me before you leave. When are you leaving?" Carol laughed and I laughed with her. "Saturday morning," I answered.

"Okay," followed by a pause, "I could pack a case and be with you within the hour allowing you three nights and if you are of a mind three mornings to ravish me at will."

I told her I would be rugby training Thursday evening including a few beers after training, but if she wanted to pack a case, feel free, she was most welcome.

Before breaking the call I said, "Carol, nothing changes, we do not have a future." She chuckled, "I know but I do enjoy being with you and I adore your love-making."

I was sitting reading when the door-bell chimed. I let Carol in. She looked at me saying, "I'll go if this is not what you want. You look like you have lost a fiver and found a penny."

"No, no I am engrossed in my book. Don't worry I want you to stay," I smilingly responded.

I took her case and carried it into the bedroom I said, "There isn't much space you may have to live out of the case. There is space, however, in the wardrobe if you need to hang clothes." Carol removed her coat.

She was wearing a short, dark blue mini-skirt and a light blue blouse with a pullover in darker blue. She looked good and I told her she looked terrific. I said, "If you want a drink I have tea and coffee, and tea and coffee and oh yes, water." Carol's face beamed she said, "I took the liberty of bringing two bottles of wine with me, one white and one red."

I wasn't in the mood for alcohol, which I apologised for but I would open a bottle for her if she wanted. She assured me she was fine and an alcohol free evening would do her complexion the world of good.

"Do you drink every night?" I queried.

"Loneliness, which has worsened following the evenings I have enjoyed your company, all I do now is sit in my flat, Sheila is out with Bobby her boyfriend, and think of you."

Her words worried me. I immediately thought I had made a mistake inviting her to stay for a few nights. I said as much.

Smiling she said, "Don't be so conceited there are plenty of men out there and they're not hard to pull. If I wanted one I could soon find one."

"Carol if this is going to be the level of our conversation I will call a taxi and you can go home, with your two bottles of wine and drink yourself silly." I was being unreasonable and I knew it. I instantly apologised. I said, "I'll tell you what I'll have a glass of red with you."

She laughed. "I'd prefer a cup of tea"

I couldn't understand why I was so het-up; was it because for the first time since Sophie I had dropped my guard or because I had invited Carol into the sanctuary of my flat, or a combination of the two. I recalled Steph moving in for a week or so deciding her stay to be unrelated because I was aware she would be flying home to the US.

All this crowded my brain when Carol said, "Richard it is sometimes good to talk about things, no matter how unpleasant. Talking provides a release. However, if you don't want to that's fine too."

I turned away from making the tea and looking at Carol I said, "Carol it is very complicated and what happened temporarily destroyed me. My recovery back to normality took a very long time. I submerged myself in work to bury the pain. Sometimes the pain re-visits and I have to once again fight it off."

Pouring the water for the tea I resumed, "The evening I entered the pub and started talking to you and your friends I sought redemption, if that is the right word. Your humour and your company were a Godsend, but I cannot, and will not be drawn into a close relationship again. If it should fail, for whatever reason I wouldn't survive."

I carried the mugs of tea into the living room placing them on the coffee table. I turned the music over before sitting in father's old chair. Carol smiling said, "That chair suits you it is as if you were paired together."

I smiled too. "Actually it was my father's however he moved out of the house leaving me and….and another person to share. The chair, I suppose you could say is my inheritance."

She laughed but was quite aware I had been very close to revealing Sophie's name. Carol, holding the mug in her hands, taking a sip from time-to-time asked about my family, whether I had siblings, why my parents were both living in the north of England.

I briefly provided an abridged description of boarding school and university. I described my grandparents and how they, in particular my mother's parents, had been influential in moulding me into what I am today.

I mentioned both businesses my parents had individually built, adding there business interests were contributory towards their separation and consequent divorce. After I had finished I felt uncomfortable. How had she wheedled the information?

The realisation hit me that she hadn't wheedled, she only asked a couple of simple questions. I decided to provide more detail than she actually asked for.

Carol put her mug down and took my mug from me. She sat in my lap putting her left arm across my shoulders. "I have two sisters, both younger who live with mum and dad. I went up to university to read biology but dropped out after my second year. Not because I failed but for a boy, a big mistake. I have said to myself on many occasions I should return to complete the course and gain a degree."

"Why don't you?" I asked.

She thought for a moment. "I don't know I seem to have ready-made excuses not to. To be quite honest the hairdressing business provides a good life. In fact Sheila and I are discussing selling our flat and purchasing our own flats or houses. She is besotted with her Bobby talking about marriage and children and home-building, which makes me feel lonelier than I already am."

"Why hairdressing?" I asked.

"Accidental I assure you. Sheila is highly trained a really good stylist but doesn't have an ounce of business sense. We drifted together, I undertook a quick-fire course and bingo we opened a salon followed by a second one and are now looking to opening a third as soon as we can identify the right location."

I said, "Sounds good to me especially if hairdressing, which I am sure it will, continues to be in demand."

"Ugh," she exclaimed. "As a young girl I saw myself as a biologist travelling the world studying the natural world, using the latest scientific tools and techniques in both laboratory settings and the natural environment, to understand how living systems work. A dream I gave up for an idiot boy and a more idiotic girl, me."

"My advice," I said, "Is to sell your share of the business to Sheila, return to your studies and go out and travel the world doing what you want to do, doing what you dreamt of."

Carol laughed. "You make it sound so simple. Perhaps I will." I looked up at Carol, she leaned towards me and we kissed. She stood and walked to the bedroom. I followed.

Throughout the night we made love, sensitive love, caring love. We immersed ourselves in gaining maximum satisfaction for each other. We trembled, and cried out and we were constantly orgasmic. I climaxed, Carol climaxed. Carol climaxed, I climaxed. There wasn't any heavy thrusting, powerful ramming just tender love-making, which brought wonderful gratification for both of us. It was a night of sensuality, giving and taking the capacity for the enjoyment of our senses.

I quickly realised Carol, because she wondered around the flat naked allowing me to enjoy her had a similar loveliness to Sophie. She didn't have Sophie's height or her luxurious auburn hair but she did carry herself proudly and sensually. Watching her motivated me to telephone Doug begging for a day off because I had forgotten to buy some Christmas presents. Doug being Doug laughed saying if anyone deserved the odd day off it was me.

The day began with coffee and toast. Carol wanted to do some shopping so we walked to the bus-stop. In town she purchased a few items from a chemist and groceries from a supermarket. I carried the shopping bags. I splashed out and bought a newspaper. The expedition, in fact, turned out to be quite therapeutic, which surprised me and also worried me. I didn't need domestication.

Wandering amidst the hundreds of last-minute Christmas shoppers proved to be enjoyable caused by a sense of happiness the shoppers were naturally discharging. I felt pleasure when we were in a book shop and Carol purchased two biology text books.

I said I would buy lunch, recommending the Dolphin hotel. Goodness knows why I recommended the Dolphin; I hadn't dined there or even been in the place. Perchance my recommendation paid dividends-- the food and service were first class. We shared a bottle of wine, which Carol insisted on paying for.

We made it back to the flat unpacked the shopping and opened one of the wines Carol had arrived with. We listened to music and talked about insignificant things until Carol abruptly kissed me. Not a kiss demanding a response but more of a motherly kiss. I laughed asking her what the kiss was for.

For the first time Carol became all coy not wanting to answer. Smiling I spoke for her, "Maybe it is because you are feeling something special and you wanted to kiss me to see it I was real."

Carol burst out laughing the coyness rapidly dissolving. "Of course not, you idiot it was because I am overly fond of you, which I know is stupid because you will not break free of whatever is holding you that is why I kissed you, because I feel sorry for you."

I didn't want Carol or indeed anyone else feeling sorry for me I had experienced all that and I certainly didn't want it again. I told her this, but badly, I admonished her, which was out of order.

I found myself, yet again apologising for flying off the handle. Carol accepted all I said in good faith. She was in fact smiling broadly. She said, "Do you know this year is a leap year and I could propose to you. However, I won't waste my time because you will say no, won't you?"

I nodded. "I would; there are much better catches out there than me."

Carol, all smiles retorted, "I doubt it. You are as I told you different, whether you like it or not you care about women. You don't want to hurt them but you will simply because of whom you are. That doesn't make sense. What I mean is you have a need for women, you enjoy their company and you love being with them but the invisible shield you surround yourself with is impenetrable."

Sitting on the sofa Carol lifted my arm to encircle her nestling into my chest. She said, "Richard start talking and tell me everything. In two days' time I will be out of your life, so tell me and don't hold back. I promise you will feel relieved to have unburdened the weight you so arrogantly carry."

I stayed silent for several minutes knowing Carol waited, knowing I would unburden. I began talking leaving nothing out. I talked for a very long time. The tale started on 7th August 1967 and ended 7th August 1971. I didn't cry, nor did I feel any anguish. I did feel the weight lift.

When I had finished we were sitting in the dark. I eased Carol off and switched on the lights, dimming the brightness down. I pulled Carol to her feet and took her to bed. This time there wasn't the sensitivity of the night before. I pummelled Carol and she wanted me to pummel her she knew as I knew that this was the end, Carol and Richard were over and Sophie remained somewhere, she would always be somewhere.

Late into the night we talked of how she had wanted so much to free me of Sophie. I thanked her for listening to my sad tale. I expressed she had made a difference, but too late. I admitted to her she had lifted the burden and she had also been instrumental in unloading my arrogance, my conceitedness.

However, I wasn't for changing. I carefully explained that there wasn't a woman on earth who I could entrust with my love and affection, emphasising not because the woman couldn't be trusted but because of life's habit of destroying people and their futures, denying love and happiness and causing so much pain.

I emphatically expressed I couldn't survive another lost love, so my only defence was not to fall in love. Carol understood and comforted my sadness.

Carol stayed on until Saturday morning. We didn't make love but we did cuddle and we did talk. We were both aware another time, another place we would have survived, but I had changed and Carol for all her want could not return me to what I had once been.

Carol was a very special lady and although we didn't have a future she would remain a part of me as Sally, Ruth and Sophie, for various reasons, had.

Saturday morning the booked taxi arrived to take Carol home to her parents in Park Gate. I fitted two panniers to the bike loaded them with the Christmas presents I had for mother and Grandma Jean and clothes. Inside two waterproof bags I rolled the rest of my clothes and washing kit working hard to limit any unnecessary creasing to the clothes before affixing them to the panniers. I dressed in the foul weather gear climbed astride and headed for Lytham St Anne's.

Chapter 17 - Christmas 1972

The ride to Lytham flew by. I used stretches or road to blast the bike driving the Bonneville to maximum output, intent on blasting the past weeks out of my system, especially Carol. Jenny and Stephanie and the others didn't matter, but Carol did. My last words to her as she climbed into the taxi were, "Read your books, go and study, get your degree and go travel and realise your dreams."

I slowly followed the houses looking for mother's number when I espied her in the bay window of her house. I turned into the drive. Mother followed by Grandma Jean came out to meet me. I hugged them both. Grandma disappeared. I thought tea and crumpets remembering my childhood. Sure enough after I had unloaded the bike pushed it into the garage, removed by gear I walked into the kitchen to be greeted by the expected tea and crumpets.

They wanted all my news, which I willingly expounded. They were thrilled for my success and wanted to know more. Was there a girl in my life? Who were my friends? Was I playing rugby? Over time in between mouthfuls of buttery crumpets I answered all their questions. Mother explained she had arranged for dinner in a pub in the centre of Lytham she thought I would enjoy. It was a rugby pub.

Mother led me to an outhouse overflowing with beer, wine, spirits and soft drinks. I asked why so much did she intend to throw a party? She laughed, "No my dear son it is for your grandmother, me and you to celebrate Christmas."

She thanked me her birthday present a scarf and brooch combination I had found in one of the stores in Southampton. They both thanked me for the Christmas cards I had posted. They queried how long I would be visiting, one week explaining one week with them and one week with father and Tina.

For the rest of the day I they fussed over me. Mother ironed my creased clothes and produced trousers and shirts, underwear and jackets insisting I tried them on, which I gladly did. My size remained static so having remembered from my last visit the sizes were spot-on. I said, "I'll go for a jog, have a bath and we can ready and try this rugby pub."

I changed into running gear and set off. Mother resided on North Promenade. I left the house crossing the road to follow a path leading towards the centre of Lytham. I ran hard for a while before reducing speed into rhythmic trot. I reached the town centre turned and jogged back. My distant meter registered seven point three miles, which pleased me.

Mother insisted on running the bath albeit I had changed my mind preferring a shower. Nevertheless I lowered into a hot bath, which felt good. I dozed off feeling mother shaking me. I received a lecture on drowning when sleeping in a bath.

Mother had booked taxis for collection and pick-up after dinner. The taxi pulled into her huge drive at seven-fifteen, fifteen minutes late. I helped Grandma into the front seat and joined mother in the rear. I asked mother to remind me of her age. Fifty-one she told me. I remarked how good she looked for an old biddy, which copped me a clipped ear.

The taxi dropped us off at the incorrect door. We had to traipse through the main bar to reach the restaurant, which I didn't mind because I had the opportunity to size up the customer base. I decided it looked interesting, underpinned by the number of attractive girls.

The menu geared for Christmas offered too many pork and turkey dishes, limiting choice. Mother chose pasta, I whispered it would be out of a packet. Grandma, after a great deal of thought chose lamb stew. I plumped for a fillet steak. I ordered a bottle of red wine and a jug of water. Mother decided she wanted a dry martini, asking the waitress if the bar staff could mix one. The girl went off to ask. She returned full of smiles advising mother the landlord would mix her one. Grandma decided to have one also so I said make it three.

I excused myself and went for a wander in the bar. I scanned the bar seeking a target knowing tonight wasn't the night. However I decided that if I could make contact with a girl, it may pave the way for tomorrow evening, Christmas Eve.

Whilst scanning I took note of the rugby memorabilia, very impressive. I could feel eyes, not sure whether male or female I used the massive mirrored gantry to search who the eyes belonged to. I spotted her, a tall brunette with mid-shoulder hair and a pretty face. I continued inspecting the rugby memorabilia working my way to where she sat on a stool with another brunette, also attractive.

Levelling with where they were seated I said, "Do you play rugby?" The second brunette answered, "Only with rugby players." I looked straight into her eyes saying, "Your luck is in you have just found one."

The first brunette laughed. "Hello Richard." I was snookered how did she know my name? She noted my uncertain expression. She said, "Leopard." Stunned I said, "When."

"You went down after my first year. I was a fresher, one of many who came to watch you and Hugo and Ben, James, Craig and others play for the college and the university."

"Well, well," I said. "What a coincidence, what are you doing in Lytham?"

"I live here," she replied. "More to the point what are you doing here?" she asked.

"Ah good question," I said. "I am here to visit my mother and grandmother who live on North Promenade we are next door in the restaurant, which I have to return to or they will send out a search party."

I asked their names. The second brunette, not wanting to miss out replied, "I am Geraldine, Gerry for short and she's Melissa, Mel for short."

Melissa said, "Go have your dinner, we will still be here when you finish."

I bowed and returned to mother and grandmother who were indeed in the throes of sending the waitress to find me. Sitting, Grandma said, "Where have you been?" "Coincidentally I bumped into an old acquaintance from university," I replied.

Mother raised her eyebrows, "Here in Lytham?" I smiled saying, "No mother I just popped into Preston and there they were."

"They?" queried mother.

"Yes there are two of them," I retorted.

"They're girls aren't they?" demanded mother.

"Yes, mother they are girls." I lifted my martini, it was good.

"I suppose mother and I will be going home without you." said mother. I shook my head saying, "Probably." Mother wasn't finished

"When will you learn to keep it in your trousers and I don't want you falling in love again. It near killed your father and I watching you suffer when poor Sophie died."

She immediately realised what she had said. "I am sorry Richard but I did warn you a long time ago."

"No problem I no longer fall in love, I only enjoy," I sarcastically responded.

"Richard, do not become upset, I am truly sorry."

Grandma butted in. "Let the boy alone he is only young once."

Mother actually laughed. "You're right mother he is, isn't he. However, I will not accept your disappearance you are here to enjoy Christmas with us, remember? You'll be out all night tonight and thereafter we will hardly see you."

"Jesus mother I've just met the girls," I replied. Grandma said, "Don't blaspheme." I apologised to Grandma and promised mother I would not disappear.

After dinner I escorted mother and grandmother to the taxi ensuring they were safely seated, I went in search of Melissa and Gerry. The bar by now and being Christmas had filled out, the noise overbearing and the men, I noticed, outnumbered the girls three to one. After navigating through the throng to find them still sitting on the stools by the bar, I expressed my surprised that they were not surrounded by guys.

They both smiled when Melissa asked if I would like a drink. I opted for a tomato juice. She said, "You still jog and train then." I laughed.

"I do and I doubt whether I will ever stop."

Gerry said to Melissa, "Tell him what you just told me."

A flash of anger, gone in a trice swept over Melissa's face. Melissa gave Gerry a "shut-up look", wasted because Gerry expounded how during college I became famous for my celibacy because of a girl called Ruth, who had walked out on me. I roared saying, "Not true although I did become celibate because of a girl, a girl who has gone but fondly remembered."

Gerry, not to be dissuaded added that according to Melissa I only had to click my fingers and any girl on campus would have willingly shared my bed. I enjoyed Gerry, I didn't particularly like her, for she was the type who told tales and couldn't be trusted. Melissa, I could see fumed, steam escaping from her ears, metaphorically speaking.

Changing the subject I asked, "What is happening in Lytham tonight and tomorrow night?" They replied with blank faces. Gerry making sure she was the spokeswoman said, "This is Lytham not London."

"Come on," I said "There must be something happening somewhere."

"Preston," Melissa contributed.

"Preston is miles from here, there must be something local," I exclaimed.

Melissa responding again said, "Blackpool."

"What were you reading, geography, I am not here for lesson on Lancashire's hot-spots." Melissa finally smiled. She had one of those smiles good actresses use when seducing the film's hero.

At that moment a guy came over pinching Gerry's bottom. She screeched like an owl turned and said, "I knew it was you Brad you have the sexiest pinch in Lytham," Melissa said "Meet my cousin. Brad this is Richard, Richard meet Brad."

We shook hands. Melissa resuming said, "Brad is Gerry's love, but Brad ignores the fact." This time Gerry transmitted dirty looks. I decided I had had enough.

"I am off, see you around. If I don't see you before have a grand Christmas." I walked towards the door or rather I started to fight my way through the packed pub to get to the door.

Outside the drizzle persuaded me to look for a taxi. I spotted a sign indicating Lytham railway station, hoping there would be a taxi rank at the station I followed the sign. A timid voice behind said, "Do you like walking in the rain? I do."

Melissa was standing ten yards back. "Sometimes but preferably when it's warmer," I replied

"Do you jog in the rain? Do you play rugby in the rain? I know the answer to both questions is yes. I like to walk in the rain, walk with me, please." she asked. I shrugged, put out my hand for to come and hold it. Melissa walked towards me and grasped my hand saying, "This way."

I realised we were walking towards the beach recognising where I had turned and back-tracked the earlier jog. A stiff breeze blasted in off the sea intensifying the strength of the drizzle. "Come off it Melissa, this is not about walking in the rain we can hardly stand, what is it?" I said in a raised voice to overcome the sound of the weather.

"Oh but it is," she said. "This is me at peace no matter how strong the breeze or how heavy the rain."

"Melissa I will walk with you and probably catch a cold but you have to explain what peace, what kind of peace you are looking for."

She abruptly changed direction tugging me with her. She gripped my hand tightly. We entered a street walking faster she said, "What time is it."

"Just after ten, why?"

"I want you to meet my parents," she replied.

"Why?" I queried utterly confused.

"Because I do," she retorted clearly agitated.

I thought, good grief I have landed myself with a loon. We had walked clear of the breeze her heels could be heard clip-clopping on the pavement. Ahead I noticed the lights of a pub.

At the pub we turned right crossed the road and entered a small, but friendly-looking bar. A voice shouted, "Hey-up George here's your lass." The bar was busy with patrons with an average age around mid to late forties.

A man emerged from a group stood at the bar. "Melissa who is that with you?" Melissa said, "Dad meet Richard he rescued me from the Leather Bottle."

He was a big man he pushed his shovel-sized hand out. After shaking hands he offered to buy a drink. I asked for a pint of bitter. I thought tomato juice wouldn't go down to well in this company. He ordered the pint and asked Melissa what she meant by rescue.

Melissa, having dug a hole now had to dig herself out, I waited. "Oh dad, Gerry and me were talking and all these blokes kept trying it on and Richard walked in came over close to where we sat. I recognised him, realising we had crossed paths at university. Talking to him kept the wolves at bay."

I thought, shit where did she unravel that from. I looked at her nose, it wasn't doing a Pinocchio. I wondered, perhaps she was looking to be a playwright.

From the anonymous voice when we entered I presumed his name to be George. He passed me the pint. I said, "Cheers George," and gulped half the pint in one.

"You needed that son," he said.

"I think I did, you daughter had us walking in the wind and rain," I responded. "Aye she'll have you doing that alright, that's where she finds her peace. But bugger if I know what she's talking about, hey girl," Melissa smiled coyly. I thought, she knows how to manage her father.

Melissa pulled me towards a small empty table close to the door. George returned to his group. "Where is your mother, you said to meet your parents?" I asked.

"She'll be out back in the kitchen with Doris, the landlady" I raised my eyebrows. "You wanted to know where the action would be tonight, it will be here.

After closing there is a private party, mum will be with other ladies preparing the buffet." The more time with this girl the more I became confused. "What party?" I asked. "Christmas party, you dope." Did she just call me a dope?

"Melissa you have to stop talking in riddles, you are confusing me," I said. She laughed and I noticed her father turn and smile. He came over "Good start son, first she's laughed in a week." He went away back to his friends. "Melissa, help me out and explain."

She held my hand, "I am the happiest I have been since I came down from university, thanks to you."

"Me," I queried.

"Yes you. You walked in the rain you came and said hello to my dad, you'll meet my mum and we'll have great party, I promise."

I finished my beer went to the bar and ordered a refill. It was on the house for Christmas. I thought I am in never-never land, where the hell was I? At the table I apologised to Melissa for forgetting to order her a drink, I asked her what she would like. "Rum and coke with ice and lemon please." I fetched the drink. She took a goodly swallow.

Melissa re-engaged with my hand. The door sprung open, giving access to a band struggling with instruments and amplifiers and huge speakers. I looked at the pub, once they had put there paraphernalia together there wouldn't be any room for customers. As for the speakers they would blast away any strays left behind.

However they tracked through the pub out through a door. George's group helped the band, so I helped also. Carrying one of the speakers following others I came to understand. Through the door, a hall decked out in Christmas decoration, a huge tree and twenty or more women busying themselves preparing a buffet startled me.

Sitting back at the table, this time I took Melissa's hand. She smiled. "Why didn't you answer my questions were you planning a surprise?" I asked.

"No not really just waiting for things to liven-up, which they will shortly."

The door burst open again, this time hordes of people walked in. The bar became a melee of people hugging, shaking hands and pecking cheeks. I was definitely in never-never land, or I was dreaming or I had lost my marbles, one of the three.

"Who are all these people, why arriving so late?" I asked.

"They've come down from the Lake District. Andy, the landlord has a brother who owns a pub up there, somewhere near Grasmere. The Christmas party alternates annually between here and there."

"What about the neighbours when the music starts?"

Melissa now relaxed and smiling happily answered, "They won't care because they are either here or will be here. This is a very, very family orientated pub." I could hear the musicians tuning their instruments. Melissa taken my hand said "Come and meet mum"

In the hall I noticed a bar over in a corner with two guys serving the thirsty arrivals. A very glamourous dark haired woman called, "Melissa." We answered the call and crossed the hall to the buffet.

Melissa said, "Mum meet Richard."

"Hello," I said.

"Hello to you. Where did you find him Melissa?"

Melissa laughing retorted, "Believe it or not years ago at university. He strolled into the George a few hours ago with his mother and grandmother and here we are."

Daphne, Melissa's mother wanted to know who my mother was. I explained she had sold her business, moved first to Freckleton and now to Lytham. I couldn't stop looking at Daphne, she was absolutely stunning. I tried to gauge her age, I could have been there all week needing to double whatever figure I came up with and still have got it wrong. Melissa whispered "Forty-four, beautiful isn't she?" I nodded dumbly.

The people from the pub and many more started to drift in. Melissa tugged me over to a round table. "Dad's table," said Melissa. The band started playing belting out a Rolling Stones' number. The sound, deafening, the speakers were modulated.

Melissa asked me to dance. Although the floor tended to be short of people I agreed to dance. I danced to rid myself of the last twenty-four hours and Melissa danced to rid herself of whatever her demons were.

We continued dancing, dance after dance. Melissa danced sensuously, very sexually, which I loved, her dancing did worry me a tad; I wondered if her parents could see what I was seeing.

When the music slowed she pushed into my arms. Her pelvis, not permanently, grinded into mine, she would grind and withdraw not wishing to draw attention to our dancing. She kissed my neck and ears. My eyes rarely strayed from her parents, albeit they didn't seem to be bothered.

As it turned out the party was very lively and the people very friendly. At one stage, probably for twenty or so minutes we had a fantastic session when we danced the Lambeth Walk and Big Apple, and the Rumba, Cha-Cha and Conga.

Melissa had been right everything in Lytham happened in her parent's local, a discreet pub round a corner amidst a town sleeping oblivious to a hundred plus people thoroughly enjoying the advent of Christmas.

Gerry and Brad arrived shortly after eleven-thirty, both the worse for wear. They received short shrift from George's brother, Stan, Brad's father.

Melissa and I were the permanent dancers we danced to everything going, not necessarily getting the steps right but we definitely tried. Around about two in the morning Melissa asked me to walk her home, saying it wasn't far. I saw her talking to her parents who looked at me.

So I went over to saying, "Melissa has asked me to walk her home, if you are concerned, no problem. However, I need to make tracks. I am tired-- I rode my bike a fair old distance earlier today and have been on the go ever since."

George suddenly all ears yelled, "Bike? What bike?"

"Triumph Bonneville," I answered.

"Blimey, some bike, I would like to see it." I immediately saw a way round gaining the go-ahead for me to walk Melissa home.

I said, "Write your address down and I'll pop round tomorrow afternoon." His instant response, "No need, you'll see where we live when you walk Melissa home." Just to be clear I said, "Are you sure?" I looked at both parents. I had the green light.

The walk must have taken a good twenty minutes after half of them I had said, "I thought you said your house was not far." Melissa hanging off my arm said, "Another few minutes." We finally made it to Melissa's parent's very smart, older style property, located towards St Anne's.

She unlocked the door and pushed me in to the hall. Melissa pushed close to me offering her face to be kissed. Gently I kissed her lips and eyes running by hands over her back and down to her bottom. She whispered, "I've been waiting for this moment all night I thought it would never come."

She pushed her pelvis against me. I slipped my hand into her tights and under her panties to tenderly squeeze her bottom. She pushed her bottom out enjoying the feel of my hands as they enveloped her buttocks. Her hand was fumbling for my zip.

I whispered, "Melissa we have to stop." Her hands were busy releasing Jolly Roger. Sharply I said, "Melissa, stop," and pulled away from her re-zipping my trousers. Her face portrayed hurt.

I quickly pulled her close whispering urgently, "Melissa this isn't the time or the place. Your parents could walk in any minute." She looked at me her face displaying concern saying, "They'll be a while."

"And if not?" I asked.

She pulled clear of me, straightened her clothing and wandered into a room collapsing into an armchair. I followed. "What's wrong Richard?" she asked her eyes firmly fixed on mine.

We were in a comfortably furnished living room with a white piano positioned in a corner. "Are you the family pianist?" I smilingly queried. Ignoring my question she repeated her question, "What's wrong Richard?"

Sitting on the arm of the chair I tenderly ran my fingers through her thick dark hair. Composed I said, "Melissa there isn't anything wrong, I promise you. You have to understand, I am not seeking a quick in, out, thank you mam, nor am I interested in garden sheds, up against walls or grabbing a few minutes in a hallway. If that is what you want there are a hundred guys in Lytham who will willingly oblige you."

She pushed my hand away. Her eyes, as big as saucers looked at me, a mixture of anger and pain summarised her lovely face. "What is it you want Richard? To play with my feelings, to make me beg, what do you want?"

"I didn't want to upset you Melissa," I whispered "I want the same as you but lovingly and tenderly."

I heard the front door open. Daphne called, "Melissa."

"In here mum," Melissa called. The room blazoned as Daphne switched the lights on. Her mother's face showing concern looked at us both, seeing where and how we were sitting, she smiled.

Daphne all smiles said "Cup of tea Richard, or coffee?"

"No I am fine thank you, I must be off." George appeared, standing behind Daphne. "You don't have to go because we have come home, sit and chat a while." I thanked him and Daphne and enforced my decision to depart.

They left Melissa and me alone. I leaned down and brushed my lips on hers saying, "I'll call round tomorrow to show your father my motorcycle. If you are still interested I would like to take you out tomorrow night to celebrate Christmas, are you?" She nodded.

I called to George, "I'll pop round tomorrow to show you the Bonneville." He came through from the rear of the house. "What time?" he asked. I smiled.

"One hour after I wake-up and before you ask, I have no idea."

He laughed saying, "I'll be here."

Melissa came to the door and kissed my cheek. She held onto me whispering. "I have so much to tell you and I will."

I could feel an earthquake, Mother's hand grasping my shoulder, when I opened my eyes Grandma came into focus smiling. I am sure they wanted to hear the sordid details if any of the previous evening's escapade. When they asked where I had been and what I had been up to.

I simply told them I had ended up at a party in the backroom of pub. Drank too much and eventually after walking up and down streets for half the night, which was true, specifically after I exited Melissa's home, I found the house. They told me they were off into Blackpool to shop and would be home after four. I said fine, I would go back to sleep.

I heard mother's plush car pull away. Before falling asleep I had determined upon an action plan involving a caravan. I jumped out of bed ready to put my plan into action. I had to find a caravan site and hire a caravan for the week. I also needed a crash-helmet for Melissa, one which would fit her father. I suspected he would be looking for a ride.

Riding the Bonneville in and around St Anne's I finally located a post office. I asked the postmaster if there were any caravan sites within easy reach. He directed me to one a mere ten minute ride out of Lytham.

I swiftly found the Caravan Park. I rode round trying to locate an isolated caravan. Thinking, I doubted the caravans if any were in use Christmas Eve. I knocked on the door of a large white house.

A chap answered, who I asked if I could hire a caravan for the week. He gave me a strange look. He wanted to know why I needed to hire a caravan. I asked him if he remembered, during his courting days, how difficult it could be to find privacy to share with his loved one.

He rolled-up saying, "I love it you want somewhere for a little slap and tickle." I wasn't au fait with the expression "slap and tickle" so I told him I wanted somewhere quiet where my fiancé and I could be alone, without either of our families chaperoning. Chuckling he stated he would gladly help me out.

He asked for fifty, after some haggling we agreed on thirty pounds. He walked me into the park, heading towards a group of four caravans. "Take the end one," he said. "You'll have all the privacy you want." He continued to chuckle.

He presented the caravan, consisting of two bedrooms, one with a double bed the other contained two singles. A large living area with a kitchen sited midway. He demonstrated how the heating system worked. He made sure there was a good gas supply and the water switched on. We swopped keys for money and I departed. He still chuckled.

I rode to Melissa's house, which took some finding. I found it, albeit the entire street looked similar. When I knocked Daphne opened the door, she smiled, "Come in Richard, they are all waiting patiently for your arrival."

Melissa exited the living room and kissed my cheek. She looked wonderful. George followed, he said "I see out the window it's a bonny bike. Do I get a ride?"

"Of course," I said and tossed him the crash-helmet I had just purchased in Lytham. He put on a heavy coat and waterproof trousers. We climbed astride and we were off.

I headed towards Preston joined the A5 and let rip for Lancaster, turned towards Morecambe followed the signs to Heysham looped back onto the A5 and blasted back to Preston and into Lytham. The journey lasted eighty minutes and he was cock-a-hoop.

Back in the house George held court talking of his love for motorcycles. When young he had been an avid Vincent fan, owning three before Daphne made him give motorcycles up. However, he failed to say, Daphne interrupted, he had a bad crash causing family heartache, money problems and a three month stay in hospital. He waved the crash away saying he was unlucky.

Daphne startled me when she asked for a short ride, not on the day but perhaps Boxing Day. Melissa pushed for a ride immediately. I told her she would need warm clothes.

When she returned I said, "I'll repeat the ride I did with your Dad but at a slower pace." It took twelve minutes to reach the caravan site. I parked the bike outside the selected caravan opened the door and ushered Melissa in.

Her shock evident I quickly explained the caravan interior. She wandered inspecting the bedrooms before saying, "Why Mr Chambers are we here?" I ignored her question. I turned the heating on.

Turning towards her I said, "Last night I may have upset you, which wasn't intended and I am sorry. Melissa I am not a "bang, wham, thank you mam". If we are going to become lovers I want you to thrill in the experience. I want to thrill in the experience. Hence, this, my lovely girl, if you agree, and I hope you do, will become our love-nest for the next few days."

Melissa leaned into me kissing my eyes and lips. Her arms encircled my neck she was pulling me down onto the long settee. Gently I removed her arms and lowered myself to sit alongside her. I lovingly placed my hands onto her cheeks, tenderly kissing her eyes, nose and lips.

After a moment I ceased my kissing and caressing holding her with my arm saying, "Your mother and father, particularly your father are very protective, quite rightly, of their gorgeous daughter. When you were at college there philosophy was simply what the heart doesn't see it can't grieve. Nevertheless, we are now in their backyard so to speak, which means we have to gain their trust."

Melissa leaned forward to kiss me, as she moved closer I pulled her into my arms holding her firmly. Giggling she tried to wriggle free. In a serious tone I said, "Listen Melissa, what I am about to say is important." She went still and I released her.

"In a few minutes we are going for the bike ride after which I will return you home. I will, hopefully borrow mother's car, collecting you at seven-thirty. When I collect you I will ask your father what time he wants you home. We will then know how long we will have together, okay?"

She nodded. I kissed her lips saying, "Right let's hit the road I need to deliver you back to your parents cold and windswept." I dropped a cold Melissa home reminding her I would see her later.

Once home with mother I enjoyed an early dinner with her and grandma, showered and shaved, sprayed cologne liberally over my body, dressed, kissed parent and grandparent goodnight and went in search of sexual release.

George answered the door inviting me in. Daphne, busy in the kitchen came through offering refreshment. George asked where Melissa and I would be at midnight. I seized the opportunity. "George, what time should I bring Melissa home, I ask because the time you decide, decides where we will celebrate the coming of Christmas Day."

He gave me an old-fashioned look. I had wrong-footed him. Hesitating for a moment he said "What have you got in mind." I wasn't sure if he was asking what time would be suitable or where were we going.

I chanced my arm; "I discovered yesterday there is a nightclub, not a disco, called the Gaiety, which is putting on a cabaret and dancing for couples, no riff-raff, but it is in Preston and doesn't close until two in the morning."

I could hear his brain ticking over. "Why not, it is Christmas after all, young people should enjoy themselves. Daphne," he called.

"Yes George," Daphne, in the kitchen called back in an "I'm busy" voice.

"Richard has asked if he can take Melissa into Preston until the early hours, what do you think?" Drying her hands on a cloth Daphne entered the room smiling.

"George she is your daughter you set the rules, remember." He looked at me then Daphne.

Melissa entered the room looking gorgeous. I said "Melissa you are beautiful." Her father said, "God Melissa you look fantastic." Melissa curtsied. Her mother hugged her, which was the last thing Melissa wanted being worried about her hair and make-up. She said, "What's all the shouting?"

George answered, "Richard wants to take you to some club in Preston, which doesn't close until two." Melissa's eyes sparkled, "So, I am twenty-two." George clearly frustrated said, "Okay but you must be home by two-thirty, or two forty-five at the very latest." I promised Melissa would be home.

They followed their daughter outside George seeing the car whistled "Some car you've got there son" I helped Melissa into mother's three week old BMW 3.0 CS, an amazing car with power steering and a fuel-injected straight 6-cylinder under the bonnet. Melissa blew a kiss at her parents and I pulled away.

At the end of the street I turned left heading towards Lytham centre. I pulled into a lay-by. I said, "There is a club in Preston called the Gaiety, which doesn't close until two, there is also the caravan. You look too beautiful to waste on a caravan, however the club will not liven up until ten onwards. So Melissa what do you want to do?"

With absolutely no hesitation she said, "Take me to the caravan we can go to the club after you have made love to me."

The caravan was chilly. I quickly switched the electric heaters on and remembering Sally and the barge I lit the gas rings and oven leaving the oven door open. I turned the lights on and closed the curtains. And then I took Melissa into my arms.

Very slowly I nibbled her ears and kissed her neck. I lifted her face and kissed her eyes and her lips. I started to undress her. I removed her short coat, carefully placing it on the dining table. She stood looking at me.

I kissed her once more, brushing my lips over her ears, neck and lips. Gradually I removed her clothes, her jacket and skirt, then her blouse. She was braless, I nibbled her nipples, she moaned. I dropped to my knees and eased her tights and panties off.

Naked as the day she was born I kissed and caressed her body, she was shivering, not with the cold but from the caressing as I awakened her sexuality. I swiftly disrobed, Jolly Roger stood erect.

My love of women is enhanced by touching and admiring their bodies, which portrayed me as a mercenary, I wasn't. I simply adored looking at naked women. I kissed her nipples. I sat on the settee using my hand to turn her one way and the other. I kissed and nibbled her bottom. I run my hands up and down her legs, over her tummy and tickled her back.

Melissa wanted me to enter her, which would have been easy. I would have climaxed and that would have been it. But that is not me I want to enjoy, I wanted Melissa to enjoy.

I changed places with her so she was sitting and I was standing. I rolled Jolly Roger over her cheeks and across her forehead, I slipped him into her mouth, withdrew him and using Jolly Roger I stroked her face. She gripped his shaft forcing her mouth to take him. I moved slowly in and out, not too deep.

She was sucking and licking and sucking. I pulled away and led her to the double bedroom. Laying her on the bed I explored her body with my tongue and lips. Melissa squirmed, her legs kicking. I gently eased her legs open lowering my head to suck her vagina. I sucked her juices. I assaulted her clitoris with my tongue until she was crying out. She started laughing.

I continued to suck and lick her clitoris she jumped up sitting straight pushing my head into her. She collapsed onto her back. Her juices were all over the bed cover. I raised myself above her and guided Jolly Roger into his resting place.

She cried out, grabbing my arms she pulled her hips up to meet my first thrust. I thrust once more removed Jolly Roger and lowered my head assaulting her clitoris. She pulled on my shoulders and my arms, desperate for Jolly Roger to be inside her. I once more entered her this time I rammed hard.

Her legs went high and her hips drove up. I began a rhythm increasing tempo then slowing. I would drive hard, return to the rhythm. Melissa screamed. She wrapped her arms round my neck. Her legs were beating a tattoo on my shoulders. I drove hard and harder. Melissa yelled and yelled.

Suddenly she tried to push me off I wouldn't budge I had to climax, my sperm had to spread throughout her vagina. Jolly Roger relented exploding my spunk deep into her. I stopped. Melissa held onto me crying out, speaking unintelligible words.

I withdrew my penis and rolled onto my back. Melissa threw herself over me her mouth searching for mine. I pulled her back wanting to cuddle, she relaxed, her head falling onto my chest. I stroked her shoulders and her back. I lifted her face kissing her passionately. She whimpered.

I kissed her once more and her arms encircled me. She spoke in a whisper, "Richard I have wanted you since the first night I saw you in the Leopold with Hugo and the others. I have wished for nothing else." There wasn't much I could say.

Melissa looked at me and smiled her fingers running up and down my chest and stomach. Very quietly she said. "Absolutely amazing, the sensations were incredible."

Her hand searched for and found Jolly Roger. Her head, her tongue and lips running down my body took him into her mouth. Gently, extremely gently she sucked moving her head up and down along his shaft. Her touch, so very light, her lips so sensitive, I started to feel tingling in my loins. Jolly Roger hardened. Her sucking became more urgent.

I drove my hips up to meet her mouth. Melissa gagged letting go. I swiftly pulled her up and over Jolly Roger she settled herself astride and started moving. For a while I lay still, enjoying the sensations caused by her urgent thrusting. Urgency made both of us begin to drive. I took control, holding her and using the strength of my arms to lift and pull her down.

I slowed to keep the pace steady making sure the whole of Jolly Roger entered her. Every third or fourth downward motion by Melissa I lifted my hips and drove that little bit deeper. Each time she squealed. We continued for a long while. I could feel her experiencing minor orgasms, making her want to speed the rhythm but I continued to control her movements.

She started to whine, a continuous whine. She threw her head back and her whine increased in volume to a howl. I needed to drive, to ram. Without decoupling I moved Melissa below me. I started ramming. I became a steam engine driving hard and harder. I pummelled her, I pounded into her and I drove as deep as I could. I pulled her legs up and forced them over her head to drive deeper.

Melissa, her throat emitting a series of strange noises began to pant. I pushed her legs further back until her toes were touching the caravan's walls. I rammed as hard as I could, once, twice, thrice and again and again. Melissa shrieked, she screamed, she cried for me to stop. I stopped she cried for me not to stop.

I rammed in time and time again. Her body lifted clear of the bed holding onto me as I drove deep inside her. Her screaming and yelling stopped, her body crumpled, she began to shake, to sob and then she exploded lifting her hips high. I exploded too, my sperm washing over her vagina walls.

Melissa kept saying "Oh my God, oh my God." She lay quiet, still inside her. She spoke "I loved it, every sensation, every feeling, every orgasm but most of all the orgasm, the one with the tingling, the electricity. I couldn't imagine such a feeling, such a feeling existed, oh my God Richard."

I withdrew Jolly Roger pulling Melissa into my arms. I caressed her, kissed her neck, run my hands over her breasts, I gently squeezed her nipples. She kissed my chest and my throat, her hand on Jolly Roger. Above her head I checked my watch. "It's time to go dancing and time to celebrate Christmas." Melissa said "Can we stay here, please. I want to be with you, you and me."

I didn't, I needed people, crowds to wash Melissa away. I had one huge problem. Although I had changed inside, once I was with a woman, some women, such as Melissa and Carol, I softened, which I did not want.

Women like Stephanie, the American and Jenny the older woman and all the others, the Verity's' and Rebecca's' were fodder, pick them up "wham-bang, thank you mam" women. The Melissa's and Carols of the world were not, they had something extra that impacted on my thought patterns. I said "No Melissa we have to go to the club, you have to look as if you have been partying when I take you home just in case your father is waiting for you."

I discovered Lifebuoy soap still in its wrapper in the small bathroom's cabinet and lifted the settee to gain access to the towels the caravan owner had shown me. I gently washed Melissa's vagina, her bottom, tummy and legs, which were all sticky from our love juices and the remnants of my sperm. I cleansed myself.

We dressed and set off for Preston. We arrived at the club at twelve-fifteen, the door wide open and there wasn't any sign of bouncers. The noise from the club extraordinary loud, everyone singing what I considered a dreadful song called "Long haired lover from Liverpool". Thinking quickly I took Melissa's coat run back to the car leaving her exposed, returning we descend into the club. I bouncer stopped us. I inclined my head towards Melissa and winked. He let us in.

We circled around the massed crowd crazily bopping on the dance floor to the bar. I ordered three red wines, two for Melissa and one for me. I needed her to smell of alcohol. I left the glasses in the care of the bartender and steered Melissa onto the dance floor.

Mercifully the singing stopped and the music started. We swirled and jumped, rocked and rolled, leaped and twisted, Melissa began to move and boy oh boy, could she move. I pushed guys away who were trying to take her over. She shimmied and shimmied, shook and shook holding my arm not letting go.

We danced and danced, the music tempo slowed and we smooched, pelvises grinding. Once more the music changed. We left the dance floor I retrieved the drinks from the bartender and we sipped the wine.

I looked up at the imitation of the famous Grand Central Terminal clock in New York noticing it read one-fifty. I once more led Melissa onto the dance floor. We locked together and smooched until the last song, "Nights in White Satin" by the Moody Blues played to an end. We kissed for a long time. Our drinks were gone, I looked to the bartender; he shrugged his shoulders and pointed at his wrist. We joined the throng exiting.

I delivered Melissa to a waiting George at two forty-six, one minute late. He asked me in for coffee, which I thanked him for but declined. I pecked Melissa on the cheek saying "I hope I can see you again." She smiled.

"Boxing Day I'll be free."

I asked for her number she wrote it down on a pad by the telephone. I said, "I'll call you on Boxing Day, perhaps we could pop to Blackpool and see the illuminations." Her father witnessed the whole charade, satisfied his daughter had been a good girl. I inwardly smiled.

151

Christmas lunch with mother and grandma proved to be great fun, we did drink a tad too much before and after. However, both ladies were happy. We had the customary roast turkey, and all the trimmings, and Christmas pudding without sixpences.

Mother moaned, Grandma groaned and I ate a delicious meal. During lunch I told story after story, which they enjoyed albeit mother on occasion did lift her eyebrows, so would have I if listening to the exaggerations I comically expounded.

I volunteered to wash up. By the time I had finished they were both flat out in armchairs fast asleep. After lunch mother gave me five hundred pounds and Grandma gave me a hundred wrapped in baking paper. Don't ask, I didn't.

Flabbergasted yes, happy doubly so, grateful definitely, beholden most certainly, I imagined how Rockefeller must have felt.

Boxing Day I took Daphne for a spin on the bike, which brought back memories of her courting and early married days to George. I thought she would have quizzed me regarding Melissa, but not a word. After Daphne's ride Melissa and I said we were off to Blackpool, which of course we had no intention of any such thing.

Boxing Day onwards for four days, we returned to the caravan, to make love, have sex. I purchased wine and soft drinks, milk and tea, and sugar. I also bought soap and a flannel.

I didn't get to see Blackpool's famous illuminations, much too busy exploring and enjoying a very sexy Melissa. Friday afternoon she decided to tell "all". Actually her story proved to be a damp squib.

Apparently the story of Ruth and I is now written into the university's book of legends. Our love became the envy of all girls, of which, not one, could understand why Ruth ditched me.

Danny Bowden, she explained ran a book where the girls could donate a pound. If a girl bedded me she would collect the winnings less ten per cent for Danny. The book collected one hundred and thirty three pounds. A secondary prize could be won if a girl actually gained entry into my flat without getting me into bed. The prize for entry into my flat, forty per cent of the takings, leaving the unsuccessful girls, to collect half their money and Danny would keep the balance.

However, if all failed, Danny kept the pot, although he did throw a party in the Union Bar. I remembered hearing of Danny's party, recalling a few rumours flying around but I took little notice regarding girls bedding me, at the time I was focused on Sophie.

Melissa in a "tell all" mood would have continued, however I stopped her. I had no interest albeit she insisted on recalling how the girls talked about Richard Chambers and Hugo, and Ben, James and Craig. They would sit in the Leopard waiting until after a rugby training session, waiting for the guys to walk in.

She explained how the Leopard became her local but I rarely turned up. Aggrieved I said, "Melissa enough you make me sound like a celebrity, and I assure you I wasn't and I'm not."

She chuckled. "Ah, ha you see you were, girls wanted to be close to you, even talk to you."

Angrily I cried, "Stop, enough you are talking out of the top of your head." She relented.

We were naked and Melissa lay nestled in my arms. We had just finished making love when she started talking once more. "Tomorrow you leave to visit your father, leaving me. Will we see each other again? How often do you visit your mother? Will you keep in touch? What am I going to do when you have gone?"

Question after question I became irate. Keeping calm I said, "Melissa this is a Christmas holiday romance. We are two people who wanted to share some magic moments, which we have, now it is over. I get on with my life and you get on with your life."

I felt her body shake and then the tears started. Her voice quivering she said, "Life is not like that Richard, you don't just pick people up use them and discard them. There is responsibility, there are feelings, and there is a need people have when they do feel. I will not be discarded. I love you."

My voice stern I said, "Melissa you cannot love me you have known me for five or six days." Perturbed I resumed, "Melissa, you know absolutely nothing about me, where I live, where I work, where I am going in the future, what I want to do in the future. Nothing, you know my name, you have heard stories about me and all of a sudden you are in love. You are being ridiculous, bloody ridiculous."

Sobbing she cried, "I loved you in the Leopard, I loved you through college, I loved you when I saw you in the pub and I have loved you more every day since. I am not ridiculous I am a woman in love."

I had to laugh, I tried not to but I did. "Melissa, please listen to me, I am heading for Newcastle where I will meet another woman who I will have sex with. I will return home where I will have sex with many women. I am not the marrying type. I love women for being women, I love to look, touch and have sex. I am a very uncaring person."

Her voice breaking she whispered, "Why are you doing this, why are you trying to hurt me. I will wait for you. I will remain true. When you tire of women I will be waiting."

I pushed her off of me. "Get dressed I am taking you home." She shrieked back at me, "You get dressed, you go home I am staying here." I thought "fuck this" dressed and went, five minutes later I returned feeling guilty as hell. I took her in my arms saying, "I'll strike a deal with you but you must promise to honour it."

Melissa nodded saying, "I promise."

"Okay this is the deal. You ask your father if you can come with me to Newcastle. If he says yes then you come. After Newcastle I will drop you off at home, we say goodbye, goodbye forever." She sobbed louder and nodded her head.

I removed my clothes and climbed in the bed beside her. I cuddled her until she stopped sobbing. I said, "Melissa, I have loved two women in my life, for one reason or another I lost both. I will not fall in love again."

A strangled sob and she hugged me holding on with all her strength. We continued to cuddle half asleep both lost in our own thoughts. Abruptly I sat up. I whispered, "Melissa this is either our last night in Lytham together or you are coming with me to Newcastle. We need to speak to your mother and father."

We washed and dressed I swiftly negotiated the roads to her house. It was in darkness. I shot to the pub. Her father stood at the bar with his pals, Daphne with a group of ladies sitting at a table.

Melissa followed as I approached him. I said, "George could I have a private word?" He excused himself and followed me to the door. I noticed Daphne stand and walk over. I waited before I said "Melissa and I would like to spend New Year together at my father's in the northeast. I am leaving tomorrow. I am asking you if Melissa can come with me."

They looked at each other. A slight smile appeared on Daphne's face. George looked like he had been hit with a wet fish.

I felt for Melissa's hand and led her to the bar leaving her parents to discuss my request. After a moment George returned to his pals. Daphne came over to Melissa and me. She looked at me saying, "Have you and Melissa been sleeping together?" I nodded. "Where?" She asked.

I told her. Her eyes brightened. "Do you love her?" I shook my head. "What happens after New Year?"

"I bring her home we say goodbye and we return to our lives." She looked at Melissa. "What about you madam?"

Melissa thought before answering, "Mum I am very fond of Richard and I would like to be with him over the New Year. I know we do not have a future. He has been very candid with me."

Daphne smiled, "So be it go and enjoy but I do not want any moping around the house when Richard brings you home. As for you young man, you are a very honest person, which I admire. You will probably break her heart, which I will have to mend, but we'll cope won't we girl?" Melissa nodded.

Daphne called George over. He said, "Look after her and bring her home safely." We shook hands.

I had two problems. One major, luggage, the other minor, although I didn't think it would be a problem, I needed to telephone father and tell him I would have a girl with me. I couldn't do much about the luggage problem until the morning.

I called father. He laughed, adding Melissa would be welcome. He explained Tina had been busy selling me to any girl who would listen. We said a few more words I asked him to give my love to Tina and he the same to mother.

I invited Melissa and her parents, after I had checked with mother, to dinner. Mother in whatever time she had went to town. She, with Melissa's help prepared a sumptuous dinner of Salmon cakes, followed by Rack of Lamb served with cranberry and shallot sauce with potato pancakes and green beans.

For dessert she would offer either cheese and biscuits or apple and cinnamon pie with cream. Melissa had a great time and told me how very impressed she had been with mother's flair in the kitchen. Although their meetings had been brief mother and Melissa seemed to get on well.

Grandma Jean, as long as she could reach for her brandy, which mother controlled, was happy, she looked at me and smiled.

Melissa wanted to bathe and dress, so I whisked her home. She returned at seven-thirty with her parents.

I seated Melissa and parents in the living room, a room at least twice the size of Daphne and George's. I watched them inspect the furnishings. I opened the huge wooden doors into the dining room so they could see mother's magnificent table and the bar where I would serve drinks from.

Mother walked in and said "Champagne" I opened two bottles. Grandma wondered in, after introductions, typical of her approach to life she said "So you are the parents of Melissa who has deprived me of my grandson's company" Mother said "Hush Jean" Grandma laughed "Why hush. You only have to look at the girl to see why he prefers her company to mine." Grandma had broken the ice.

We sipped the champagne swopping tales. George, let slip he managed the local colt team for the rugby club. He said, "I hear you play." I smiled.

"On occasion." Melissa jumped in. I instantly thought, "oh no".

"Dad, Richard played for his college and the university, and he turned down the chance to train with the England set-up wanting to put his studies first."

I saw George's eyes appraise me. "Flanker?" I nodded. "Are you still playing?" he queried. "I skipper a team," I replied

"Which team?" he asked. I told him, his eyes opened wide. I had a friend for life. The second bottle nearly empty, mother told me to open the wine asking our guests to sit at the dining table.

155

Through dinner George and I talked rugby. He asked me, if when visiting mother, would I join him at the rugby club one night for a few beers, I said I would. Grandma and Melissa were talking, Grandma recalling the holidays I would spend in Silverdale, describing a young boy who had ants in his pants and who was always out and about.

However, the most obvious union was Daphne and mother as they laughed and told stories all through dinner.

Dinner over, mother resisted all offers of help. I knew she would rinse the plates and dishes to get the worse off leaving the washing-up for her lady who cleaned. Melissa whispered that her parents had agreed to her staying with me all night in the caravan.

Mother overheard. "What caravan?" Daphne laughed out loud she said, "He hasn't told you," she laughed again even George smiled. "Your wayward son has seduced my daughter and kept her under lock and key in a caravan up at the park." Daphne laughed uproariously, Melissa reddened and I poured myself a drink.

Mother said in her "I am your mother" strident voice, "Richard, explain yourself." Daphne chimed in, "Has he told you he is taking Melissa to Newcastle tomorrow." I thought here we go.

Before she could admonish me I said, "Mother, Melissa and I wanted privacy so I rented a caravan to have privacy. As for Newcastle we only agreed that a few hours ago and I haven't had a chance to tell you."

Mother retorted, "Does your father know?"

"Yes I telephoned him when Melissa and I came home," I retorted back.

"You have told your father but not your mother."

I wasn't sure whether mother was making a statement or asking a question, I treated it as a question. "Mother, I apologise, everything happened so fast." George said "You can say that again" Melissa laughed saying "It's like watching a comedy at the theatre, absolutely brilliant" Daphne laughed, mother laughed we all laughed.

Tucked up in bed in the caravan Melissa giggled. "What's so funny?" I asked. Still giggling she answered "Parents." I chuckled. The night, extra luminous from a bright moon I opened the curtains above the bed to let in the moon's lunar reflections, Melissa kissed me and I returned her kiss.

With little foreplay and with Melissa on her side her bottom pushed out towards me I eased Jolly Roger in through the opening of her moist vagina. A gentle moan escaped her lips, the moment romantic, enhanced by the shine of the moon. I slowly pushed Jolly Roger all the way and lay still. Melissa fidgeted wanting movement she pushed back in to me. I stay still relishing the feel.

Melissa accepted the stillness, a little whimper sounded from deep down. She said, "Wouldn't it be wonderful to lie like this forever?" I smiled, she couldn't see the smile, but she knew. I pushed moving my hands to her breasts, such lovely breasts, round and firm with sexy little nipples, which I gently tweaked. Melissa pushed back once more.

I started the movement she wanted. In and out, in and out, withdrawing my penis to her labia lips before sliding it back in. I could feel the urgency rising in her movements. I doggedly refused to be rushed.

I gently pushed in and gently eased back. Every now and again I would ram hard. Melissa in response would squeal. She let out a long sigh whispering, "I love the feel when you push hard." I pushed hard once more, Melissa sighed. Suddenly her body quivered and she panted, unexpectedly climaxing.

She cried out "Hell Richard what happened?" I chuckled.

"You climaxed."

"I know that you sod but how?" she asked. "We are not moving, well just a little but not enough. How did that happen?" she asked again "It's called coitus, or sexual intercourse or physical intimacy, which sometimes causes girls and boys to climax." I laughingly responded.

Her climax signalled me to start making love. I increased the tempo, she did likewise we were pushing and driving, thrusting and shoving trying to ride a great big wave. I climbed on top, Melissa on top, and she lay on her side, wherever we were we thrust.

I decoupled stood to the side of the bed turned her onto her front pulled her hips up and attacked her doggy style. She screamed and I mean screamed. Her juices were splashing down my legs and I rammed. Every ram commanded a yell from me and a scream from Melissa.

Orgasms started flowing through her. I rammed harder I wanted to come in her mouth, we hadn't before but now I did. I could feel Jolly Roger readying for the explosion. I felt my sperm boiling. I whipped Melisa over straddled her and forced my penis into her mouth. She accepted it willingly.

I exploded, she gagged but gamely sucked. The sperm kept flowing. Fully expended her face was awash with my sperm, it leaked through her lips, she tried to swallow the discharge, her mouth full of my sperm.

My discharge happened too fast, the experience of power dissipated. Melissa in a little girl's voice said, "I haven't done that before. I would only do it for you. The funny thing is I liked it, I felt strong." She laughed using the sheet to wipe her mouth.

I climbed from the bed returning with a damp flannel I wiped her face, her vagina and the crevice between her buttocks. She said, "You are so loving and so caring and you worry about me. I know you are worried about delivering me home to my parents." She laughed. "Did I just say delivering I made me sound like a parcel. But you are, aren't you." she leaned over using the moon's light to look into my face.

She resumed, "Richard I made a promise and I swear I will keep the promise. No histrionics, no crying just a simple goodbye and a kiss on the cheek, perhaps a wave if I feel in a good mood." She smiled at her own comment.

I was wide awake at six with Melissa clasped in my arms. I had an erection. I gently climbed over and lay behind her. I could feel her warmth. I guided Jolly Roger up between her legs to touch her labia lips using my right hand round the front of her body I steered him to her opening.

Satisfied I was on target I very gently and very slowly pushed. Whoosh she was so wet I drove right up inside her. Melissa yelped and squeezed her legs in defence. I pushed and pushed, she laughed and pushed back. She accused me of thievery for taking her without her say so. Swiftly I unloaded my sperm and deflated. Melissa laughed saying, "How the mighty fall."

Chapter 18 - New Year 1972/73

I left the key in the door as instructed by the owner and escorted Melissa home. Her father just leaving for the colt's rugby training. He wished me well and a happy New Year adding to look after his daughter, which I promised to do.

I rode home. Mother cooked bacon and egg, fried bread and grilled tomatoes, which I smothered with HP sauce. I showered and headed for Blackpool to locate a motorcycle shop. I had two addresses taken from the telephone directory.

I had been searching for half an hour when I chanced on a policeman. I gave him the shop's name. He explained they had moved to larger premises and directed me. I found the shop. Told the guy what I wanted.

He had the perfect solution a bracket that fitted to the bike's structure plus two metal rods that stood perpendicular to take the weight. I listened, deciding his solution to be a very ingenious piece of equipment. One of his men fixed the apparatus. I also purchased waterproofs for Melissa and a waterproof sheet to cover the luggage. My Christmas money came in handy.

I stopped off at mothers, packed my belongings and loaded the bike. I hugged mother and Grandma promising to re-visit In March. They waved goodbye from the gate.

After Daphne let me in and I looked at Melissa's luggage I could have cried. "Melissa, sweetheart," using my "now then little girl" voice, "Where am I going to load all of that. Look out of the window, do you see a Pickford's truck, what no Pickford's truck?" I jokingly asked.

Continuing I said, "Perhaps if you look hard enough you might just catch sight of a little two wheeled vehicle parked to the right of the window, which means it is re-pack time."

Daphne smiled. It was obvious it was the New Year gown and accessories that were taking the space. After some thought without coming up with an answer I capitulated and said, "I'll tell you what leave all that behind and I'll buy you a New Year present of a gown and the bits and pieces needed. What do you say?"

Her arms wrapped round my neck and Melissa heartily kissed me. Daphne smiled and said, "You are a very lucky girl." I loaded the bike stacking the bags and cases once, re-stacking twice, before third time lucky I managed to load the lot.

Kisses and hugs for Daphne and we were off. Whickham, here we come.

I had given the atlas some heavy studying, deciding to head north to Carlisle and cross country on the A66 to Whickham. A brilliant deduction we were in Whickham in time for the pub at lunchtime arriving just after midday. Tina and father made a huge fuss of Melissa. They showed her the bedroom, with bathroom.

Downstairs in the kitchen, after we had discussed the journey, weather, Whickham and the local pubs I explained we needed to find an evening gown for Melissa. Tina advised Fenwicks or Debenhams, two large stores in Newcastle, deciding Fenwicks would be our best bet. Father told me to find Grey's Monument in the centre of Newcastle, close to all shops.

When we had found the gown we would meet Father and Tina in their local pub, approximately four hundred yards from the house. Father also gave me keys for the house and garage.

Fenwicks had a huge selection of evening gowns and I think Melissa tried them all on. However, she did look magnificent in most. Somehow I had missed the curvaceousness of her body, which the gowns demonstrated reminding me I had a gorgeous woman sharing my bed.

While I sat and observed Melissa and the various gowns she tried on, I began to realise just how much of a voyeur I had become. I loved watching and studying women. They come in all shapes and sizes and they intrigued me. I loved the fashionable short skirts, knee high boots, cocktail dresses and evening gowns, high heels and long, long legs and expressive attractive bottoms. I loved the many hair fashions. I quite simply loved women, full stop.

The lady serving Melissa interrupted my thoughts asking if I had made a final choice. I hadn't realised I had been appointed as the decision maker. I held a short conference with Melissa. Together we decided on a pale green, strapless gown with a tantalising side slit, which reached halfway between her pantie line and knee. She looked incredibly sexy.

After the purchase, the price knocking me into next week we sauntered the store searching for accessories. I also realised I loved the Geordie accent enjoying listening to the counter assistants as Melissa busily spent my Christmas money.

Walking back to the bike a very happy Melissa, acting coquettishly, asked if I had a tuxedo, which I did having purchased one at a sale for a wedding reception. I had left it behind when I moved from Hove to Southampton leaving it with an assortment of other belongings for father to move to Whickham.

We dropped the purchases off at the house and strolled to the pub. The first indication that father and Tina were regulars was the sign reading "KEEP OFF TINA AND DICK'S" affixed to the wall above where they were sitting on two stools. I couldn't help noticing Tina displayed an awful lot of thigh.

I heard father's voice. "Hear they are." I acknowledged his wave. Two stools swiftly materialised for Melissa and I, and introductions made to a dozen or so regulars. Father ordered the drinks. Melissa entering into the spirit of the company ordered a whisky and lemonade. I noted that they served her a double.

Looking around the pub I noticed a glazed section where people were dining. I espied a woman, dark with long hair curled into a bun, delivering plates to a table. I said too loudly, "Jesus Christ Ruth." Melissa's hand was on my shoulder holding tight. She saw the woman.

Father asked who Ruth was. I indicated the waitress. He laughed, "That's Catriona, she's a lovely girl. Has a little boy, her husband left her for a young slip of a girl." I felt Melissa's hand relax its grip. I turned back to Melissa and smiled, she kissed my cheek.

I wanted to meet Catriona.

Until closing time we gossiped, Tina bombarded Melissa with questions regarding her gown and her college days keeping her occupied. Father asked after my work and stressed his pleasure upon hearing I was doing well.

He described R J Construction's success, which now ran to over two hundred employees. Johnny, father's partner's family had relented and moved to Gateshead. Wexford a great guy, I heard had proposed to local Geordie girl in the summer. He had taken the girl home to Eire to meet his parents. Little Brian, Dennis and Jerry were still with him as was Casey and a few of the others. Most had gone home for Christmas.

Come closing time we walked to father's house. Melissa and I unpacked and lay on the bed. Melissa asked what would have happened if the woman had been Ruth. I didn't answer simply because I didn't know.

After a while I said, "Nothing, I would have taken you over to meet her, said hello, wished her well and said goodbye. Ruth is the past she is now dead and buried."

I wanted Melissa. I told her to stand and undress. She obeyed. I watched taking in her round breasts, her slim waist and lovely hips. I asked her to turn round. I looked at her bottom, a perfect sculptor of what a bottom should look like. Fleetingly I remembered Sophie's bottom. Jolly Roger was erect.

I lifted my hips and removed trousers and boxers. Melissa leaned over to remove my shirt. I sucked her nipples. I quietly said "Suck me" she lay across and took Jolly Roger into her mouth. She gripped the shaft and moved it up and down into her mouth.

I said, "Take your time I want to savour every touch and every feel." I let her suck and lick for a long time. I wanted to feel her sucking me. She never wavered she worked and worked. I thought her mouth must be aching.

I pulled her hair and dragged her up to kiss her. I run my hand down to her vagina and inserted my fingers. She was wet, very wet. I pushed her head back down and pulled her legs round so her vagina was available for my mouth.

I sucked her vagina hard causing a vacuum. I heard her moan. I thrust my hips up to meet her mouth. She gagged. I concentrated on her clitoris. Her sucking of Jolly Roger as clitoris sensations took over became erratic. I held her head whispering, "Suck" she obeyed.

Abruptly I pulled her up, lifted her legs and rammed hard. She squealed. I rammed and rammed. I stopped, telling her to suck me. I repeated the move ramming into her. I rammed again before ordering her to suck. I shot my load into her mouth she swallowed and swallowed. I asked her to lick the head of my penis. She looked at me and told me she loved me.

Melissa snuggled into my arms I lay thinking. I had just fucked Ruth. Melissa wasn't there. I had wanted to hurt Ruth for the hurt she had given me. But Melissa had read my treatment of her as love.

I pulled Melissa tight and whispered, "Sorry" She lifted her head asking what I was sorry for. I said, "For doing what I just did."

"Oh Richard," she cried. "I loved it. It was fabulous I enjoyed your sperm I love the taste and the feel in my mouth."

I thought "one day I will understand women", not today obviously, but one day.

I decided I needed a shower. Melissa watched from her grandstand seat on the toilet lid. She reached through and held Jolly Roger. She said "Your penis is so beautiful."

"Jolly Roger," I said. She looked at me with a blank expression. "That's his name. He was christened by a lady a long time ago. The name has stuck." She giggled letting him fall "What a great name, Jolly Roger" she said the name to herself several times.

Melissa replaced me in the shower. I decided to wash her. Tenderly I used the flannel to wash her from top to toe. Melissa enjoyed my loving attention. She started to massage her clitoris I watched her face. Her expressions repeatedly changed. She smiled, she laughed, she grimaced and she sighed regularly. I saw her climax start, her body shudder, and her face shone a beautiful picture of pleasure.

I guided her from the shower gently leaning her across the sink and entered from behind. I gently pushed in and out. All I wanted was to come. It didn't take long. She must have felt my sperm because she sighed saying, "Oh Richard."

I tugged her into the shower, the water still running. She was giggling, holding onto me. I washed between her legs she pushed against my hand. I slipped my finger into her anus she shrieked and pushed me away. She looked at me hard I stared into her eyes. Her bottom was mine I could see it in her eyes.

Melissa asked to borrow an iron. Tina produced ironing board and steam iron and a cloth for Melissa to press a short black dress. Back in our room I watched her dress. She put on her panties, then tights before donning the little black dress. Her firm breasts discarded the need of a bra. I sat in silence as she brushed her hair and applied make-up. She slipped her shoes on, the whole episode proved very sexy.

When she had finished I walked behind her and kissed her head. Holding her hand I paraded her for my visual pleasure. Her gorgeous long legs, sculptured breasts and her curvaceous figure encased in the little black dress presented a striking, stunning woman. She looked so young, innocent yet sexy, I couldn't figure it out.

I told her she looked beautiful, sexy and sumptuous wrapped in one big parcel for me to open later. She didn't believe me so I pushed her in front of the mirror and said, "Look, have a good look. You are a delight, a beautiful woman."

She turned this way and that way still not satisfied. I reiterated how beautiful she looked. I run my hands over her body and nuzzled her neck. I whispered "Melissa you are a joy to look at, you would excite any man." Provocatively she asked if she excited me. I hugged and kissed her affirming she did.

She kissed me forcing her tongue into my mouth. Taking a breath she said, "Are you going to?" "Going to what?" I asked. She didn't answer my question instead she said, "I won't mind if you want to."

Exasperated I said, "Melissa I do not have a clue what you are muttering about." She smiled. "Your finger." I switched on.

"No I am not," I answered.

I went downstairs leaving her confused, knowing damn well I would, but not until she had nagged me to do so. I heard her close the bedroom door I went to meet her at the stairs. Standing on the bottom stair she matched my height. I kissed her and reiterated how beautiful she looked. Father came into the hall and whistled. Tina came to the top of the stairs, I whistled.

The nightclub seemed quiet when we arrived. Father, once more well known, was shown to one of three raised tables overlooking the other tables and the dance floor.

Father asked Melissa if she liked champagne. Satisfied he ordered a bottle for Tina and Melissa and two large brandies for him and me. He started talking to Melissa. I asked Tina how life was in the cold north her answer was, "The weather may be cold but the people are warm." I couldn't odds that.

I asked if she had made any friends, two by all accounts, Dulcie a Welsh girl in her late thirties and Sam, late twenties, a Polish girl teaching English, which Tina found hilarious, so did I. Making certain Melissa was

163

absorbed by father's charm I asked Tina about Catriona. Tina glanced at Melissa saying, "Not for you, she is off men, for the immediate future." I nodded.

The club, which wasn't too large started to fill from ten onwards, mixed groups arrived. There were a few men in pairs and several groups of women. The women impressed me they were all half naked. I asked Tina. She couldn't explain it putting it down to being a Newcastle phenomenon.

The seven piece band with two singers, one male, and the other female started their act at ten-thirty. By eleven the club rocked and rolled. I hadn't seen so many desirable women under one roof for a long time. One or two were delectable.

There were a few couples dancing but mostly it appeared to be groups of women. Melissa wanted to dance. I slow danced allowing me to scan the females. I thought this is the place to be, forget Southampton. Melissa began to act very sexily, I responded putting my hands on her bottom.

We danced the night away, I must have been of the floor for a good hour before the band took a break and the DJ turned his turntables. We returned to the table. As we passed one table a hand touched my leg I looked into the very blue eyes of a blonde. She smiled. I smiled and carried on guiding Melissa.

Melissa gulped her champagne. The waiter appeared and refilled her glass. She drank the refill quite fast. The waiter was back in a trice refilling once more. There were two guys leaning over the table, obviously friends. Tina and father were busy talking to them.

Melissa pulled my head down and nibbled my ear. I put my hand on her knee. She wiggled whispering, "I want to go to bed" I couldn't help it I said "Hang on I'll ask the waiter the way to the beds." She whispered, "Feel me I'm wet."

I glanced quickly round the room; the table clothes touched the floor. I ran my hand up her short skirt. She was indeed wet. She whispered urgently, "Richard I need you now"

We were miles from home, strangers in a nightclub in the centre of Newcastle and my girl wanted sex. There wasn't much I could do and I told her so. I looked at my watch, nearly midnight, leaving two hours before we would set off home. I nudged father, he leaned back. I said, "Melissa has drank too much I need to take her home." He nodded, we said goodnight.

Outside the club there were a couple of taxis. I gave the address and the driver navigated clear of Newcastle. Melissa kissed me and held Jolly Roger. I paid the taxi and opened the door. Melissa grabbed my hand and yanked me upstairs. In the bedroom she pulled up her short dress, pulled of her tights and panties wanting me immediately. I told her to get into bed, which she did. I slowly undressed.

I climbed in with her. Melissa's head dived straight down her mouth sucking Jolly Roger. I pulled her off and laying her on her back I forced her legs high and back. I drove into her she yelled, screamed and climaxed within seconds. I kept driving in and out she shouted, "More, more." I gave her more.

I turned her onto her knees and went in from behind. I turned her again onto her back and drove in and in. I started to pummel faster and faster. She fought back trying to match my drive. She screamed constantly. Her body trembled, going through spasm after spasm. She told me how much she loved me.

I couldn't come but I remained hard so I kept driving in. She pleaded with me to stop. I stopped and she burst into tears. I cuddled her she pushed me away. "I'm crying for joy," she yelled. "So much pleasure I didn't know it was possible."

Melissa snuggled into my arms. She ran her hand up and down my legs, the stroking gradually slowed and stopped Melissa fell asleep. Satisfied she was out for the count I eased her free from my arms and climbed out of bed. I pulled on a dressing gown and put my boxers on.

In the kitchen I made a sandwich and a mug of tea. I was sitting in the kitchen when Tina and father arrived home. Tina showed real concern for Melissa pointing out she must have drank a whole bottle of champagne. I explained I had put her to bed. Tina kissed my cheek, said goodnight and ascended the stairs.

Father passed me a note saying, "When did you get time to chat to a woman?"

"I didn't." I retorted. The note written in a beautiful script said *"I will be in the Criterion for lunch between twelve-thirty and thirteen forty-five, 3rd January. It would be nice if you could make it, if not don't worry, Debbie"* and a telephone number.

Father said "What do you make of that?" I told him I had no idea. I asked what the girl, who delivered the note looked like. He didn't know a waiter passed the note while Tina powdered her nose. Father, glanced at the note and put it in his pocket. I asked father what his plans were for the 3rd.

"Work, what's yours?" he asked.

I said, "Is it okay if I come with you and shoot in to town to meet the mysterious Debbie?" He indicated upstairs with his head, "What about Melissa?" I thought for a minute. "Perhaps she can help Tina with shopping or they could go to the sales, or something."

He laughed. "Your mother telephoned Saturday after you left Lytham. She complained that you couldn't keep it in your trousers. I now see where she was coming from. We'll work something out."

Melissa shook me awake. "Yes oh beauty in the sky," I smilingly asked. She leaned over me and kissed me on the eyes followed by my lips. I put my arms round her. "It was wonderful last night," she said.

"What was?" I asked.

"The love-making of course," she replied smiling.

"I want you now," she said.

"You'll have to wait I need the loo," I replied.

"What happened to romance?" she queried.

"It's about to get flushed down the loo," I replied. She smiled.

I returned and jumped back into bed. "Talk to me Richard," she insisted "About what?" I asked.

"Something and nothing, just talk to me, please."

"Okay, if you really want to talk I'll be serious for a moment. I am going to take you home on the 6th January, we are going to say goodbye and unfortunately our romance ends. We have a deal, remember. You have to stop telling me you love me. You have to come to terms with the fact I will be out of your life. And you have to accept I have not altered from my original statements. I am Richard Chambers, the cynic, the womaniser, you will not change me."

"Haven't you got one nice word to say about me?" she demanded.

"Melissa I could write a book about you, you are a very attractive woman, you are very sexual and you love sex and I think you are gorgeous. You are a sensation in bed and I am extremely fond of you and I hate what is going on. I wish a thousand and one other things. However, I cannot change what is past. But please, always remember I have loved you, I have loved being with you and I have loved you for the days we have and will be together. Beyond those realities I cannot commit or add any further words."

Melissa quietly said, "Actually, I am slowly realising I am not in love with you but infatuated, the result of a college crush." I stayed silent. She continued, "I have come to realise living with you would be a nightmare. I could never trust you. No, you are right Richard we enjoy what we have and say our goodbyes. Now make love to me."

We made love slowly and sensitively. No driving, no pummelling just tender love-making. Tender touches, soft kisses, fingers intertwined, we moved together, synchronised, expelling feeling.

We both reached a climax, virtually simultaneously. When I spurted my sperm she whispered, "I feel you coming. I haven't felt it before. Does the feel of your sperm mean something special?"

I whispered, "Yes, it means we are very fond of each other and we are very compatible, sexually."

"It also means if we had met under different circumstances, perhaps a year or so ago, things could have been much different. Cruelly, we didn't meet, which is why we are here, both knowing we have a few days before saying goodbye."

Melissa chuckled, "I would like to make love again exactly as we just did. It was distinct, the feeling quite amazing, I tingled."

"We will," I sighed.

"Richard, will you remember me or will I be forgotten, another conquest?"

"I'll remember Melissa," I whispered.

Most of the day was spent in bed. I heard father shout he and Tina were going to the pub during which time Melissa and I enjoyed two tumultuous sessions of sex. Both sessions were hard sex, no quarter given.

We tried many positions, most of which I remembered from the Kama Sutra I had secreted away from father's bookshelf in Hove. Melissa had great fun, loving all the different positions we were trying, sometimes we ended up falling about laughing and giggling.

It was during those two hours I realised Melissa had changed; her college crush had evaporated. I had been reduced to a man who was great to be with and great to have sex with. The tables had turned causing me to become attentive and desperate to please her as opposed to the first few days we were together, when Melissa worked so hard to please me. I quite liked the change, I felt less guilty and more caring.

We were in the kitchen frying sausages for sandwiches when father and Tina returned. They said hello and went to bed. I was aghast; parents don't go to bed and have sex with their offspring in the house. If they did, they were very quiet.

New Year's Eve and father and I were enjoying banter and a brandy in the dining room waiting for the ladies when he asked if I had serious intentions regarding Melissa. His timing couldn't have been better, Melissa entered the room.

She answered, "No he hasn't, nor have I with Richard. We are having fun, enjoying being young before we are married with a house full of kids." She laughed, father smiled and I went to Melissa and hugged her.

I looked at her she was astonishingly beautiful. The gown fitted perfectly, beyond perfect. She twirled and kissed my cheek, I felt a tug at my heart strings. I couldn't take my eyes off her and she knew it, the tables had truly turned I had become her paramour, her lover to use and discard.

Tina joined us looking very attractive in a black gown decorated with sparkling sequins. Before leaving father mixed cocktails, I watched in fascination as he poured gin, Grand Marnier, Cherry Liqueur, pineapple juice and lime juice into a cocktail shaker and energetically shook it before pouring it into two tall glasses to which he added garnish and club soda producing, he told me, Singapore Slings for Tina and Melissa. He mixed dry martinis for he and I, which were very good.

We were finishing the drinks when the door-bell rang. I answered the door surprised to see a burley policeman. Father behind me called, "Come in Dave and meet the family." He already knew Tina who hugged and kissed him on the cheek. We shook hands as I watched his eyes roam over Melissa.

He refused a drink saying, "Later Dick, too early." The next surprise, we were being chauffeured in a police car to the nightclub, The Mighty Quinn. Father seated in the front with the two ladies and me in the back.

The Volvo estate, with blue light flashing passed cars as they pulled over, jumped a red light delivering us to the club within minutes of leaving the house. Very impressive I thought. Dave and father had a few words while Tina led Melissa and me into the club.

Once more Tina and father were well known. We were escorted upstairs to private rooms. Our table, a booth centrally sited provided a view through tinted glass to the hordes below shimmying and shaking and also of the room we were in.

Without a word being said, two ice-buckets with champagne bottles were placed close to the table and several small plates of canapés appeared. One of the waiters poured the champagne. Father followed in a few minutes later. A guy in a tuxedo met him. They whispered a few words. A bottle of Hennessey cognac was served.

Father poured a dash of brandy into each champagne glass, making the bubbles more effervescent. Father wasn't Ken who constantly called for toasts instead he lifted his glass and simply said "Happy New Year." Melissa sipped her drink and linked her arm into mine. She leaned close and kissed me.

The private rooms had a very small dance floor. However, the one we were overseeing was huge. Melissa wanted to go down and dance. Minus her coat her pale green gown expressed her beauty. I noticed eyes following her as we descended the stairs. I felt good and I know Melissa did I could feel her happiness.

The more we danced the more provocative Melissa became. She was putting on a show, which reminded me of Sophie and her little saying, "give them something to write home about".

I threw myself into dancing inventing new steps as we danced. I would squat, kick, turn, throw my arms in the air and pull Melissa into my arms twirling her. We were having tremendous fun.

When the mood change and we smooched she again reminded me of Sophie and the close-up dancing we had enjoyed. Why, after all this time, was I being reminded of Sophie. It dawned on me, a beautiful woman and a New Year bash combined brought Sophie back.

I told Melissa I had had enough and needed a break. We returned to the booth. Two ladies and a guy were crowded into the booth. I was immediately attracted to the blonde, very slim and elegant with a beautiful face and long flowing hair, a gorgeous specimen of womanhood.

They stood as we approached. We were introduced to Dulcie and her male friend Chas and Sam, the Polish English teacher. When I shook Sam's hand I experienced an electric shock rushing straight to my loins. Sam graciously smiled. Dulcie and Chas on the other hand gushed forth with nonsense looking to impress.

Melissa sat next to Sam and I squeezed in next to Chas. I was hoping we wouldn't be stuck with him and Dulcie albeit Sam was most welcome. Dulcie and Tina were discussing gowns with Melissa on the fringe of their conversation.

Chas was talking football, which neither father or I were interested in. He harped on about two players Malcolm McDonald and Terry McDermott.

I looked up to catch Sam looking at me. She didn't turn away, just looked at me. I leaned across and asked, actually I had to raise my voice, how she, a Polish girl had ended up teaching English in England. Her smile was warm and her face glowed. I was enthralled.

Because of the other conversations bouncing around the booth she shook her head and mouthed "later". Melissa asked me to dance on the small floor where half a dozen couple were smooching. I took her hand and led her to the floor.

Immediately she was in my arms she said, "I see you are lining-up your next conquest. Just remember you are all mine until the sixth."

I laughed saying, "What the heck are you talking about?"

"Don't treat me as if I am idiot, you know what I mean," she retorted.

I pulled her close and kissed her cheek. I whispered, "Sam is not my next conquest as you so blithely put it. For a start there are three hundred plus miles separating us. She is a friend of Tina's and I would not be welcome if I came in between Tina and her friend, so young lady forget you morbid thoughts, forget about conquests and concentrate on me." I won that round. Melissa looked into my eyes, smiled and kissed me on the lips, a lingering kiss.

As we danced I watched waiters delivering food to the table. Dulcie, Chas and Sam had disappeared. We returned to the booth. The food consisted of an array of buffet finger food, an excellent selection. The club didn't lend itself to three course dinners, well not on New Year's Eve.

The evening moved fast. Melissa and I were constantly in each other's arms on the small dance floor. She was quite content to be with me enjoying the attentiveness I was showing her. Father and Tina also danced, father demonstrating his flair for ballroom dancing.

Close to midnight the floor flooded with people, some were dancing in between the tables. The countdown commenced, 1973 only seconds away.

Melissa holding tightly onto my arm pulled my head down and smothered me in kisses. I responded fervently. She would not let go of me, or I, her. We kissed and kissed through most of Robbie Burn's Old Lang Syne.

Sitting in the booth, father and Tina dancing Melissa very seriously thanked me for bringing her to Newcastle expressing the night's party had been fantastic, she had loved dancing with me and she would miss me for a while when we parted, but in due course I would be a memory, a lovely memory, but nevertheless a memory.

I was relieved to hear her words. She had taught me a valuable lesson, which was the ease in which I allowed myself to become entangled with beautiful women. I wouldn't allow it to happen again. Who was I kidding?

The club's patrons were jumping celebrating 1973 with gusto. We danced some more, kissed and hugged becoming loving friends as opposed to long-term lovers. Sixty per cent of me was pleased I had invited Melissa, thirty percent wasn't and the odd ten percent slightly confused.

Just after two, a tuxedo guy entered the private lounge and whispered in father's ear. Father announced our chauffeur had arrived. A waiter delivered the lady's coats and we departed joining the exiting throng. The streets were alive with Conga dancing, couples hugging, and general mayhem. I decided I liked Newcastle.

Once more, blue light flashing we raced home. Dave pulled into the drive. Three or four people were congregated by father's door. Several people were wishing us New Year from afar obviously heading for his house.

Before we could enter the house we had to participate in a ceremony called First-Footing. Dave the big dark haired policeman produced a coin, a lump of coal and a bottle of whiskey. He led the procession into father's house. The ceremony, which is steeped in folklore supposedly, brings good fortune for the coming year.

Father, unbeknown to Melissa and I had prepared the kitchen as a bar, consisting of a small barrel of beer an array of spirit bottles, mixers of every flavour, wine and cider. From the freezer he produced a huge bag of ice and tipped the contents into a large bowl.

To the left Tina with help from Melissa removed wrapping from what seemed like an outside caterer's buffet. Music started playing and the conversation took off. Melissa suddenly found herself in demand being whizzed around the living room floor. Someone decided there wasn't enough room and the furniture disappeared into the hall.

I found a corner and was quite happy watching proceedings. I was also becoming slightly tipsy. Not too tipsy to see Sam arrive, she indicated, with a surreptitious movement of her eyes, upstairs. I waited a second to check if anyone had noticed her arrival, satisfied they hadn't I climbed the stairs. She was standing in the entrance of the box room, she beckoned and I followed.

She put her finger to her lips. Whispering she said, "We have two minutes before you will be missed. Who is the girl, what is she to you?" I thought "shit" this is one direct girl.

I whispered back, "A Christmas romance, which has extended to include the New Year" She nodded, "When you visit your father I will be here, now go." She opened the door and pushed me out.

I returned down stairs returning to where I had stood previously, confident I hadn't been missed. I watched the door. A little while later Sam descended the stairs and left the house.

Melissa clasped my hand telling me that wherever I was, I wasn't with the land of the living and added I looked half sozzled. I smiled inanely to confirm her observation. Melissa put her arms round my neck and kissed me very warmly, which became very sexy, which became very urgent.

With a huge smile I whispered, "Don't tell me you're wet and you are in desperate need of Jolly Roger." She laughed gaily saying loudly, "Yes you're dead right." No one noticed, the buzz of the room and the music combined drowned out her voice. I said, "We'll have to wait a while." She nodded asking me to fix her a drink, whiskey and lemonade.

We had to wait a long time by which time I had sobered up. However, Melissa was dead on her feet. We said good night and Happy New Year to the remaining revellers and I tossed Melissa over my shoulder, she responded with a squeal and in good fun called out, "Take me to bed Mr Caveman."

I swiftly undressed the both of us. Jolly Roger stood erect, waiting, I looked at Melissa, she seemed to become more pleasing to the eye every time I saw her naked. She lay on the bed lifted her legs. Without any foreplay I gradually forced Jolly Roger into her very red and very wet vagina. Melissa drove her hips towards me saying "Do it Richard don't play games," I rammed in, she moaned, holding her hand over her mouth.

The more I rammed the more she moaned. Her hand left her mouth her hands grabbing the back of her legs she pulled higher and I drove in deeper. She climaxed, I climaxed but Jolly Roger wanted more. I continued driving.

Melissa was having orgasm after orgasm, she started giggling. I queried with my eyes, "I don't know," she hoarsely whispered. I climaxed again filling Melissa with my hot sperm. She whispered "Why am I feeling your sperm?"

"Because you love it," I replied adding, "And there's plenty more to come"

I stood up, deciding to have a shower. I took her hand and pulled her with me. In the shower we washed each other with Melissa falling to her knees to wash Jolly Roger with her mouth. She giggled again. I asked why all the giggling.

She didn't know putting it down to happiness and the wonderful time we were having. Jolly Roger once more, wanted attention, I turned Melissa to face the wall and bending my knees pushed him up into Melissa.

She squeezed her legs together and for the first time she used her vagina muscles, which was excruciatingly sexy. Using her hand she removed Jolly Roger from her vagina and placed him against her anus. I pulled away. Angry I re-entered her vagina I rammed hard and harder. Melissa shrieked. I rammed until I exploded into her. She cried out.

In bed she said "I wanted you to do it." I rolled onto my side and proceeded to give her a lecture on anal sex. I explained all the things I had once explained to Sophie, the intricacies Sandra had taught me. I added at the end I wouldn't have anal sex with her saying if she ever felt the urge again to save it for the man she decides to marry or live with, not for me. She kissed me saying "You are such a strange man, albeit a lovely man."

I returned to consciousness at four in the afternoon, Melissa in a deep sleep, quietly snored. I carefully removed her arm carelessly lying across my chest and climbed from the bed. I located a pair of jeans and a polo shirt, pulled clean boxers on and dressed. The house was silent.

A graveyard of bodies awaited me in the living room. Well, two guys and a woman wearing pink panties. I tip-toed around them to retrieve my bike keys from the mantelpiece went into the hall and put on my leathers, making sure I had a door key I exited the house pulled my bike from the garage and sped off to goodness knows where.

I headed into Newcastle, picked-up on a sign to Tynemouth turning to head in that direction. From Tynemouth I followed a coast road through Whitley Bay and onto Blythe, a depressing town. I continued north joining the A1 and following it to Berwick upon Tweed.

Leaving Berwick I followed a signpost indicating Coldstream, reaching a junction I turned left towards Newcastle. Two hours after leaving father's house and a quarter of an hour after opening time I entered the pub. I ordered a pint of bitter. The guy serving said, "Aren't you Dick's son?" He pushed out his hand. "I'm Dougie, the landlord I think you met the missus." I shook his hand confirming I had met his wife and I was Dick's son.

I found a seat near the door people watching. I scanned the pub hoping to see Sam or Catriona. Listening to the buzz of the pub completely absorbed I glimpsed a shadow in the restaurant, Catriona stood to the left of the restaurant door tying an apron around her slim waist. I watched her curl her gorgeous long black hair into a bun.

I stared, fascinated, I couldn't help it, and she looked so much like Ruth. She busied herself tidying tables, polishing cutlery and rearranging small table bouquets. At that moment Ruth came flooding back remembering the Christmas and New Year we had shared in the Cotswolds. I felt my eyes well, I drank my beer and left.

I freewheeled down the small road to father's house parked the bike behind his car and went in the house. Father and Melissa were in the kitchen. Tina apparently felt fragile and would stay in bed. I thought where I have heard that before.

Melissa came and cuddled me wanting to know where I had been. I told her, leaving out any mention of Catriona. We dined on leftover food from the buffet and watched television. Television bored me I couldn't and wouldn't come to terms with it.

I searched through father's bookshelves. Quite surprised I discovered Cromwell, Our Chief of Men by A. Fraser. I asked him why this particular book, he explained his interest in history, specifically history relative to England. I borrowed the book, said goodnight and went to bed hoping Melissa would enjoy television for a while.

Melissa came to bed an hour later, she kissed my cheek and entered the bathroom. I listened as she brushed her teeth and spent a penny. Naked she climbed in beside me. Kissed my cheek once more and turned on her side and closed her eyes. Sometime later I put the book down and switched off the lights.

I lay thinking, it was over, we had indulged in heavy sex for a few days, and it had been fantastic. However, her coming to bed turning and going to sleep signalled we were done. Not sexually, we would enjoy the few days we had left but then it was over.

I started to think, how does a marriage work? You fall in love, marry, fuck yourselves senseless for few weeks, or months, before routine sets in. Work, perhaps children, even lovers enter into your life. Sex is permanently on the back-burner, there simply isn't time, or tiredness prevails or love ceases. But you carry on regardless.

Yes there is affection and occasional sex but on the whole you are only two people amidst millions of others going through the same routine. Bed, sleep, work, eat, television, the odd beer, bed, sleep, work and over and over and over.

My last thought revolved around whether Sophie and I would have become routine. I decided not, Sophie wouldn't have allowed routine.

I didn't bother to meet the mysterious Debbie although I did call her saying the next time I visited my father, if she was still interested, I'd telephone her. My proposal satisfied her. She asked one or two questions regarding Melissa, father and Tina. What I did where I lived, normal stuff.

I asked nothing of her. If I did choose to meet her I wanted to be surprised not forewarned or forearmed come to that, half the fun is in discovery. I didn't see Sam again, nor did I venture into father's pub looking for a ghost from my past.

Melissa and I continued to enjoy each other's company and sex. After my lecture on anal sex, she didn't raise the subject again. A few days later we thanked Tina and father for a great New Year, called Melissa parents and my mother expressing we would be back in Lytham by late morning.

I dropped Melissa off at home enjoyed a chat and a cup of tea with Daphne. Melissa walked me to the bike. Hugged me tight and thanked me for being a gentleman and for being fun expounding the fabulous time she had enjoyed for the past ten days.

Her last words before a final kiss were, "Thank you for being Richard Chambers. Whoever she is, wherever she is, she will be getting a marvellous man."

I walked into my cold flat early evening. I turned the heating on put a record on the player opened a can of beer and mused over Christmas 1972 and the coming year, 1973. Finally I telephoned Carol leaving a message on her answering machine, wishing her a very prosperous and educational 1973.

Chapter 19 – Hartlepool and a Freighter

On the 8th January I ventured into work ready to listen to a dozen stories relative to the past two weeks festivities. I wasn't interested but I would put on a brave face smile or laugh at appropriate times. I certainly wouldn't be exposing how I had spent the festivities.

I somehow got into the habit of calling Debbie in Newcastle every Sunday morning. We would talk rubbish, express a desire to meet and go through the same conversation a week later. I think the mystery of her, especially the note and the beautiful script kept me interested.

Carol and I would meet from time to time, make love or not, if it happened fine, if not also fine. We were friends, good friends. Early February she told me she had enrolled to complete her degree.

I was so pleased for her. I took her out for dinner to celebrate her decision to return to her studies and how confident I was that before long she would be realising her dream. After dinner we returned to my flat. We made love, caring love, delicate and receptive love, we explored each other's bodies, we kissed and caressed, sometimes we talked, but mostly we made love.

Carol and I also ventured out for Valentine's Day. She insisted it was her treat. During dinner she described how she and Sheila had reached an agreement with regards the flat and the business. The business now consisted of three salons, all were doing well. Sheila would take over the mortgage payments for the flat, which she and Bobby would move into after Carol had departed. They were due to marry in the summer.

In return Carol would sign over her share of the flat. However, Carol would maintain fifty percent ownership of the salons contributing her knowledge, specifically management accounts and critical decision making and business advice. The ownership extended to beyond the three salons meaning if the numbers increased so did Carol's net worth. Carol was very happy with the arrangement. The documents were being drawn up by the solicitor the business used.

When we left the restaurant Carol politely but firmly resisted my suggestion to share my bed. She made it very clear she could not go on being a part-time lover. Friendship was fine, she would still like to meet for a drink or a meal but no more making love. Carol stressed she was already half in love with me and she didn't want to fall any deeper not knowing whether I would commit to a long-term relationship, or not.

As we kissed goodbye she did say she would use her studies to erase me from her memory. Adding, with a wistful smile she would be trying, hoping for success.

Towards the end of February Doug called Jimmy Johnson an electrical engineer assigned to my team and me into his office. He asked if we had heard of Hartlepool. I answered "Wasn't there something about a French general and a monkey?"

Doug roared, "That's right, they thought the bloody monkey was a French admiral so they hung it."

After the laughter subsided Doug explained a bulk freighter berthed in Hartlepool had a few problems. Specifically, the electrical supply, which periodically tripped out and two diesel engines that only produced half-power. Both Jimmy and I, as Doug had, guessed what the problems were and the symptoms.

We would be leaving Wednesday, flying to Newcastle from Southampton where a guy would meet and greet and deliver us to Hartlepool. I opted to ride my bike.

Final arrangements, including secure transfer of tools, equipment and test equipment were in place by Tuesday afternoon so I decided to leave later in the afternoon. I called father and Debbie. I also telephoned Carol.

It poured all the way to Newcastle; the bike and I were sodden. By the time I arrived at father's house I had decided the time had come to wave the bike goodbye and find a decent car. Admittedly, the bike, particularly in the warmer months had been great fun, the winter months however, were on the whole, miserable. Tina made me welcome running a hot bath and serving tea and a sandwich.

Tina asked after Melissa and my work, once I had answered conversation died, we didn't have a great deal in common. I walked up to the pub grateful the rain had rained itself out. I had a couple of beers noted Catriona wasn't working and returned to father's house. He wasn't home, something to do with burst water mains.

I left my bike out to leave access for father's car and went to bed. I left for Hartlepool at six-thirty and arriving for seven. I searched for a café and treated myself to full English, the first for a while. I found the harbour masters office, following several telephone calls and after showing all the relative documents I secured a dockyard pass.

Jimmy wasn't due until four in the afternoon. I found the ship, the Range Extender and met with the ship's engineer and skipper. Both were foreign, Egyptian, I think, which caused a language problem.

Nonetheless I was given access to the ship's engineering rooms. As soon as I saw the state of the machinery and the equipment I immediately recognised there would be a few long, long days to diagnose the problems. The whole bloody ship was a floating disaster. How it had made it from Bremerhaven to Hartlepool was anyone's guess.

I telephoned Doug explaining it would take a week to fully inspect, diagnose and log the defects, possibly longer depending upon what we discovered during initial inspections. I recommended he called the owners to check exactly what they would require. I gave him father's number asking him to call after seven.

Jimmy arrived and we inspected the ship together, he noticed massive electrical issues, stating much work would be necessary to make the ship safe and reliable. I dropped him at the guest house and we agreed to meet in the morning.

I arrived home to find Doug talking to father. He winked at me and passed the receiver. Doug advised we had twelve working days to inspect and provide a comprehensive report completed in three sections, one mechanical, one ancillary and the other electrical. Peter's team would prepare a provisional cost against the report thereafter the owners would make a decision.

I joined father in the kitchen, he looked whacked. Apparently they were cutting a deep trench across open land when they hit an unmarked water main, causing havoc. He didn't leave the site until six in the morning returning at midday to check everything was okay.

Tina, Dulcie and Chas were in the pub. Father, before going to bed asked a few questions regarding my unexpected arrival. He seemed pleased I would be around for a couple of weeks. I checked my watch: seven-thirty. I called Debbie we talked for a few minutes before I suggested I would pop round to see her with a fish supper and a bottle of wine.

Debbie lived on the top floor of a three storey block of flats in Jesmond opposite the Town Moor. It took some finding but I managed after asking a young couple walking their dog. She opened the door, I had been expecting a blue-eyed blonde instead a magnificent auburn-haired goddess greeted me, wearing jeans and sweater but looked absolutely divine.

She said, "Hi Richard meet Debbie", and laughed and what a laugh, it was pure music. Enjoying the moment she said, "Come in and explain the shocked expression and the hair standing on end." She had a sense of humour, I thought, marvellous.

I followed her into the kitchen where she unwrapped the fish and chips and proceeded unceremoniously to dump them onto hot plates picked up two glasses and led me to a small dining table.

A corkscrew waited on the table and I opened the wine. Laughing she said, "Who were you expecting? A blue-eyed blonde". I gasped. She laughed. "I dared her, Krista, to touch your leg." She laughed again. "When you looked at her and smiled I knew you were a free man hence the note, the telephone calls, the fish supper and the wine."

Debbie worked as a laboratory technician at Newcastle General Hospital and had done so for three years. She was single, twenty-seven, considered marriage uninspiring, although suspected that one day it would happen. Didn't have a steady and hadn't for two years. She said, "Your turn."

I told her about Sophie, my work and the life style I had chosen after Sophie's death. I mentioned Carol, a good friend. I talked rugby and explained why I was in Newcastle. She asked after the glamorous girl she had seen me with New Year's night. I described Melissa and me as a girl and boy who enjoyed sex. She laughed uproariously. I helped her wash the dishes. She commented, "You're house-trained as well, a bonus."

For the rest of the evening we talked about life's shortcomings, travel, rugby briefly, but mostly our jobs. She thought rushing here and there repairing ships sounded romantic, much better than arriving at the same laboratory morning after morning. Just after ten she ushered me out of the door inviting me to have dinner with her Friday night.

Thursday Jimmy and I set to at seven-thirty until eight in the evening. The ship was filthy and consequently we were filthy. After eight we sat in the ship's mess room and prepared the first of many pages, which would form the report. I dropped him off once more and gunned it back to Newcastle.

Friday was a repeat of Thursday. The ship was in shit-state, it would take weeks of expensive costs to make it seaworthy, including the provision of maintenance regimes, spare parts lists and competent engineers to keep the ship maintained.

Both Jimmy and I were of the opinion the ship's engineer and his team were out of their depth, which we would include in the final report.

We called Doug at five to give him the update he had requested. I called Debbie at six advising I wouldn't get away until eight or nine. She said, "So I cook later, no problem." I arrived at fathers at seven-thirty, bathed and shot round to Debbie.

She opened the door with a bright smile-- she looked sexy dressed in a mustard-coloured, knee-length skirt and white blouse wearing an apron. It was the first time since Sophie I had considered an apron sexy.

I carried a bottle of expensive red wine, my contribution to the dinner. She took the bottle saying, "You know your wines then?" She headed for the kitchen and I headed for the corkscrew, which wasn't on the table. Debbie was laughing dangling it between finger and thumb.

She checked the food and taking my hand led me to the settee. We sat together thighs touching. I couldn't stop myself I took her glass and leaned into her and kissed. She pushed me off. Smiling she said, "Steady boy we have all night, if it happens great, if not there is always another night."

I said, "Too late, it happens now."

This time her arms went round my neck and we were kissing fiercely. My arms were round her back and across her bosom. I was bloody well near eating her. I smothered her with kisses to her face, her ears, neck and throat. My hands stayed away from roaming over her body. Debbie returned my sudden assault with passion.

We were wrestling each trying to get the upper hand. Our tongues battled for supremacy our legs were crossing each other's and we were starting to explore bodies. Debbie using her strength pushed me off saying, "Food now or later."

"Later, much later," I replied.

She took my hand and led me into her bedroom. The room was large the bed huge. She started to undress. I stopped her. "I will undress you." She smiled coyly.

I slowly undid the buttons of her blouse, as I removed it I kissed her beasts above her bra. I undid the bra freeing her beautiful breast with her erect nipples. I nibbled her nipples. I kissed her shoulder and ran my tongue down her tummy. I turned her round and ran my tongue down her back and up across the back of her shoulders.

I dropped to my knees undoing the skirt's zip. I slid the skirt over her hips. I licked her tummy and ran my tongue above the elastic of her tights. I very gently eased her tights off. As they moved down her legs I nuzzled her Mons Venus with my mouth. Debbie moaned.

I clasped her firm buttocks and pushed her vagina against my mouth. I pushed my tongue to the side of her panties crutch. I could smell her sex. I pulled her panties down with my teeth. I ran my tongue all over her legs. Finally I had her naked. Debbie was mine from the top of her head to her toes all mine. She knew it and I definitely knew it.

She pulled at me trying to strip my clothes away, I helped her. Seeing Jolly Roger she held him firmly. She used him to pull me towards her. She collapsed onto the huge bed her hips balanced on the edge and opened her legs. I guided Jolly Roger to her vagina's entrance pushed in an inch or more, withdrew and dropped to my knees, my mouth and tongue started sucking and licking her vagina, she was moist not yet in full flow. I wanted her juices to flow.

I worked tirelessly sucking her vagina. She pulled at my head she wanted my tongue to tantalise her clitoris. I moved to her clitoris, it was large enough to suck. I sucked it into my mouth and tenderly nibbled. She went crazy her juices started to flow the tap open. I alternated between vagina and clitoris. She yelled "Richard, fuck me" I stood and rammed hard into her she screamed.

I held her legs up and drove in. Gradually I eased her legs over her head driving in deeper. She thrashed shouting "Who are you?" I stopped. She let out a shriek and screamed blue murder. I started driving, thrusting and ramming as hard as I could. I was coming I told her she grabbed hold of me and drove up towards me she cried out and I released my sperm as deep as I could. She drove up and yelled, "Oh my God I'm orgasmic. I am bloody orgasmic, oh my God."

I withdrew from her she sat up and pulled me into her bosom suffocating me with her breasts her teeth biting chunks out of my shoulder. Debbie started to rock, a low moan forcing itself from her throat. She shuddered and opened her legs pushing her vagina hard against my thigh and rubbed her vagina up and down, all the time moaning.

Sitting on the edge of the bed her legs encircling my thighs she passionately kissed me. She moved her body against me positioning her vagina until a half erect Jolly Roger slipped in. She didn't want movement just the warmth of him inside, although as I thought, he began to grow.

She looked deep into my eyes holding her hazel eyes steadfastly locked into my blue ones. She gently kissed my nipples, re engaging our eyes she said, "Who are you Richard? I am twenty-seven, closing on twenty-eight and I have just had a great orgasm. Stop I rephrase multi orgasms. So I repeat my question who are you?"

I whispered "Would you like to try for more?"

"Yes," she whispered.

I smiled and kissed her nose and her eyes. Jolly Roger now fully erect, I tenderly pushed him in deeper she pulled herself closer with her legs.

I pushed her back onto the bed, decoupling for a moment until I had Debbie on her back and her legs high. Her vagina was very red and very wet. I hovered above allowing Debbie to guide Jolly Roger to his favourite home.

I pushed in slowly until I could not push any further. I began a rhythmic motion keeping a fixed pace. I concentrated on kissing her warm mouth nibbling her ears and running my tongue around her neck and throat. I nibbled her throat. I pushed her legs higher and pushed harder. Debbie responded forcing her hips to meet by thrusts. Gradually, without losing control I increased the tempo. I saw her smiling, her lips began to quiver.

I pushed harder increasing the rapidity of my thrusts. Her nails dug into my arms I started to pummel forcing her legs further back. I yelled shouting at her to thrust up. Her scream started and continued. Her body started to tremble. Her juices were making a sloshing sound every time I rammed home.

She tensed and relaxed and tensed again she became a wild creature tearing at me. I could feel my own spasms. I was coming, I exploded, and she screamed and squeezed her thighs against my hips. She cried out and dived up to grab my neck pulling me down to kiss me. Her tongue was deep in my mouth.

She squealed, shuddered and cried out once more before letting go of my neck and collapsing below me. She looked at me intensely. She whispered her voice breaking "How, how do you do that. It's astonishing. I feel waves of pleasure pulsating through me, how Richard, how."

I rolled off of Debbie and lay on my back. I was wet with sweat. Her body glistened in the bedside light. I roughly pulled her over into my arms. She surrendered, completely lost, her head resting on my chest as I tenderly stroked her rich auburn hair. An image of Sophie appeared and disappeared.

Chuckling she said, "The lovely dinner I prepared and cooked will be ruined."

"No it will not, it will be slightly overcooked, but delicious."

She climbed from the bed, I watched, she looked magnificent, probably the most perfect body of all my conquests. She was taller than Sophie, her legs longer, her bottom not quite as perfect as Sophie's, but her breasts and her nipples and her wonderful protruding clitoris were superb.

She was as unashamed as Sophie at ease to walk naked through her flat. I asked for the bathroom and if I could have a shower. Debbie called back "I'll check the burnt offerings and we'll shower together afterwards you and I have some serious talking to do."

She came into the bedroom all smiles. "Not bad, the burnt offerings are edible. Right young man," she opened a door, "This is my bathroom, which I love." I followed her in. It was very spacious consisting of a walk in shower, a bath large enough for three, a bidet and toilet plus a sculptured wash basin.

I laughingly asked if she could swim. She turned to face me. I swim and I bathe, I love bathing, whether in my bath, under the shower, in a swimming pool, a lake or the sea. I love to be in water. Water is my security blanket. She switched on the multi-spray shower.

She took my hand kissed my fingers and guided me under the sprays. She held my penis, waving it one way and the other. Jolly Roger thinking its play time started to harden. Debbie quickly let go. "Does that thing ever take a rest?" she asked.

"Most of the time, he only comes out to play when he has a playmate, which is not as often as he would like." I replied with a smile. "I bet you say that to all your lady friends," she commented. "No, I can honestly say those words were spoken for the first time."

We rubbed each other dry I put on boxer shorts Debbie in her apron and panties. She served dinner of very tender lamb shanks, coated in mint, crispy roast potatoes and cauliflower served in cheese sauce. We talked and laughed and drank the wine.

I helped her once more to wash-up. She kept kissing me. Laughingly she said, "I am checking to see if you are real or I am dreaming." I placed my hand on her bottom, creeping under her crevice to touch her vagina. "Enough Richard, please enough." She was laughing. "Unless you are rushing off we have the whole night before us. And the weekend if you want to." She blushed slightly.

We went back to bed. We snuggled close. Debbie asked my age. "I did tell you the first time we spoke on the telephone," she shouted. "Twenty, something."

"Close," I said. "I am twenty five and a few months."

"Where did you learn to be such a wonderful lover?" she asked. "Hold up girl who says I am a wonderful lover, only you," I retorted.

"No, you know you are. You know exactly what to do, when and how, you are an expert" she exclaimed. I said "I am only a wonderful lover if the woman I am with is responsive. No response, no wonderful lover."

She thought for a second. "You are an F-I-B-B-E-R."

"Why would I fib?" I asked.

"I don't know, perhaps shyness, but I think not, but you are fibbing aren't you?" I didn't want to roll out the Sandra saga, nor did I want to talk of women sounding as if I was boasting or something. I thought of Ruth and Sophie.

"What I am going to say is a one off. What I say is for the first and most definitely last time. In my short life I had two wondrous long relationships, one much longer than the other.

The first was Ruth. We lived together during my second and her final year at college. We were inseparable and we made love often, very often. During our love-making we learnt how to please each other. Sometimes we experimented but most of the time we wanted to please. The second love was much more dynamic." Debbie interrupted "What happened to Ruth?"

I resumed, "Ruth completed her finals gaining a first. We had one last weekend together before she disappeared to Israel and in to a Kibbutz. We had committed to each other for the future. However, she lied to me. In fact I discovered a few untruths. The untruths, in her defence, were because she wanted what we had to continue but thought future happiness unobtainable."

Debbie asked why. "I think," I paused. "Because she believed or was aware her family would reject a gentile, a Christian."

"How long did the relationship last?" she queried.

"Ten months."

I continued, "The second relationship was much stronger, more loving and more genuine and we loved each other beyond all imagination. We were very fortunate we, thanks to my parents, had a four bedroomed house, two good cars and a life, the envy of many.

We were known locally as the "perfect couple" and the "ideal match". Her name was Sophie. She was amazingly successful both at college and work. However, we were ardent lovers we explored and experimented. We

182

would do anything for each other, anything. So during the four years, yes four years we were together, we did a great deal of experimenting. You could say practice makes perfect."

"What happened to Sophie?" she queried.

Very quietly I said, "She died in a car accident two weeks before our wedding."

"Do you know what is really upsetting is that it took me the best part of fifteen months to forget Sophie and you, Debbie are her double. You are the first woman I have been with who has auburn hair, the same colour as Sophie. I had purposefully steered clear of women with auburn hair. You are slightly taller but otherwise you are so much alike, so much."

I could smell Sophie. I closed my eyes and prayed Sophie would leave me.

I woke up with my face nestling against Debbie's bosom. She was sitting-up her back leaning towards the bed head. Her hand was gently stroking my shoulders and back. I sat up and Debbie smiled a wonderful loving smile. I kissed her.

I apologised for Sophie's ghost before saying, "She's gone." Debbie took my face between her hands and tenderly kissed me. She said, "I am at a loss. I don't know what to say or what to do. I feel useless."

I laughed, I don't know why but I did. I said, "We can make love, tender love."

Debbie said, "Yes please I would like to."

I gave my whole being to Debbie, I loved her as I would Sophie, and I showered her with my love. I explored her body. I rolled her one way then the other. I laid her on her front and on her back. I opened her legs and closed them. I kissed her knees, her ankles, her toes. Debbie moaned and gasped.

I ran my tongue up her legs and down, the tops of her legs and her bottom. I run my fingers over her breasts and squeezed her nipples. I ran my tongue up her arms over her shoulders. I nibbled her neck, and ears. I gently sucked her fingers. Her head thrashed from side to side.

I rolled Jolly Roger over her face, across her breasts, under her arms and teased her vagina. I ran my tongue down through the crevice of her buttocks. I flicked her anus with my tongue and she pushed back. I rolled her over and sucked her vaginal juices I tormented her clitoris. She was panting and trying to pull me into her. I resisted. I gently inserted my fingers in her vagina and licked her juice.

I forced my penis into her mouth. She held on not wanting to lose it. I took it out. I pushed it into her vagina and let her suck her own juice. I drove hard into her and withdrew and I sucked her vagina until she was screaming. Debbie was pleading, crying out for me to fuck her. I wouldn't stop. I continued to caress with hand and mouth. I went all over her again and again. I forced my tongue into her anus. Her vaginal juices were soaking the bed sheets.

I pulled her up on to her knees, squatted behind her and rammed as hard as I could into her. She collapsed onto the bed with me on top of her. I forced three pillows under her hips and mercilessly rammed. I rammed and rammed.

I stopped turned her onto her back lifting her legs and pushed them over her head and rammed into her again. She was howling, screaming crying for more. I pummelled with all my strength. I climaxed, once and kept ramming. I climaxed once more. Debbie was convulsing, jerking and spams were running through her body she cried for me to stop. I withdrew and placed my penis on her face. She tried to lick it. I let it slip level with her mouth. She opened and took it in. She tried to angle her head so I could get deeper. She was gagging. I could feel the tightness of her throat.

I pulled out and rammed back into her vagina. I pushed her onto her front preplaced the pillows and gradually entered her bottom. She pushed back yelling "Nooooo". I started to drive in and out. She was meeting my thrusts crying out "harder". I rammed hard. Debbie shuddered and yelled. I climaxed my sperm rushing into her bottom. She clenched her buttocks and screamed.

Deflated I gently withdrew. She pushed me onto my back and lay on me kissing me and kissing me, licking my eyes and my ears. Hugging and squealing she crumpled into my arms. We lay still for a long time. No words were spoken. We gradually regained control of our breathing.

Debbie said, "If a woman was ever ravished I am that woman. It was remarkable, astonishing and beautiful, oh so beautiful."

I said, "Remember our little conversation about response. You responded, I responded. You wanted more, I wanted more. You demanded, I demanded. We have just made love, had wild sex but neither of us could be termed an expert we were two people who responded and reacted to the demands of our bodies, our inner needs and to the sex we wanted so much. You Debbie are one hell of a woman, probably the sexiest I have ever made love to."

She laughed, "Was that supposed to be a compliment?"

"Yes, a very well deserved complement," I laughed.

Looking into my eyes she said, "Could you do it all again?"

"With you yes, with another woman, no." She kissed me hard, very hard. I held her tight. She was mumbling about sex and how wonderful it was. I closed my eyes, her mumbling became distant.

Debbie was still in my arms when I wakened to an alarm clock buzzing followed by a DJ talking about the weather and then music. Debbie's hand went in search. I lifted my body and put Jolly Roger in her hand.

She jumped up and squealed. "No Richard, no more. Go to sleep." I closed my eyes once more listening to a familiar song I couldn't name, which faded into the distance. Debbie was in my arms her head resting on my shoulder, she was smiling.

I was awakened by a beautiful naked lady. She was holding a mug of coffee. I forced myself to sit up. Debbie seated herself on the bed and leaned in and kissed me. "Good morning Mr Response man, Miss Response lady is cooking breakfast."

I placed the coffee on the bedside table and pulled Debbie into my arms. She was fresh her body odour delicate. I nuzzled her nipples and pressed my hand against her vagina. She gently pushed me away saying, "Go shower, you stink of me, breakfast in ten minutes."

I swiftly, using a rough sponge, scrubbed my body, wrapping a towel round my waist I sat at the dining table. Debbie, her cheeks rosy from the heat of the stove rushed in with two plates of scrambled eggs, bacon and button mushrooms. She rushed backed to the kitchen, her buttocks suggestively swaying, returning with toast and a coffee jug.

She removed her apron leaving her in panties and Jolly Roger stirred. I placed my hand inside her thighs and kissed Debbie passionately her arms wrapped round my neck. The returning kisses were exciting Jolly Roger. She slapped him and lifted her cutlery.

The dishes washed, dried and stowed I telephoned father. He asked after Debbie, which I answered truthfully by saying, "She is another Sophie in stature and looks." He groaned before advising Doug had called. He gave me a number to return the call.

Realisation dawned when I recognised that Debbie's similarity to Sophie. I could mention her name in conversation, I could think of her. The terrible exposure of my past and Debbie's positive reaction had cured me. At long last Sophie would fade away, not completely but far enough to free my spirit to change my character once more.

I telephoned Doug. His concern was progress and the constant demands from the ship's owners. He was emphasising strongly that the owners, a Middle Eastern consortium, managed several ships, discreet research had revealed they were poorly maintained and in need of urgent repair works.

I laughed saying, "I can see the pound notes registering in your eyes." He laughed replying, "Think of the bonuses." We said goodbye. His mention of bonuses was ringing in my ears, when I remembered I was thinking of exchanging motorcycle for a decent car.

Debbie, her apron once more removed, her nakedness enticing, was standing framed by the kitchen architrave. My mind flashed back to Sophie stood in a similar position in the London hotel. I quickly crossed to her taken her in my arms, hugging her and nuzzling her neck. She whimpered.

Her eyes found mine and she nodded. I lifted her and carried her to the bedroom. Within seconds I was deep inside Debbie's warm vagina, steadily but forcefully driving into her. She lifted her legs and I began to pound. We were both yelling and we both climaxed. We rolled together clasping tightly. Debbie said, "Do you ever tire?"

I laughed. "Take a good look at yourself woman, how could I possible tire when you are constantly parading your beautiful loveliness."

Once more we showered. We remained naked. I was sitting on the settee watching her search for a photograph album. I asked her to walk back and forth so I could watch her walking. Debbie gave me a very old fashioned look but she did walk for me.

I adore women, their shape and their movements. I am the consummate voyeur. A botanist can display the most beautiful flowers and expound their beauty. An arborist will find beauty in oaks and planes and eucalyptus trees. An architect will talk for hours on the beauty of buildings, their design, shape and the moving parts that make a building breath. A zoologist will exclaim the beauty of the thousands of animals that roam earth's surface and swim in the lakes and oceans. And I would agree with them all, but, I would always argue that true beauty, the most pleasing beauty can only be defined in a woman, in her body, in her soul and in the purity of her exquisiteness and uniqueness.

Debbie raised her eyebrows obviously starting to consider me to be a weirdo said "Finished". I smiled at her. "For the moment." She returned, searching for the album.

Before she could open the retrieved album I said, "Debbie, this coming week and the following week will end and I will return to Southampton to my flat and work. It is doubtful I will return, except on odd occasions, perhaps for a weekend to visit my father or the odd work assignment" I took a deep breath continuing "Which means this relationship, our relationship and any future relationship is curtailed by circumstance."

I took her hand in mine resuming I said "We could sit here and make promises, swear everlasting togetherness both knowing that unless we are in the same town, seeing each other constantly, the relationship will wither on the vine. I have to make this clear I do not want to walk away with either of us expecting more in the future. Such an expectation would be grossly unfair for us both."

Debbie considered my long oration. "God Richard you are such an honest man. You actually care for what people feel and think. That is so rare today, so very rare. Yes I realise our relationship, as you put it will be short, so we are obliged to enjoy every last moment. However, I may decide to apply for a posting to a Southampton hospital, what then."

I half-expected Debbie's response. "I still cannot guarantee we will remain a couple, I just can't. If I thought for one moment we could build a life together I would encourage you to seek a posting south, but I do not know, and if you are honest you don't really know. We may be sexually suited, which is fantastic, but it doesn't automatically make us compatible." She nodded.

"I know," she laughed. "Therefore, we, as I said a moment ago, are duty bound to enjoy what we have for as long as we have it."

The rest of the weekend, after I had shared Debbie's life through her photograph album, was devoted to the bed, or the floor, or the settee or wherever we decided to make love, have sex. We revelled in our debauchery, revelled in the thrills and revelled in good honest open sex.

During the two weeks while Jimmy and I worked exhausting hours and compiled copious material for the report Doug had demanded I introduced Debbie, one evening, to Tina and father. They immediately identified Sophie and it showed. Debbie made light of the similarity explaining I had told her about Sophie and the likeness.

I moved into Debbie's flat. No matter what time I arrived at her flat, no matter how filthy there would be a bath or shower followed by food and sex. We could not get enough sex. We experimented, we explored and we enjoyed, it was marvellous. I savoured every moment as I know Debbie did. I did learn that she was no stranger to anal sex and loved it as Sandra and Sophie had. Her previous lover had introduced her and she had quickly come to enjoy the sensations that accompanied it.

On the 7th March Jimmy and I completed our exhausting inspection of the wrecked freighter. We would spend the 8th finalising the report and undertake a final tour of the ship. I telephoned Doug late on the 7th informing him of our progress and the decisions we had made. He listened before stating he wanted us both in the office the morning of the 10th, a Saturday, to meet with him, Pete and two of Pete's team.

Returning from Hartlepool I called in to see Tina and father, explaining my work was complete and I had been ordered back to Southampton, travelling Friday. They suggested dinner with Debbie in the Highwayman Thursday night. I agreed subject to Debbie. I walked into Debbie's flat catching Debbie in the throes of ironing a pair of my jeans. In fact due to the limited clothes I had packed Debbie and I were constantly washing and ironing. I told her of the situation. She agreed to dinner. I telephoned father.

I showered and ate the dinner Debbie had prepared. We undertook our household chores, after which we sat on the settee.

Debbie started talking. "Richard, I have come to realise you have used me, which is not a problem-- you have been wonderful. I have used you too, to enjoy wondrous sex. I also realised you have never lied, or tried to build something which couldn't be built. You told me at the beginning the relationship would be short. I said fine let's enjoy what we have, and we most definitely have enjoyed the time together we have been blessed with."

She stopped to consider her next words. "But you are very disparaging, an out and out womaniser, who has constructed an impassable persona simply because you are terrified of finding and once more losing love. Richard what you don't realise is the hurt and damage you cause the many women you charm and seduce. I am one, there were many before me and there will be many after me. I ask you, no I beseech you to reconsider your lifestyle, your cynicism and allow love to filter into your heart."

During an enduring silence I thought of Carol, Melissa, even Cheryl, Suzy and Sandra and many others. Debbie was quite correct and I had no defence against her deliberation.

However, I had chosen my way of life and although she considered it cynical and enigmatic I was not ready to love again, I doubted if I ever would be. I could not and would not commit to something that might break. I considered her words recollecting that Debbie had recognised I did not lie and that I was honest and open.

Expressing a wry smile I said, "I do fall in love with women, I love and adore all women. And when I hold a woman and when I make love with a woman I am in love, deeply in love."

I tried to describe how I loved every last woman, even the one-night stands and the longer relationships of this world and how special they were.

I did agree, however, with Debbie when she rightly said I had built an impassable persona, but there again, she didn't live with it, I did.

She explored by asking specific questions, my thoughts. When she finished, she said, "I feel sorry for you, not as much as you feel sorry for yourself, but I do experience sadness for you and your future."

We went to bed and made very tender love. We were saying goodbye. I realised Debbie would expect me to move out in the morning, she needed to return to normality and begin the process of forgetting I ever existed.

In the morning I packed my belongings and lugged them down to my bike closeted in Debbie's storage in the basement. She made coffee and eggs on toast. We ate in silence. I helped her to wash and dry the dishes. We sat for a while holding hands.

Eventually I had to leave, we hugged and kissed and said goodbye. I loped down the staircase to my bike. Debbie was tearful, but that was how it was, I wasn't going to change.

I followed the van transporting Jimmy and our equipment to the airport. We ensured the tools and equipment were passed to the cargo section. I walked with Jimmy to the passenger terminal, stood-by while he checked in. We would meet Saturday morning sharp at eight.

Dinner that evening with Tina and father, without Debbie, was also quiet. The dinner, I chose steak, which was good, but the two bottles of red wine were better. However alcohol does not cure it only delays. In the morning I loaded the bike and headed south.

Chapter 20 – Work, Promotion and more work.

When I arrived at the office Saturday morning Doug and Pete were waiting. The report collected from Jimmy when he landed was spread over the meeting room table. Doug expounded the value of a good report, congratulating Jimmy and me.

Jimmy arrived at eight-fifteen, looking terrible. He explained he had missed his brother's birthday whilst in Hartlepool, the family and he had celebrated from the minute he arrived home until the early hours. He reeked of alcohol. He was busily sucking on Fishermen's Friends, trying to rid himself of his terrible breath.

Pete's two guys followed Jimmy in. Eleven hours later, a hundred cups of coffee and after a great deal of cursing and regular debates, we finally agreed a price to undertake a near complete overhaul of the ship's engineering systems and machinery.

It was decided if the price was accepted I would lead a seven man team, with Jimmy as my number two. However, in the price we recommended that the ship should be towed into Wallsend, north of Newcastle because the dockside facilities were much more readily available. Also, if the ship required to be worked on in dry-dock, dry-docks were available in Wallsend. For dry-docking we submitted a provisional sum to cover the cost plus Maybury's mark-up.

Jimmy and I were given Monday off. We decided to meet for lunch over his way, in Woolston. We met at the pre-determined time and got pie-eyed. How it happened neither of us knew, we started drinking at twelve-thirty and were drunk by one-thirty and legless by two-thirty.

Somehow we made it to his parent's house. I woke up at seven, crashed in a chair, with a head the size of Birkenhead, it hurt. Jimmy's mother fed me pain-killers and served a terrific beef stew, which was more effective than the pills. Jimmy accompanied me to the working man's club where we had drunk ourselves daft to retrieve my bike. I waved good bye and headed home.

The flat, which hadn't seen a duster or vacuum cleaner for weeks, stank. I rolled up by sleeves and attacked it. As I scrubbed and cleaned Birkenhead dissipated although the Featherstone's upstairs did complain around ten o'clock regarding the noise I was making.

Tuesday, fresh as a daisy, I arrived in work early. Due to my absence on my desk sat a ton of paperwork, outstanding invoicing to be passed to accounts for billing and February's monthly report to write were just two of the tasks.

Doug walked into my office with a coffee for each of us. "How's it going Richard?" he asked. "Good Doug, why?" I retorted.

He laughed. "You're our travelling man so if travelling is needed I knock on your door first." I smiled at him.

"I didn't hear any knocking."

"That's because I am the boss," he laughed. He continued, "Anyway there is a three, possibly four day repair of a tanker in Falmouth, do you fancy it?" he queried.

"What's the problem?" I asked.

"The boiler is losing pressure, suggesting some heavy leaks of super-heat. The ship's engineer has shut down the engine and boiler rooms and switched to shore power," he explained.

I said, "I'll need a team."

"No problem, choose who you want—they're your guys."

I looked at him. "My guys?" I queried.

"Oh, didn't I tell you Terry Groves, your old boss has gone back to sea to get over his divorce, leaving you head of National and International Emergency Services?"

"Oh fuck," I said. Doug laughed and exited my office. At the door he called back, "You had better get your team together and tell them before the rumour mill takes over."

I was one of three team leaders who reported to Terry. I was unsure how engineers were assigned or what my new division consisted of. I contacted personnel asking for a supervisor armed with the information I was requesting to be in my office within thirty minutes. I put the receiver down saying to myself, "start as you mean to go on."

I called mother and father to inform them of my unexpected promotion. Both wanted details I couldn't yet provide. I promised to call then within a couple days with an update.

While waiting for personnel I considered the size of my empire. I had a team of six mechanical engineers, four electrical engineers and one hydraulic engineer, seven technicians and two support admin, two drivers, and one procurer, and one store keeper.

Shit, I thought I hadn't realised my team was so many, twenty-four people in my team, how many in Charlie Reynolds and Martin Stevens' teams. I was cursing to myself when there was a knock on the door. I called, "enter". A tall, very gorgeous, very lithesome and extremely attractive redhead entered who I hadn't seen before. However, I rarely visited head office.

She came forward her arm outstretched. I stood and shook her hand. I said, "And you are?"

"Christine Clarke, commonly known as CC," she replied with a nice smile displaying even teeth. I noticed her faint freckles, they excited me. She handed me an official letter.

I told her to seat herself at the small meeting table, asked if she would like, tea, coffee or water. She asked for tea. I called through to Janet, my girl Friday ordering tea and water. I opened the letter-- it was from Mr Maybury officially advising of my promotion.

I looked at the salary, which would be paid monthly and broke out in a sweat. Four hundred and seventy-three pounds plus a whole list of additional items I didn't know existed. I whispered, "Oh fuck."

CC said, "Pardon Mr Chambers." I laughed out loud.

I moved to the meeting table. "Okay before we start tell me who you are and where you fit in." CC explained she was the National and International Emergency Services personnel supervisor with a team of three, one payroll, one union liaison and the third her assistant.

Answering my questions she had been with the company two and a half years. She had gained her degree from a certain West Country university. I told her my name was Richard, not Mr Chambers. She smiled. Apparently my predecessor always insisted on Mr Groves. I laughed saying, "I ain't Terry Groves."

For the next hour or so I learnt I now had seventy-two staff, eleven vehicles, three stores, and a tool and equipment area, managed by Casey at the main warehouse. I had a small design team of a manager plus three back at head office.

I now understood the huge salary; my responsibility was massive. Once more I whispered under my breath. CC heard me and smiled. I said, "What good are you, your team and the design team stuck in head office?" She shrugged. "Who says you have to be there?" She told me Gareth Holdsworth Head of Personnel and Commercial was her direct boss with a dotted line into me.

I mused over her answer. Gary was an okay guy, one of the directors, an ex-engineer who found himself managing personnel and commercial. I said, "I'll have a word whether I will get anywhere has to be seen but personally I would rather have all my team included dotted lines with me." She actually laughed.

I said, "What's the word at head office?"

"We have received seven requests for transfers to your team," she answered.

"You're shitting me," I said and immediately apologised. I wasn't used to having females in my office, especially good-looking ones.

CC laughed saying, "I've heard worse."

"What else?" She smiled.

"Everyone knows Mr Inglis is not particularly fond of you. However, and it is hearsay, he threw a cup at the wall in his office, fortunately the cup was empty."

I roared and she laughed too. I had to ask, "Am I higher than him on the company's organisational chart?" She nodded taking from her pile of files and paperwork the new organisational chart.

There I was in all my glory, still only twenty-five and sitting one tier below the board. I said to CC, "This calls for a celebration, what are you doing tonight? Are you married, courting or anything?"

She shook her head. "Well," I said, "Do I get to buy my personnel supervisor dinner?" She thought before saying, "There is a company policy which forbids liaisons between employees but if you can keep a secret, so can I."

"Where do you live?" I asked.

"I share a flat with my sister close to the Duke of Wellington," which was close to head office and a matter of yards distant from my flat.

I followed through with what food she liked, or would she prefer to just have a beer or two. No she would love to have supper somewhere and she enjoyed most cuisines. I said, "I'll meet you in the Wellington at seven-thirty, okay?" She nodded and said that would be fine.

I asked her which she preferred Christine or CC. Her answer was CC at work was fine; out of work definitely Christine. I said, "Okay Christine, see you soon and oh yes, before I forget. Arrange for my teams to congregate in Casey's warehouse for ten in the morning and you be there."

She presented me with all the files and a ton of paraphernalia before I walked her to the office door where a driver was waiting to run her back to head office. I went to investigate my new office, which was at least, if not more, twice the size of my existing one.

I knocked on Doug's door and walked in. He looked up "Well" he asked. I said "Unless you insist I would prefer to give Falmouth a miss and send one of the others plus team. I'll organise and be available twenty-four, seven. I have just been with personnel and I now see what you have so kindly dumped on my desk, and yes before I forget, thank you for the trust and support. I will work damn hard to ensure I don't let you down."

"Sit down Richard." I sat opposite him. "For some unfathomable reason you are suddenly Maybury's shining star. I know I can say that without you becoming impossible to work with because your head isn't stuck up your own arse. You have no idea how your dedication, exemplary work and customer relations has increased turnover and profit."

"Maybury and the board think the sun shines out of your arse. Fortunately, or depending which way you look at it, unfortunately, I know you better than they do. So I stopped an alternative promotion. They were going to build a division around you relative to business processes, business development and fuck knows what else. You would have been wasted. Hence as soon as I heard Terry's news you were always going to replace him."

He looked at me. "Anything else?"

"Not at the moment but I will become a pest for a couple of weeks. He smiled.

"Who says you aren't already. As for Falmouth, it's your baby you decide but don't balls-it up." I saluted and exited.

For the four hours before I was due to meet Christine I put together the Falmouth team giving them a stern lecture on cost, time management and customer relations. I put Jimmy in charge.

He and I sorted his needs and arranged transport. I then called in one of my drivers and storekeeper to move my office. When they had finished I roughly prepared notes for my introductory speech to my very big team. It took ages before I was satisfied.

I briefly thought of Sophie knowing she would have been so proud. I called my parents once more to bring them up to speed. I left the office heading for the Duke of Wellington and Christine.

I was five minutes early. Christine and another red headed girl were standing at the bar. I walked over. Christine introduced her sister, Charlotte, who had insisted on keeping Christine company in case I was late. I was grateful to Charlotte for her presence, which gave me the opportunity to take my bike home and put on a clean shirt. I ordered refills for them saying I would be half an hour.

I swiftly returned, when I walked in they didn't notice, they appeared to be arguing. I breezed over smiling and joined the two girls. I thought what the hell and invited Charlotte to join us.

I noticed Christine's grimace and her "don't you dare" stare at her sister and the discreet kick to her sister's shin. Charlotte thanked me saying another time and departed. I said to Christine, "Do you often kick your sister's shin?" She went bright red and I laughed.

I bought a beer and refilled her white wine. We moved to a table near to the exit to the gardens. We must have talked for good hour and a half and two drinks albeit I switched to wine.

Without little effort I learnt all I needed to know about Christine and a fair amount about Charlotte. They were orphaned along with a younger brother, Charles when they were nine, twelve and fourteen. Christine now twenty-three was the elder.

Their Aunt Sadie and Uncle James took them in. James worked as an investment banker based in Hong Kong so they were shipped to Hong Kong where they enjoyed a privileged life. Charles still lived in Hong Kong, the two girls returned to the UK for university and careers hence they shared a flat paid for by Uncle James.

Charlotte had attended the same university and worked for the local council in the planning department for road infrastructure improvements, which she was good at. Actually Christine appeared to be proud of her younger sister.

She pushed for information regarding myself but I was careful what I said-- I didn't want another Melissa or Debbie. I told her I was free and easy with no fixed agenda, just a guy who loved work. She laughingly asked whether I was destined to spend my life in permanent bachelorhood becoming an old roué.

I answered truthfully stating I didn't intend settling down for a very long time, emphasising I loved freedom and work too much. Afterwards I thought what a stupid thing to admit to. I was challenging Christine to change me, or was I being pig-headed? I wasn't sure.

We had dinner in a trattoria I knew. In fact, mother had introduced it years earlier. The ambience was good and Christine relaxed and enjoyed herself. We had a laugh about her sister and herself when she told me the story of a particular time she was lost on her second day at university, unable to find the right building never mind the lecture hall.

After dinner I walked her home. I escorted her to the first floor. She invited me in for coffee but I cried off, blaming work. I saw the disappointment in her face and very nearly changed my mind. I kissed her cheek and asked her if I could see her again, which she agreed to.

I said, "This Saturday I need to buy a new suit, maybe two," adding, "Ladies are much better than men in choosing clothes." I suggested she could help me select, followed by lunch. Her smile would have lit up Southampton City Centre. I kissed her cheek once more and evading her grasp. I said, "See you tomorrow."

The walk home I concentrated on how to keep Christine at arm's length and remain friends.

Once home I enjoyed a shower before checking the flashing answering machine. The first message, from mother, she wanted to know more about my promotion, the second from father demanding the same. The third, from Debbie, chastised me for not calling her Sunday asking if she was off my list. The fourth, from Carol moaning she hadn't seen me since Valentine and had I given up on her.

The last one was from Doug; he said, "You won't believe this, we've got the freighter overhaul. Old Maybury wants to give you a bonus, don't worry I've put a stop to his silly notion." He was laughing.

Wednesday morning I jumped out of bed bright and early and went jogging, my first for a long, long time. Three miles and I was shagged out. In the office I waited patiently for Doug's call to his office regarding the Hartlepool freighter, the Range Extender or whatever it was called. However he was at head office.

At nine forty-five I rode my bike down to the Warehouse. I said good morning to Christine, calling her CC asking if the teams were all present.

She explained we were waiting for half a dozen engineers who were on their way.

She proudly introduced her team and the design team headed by Terry Whitehead. I chatted with them for a while. I cornered the two remaining team leaders, Charlie Reynolds and Martin Stevens knowing I had yet to replace myself. I wouldn't rush I wanted to get to know everyone. I looked at my watch deciding I would give the missing six until five past. I wondered amidst my old team getting congratulations and handshakes.

A mini-bus pulled up and the missing six jumped out. Casey and his team were standing to my right. Casey winked. I climbed onto a packing case. I extracted my notes and started talking. I received cheers and boos and comments but on the whole it went well, which was affirmed when other team members came over and wished me well. I climbed astride and gunned the bike back to the office.

Reception informed me Doug was waiting in the meeting room with Mr Maybury, Pete was also present. Doug got straight down to it. The owners have paid for the first inspection, every penny, which was unheard of. Payment wasn't normally received for forty to seventy days after the work had been invoiced.

However they wanted five similar freighters inspected and comprehensive reports produced plus two other ships running out of Muscat, Oman also required similar inspections. They were also willing to pay fifty percent up front subject to a pricing schedule they had asked for. In the meantime Doug, Pete and I would be flying to Muscat, to meet the owners.

I leaned back in the chair. I said, "Bloody hell, if we win work across their fleet we will earn a fortune, probably close to seven or eight million pounds." Doug looked at me with pride. His boy was on the ball. Mr Maybury said, "That much." Doug confirmed the figure.

Mr Maybury said, "Doug, it has to be Richard-- he has to run the whole operation under your supervision." Doug thought about it before saying, "Okay he manages from here making periodic visits. Don't forget he has a similar value of work dotted around the UK and Europe, he can't afford to take his finger off the pulse." For a while Mr Maybury and Doug argued until Doug told Pete and me to leave the room.

After lunch Doug came to my office and collapsed into a chair and sighed. "When was the last time you were drunk?" he asked.

I smiled. "Quite a while," purposefully not mentioning the recent debacle with Jimmy.

He said, "I am not much of a boozer but all that could quickly change if I have to put up with idiotic management for much longer."

I said, "It would be great to know what is going on."

He laughed, "If you find out be sure to let me know. Right this is it. You, Pete and I with a couple of the lads, especially Jimmy will price the inspections for the seven ships. They are dotted all over the globe."

He scratched his head, "Haven't you just decided to ship Jimmy off to Falmouth?"

I nodded. "No worries we will use Cyril, he is not as quick but he is accurate." I could hear him thinking. "Okay, you will manage the operation but you will be in Southampton for one whole week every third one. The rest of the time your life will be aeroplanes, hotel rooms and ships.

However and unfortunately to begin with, you will be based in Wallsend overseeing the fastest-ever ship overhaul. You will work every second of the day. The fleet's inspections will be managed by you but you will only allow yourself a maximum of two days aboard any one ship and I couldn't care less if you work the whole forty-eight hours, understood?" I said, "Understood."

He continued, "Tomorrow and Friday, and Saturday if necessary you and I will plan the whole operation for the inspections, although we are waiting confirmation to where the hell the ships are, which will be telexed to us by midnight. We will have to work out costs and floats, tools, equipment including testing kit, and accommodation, flights, local transport and a whole lot more."

He ceased and once more scratched his head. "The stumbling block is the Range Extender's overhaul. Arranging the towing to Wallsend and Wallsend's facilities will not be problematic. However, the overhaul and getting the work done aboard a dozen ships in the UK and Europe plus these seven bloody inspections will be. We will suffer manpower shortages and the costs will be astronomical."

He lost his thread for a moment before saying, "As I said you will begin in Wallsend and get the teams working, set work regimes. After the first week you will be required to be in Wallsend two days a week, the agreed week in Southampton and as I said flying here there and everywhere, but I suspect it will be necessary for you to fly weekends leaving the weekdays clear for work responsibilities, so young Richard you can kiss your girlfriend goodbye for a few weeks."

He was smiling, "I presume you have a girlfriend."

I shook my head. "No, I don't have time working for you." He laughed.

It was late when I finally arrived home to my wee flat. I checked the answering machine. A booming Hugo said, "Where the hell are you? You owe me a visit. Lunch, Sunday at the hotel, don't be late." I laughed to myself, how I loved that guy.

Thursday, Friday and Saturday Doug worked the small planning and pricing team late into the night. We cursed and shouted and argued until eventually Doug accepted the specifications and complex scheduling. He collected the reams of paper and extended scheduling to pass to the marketing guys to beautify for issue to the client.

I was settling in bed when I remembered Christine. The shopping expedition and lunch we had arranged had slipped my mind. I couldn't call to apologise without a telephone number. I decided to call round to her flat before I raced to Richmond to meet Hugo.

Mid-morning I was standing ringing the door-bell and knocking on the door when a voice from below called up advising Christine and Charlotte had gone out. I asked the lady if she could spare paper and pencil to leave a note. I wrote, *"Sorry, work took over. I will do my best to make it up to you. Richard"*

The ride to Richmond was quick and easy. I arrived at the appointed hotel where I proposed to Sophie, at twelve sharp. I walked through to the bar hoping to see Miriam. When I asked for her I was told she no longer worked there.

I seated myself on a stool at the bar and ordered a tomato juice to wait for Hugo. Several people and a family group came in and ordered drinks and checked their reservations for lunch.

I heard Hugo before I saw him. "King Dick you old bastard you made it then." I jumped from the stool and went to meet him. We hugged and back-slapped and laughed as we always did when we met. Miriam was standing behind him. I rushed to hug her before standing back to admire her dark-haired beauty.

It wasn't often people were given the chance to see Miriam dressed as a woman presenting her special Latino loveliness. She, as Ruth all those years ago, preferred to live in jeans and loose sweaters.

Hugo said, "Come on, I am starving," and led Miriam and I towards the restaurant. He disappeared, giving Miriam and me a chance to catch-up on news. She was working full-time as recruitment consultant specialising in the construction business. She wasn't overly fond of the work but it was easy and not over demanding.

Hugo was extremely busy, being dragged deeper and deeper into his father's businesses. From time to time they reminisced over Sophie and me and were grateful to hear I had, more or less, got over her death.

Hugo returned to the table with a waiter struggling with a huge ice-bucket containing a magnum of champagne. Hugo loved his champagne. Sitting down he said, "What are you doing 15th September?"

"Jesus Hugo that's months away how the hell would I know," I replied.

I noticed Miriam smiling she was radiant. "I need a favour," he retorted.

"What favour?" I queried.

He boomed, "I need a bloody best man," and roared. The whole restaurant turned to see the giant Hugo in full flow. I ignored him and hugged Miriam, pulling her onto my lap. He was still roaring when we stood and hugged. I stuttered congratulations kissed Miriam, shook his hand and of course told him I would be honoured.

During a loud and happy lunch our merriment spread to fellow diners. A couple of tables chorused congratulations. Hugo poured the champagne frequently and invited me to stay the night and leave early in the morning, which I agreed to, leaving me free to share in the champagne.

Miriam, who I had rarely witnessed drink more than the odd glass of alcohol also imbibed freely. I surreptitiously paid the lunch bill by way of my celebration of their impending happy day. I did remember Sophie a couple of times, but not for too long.

We ordered a taxi to take us to his flat on Richmond Hill, which, if it wasn't for the intake of champagne we could of easily walked. In the flat he abruptly, without explanation, lifted his big legs onto the leather settee closed his eyes and went to sleep. Miriam threw a blanket over him.

She and I moved to the kitchen where she made a cup of tea before ordering a taxi for six in the morning to return me to my bike. We talked over the past and discussed her future with Hugo.

We laughed over Gertie and her whimsical way, wondered how Jessica and Simon were getting along and generally explored common ground, which revolved around Hugo, rugby and her friendship with Sophie. I remained objective throughout signalling yet further that Sophie was a memory, not to be forgotten but to be stored away and remembered as a significant phase in my journey of discovery.

Miriam, obviously very much in love explained why they had waited so long before deciding upon a date, which as I expected had a great deal to do with Hugo and the huge responsibility his father forced on him. I was extremely pleased for them both.

Around seven Hugo made an appearance, apologising for sleeping, blaming his father and the hours he worked. Miriam reminded him of rugby training and the game he played for his London club every Saturday might also contribute to his tiredness.

Hugo and I went for a walk down the hill into Richmond discussing the wedding, which would be held in his family's chapel followed by the reception in the family home. He too reminisced for a while, particularly remembering with fondness our university days and when we lifted the UAU rugby cup

He did mention, in passing, both Ruth and Sophie but didn't labour upon specific points. We walked back up the hill to enjoy a fry-up prepared by Miriam. I cancelled the taxi simply because Hugo's flat, close to the hotel, would only take a few minutes to walk to collect my bike.

199

I awoke early, sneaked out of the flat and collected my bike. I arrived back in Southampton by seven. I changed into slacks, shirt and tie and rode into the office ready to start what I knew would be a tough period with no quarter given.

Pete, Doug and I had three days in Muscat meeting the owner's representatives. After which we worked, we sweated and we cried for nineteen weeks. We didn't stop and I did, on many occasions, go without sleep.

My teams were supreme they worked and worked, killing themselves for Maybury. We completed the Range Extender's overhaul in four and a half weeks, an amazing achievement.

We watched her sail out of Wallsend and got drunk, not legless, just drunk. I gave the guys the rest of the week off to see their families and catch up on much needed sleep.

Meanwhile, as predicted by Doug I flew most weekends and worked non-stop as did every engineer, technician and support team member. The comradery was amazing. We were bloody efficient and extremely effective. I praised and hugged my guys.

Now and again we would have a good drink. But work was always the priority. As quick as we put one job to bed another new one sprung-up. Maybury's reputation was sky-high, work poured in through the door.

We completed the inspections a fortnight ahead of schedule and submitted the costs for the repair and overhaul works. Within days of a report and cost being submitted Maybury received the order for the repair and replacement work including the promised fifty per cent up front.

We had teams working in Simonstown, South Africa, Oman in the Middle East, the Azores in the Atlantic and Manila in the Philippines. I visited and stamped my mark. I put on overalls and wielded spanners and screwdrivers, often covered head-to-toe in grease and oil, and I loved every minute.

We started the intensive work programme 26th March and completed 2nd August. During those nineteen weeks we completed all the outstanding UK and European works, the seven outstanding inspections, and eight overhauls including the Range Extender.

For the UK, European and seven ship fleet work we achieved fourteen point seven million pounds in revenue. The most incredible news I discovered during a business development management meeting, so incredible I had to ask for the figure to be repeated, my division had secured positive new work orders for a further nine million pounds. Doug and Mr Maybury were over the moon.

Doug accepted his promotion to the board with a wry smile. Pete replaced him as my boss, albeit he only had a couple of years before he would retire. My title was changed from Divisional Manager to General

Manager, Maybury Marine National and International Ship Repairs. However, the biggest shock came when Doug called to say my teams had been awarded two hundred thousand pounds in bonuses. He quietly added I had been awarded twenty thousand then roared.

I recruited Christine to help me work out how to share the bonuses fairly. She devised a scheme based on hours worked, time away from home and extraordinary circumstances such as working in high temperatures and local conditions.

How she did it I don't know but I was very impressed. I suggested the scheme should be issued before payments, so all the teams would understand how individual bonuses had been calculated. We didn't receive one complaint or grievance.

There is always a downside. I lost the rugby team captaincy and was unavailable for selection for all teams until I returned to full training. Fortunately the end of the season ensured I didn't miss many games. I understood as did the club. I wrote a letter explaining work pressures and international travel.

I kept Carol abreast of events and we did manage a late supper. My parents were immensely proud and demanded to see me. Debbie let it be known I would always be welcome to see her whenever I was in town, not for sex but for dinner or drinks. We met twice while I worked in Wallsend enjoying dinner, and sex, for which she hated me for.

I did go out looking for sex. I proved successful on several occasions. There was Beth a window dresser, another Carol, a secretary, Penny a coffee-bar manager and Kate a barmaid at a local hostelry, and Deidre an out and out sex machine who hung about for a couple of weeks.

However, Christine was always on my mind. I managed in the early weeks to keep away from her but personnel's involvement organising flights and accommodation and expense floats and payroll for my teams meant we constantly worked together. Naturally, therefore, when in Southampton, we were spending work time together, which eventually led to a few dates and then on to regular dates.

However, I didn't try to seduce her, nor her me. I steadfastly remained the gentleman fighting to ensure I didn't find myself entangled as I had with Carol, Melissa or Debbie, albeit Debbie and Carol had worked out, we were good friends.

If for one reason or another I didn't get a chance to speak or see Christine I would become irritated, and then I would berate myself. At the time I didn't realise it but day by day Christine was gradually capturing my heart.

Chapter 21 – Gertie, Catriona and the Letter

Towards the end of July, late one evening, I received an unexpected telephone call from Gertie. She would be in Southampton for a week playing violin in an orchestra staging Elgar's work at Southampton's Civic Hall. Gertie not one to pull punches asked if she could move in with me for the week. I explained I only had one bed and that my flat was small. She complained I was brushing her off demanding to know if I was courting, or as she put it "hooked-up".

I mentioned both Carol and Christine, stating I wasn't "hooked-up" but they were companions and Christine in particular was a regular date. The questions kept coming, which I answered truthfully. In the end we agreed to meet for lunch on the Saturday she arrived in Southampton.

I met her in the hotel reception area and we walked to Miranda's, a new bistro recently opened on Commercial Street, for lunch. Gertie, a very beautiful woman, badgered me about my life, what I was doing where I was going. She was not really interested in my responses, but that was typical Gertie. After lunch I walked her back to her hotel. From her handbag she produced two tickets for the evening's opening show.

I was leaning forward to kiss her cheek when she said, "Sophie's gone, Richard-- you can't live your life dreaming of what is dead and gone." Gertie didn't know but at that moment I came the closest I ever would to hitting a woman. I turned leaving her standing on the hotel steps and walked away.

I didn't use the tickets. It was midnight when my door bell was chiming its irritable chime. I staggered from bed pulled on a pair of tracksuit bottoms to answer the door. It was Gertie. I said, "What are you doing here. How did you find where I lived?"

She burst out laughing. "Do you know how many R. Chambers reside in Southampton, according to the telephone directory there are four, and you were the third on the list." Gertie pushed passed me and entered the flat. I followed and she said, "It is small isn't it," indicating with her arm the full expanse of the living room.

Continuing she said, "I have come to apologise I was out of order and very crass. I should not have said what I did and I certainly should not have mentioned Sophie. The words just blurted out. You are the only man to brush me off and, because I am a selfish cow, it hurts." She sat down on the settee saying, "Do you know how to make a cup of tea?" I walked into the kitchen.

I expected her to follow but she didn't. I kept my own counsel, remaining in the kitchen waiting for the kettle to boil and make the tea. I carried the mugs into the living room there was no Gertie. I knew she was in my bed. I carried the tea through placed a cup on the bedside table walked back to my side of the bed put my cup down removed my tracksuit bottoms and climbed into bed.

We didn't say a word. I roughly pulled her into my arms and kissed her. She responded, her hand immediately searching for Jolly Roger. He would always let me down, utterly unprincipled, jumping to attention the minute her hand made contact. I pulled the bedcovers off and callously pushed her head down.

Gertie quite happily took him into her very experienced mouth and made me yell until I exploded into her mouth. She continued her manipulations keeping him hard. She pulled me over her and I fucked her hard, she wanted rough and hard and I made sure I gave her what she wanted.

Lying on our backs, Gertie chuckling, she said, "I always knew you were a good fuck from the first time I looked into your blue eyes in Eastbourne and they said take me to bed." I said, "Gertie, you got what you wanted now shut up." She laughed, "You got what you wanted too. How long has it been?" I ignored her.

Sometime in the night I found myself caressing her body and running my hands down her tummy to push my fingers into her wet vagina. She turned her back on me and I pushed Jolly Roger into her again. She moaned and said, "That feels good." I built myself into a frenzy gripping her hips and driving into her.

She was yelling very unladylike and the Featherstone's starting banging on the floor above. I laughed and rammed harder wanting Gertie to scream louder, she didn't let me down. I exploded into her for the third time and she shrieked long and loud. The Featherstone's gave up their banging. She said, "Can I move in now?"

I said, "Why not."

In the morning I left a note and a spare key and went jogging. It was Sunday and the weather for a change was bright. I jogged for miles, panting and puffing forcing my body into pain. Exhausted and breathing heavily I realised I was outside Christine's flat. I climbed the stairs and rang the bell. Charlotte wearing a dressing gown answered inviting me in and shouting to Christine "Lover boy's here." I smiled to myself thinking, "lover boy".

I was in their flat for the first time. I was admiring the discerning furnishings when Christine peeked through the slightest opening of a door at the bottom of a short corridor.

A few seconds later she staggered into the room also wearing a dressing gown. She looked at me as if I was demented before saying, "What are you doing here, you're all sweaty." I smiled replying, "Is that the way to say good morning to "lover boy"" putting strong emphasis on "lover boy". She smiled. "I'll kill my sister, that's her nickname for you."

In a serious tone she asked if there was a work problem. I shook my head and explained an unexpected friend had arrived from London for work reasons and would be staying in my flat for the week and I would not be able to meet her during the week.

She nodded, opened the door and said, "See you at work." Christine was no one's fool-- she knew instantly my guest was female, how she realised I couldn't figure.

I jogged to the flat hoping Gertie had gone to collect her things, but no she was still in my bed. Hearing me come in she walked naked from the bedroom and wrapped her arms round my neck and kissed me. She said, "I just love sweaty men." Her hand squeezed Jolly Roger and of course he stirred. She said, "Let's shower together I love it all wet."

Gertie, thank goodness, set off for rehearsals at one promising to return with her belongings at about five. I went into the office to catch-up on my big hate, paperwork. I returned to the flat at five. Gertie was busily unpacking her things. She said with a huge smile, "Once more Richard and then I have to get ready."

I shook my head. But Gertie, the ultimate temptress, before I realised she had me on the settee, sitting astride driving up and down.

Gertie for all her air and graces and her elegance was the consummate sex fiend. She wanted everything non-stop, night after night. I drove Jolly Roger into her orifices relentlessly. Every moment we were in the flat together it was ceaseless raw sex. She was insatiable and when I mentioned this she agreed saying "Great isn't it." Pointing out she hadn't seen me slowing down. Gertie always laughed, life for her was one big game.

Saturday morning and for the first time during the week I woke up happy knowing the concerts were over and Gertie would soon be out of my life and on her way back to London. No such luck, she decided to return to London, Sunday.

Although it sounds as if I constantly moaned with regards Gertie, which I suppose I did. She was however a very beautiful and a very highly sexed woman and I did enjoy the sex. It was raw and we both knew it wouldn't be permanent, a blessing. Her final words before she climbed into her car Sunday afternoon were "You are one of the best, I might come back for more" and laughed, she continued to laugh as she pulled away.

The following week I didn't see Christine once. I did spend a couple of days in Greenock with Jimmy going over an engine overhaul. Back in Southampton and still getting the cold shoulder from Christine, I decided I needed a long weekend to sell the bike and buy a car.

In the space of one day, Friday, I sold the Bonneville and purchased a six month old Volvo 1800ES finished in racing green taxed and insured for the open road. I test drove it to Bournemouth and back very pleased with my purchase.

I called the office from a telephone kiosk and asked for Christine, when I was put through. I said, "Hi can I meet you tonight, I have something I would like to show you?" Her cold voice came back. "Has she gone then?"

Irate I said, "Christine we are not officially courting, we are not engaged and I have not bloody well proposed to you so get off you high horse and answer my bloody question." She hung up.

The following week I returned to Greenock working with Jimmy to oversee some major lifting works which involved cutting away the deck of a ship to lift a generator out and replace with new.

Chapter 22 - Margaret

During the week we were in Greenock I became entangled with Margaret, a model. I noticed her with two other models, one male, the other female, modelling fashionable jeans for a popular brand. A woman shouted issuing instructions directing the posing for three or four photographers.

Curiosity drew me over to where they were posing. A cold blustery wind swept off the river, the rawness of an industrial environment being used for the backdrop. Worming through the gathering of on-lookers I managed to get close enough to look into her eyes, they were dead. The photography completed she grabbed a large coat. I rushed forward and helped her to put it on.

With her coat on she turned to thank me. Her eyes had regained life. I smiled and started talking. I asked her if she was cold, suggesting a brandy and coffee to warm her. She didn't respond, just looked at me expressionless. I began to preach the virtues of beating colds before they could take a hold. I expressed how flu could be so depressing with running noses and sore throats. I broke the barrier down; she laughed a delightful throaty laugh.

She said, "Jesus Christ, what the hell are you jabbering on about?"

I laughed, "Christ knows I just needed to talk to you." The paraphernalia of the photo shoot closing and the gear being stowed, and disappearing onto a truck crashed on around where we stood. Her throaty laugh returned. "Alright Mister buy me a brandy and a coffee. Her eyes darted left and right, she pointed towards a third-rate hotel. "There will do."

She shouted to her companions, "Mister here is buying brandy and coffee, see you tomorrow." She lifted a huge bag up onto her shoulder. I took the bag. We crossed to the hotel. In the hotel foyer she said "Margaret," and looked at me. "Richard," I responded. She grabbed the bag heading towards the ladies saying she would dress and be with me in ten minutes. Margaret indicated the bar saying, "A double, I am bloody freezing."

She entered the bar looking for me. I raised my hand. Walking towards the table I could see she was stunning, tall and confident, a very attractive woman. Sitting she took glasses from her bag, putting them on she said, "I am as blind a bat without these," and laughed. Her eyes looked me over smiling she said "Not bad and what is an Englishman doing in Greenock, not the safest place in the world." She lifted her glass and took a gulp followed by a similar gulp of coffee.

"I am working in the dockyard for a few days replacing a generator," I answered. She laughed, "Replacing a generator? Replacing a bloody generator and he holds my coat." Her throaty laughter was exciting. I told her it was a very sexy laugh. Margaret roared, "Now where have I heard that before," followed by more laughter. "Is that your best chat-up line?" she smilingly asked.

"No, I don't have any particular chat-up lines. I look, I fancy and I start talking what comes out, comes out," I replied. Margaret taken her glasses off laughed and laughed, only quietening when she sipped her brandy. Expressing a magnificent smile she said, "So Richard you looked, saw me and fancied me and now what?"

I smiled "Your decision, dinner, drinks or cinema or, we could go to bed."

"Jesus Christ," she exclaimed, "No flies on you are there?"

Smiling I said, "Time is of the essence. Yes I looked, liked what I saw and fancied you so why beat about the bush? And why I am at it, when I looked at you modelling your eyes were dead, why?"

Margaret her glasses back on and smiling said, "Jesus Richard that is what I call a chat up line. You didn't see the goose pimples, the blue lips, only the dead eyes, now that is extraordinary. Perhaps you are different."

She thought for a moment. "My eyes were dead because the assignment is a crap assignment. I have got a week, dressed, undressed, rain or sun whatever I have to look glamorous and in love with a pair of jeans, wouldn't your eyes be dead?"

Picking up her glass I stood to refill it. She held my arm, "Not here we'll go somewhere nicer, where you can romance me and try to talk me into bed, which will be interesting." We both laughed.

She asked where I was staying. I told her the hotel in Largs. She smiled, "Oh good I live in Largs, I know the hotel, we'll go there, I know the bar, it's well decorated and it's also quite romantic, and it gets lively. Yes we'll go there." We exited the hotel looking for a taxi. On the way we stopped off at her apartment. I waited in the taxi while she unloaded her bag and changed her clothes.

Entering the hotel we chose a table over to the right of the long bar. Margaret deposited her coat at the cloakroom. Wearing a simple red cocktail dress, she looked ravishing, her blonde hair freed from the ribbon she was wearing, lay across her shoulders. She looked absolutely gorgeous and I complemented her on her beauty. Her response was a throaty laugh.

Jimmy and a couple of the lads I hadn't noticed came over. I introduced Margaret enjoying the discreet looks, she encouraged. Jimmy winked and bought the first drink before leaving Margaret and me in peace.

We were sitting close, side-by-side, I could feel the warmth of her body, particular her thighs. I enjoyed the feeling. Margaret lifted her glass and chinked mine saying, "Well Richard what do you do besides work on generators?"

I laughed. "Not much, generally, I travel the world repairing and maintaining ships." I briefly explained the last few months mentioning the hours I have spent in aeroplanes and the countries I had worked in. I immediately noticed she was impressed. "You are not just an engineer then?" she queried.

Still laughing I said, "That's exactly what I am, an engineer and proud of the fact."

"No, you are more, those guys revered you, and I could see it in their mannerisms and the polite way they spoke to you," she responded.

I didn't want to discuss my life too much I said, "Quite simply I manage three teams of engineers who do the work. I spend all day fighting with paperwork." Smiling she said, "If you fight paperwork why are you here in Greenock repairing a generator?" she asked. "Alright, alright, I yield," I laughingly cried "I am here because the job is particularly challenging and I decided I should be in attendance."

Margaret enjoyed questioning me. However before she could ask another question I asked how she became a model and whether she enjoyed modelling. Her full story, albeit glossed over followed. She was now twenty-five and her modelling days were numbered. She, although she had worked hard to become a top model, never quite made the top tier. Initially when sixteen, seventeen and eighteen she was in high demand because of her height and slimness, but as time progressed other sixteen year olds were appearing everywhere.

Although she received plenty of work, the fashion houses, except on occasion, rarely used her leaving her with jeans, and cars, and underwear, and pyjamas, frying-pans and other dreary options. She sounded sad.

Continuing she explained she couldn't complain because the money was good and she lived well. However, she expressed, when the assignments slowed or stopped, she had investments and would set-up a business relative to fashion or something aligned to the industry, probably in England.

To lighten the mood I told her she looked fantastic and she could model generators for me any day. Her laughter returned. "I think we have exhausted work perhaps I should take you to dinner." More throaty laughter. "I am a model-- I don't eat, the occasional lettuce leaf and the odd carrot, but yes a juicy steak would be welcome." We finished our drinks and caught the lift to the restaurant on the top floor.

The dinner was cheerful. Margaret regaled story after story describing disasters, great times and travel throughout her modelling career. One story which tickled me happened when Margaret just eighteen, engrossed in doing a sexy swimwear shoot in some woods, close to a beach. Suddenly a guy jumped from behind some bushes. He went to his trouser pockets causing the photographers and the support people to panic.

Margaret admitted she was scared. Anyway all he did was pull out a camera and start taking photographs.

The dinner over we ordered cognacs and black coffees. I looked to my watch-- it was close to ten. I said, "My room is down one floor, or should I take you home?" Margaret reached for my hand lifting it to her cheek she said, "How long are you in Greenock for?" I smiled. "Three or four nights," I replied. Smiling she whispered, "You're right, time is of the essence I think you should take me to bed but before you do, I pre-warn you I am an uncontrollable when closeted alone with a man in a hotel bedroom." Her throaty laugh echoed around the restaurant, raising eyebrows.

I signed the cheque and we clattered down the fire escape stairs to the 19th floor and into room 1908. Margaret remembered her coat. While she used the bathroom I descended to the ground floor to collect her coat. When I returned she was in bed feigning sleep.

I quickly showered and jumped into bed. I snuggled into her back putting my arms around her. She whispered, "I have to be on-site for the next shoot by midday to catch the sun at its zenith."

I quietly chuckled, "I am sure we can manage that."

She turned and melted into my arms. Her lips searching for mine were greeted and assaulted as I forcefully pulled her tight into my body. She fervently responded forcing herself astride my chest, for a moment she looked down at me. All of a sudden using her mouth and teeth, she assailed my body nibbling, sometimes nipping, sending electric shocks flowing through my loins. Her delightful body was alive, vibrating. Jolly Roger stood tall, rigid, and ready.

My hands were chasing her movements caressing her breasts, squeezing her buttocks and roaming freely, my fingers brushed her labia lips feeling the warmth of her vagina. My hips had a mind of their own forcing upwards, waiting expectedly for her mouth to eclipse Jolly Roger. Her head moved towards my chest her teeth nibbled my nipples, her hand slowly massaged my penis. Her manipulations were sending me wild. I could feel my sperm bubbling desperate to escape. Abruptly she stopped falling onto her back pulling my head onto her breasts. I nibbled her nipples.

She responded with urgency using the force of her demands to drive my head down to her vagina. The moment my lips and tongue touched her secret gateway she thrust her hips up using her widening legs to lift her body into a position of complete surrender. My tongue delved into her and I savoured her hot love juices.

Using her legs she clamped my head, twisted her body and turned me onto my back manoeuvring her vagina above my face. With her juices dripping onto my face she lowered her very red and very open vagina onto my mouth. I clamped my mouth hard onto her driving my tongue in search of her clitoris.

She started moving her body up and down her vagina intermittently connecting with my lips. Suddenly she lifted cleared, swinging her body to straddle my loins guiding Jolly Roger deep inside. She squealed and drove her hips down momentarily grinding her pelvis.

Time after time she lifted her hips thrusting down forcing Jolly Roger deeper with every thrust. Abruptly she leaned forward and bit my lip, and grabbed my hair, using it to force herself to push down harder. My head exploded my sperm blasted into her and she gave forth a penetrating shriek the whole hotel must have heard.

The next minute she was once more on her back her legs lifted high pulling my body over until I hovered above her. She reached Jolly Roger satisfied he had remained rigid she eased him into her very wet vagina. She thrust up forcing his full length to slide deep. She bucked, and bucked lifting her hips clear of the bed and bucked once more.

I pushed hard feeling her body respond, her legs lifted onto my shoulders, she beat a tattoo. She thrust and squealed her body demanding more and more. I responded to her demands and rammed hard and harder. I became a piston engine driving in and out with force ever increasing the rapidity of the thrusts.

I could feel her nails tearing my skin her teeth biting my arm and still she thrust her hips up I buried deep into her. Utilising all my strength I lifted her body into my chest and forced Jolly Roger deeper, she wailed, screeched and dug her teeth into my shoulder and then she started trembling, waves of ripples spread through her body, her wail transcended into a piercing shriek and she started yelling.

Abruptly she went quiet, her arms wrapped round my neck her lips caressing my neck. I carefully lowered her onto the bed lowering to lay by her side. She turned and cuddled into my chest her face hidden.

I held Margaret tightly caressing her shoulders and running my fingers along her spine. She lifted her head forcing upwards to kiss me. I stroked her hair. She kissed my eyes, cheeks, nose and returned to my lips. I looked into her eyes they were bright. She climbed over my body and began kissing my arms where she had bitten me. She continued searching for my battle scars, kissing each tear of my skin and my shoulders where droplets of blood blossomed. Her face alight with a brilliant smile she said "I warned you"

She climbed off the bed and pulling my hand forced me up and into the bathroom. We showered. I tenderly dried her body taking time to inspect and explore her delightfulness. Although slim her body curved in the right places, her breasts were perfectly formed, her nipples dark and her legs travelled down and down forever. Her bottom perfectly formed completed her exquisiteness.

Standing side-by-side I realised she was tall, much taller than I had imagined. I asked her height, "Five-eight" she responded. I took her into my arms reaching down to clench her buttocks. Jolly Roger instantly stirred. Margaret laughed saying, "No more I am going home, a model needs her beauty sleep." She moved into the bedroom to dress. I too started dressing. She said, "I don't need you to escort me home, I am a big girl." I argued I couldn't allow her to go home unescorted. She smiled.

We were opening the door to exit the room when she turned and faced me. Her exquisite face expressed a frown. I could see she was thinking she moved her eyes to gaze into mine. For a moment we stood looking at each other. She said, "Pack your case and check out." She sat on the bed and watched me pack.

There weren't any available taxis we sat in reception waiting for the hotel to call for one. Her head rested against my shoulder. She searched for my hand, squeezing, she said "You will be the first man to enter into my private world, into my home, my sanctuary." Before I could respond the reception clerk called over pointing to a taxi parked outside. I lifted my case and followed Margaret to the taxi.

In the back of the taxi Margaret snuggled close. We didn't speak. We clambered from the taxi. The driver retrieved my case from the boot. I followed her to the door and up the broad stair case to her apartment. I walked in and was instantly overwhelmed; her apartment was huge with a staircase centrally positioned leading into an attic area.

We still hadn't spoken. My mouth must have been open. Margaret said, "Close it before you catch a fly," and laughed. She waved her arm. "My sanctuary, my home and you are welcome. Come I'll show around."

The apartment consisted of a huge dressing room with mirrored wall and three floor to ceiling especially constructed wardrobes filling the other walls leaving a carefully crafted window area. The next room was smaller with a two-seater settee, a desk complete with telephone and a built-in book shelf full of books. She said, "I sit in here and read, happy to be transposed into a world of fiction."

Taken my hand she led the way across the huge living area filled with white upholstered settees, chairs, three coffee tables and attractive oak furniture. In one corner an attractive cocktail cabinet rested adjacent to a built-in bar with one stool. Margaret noticed my eyes. "When I feel lonely, which is often, I sit at the bar with a book and a brandy, or maybe a glass of wine, sometimes a gin and tonic."

She opened a door displaying a very modern kitchen, pushing open a second door leading from the kitchen she indicated her laundry area. The final room portrayed an intimate dining room furnished with a beautiful oak table and four matching chairs, a sideboard and several paintings hanging from the walls. I was stunned by the splendour of her apartment.

Pointing to the central staircase she said, "My bedroom and bathroom." I trailed behind reaching her bedroom. Once more I felt overwhelmed the room was wondrous with a huge bed sited dead centre, the carpeting was thick and the walls were again full of paintings. Besides the bed the room was shorn of furniture, the roof was glazed letting in the moonlight. I followed Margaret to the bathroom. A huge round bath again centrally positioned commanded the room, high above another glazed ceiling, to the left, a wash basin and a door leading to a water closet and bidet.

I sat on the edge of the bath and looked and looked. Margaret's throaty laugh reverberated off the walls. "Well say something," she cried.

For a moment I was speechless, eventually I stammered, "I'm astounded, it's magnificent, I've never come across anything like it, its bloody magnificent, a palace." She laughed saying, "My sanctuary now defiled by a man, you should feel very special, very special indeed."

Taken my hand she tugged me into the bedroom and down the stairs. "Bring your case." I obeyed and followed her into the dressing room. Making space she instructed me to stow my clothes. "I think a coffee and brandy are needed don't you agree?" she asked. I dumbly nodded. Margaret once more laughed.

Again I found myself following her as we crossed to the kitchen, I considered myself a lap-dog seemingly always trailing behind Margaret, to heel. Passing the stairs I deposited my washing bag on the third step.

Swiftly she filled a coffee machine with beans and after checking the water level switched it on. Yet again I was following her this time towards the cocktail cabinet where she poured two liberal glasses of brandy.

Passing a glass to me she said, "I've yet to understand why I invited you into my sanctuary, I have resisted for five years, keeping men at arm's length, out of my life, using them for sex when needed, and all of a sudden I invite a generator engineer, I ask you a generator engineer, explain that to me please do."

I had never felt so hopeless, so completely overcome, speechless, dumbfounded, whatever, I felt useless. I couldn't even speak. Margaret, thank goodness, took the brandy from my hand placing it on the bar. She forced herself into my arms, "Say something, Jesus I can't talk for both of us." I remained silent. "Right," she said. "I am going to drink my coffee and brandy and go to bed, any comment."

Finally I discovered my tongue. First I looked at my watch. I said, "It's just gone two I have to be up and at the ship by eight, so bed is a good idea. I'll give coffee a miss." I gulped the brandy. I took her hand and pulling her after me I said, "You don't need coffee either." I recovered my washing bag and we climbed the stairs.

We quickly disrobed entering the bathroom to stand side-by-side brushing our teeth. Moments later we were in bed and embracing. We kissed, our hands exploring, her hand found Jolly Roger simultaneously my hand smothered her vagina. I rolled Margaret onto her back, lifted her legs gently forcing them apart.

Tenderly I forced my penis into Margaret's welcoming vagina. My movements were tender, I slowly inserted Jolly Roger until our pelvises grinded together, she lifted her hips to enforce deeper penetration, very gently we moved in unison. Her legs encircled my waist her arms my neck and I sighed as I pushed hard into her.

I moaned feeling immense pleasure, the muscles of her vagina clamped tightly around Jolly Roger. She wriggled her hips side-to-side. I withdrew to the entrance of her vagina and rammed home, she screeched. I withdrew and rammed again, once more she screeched. I increased tempo and starting driving harder and harder. Her teeth found my shoulder biting deep. I cried out and shot my sperm splashing my seed over her vagina walls.

Margaret screamed "Don't stop, Jesus." I pounded into her, her teeth were biting deeper. I pounded and pounded. In response she drove her body to meet every thrust. Jolly Roger wouldn't let me down, absolutely not. He reacted positively forcing his head to crash into Margaret's cervix. Her nails raked my arms her teeth clamped hard and then she yelled, she screamed and yelled, she thrashed and kicked and she blasphemed.

Her body went limp she pulled herself up, using my neck for purchase, to grab my hair pulling my head down to meet her lips, she forced her tongue deep into my mouth and pressurised her lips against mine. She then crumpled beneath me. I gently moved to her side. Margaret forced her body against mine her arms round my shoulders, half whispering, half laughing she said, "The right decision, don't you think?"

My poor body was bleeding across my shoulders, my right arm and my back. Margaret administered little kisses before leaving the bed, returning with a damp flannel and a tube of cream. Tenderly she wiped the offended areas where she had bloodied me and gently rubbed cream over the wounds.

Margaret was alive, she smiled, her face shone, her throaty laughed burst forth, her lips caressed my face and she held me tight, very tight. She moved my head down to nestle against her breasts. She quietly said, "I know why I invited you into my sanctuary."

I listened, waiting for her explanation instead she said "You could at least do me the courtesy of asking why" she laughed. I whispered "Why?"

Her hand was lazily brushing my hair. "Because you are different, very different. I don't know what or why but different you most certainly are. Who would ever think to ask why my eyes were dead."

I whispered, "That doesn't sound like a good enough reason to me." Once more her throaty laughed escaped. "You are…, what? Unfathomable, that's it you are unfathomable. I can't figure you out. Most men are open books, you're not. You are mature, sensuous, caring, loving and extremely sexually aware, most men aren't."

She suddenly hugged me tighter. "Different, not the run of the mill, and when you walk, my God you walk proud, erect, tough, your posture is screaming look at me, that's why your men revere you, you demand respect. Jesus, you are all man, a fucking real man, that's why I invited you home, home to my sanctuary."

My eyes were demanding closure I struggled to speak. I hoarsely whispered, "Is that all."

Margaret was thrown into spasms of laughter, I heard her throatiness as I surrendered to sleep.

I woke with a start throwing Margaret off, not intentionally, my back. She grasped my arm. "What's wrong?" "What time is it?" I retorted. I looked to my watch. "Ten past ten," I yelled. I jumped from the bed Margaret followed calling, "I'll make coffee."

I rushed into the bathroom, brushed my teeth and swilled my face. Charged downstairs and dressed, rushing into the kitchen I kissed Margaret's cheek saying, "No time for coffee, I'll be back between six and seven, will you be here?"

Margaret looking gorgeous her face radiant answered, "I'll be here"

I arrived at the ship just after eleven. Jimmy looked me over. He said, "That good eh?" and laughed.

The hired crane was in position, the lift ready. I dived down the steep ladders into the engine room. I quickly checked the slinging and fixings; satisfied, I ascended the ladders to be met by a beaming Jimmy and the team. Jimmy said, "Right Boss can we get this over with?" I smiled and nodded.

One of the lads produced a mug of coffee, which I gratefully accepted. The team positioned themselves holding ropes to guide the generator through the tightness of the engine room, missing pipework and ancillary equipment. Jimmy signalled the lift to commence. An hour later, the old generator safely secured on the back of a truck I offered to buy lunch.

We crowded into a café and ordered lunch. Four pairs of eyes were looking at me waiting to hear the events of the evening before. I laughed and shook my head. I said, "No way."

The rest of the afternoon and into early evening the engine room was readied for the new generator being delivered mid-morning the following day. We checked and double checked every conceivable eventuality until we were satisfied the new generator would drop comfortably onto the steel plinth sited amidst the engine room's boiler plates. I offered to buy a beer but received polite refusals.

Jimmy said, "I imagine you should be somewhere, am I right?"

"You're right," I said, laughed and darted off towards the dockyard gates.

I rung Margaret's bell at seven-thirty, the door buzzed. I pushed it open and charged up the broad staircase two steps at a time. Margaret stood at her door a vision of loveliness wearing a short simple white smock displaying her glorious legs. I pushed her in closed the door pulled her into my body running my hands down onto her bottom and kissed her hard. She yelped "Jesus Richard," her arms encircled my waist.

Catching my breath I inhaled her aroma and kissed her again. Her arms wrapped around my neck and she responded passionately, nibbling my lips. Her throaty laugh intermingled with words gasped "If this how you are going to arrive every night you are welcome to stay as long as you want." I smiled and kissed her once more. She said "Bath time you smell of whatever generator's smell of."

We bathed together. I asked after her day. "Like any other. I wore these jeans, those jeans. I changed that blouse for this blouse. I stood this way and that way. I smiled, I didn't smile. I walked that way and this way. I lifted one leg then another. I winked and so on and so on, just another day at the office."

I smiled, cupped her face leaned forward and gently kissed her, She opened her mouth I pushed my tongue in, she bit it, gently. Her arms reached for me causing a misbalance, we toppled into the water flooding the floor.

Margaret laughed, she was always laughing. I asked her why. "I laugh when I am happy, which is not often. I am happy now, I was happy last night and I will be happy tonight so why shouldn't I laugh." I couldn't think of a suitable response.

She stood, my hands reached for her bottom pulling her vagina to my lips. She slapped me away saying, "Floor drying time, food, music, dancing and bed, and love, in that order, okay?"

"Yes Mam," I retorted. Using towels we dried the floor. Margaret slipped her smock on. I wrapped a towel round my waist.

She asked what music I liked. "I am eclectic," she smiled. She chose "Band on the run" by Wings, Paul McCartney's group. She played it loud. I asked about her neighbours. She smiled. "This house is one of my investments, my neighbours are relatives. My kid brother lives in one flat and my grandparents in another. They will not be bothered I soundproofed the floor." She pulled me into her arms and we moved to the music.

I nuzzled her neck she pulled her head back to provide greater access. I nibbled her ears and pulled her hips into mine, we grinded together. Jolly

Roger stirred. She once more laughed and pushed me away. "Lettuce leaf and carrots followed by yoghurt, okay?" I smiled answering, "Perfect."

For supper, we enjoyed a wok fried concoction of prawns, spring beans, sugar peas, spring onions and shredded lettuce, fresh bread and a bottle of white wine. The meal was superb, I thoroughly enjoyed every morsel. The wine matched the food. And yes, yoghurt provided the dessert.

Throughout Margaret smiled and laughed gaily listening as I regaled the hours I spent imprisoned in aeroplanes and sleeping in airports, trying to find hotels and working twenty-four hours a day. My reminiscing didn't stop the touching and holding hands, the kissing at regular intervals, nor the constant need to reach for each other.

We washed the dishes. She pulled the towel from my waist, ordering me to put something on, a shirt or something. I obliged, finding boxers and a T-shirt. We danced close together, we shimmied and twisted. Margaret was full of merriment, gaiety emanated from her soul, her happiness contagious, and I felt so very happy. She asked what time I had to be at the ship. I told her no later than eight-thirty. She put a new record on the player took my hand and we climbed the stairs to bed.

For three hours I lived, driven to the highest level of sexual gratification, a period in which Margaret exploited every one of my sexual weaknesses, thrived on every sexual assault I could throw at her and still demanded more. I pounded, rammed, pummelled, and I caressed and I loved tenderly. I explored her body top to bottom and back again. She explored mine.

I exhausted myself in pleasure for Margaret and for me. Eventually, shattered I heard the words, "Sleep my darling, sleep." I inwardly gave thanks and closed my eyes. Falling into a deep sleep I heard the words "my darling".

I could hear a pitter-patter; I couldn't understand the noise. I opened my eyes seeing rain bouncing off the glazed ceiling. I smiled reaching for Margaret. I was alone. I checked my watch six-thirty. I leapt from the bed and leaped the stairs. Margaret looked up as I charged into the kitchen. She smiled I enclosed her in my arms, her head under my chin. I ran my hands over her naked body delighting in its softness. She wriggled round to face me wrapping her arms round my waist. We kissed tenderly our tongues gently exploring.

I lifted her and carried her into the living room laying her on a settee. I lay atop her and kissed her neck, nuzzled her throat inviting her to open her gateway to heaven. Her legs moved I guided Jolly Roger towards the entrance and slowly pushed into her. A soft moan emanated from her throat. I brushed my lips onto hers and slowly pushed in deeper. She wrapped her arms round my neck driving her hips up to meet my push.

216

I wanted this to be slow, very slow I wanted to be inside her for a long, long time. I very slowly withdrew and slowly pushed back in thrusting gently at the end of each push. I continued and continued maintaining the utmost tenderness. Margaret writhed and shouted I ignored her. I was intent on ensuring she realised the most astonishing orgasm.

I gradually increased the tempo, not perceptible, but a slow increase. I was content to take all day, if necessary, wanting Margaret to relish every move, every thrust no matter how small. I wanted her tingling, electric pulses rushing through her loins, her vagina.

For what seemed an eternity I pushed and pushed deep into her very wet vagina. The tempo had increased significantly. I was closing in on ramming, pummelling. Margaret hadn't stopped shrieking, calling me names, blaspheming, thrusting and wriggling, crying out. The pummelling started. She was fighting to push me off, the more she fought the harder I rammed home.

All of a sudden her body tensed her nails tore skin from wherever she could. Her teeth were biting deep into my arms, my shoulders. She started screaming, screaming, yelling and yelling. Her body vibrated, it shook. The screaming became wild, uncontrollable. Her body was shaking, her mouth clamped tight onto my shoulder, she screamed, her teeth clamped again. Her body lifted, trembled, vibrated. I couldn't hold, my sperm blasted deep into her. She hit my face, she started slapping me. I pushed and pushed. Jolly Roger died. I withdrew him.

She grabbed me and kissed and kissed and bit and bit and she screamed once more. She yelled "Fuck you, fuck you, you bastard." I laughed, she laughed. She hung onto me. Her eyes closed, I kissed her softly. She kissed me back. I said, "Time for work see you tonight." Her laughter, her beautiful, beautiful throaty sound resonated, I kissed her once more.

I helped her up from the settee pulling her into my arms and hugged her hard. She responded squeezing my waist with all her strength. I kissed the top of her head. I whispered "I really do have to go work."

"I know," she replied adding, "I'll be here waiting." I asked whether she was shooting today. She was but a short shoot in a workshop where she had to hold spanners and hammers and whatever else they gave her to hold.

I arrived on site at nine. The team were waiting. They laughed when I emerged from behind a truck to cross the rail tracks to reach the ship. I was soaked.

We went below to the engine room working back up towards the deck, carefully inspecting the downward route ensuring it was completely clear of any obstructions. We had just finished when the crane arrived. I noticed towards the far side of the rail tracks a driver pulling a tarpaulin from his load revealing the generator.

Six hours later the generator fitted safely onto its steel plinth the bolts and vibration mounts torque tightened we were ready to make all the fuel, exhaust, ancillary, electrical connections, which would take a day, maybe a wee bit longer. I suggested to Jimmy an early day with an early start in the morning. He looked at me and smiled, "How early?" I looked at the team, they were all smirking. I laughed, "As early as you say".

He took me to one side. "Go away Richard, we'll work on another couple of hours and we'll see you at nine in the morning." I started to argue. "Richard, everyone knows you are the eternal twenty-four hour man, they all know you have done the hard hours. You have nothing to feel guilty about, go and enjoy."

I slapped his shoulder saying, "I owe you."

"You don't my friend, you most certainly don't."

I was ringing the doorbell getting no answer when a voice said, "Yes young man." I turned, a handsome woman probably late sixties stood behind me. "Oh hello," I said. "I'm looking for Margaret." "Are you her boyfriend?" she queried.

"No not really, a friend," I replied.

"Come in and I'll make you a cup of tea," she invited. Looking around I smiled. "Come in where?"

"I'm Margaret's grandmother I live on the ground floor."

"Thank you, I would like that," I replied.

Margaret's grandmother was unlocking the door when Margaret's voice said, "And what is going on here?"

I turned and smiled receiving a brilliant radiant smile in return. Her grandmother said "Hello dear, this young man was looking for you I was about to make him a cup of tea." "Hi Nan, it's okay, I'll make him a cup of tea," replied Margaret.

Grandmother wasn't finished. "Why don't I make you both a cup of tea" I said. "A great idea," Margaret gracefully conceded. I relieved Margaret of her huge shoulder bag and we followed Nan into her flat.

I was introduced to Granddad, Jock. I listened intently while Mary, her Nan extolled Margaret's wonderful virtues and her good heart. We have finished the tea readying to leave when Mary said, "If you are not Margaret's boyfriend who are you? She doesn't allow people into her apartment, especially men." Margaret answered, "He's the generator man Nan." I had to turn away to hide my smile. "Oh alright then," replied Nan.

We ran up the stairs into the apartment and I lifted Margaret high and hugged her tight. She was laughing her face glowing, a beaming smile lighting her face. She wriggled free and threw her arms round my neck and kissed me.

She cried out, "I have missed you, how could I have missed you? I don't know you." I encircled her in my arms holding her tight so she couldn't escape. "And why are you home, did I just say home? Why are you here so early?"

"I missed you too. I have wanted you all day," I responded.

"Jesus, Richard you haven't stopped having me, you've had me every which way," she yelled at me her face bright.

"And Jesus Christ what the hell did you do to me this morning I've been bloody wet all day. I couldn't concentrate. I couldn't stop smiling. The shoot director was angry, shouting and yelling. He nearly got the bloody hammer I was holding banged onto his head."

I gaily laughed, Margaret gaily laughed we hugged and I swung her round. We fell onto the morning's settee minus its cover, her body resting in my arms. "I had to scrub the cover after you left our juices left a great big stain." I kissed her head, followed by lifting her face to kiss her lips. "Stop Richard, stop, stop," she cried out.

"We have to slow down," she groaned. "You're insatiable I can't take much more." She lifted her skirt. "Feel I'm bloody dripping wet." I pushed her panties crutch to one side and slipped two fingers into her wet vagina. "You see what I mean. Jesus, take me to bed and get on with it."

We climbed the stairs stripped and fell into bed laughing. Jolly Roger was ready. Margaret straddled him and moaned. I thrust up, she drove down, and we were off once more driving crazily into each other. I swung her beneath me lifted her legs and pushed them back and rammed hard. She shrieked. I pounded until she screamed and screamed and was again slapping me her teeth imbedded into my shoulder. My sperm shot into her and I yelled. Margaret's leg banged onto my shoulders her body crumpled and she wailed.

I looked at her. The radiance from her face illuminated the bedroom. Her eyes were bright and her smile beamed warmth. I eased my body next to hers and cuddled her close. After a short silence she said "Tonight's the last night isn't it?" I thought, tomorrow would be Thursday my flight was booked for late afternoon. I confirmed tonight was the last night.

After a few minutes I said "I could stay over until Sunday providing I can get a flight" She said "You know where the telephone is".

I searched my gear for my flight tickets. I called the airline requesting a flight change. It cost fifteen pounds but I managed to get a seat on Sunday's late flight, departing at six-twenty. Margaret was in the kitchen. I walked in behind Margaret and encircled her in my arms. Kissed her head and said "I will be here until three Sunday afternoon." She turned and kissed me.

Turning her face up to look at me she asked, "What happens after Sunday?" I didn't respond. She continued, "Am I forgotten, just another woman you managed to bed?" I shook my head. "Of course not," I answered. "I'll give you my details; whenever you are in England call and I will meet you."

"Are you married, maybe engaged or at least a steady girl?" she queried.

"No, not married, not engaged, nor a steady girlfriend but I do meet one or two girls from time to time." She laughed loudly and kissed me. "So I become one of many who must wait for the man to choose from his Harem, wonderful, I really feel special."

All I could think was "why does life become so complicated". I said, "Listen Margaret I am here because I fancied you, remember? I am also here because I am different and because I am all those things you said, mature, sensuous, caring, loving etc. We did not commit to everlasting love, we committed to making love. I didn't try to court you I simply suggested we could go to bed."

"I know," she yelled at me. "I know, for Christ's sake I know. I want a drink, get me a drink" I went to the cocktail cabinet lifted the brandy bottle and a glass and returned to the kitchen. Margaret was leaning against the work surface. I poured a glass for her. "Where's yours?" she demanded. "I am fine thanks," I replied.

We wandered through to the living room, sitting on a settee. Margaret sipped her brandy. She whispered, "The shoot's finished. I am not needed until next Wednesday when I've a booking for sexy underwear for three days. I will be available for you to grind away at until you leave on Sunday."

"Ha-ha, very funny. I am not into "grinding away" unless the other person wants to grind away. Probably, to stop any unnecessary pain or hurtful words, I'll move back into the hotel and re-arrange my flight. There is no point in continuing if either one of us is going to regret what has happened, or what may happen."

Margaret put her glass down and forced herself into my arms. "I am sorry Richard I am being bitchy. I can't help it. You have broken down my barrier, passed beyond arm's length. My heart feels. I cannot control its feelings. It cries for you, it wants you." I reciprocated her cuddle holding her in my arms.

"And," she said sitting upright, "I have been excited, thrilled and I have gloried in the sex we have shared and I want more. Therefore you stay here and we grind together, you love me and I will love you," she laughed and cried and laughed, tears flowed down her cheeks.

I pulled her back into my arms. I whispered, "Margaret I am sorry I didn't expect to hurt your feelings and I certainly did not intend to break down any barriers I simply looked at you and fancied you. I thought, perhaps wrongly, we were both free agents free to enjoy a few days and nights and move on."

Her head buried in my chest Margaret said, "Do you know Richard, you are a bastard and you don't know you are. You adore women and therefore you think if you target one and she agrees to go to bed with you, all is fine. Well it's not, women have feelings, feelings a damn sight more real and relevant than a man's."

Her voice very quiet she resumed, "Men on the whole are unemotional- - they only want to fuck, have sex. Women do of course have sexual urges but they know they are able to choose a man have her way and move on, the man is happy and the woman is happy."

Margaret moved her head to look into my eyes. "But a man like you comes along who is all the things I said, totally different from the run of the mill and a woman's emotions, my emotions go haywire. How many women out there have you hurt, given them a few days loving and moved on leaving them agonising over who they are, not knowing why they have failed, not realising they haven't failed only that Richard the Bastard has passed through their life. You don't know do you, you don't know how many hearts you have broken. You see you really are a bastard."

Forcing herself to sit straight she held my face in her hands saying, "You are different and you honestly don't know what you do to women. Christ, look at you, you are handsome, rugged, perfectly formed and you do have an open heart but open for the wrong reasons, you break hearts."

I felt very uncomfortable, very guilty. In fact, I selfishly started to feel sorry for myself. I was arguing internally, the good side saying Margaret's right, you are a bastard. The bad side saying she's wrong you have always been honest telling the women you are not available except for sex. Bloody hell what a mess, here I sit in Margaret's apartment being exposed for what I actually am, a low-life. I couldn't think of one good thing to say in my defence.

Margaret could feel my indecision and my guilt, she could feel my discomfort. She said "Richard its fine, we will continue together having magical sex for the next four nights and probably days too, after which we move on. I have come to terms with my emotions, they are under control. Now pour me another brandy and get one for yourself and afterwards we will go and get a fish-supper, your treat."

I did her bidding. While I found a glass for myself and poured the brandy Margaret put a record on the player. Tubular Bells by Mike Oldfield filled the room. We sat close together sipping the brandies listening, there wasn't, for the moment, anything else to say.

We walked down the street to purchase two fish suppers, shared a bottle of wine, and enjoyed the warmth returning into our relationship. We went to bed and we loved, very tenderly we loved. We lay connected for long periods enjoying the feel. Every now and again I would have to move to keep Jolly Roger interested but on the whole we didn't grind, we gently loved.

The following afternoon after I left site leaving Jimmy to complete the works, ostensibly to fly back to Southampton, I returned to Margaret's apartment with a huge bunch of roses, one dozen each of red, white and yellow and a card expressing care and love.

Margaret was back to normal her throaty laughter resonating. We both smiled and laughed. I took her out to dinner, she dressed lovingly, and limited in choice I wore grey slacks and an open neck shirt.

The following nights and days were hell bent of making love. Margaret determined to substantiate her love of sex and together we wallowed.

We refused to permit time to interrupt we both wanted to cherish every moment. We loved and loved, we experienced electrifying orgasms, we rejoiced in the sensationalism of fornication. Together we climbed mountains, dived deep into oceans and floated high in the sky, immersed in pure self-satisfaction, encountering spasm after spasm of pleasure.

Sunday afternoon arrived, the ordered taxi waiting downstairs and I saddened. I hugged Margaret for one last time running my hands down to her marvellously moulded buttocks. I wanted to say a hundred words, a thousand words but she, the intelligent one, the adult one pressed her fingers to my lips.

Margaret, sitting holding my hand in the taxi, accompanied me to the airport, we passionately kissed goodbye. Sitting aboard the aeroplane knowing Margaret would become a very loving memory I felt sad. I recalled her words describing a bastard, Richard Chambers.

Although permanently scarred on my shoulders and particularly on my back and questioned unremittingly, I parade the scars proud I had been loved and I had loved Margaret.

Chapter 23 - Back to Real Life

Monday morning back in Southampton I attended meeting after meeting listening to this report and that problem. I worked late into the night. A ton of paperwork required attention, reading, comment, notes and responses were necessary.

All day I thought of Margaret, I thought of Carol, and Debbie and woman after woman. I re-visited the Cotswolds with Ruth, I boarded the barge on the Thames with Sally, I made love to Sophie and I remembered faces, or was it sex, I didn't know. I decided it all had to stop, how?

How to stop? How to change direction? I considered who Richard Chambers really was and who he should be. I thought of Catriona, and of Sam in cold Whickham. Christine took charge, encapsulating my mind. I envisaged her striking beauty her stunning red hair, her beautiful face. I knew then where my future lay. However, I had to close the book, which included Catriona and Sam.

I tried again to re-contact with Christine. I was definitely in her bad books and I couldn't think how to remedy the situation. Working late in the office, I thought, rather stupidly, "up you girl" and took another long weekend. No one argued with my extra weekends the whole company knew I rarely took leave and worked the longest hours. I drove my new car to Newcastle. I had decided to search out Sam.

It was after six in the evening when I arrived. Father's house was in darkness. I left the car and walked to the pub. Sure enough he and Tina were in their corner. They were surprised to see me. Father said, "The wanderer returns. How were your travels?"

I shook his proffered hand and hugged Tina. Dulcie and Chas followed me in. Chas bought me a beer. I described my travels and the incredible work we had completed. Father was very interested the others listened politely.

I asked after Johnny and the rest of father's men before asking about Catriona and Sam. Tina answered on behalf of Catriona saying she was still off men. As for Sam she hadn't been seen for a few days.

Tina quietly pushed me trying to discover if I had designs on Sam. I denied any interest saying I was only asking after the few people I knew in Newcastle. Father asked about Debbie to which I shrugged.

I told father I had sold the bike and purchased a car. I spoke highly of my new car describing how years earlier Simon Templar played by Roger Moore, the Saint from the television series had driven one.

It didn't ring any bells so I gave up. I said I was hungry and would have something to eat asking the company if they wanted to join me, keeping my fingers crossed they would refuse, which they did.

I thought let's have a go at Catriona. She came to meet me greeting me with a gorgeous smile. She said, "It's Richard isn't it, Dick's son."

I nodded saying, "And you are?"

She smiled. "Catriona."

"Unusual name, Spanish, Italian….?" I queried knowing damn well it was Irish. She didn't answer until I was sitting at a corner table. "Irish, my heritage is from Cork albeit my mother and father are second generation."

She offered a menu, which I declined saying, "A medium rare fillet without chips or vegetables and a side salad would be fine, and oh yes a glass of house red and a glass of tap water." She smiled and hurried away. I watched her hips sway away into the kitchen. She came back with the wine and water.

Expressing my best smile I said, "You're a gorgeous-looking girl." I was seeking a reaction. I very nearly got a glass of water in my face, not the reaction I was looking for. Instead she said, "We do not fraternise with customers," turned and marched away her hips near static. I had my reaction.

The steak and salad were served, which I took an inordinate length of time to eat. I kept my eyes on Catriona, and she knew I watched her every move. I waited patiently to order an Irish coffee when she came and cleared the table. She looked at me saying, "You are a very silly boy and don't think I haven't noticed you watching me. I think you are rude, immature and a disgrace to your father who is a gentleman."

I reached for her hand. She pulled away. I said, "Boy? I don't think so; immature? Quite possibly; as for being a disgrace to my father, I most probably am. However, I am male and you are female and extremely attractive. I am therefore attracted towards you. I would suspect I am not the first nor will I be the last to identify you are a gorgeous looking girl. If I have upset you I sincerely regret my actions and apologise unreservedly." She gave me a curious look saying, "I'll get your Irish Coffee."

While waiting, I extracted one of my business cards from my wallet. On the reverse side I wrote, *"This is my home number. If you ever feel you would like to talk please telephone, but not until after nine. Richard"*

Catriona served my Irish Coffee and accepted my card, which she slipped into her apron pocket. When I called for the bill she slipped a piece of folded paper into my hand. She whispered, "Read it later." The bill paid, I re-joined father and Tina.

Later in bed I opened the note, which said *"If you feel like talking call me after eleven thirty Thursday, Friday and Saturdays. Alternatively telephone any morning between seven and nine. I have a two and a half year old son. Catriona"*

I waited a week before I called her. I was in my office checking through the previous month's management accounts when I glanced at my watch.

For some reason I thought of Catriona. I took her note from my wallet and dialled her number.

A female voice, certainly not Catriona's said, "Yes who is this?" I asked to speak to Catriona. The voice in a venomous tone said, "There's some man on the phone."

"Hello, Catriona speaking."

"Hello Catriona," I said. "I feel like talking." In a business voice she said, "Oh yes Mr Chambers I haven't forgotten, could you call back after midday." I said I would and hung up.

I considered the circumstances regarding Catriona deciding the distance was too great, she had a toddler and any relationship could become messy. I chose not to telephone her.

However, she called me. Reception rang through advising a Mrs Catriona Buchanan was on the line. "Hello Catriona did I call at an inconvenient time?"

She replied, "Yes and no. Unfortunately my mother had called round to take me shopping."

"Sorry," I said.

"Not your fault," her instant response.

She asked me what Southampton was like, was it a big city, did it have theatres and nightclubs and good shopping. She asked what a General Manager of a ship repair business did, plus many other questions, some genuine inquisitiveness, some conversation fillers.

Her last question was, "When are you visiting Dick again?"

I swiftly answered, "If you want to meet me I'll be in Whickham late Friday night." "This Friday?" she asked "Yes this Friday," I responded.

"Yes I would like to meet," she stated.

"Okay I'll telephone you Saturday morning."

Catriona replied, "I look forward to your call, goodbye." Before I could respond she hung up.

It was gone seven before I drove away from the office Friday evening. My case on the back seat I manoeuvred my way through the Friday night traffic heading for London. Heavy traffic on the south and north circular roads slowed progress.

Finally getting onto the M1, I cruised at eighty MPH joined the A1 also heavy with traffic, getting snarled up south of Nottingham, again at Doncaster and I hit the daddy of them all at York. It was close to three in the morning when I silently let myself in to father's house and fell into bed.

Father shook me at ten-thirty we a mug of coffee. He said, "Tina thinks you have made headway with Catriona. Have you?"

"I don't know she rang Tuesday and here I am," I replied.

"Richard," the tone suggested lecture time. "You have to learn how keep control of your urges, you can't spend your life seeking out women scattered all over the country just to prove your manhood. It is about time you settled on one woman and sorted your life out. And when are you going to visit your mother she is worried about you and annoyed with your constant womanising."

I thought for a moment, "Father, I am not sure I am ready to settle. I have too much to do and too much too see, and my work keeps me pretty much tied-up twenty four, seven." He shook his big old head and left me alone.

After a shower, shave and dressed in fashionable jeans and a smart checked shirt I left the house to locate a telephone kiosk. I called Catriona. Following polite conversation she asked if I could find Birtley.

Having persuaded her I could she gave me directions off of the A167 into a residential area. It didn't take long to locate her semi-detached house. I learnt later she owned half and her estranged husband the other half.

She opened the door with her son holding her hand. She introduced me to Fergus who solemnly shook my hand. Catriona wore jeans and a loose shirt. Her face was free of make-up. I tried to gauge her age giving up when I realised the target ranged between eighteen and twenty-eight.

I attempted to play with Fergus; however he kept his distance holding onto his mother's legs. Sitting at a small table in the kitchen she briefly explained, without detail, her husband's absence. I didn't comment. She appeared to be extremely nervous. For a while we made unintelligent small-talk until becoming bored I said, "Why don't we go somewhere, you tell me where and we will go."

Catriona after first calling the pub, to report in sick, suggested Whitley Bay. I remembered passing through astride the Bonneville a few months earlier. A typical seaside town with a funfair, lots of open green areas and a very sandy beach.

Fergus had his favourite ball, which he and I played football with. I bought him an ice-lolly and a small tube of Smarties. We clambered down to the beach where I took off my shoes and socks pulled up my jeans to just below the knees and waded into the water with Fergus sitting on my shoulders. He screeched and yelled, calling his mother to come in the water.

Fair play to Catriona she removed her shoes and rolled her jeans up and waded in. We kick-splashed each other, both laughing, encouraging Fergus to shout and giggle, even more. Soaked from the waist down we retreated to the sand to lie in the sun. Fergus enjoyed himself throwing his ball into my face and onto my stomach.

Partially dry we brushed the sand off and walked towards the fun fair. We stopped off at a little café and spoilt Fergus with cream cake and a milky chocolate drink. His mother and I selected sandwiches and a pot of tea.

After the food we rode on all the rides suitable for toddlers, of which there were many. Catriona became upset because of the money I was spending. For the first time I put my arm round her pulling her into my arms telling her not to concern herself.

In my arms, momentarily, forgetting herself, she lifted her face for a kiss. Abruptly she had a change of mind not wanting to commit to this strange man who had suddenly weakened her defences.

Fergus, as we slowly meandered back to the car fell asleep over my shoulder. He had missed his afternoon nap. Catriona, lost in her son's enjoyment held my free hand. I held the door and watched her clamber into the very small rear seat before passing the sleeping toddler into her arms. Fergus opened his eyes for a moment; however, once settled in his mother's clasp he soon returned to sleep. I drove steadily not to disturb him.

Once in Catriona's house Fergus once more burst into life. He and I went into the garden to play catch-ball, his mother watching from the window. For a while I pushed him on the garden swing and played aeroplanes. Every now and again I would discreetly glance towards his mother. Her face radiantly happy seeing her son playing with a substitute father.

Catriona served minced meat, potatoes and peas for supper apologising for serving baby food. I thought the supper delicious and emphasised my contentment. Together we bathed Fergus, flooding the bathroom. In bed he demanded I should read to him, which after he had decided upon his favourite story, about dragons and princesses, I read until he closed his eyes and fell into an innocent sleep.

Catriona once more apologised, this time for not having any wine or beer. I found myself trying to convince her that I was not an alcoholic and only drank on occasion. She made a mug of tea before seating herself on the settee, her thigh touching mine. I could feel her body heat and I wanted so much to pull her into my arms and cuddle her.

However, I refrained eventually saying, "It's time I was off, we don't want your neighbours talking." She searched for my hand and held it tight. She thanked me for a wonderful day and for the attention I had given Fergus. I wanted her badly but I remained stoic not wanting to challenge her defences.

I stood ready to leave. Still holding my hand Catriona stood with me. She whispered, "Richard I would like you to stay a little while longer."

She moved to draw the curtains, turn off the overhead lights and switch on a table lamp.

I was still standing when she walked into my arms. She said, "Just a cuddle that is all I ask." I held her in my arms kissing the top of her head. Her arms were wrapped round my waist and she was holding onto me, not wanting me to leave.

She lowered to the settee pulling me down with her. She snuggled into my arms. Lifting her head she offered herself to be kissed. We slowly moved towards each other, both hesitant before our lips connected. Her lips firmly on mine her arms encircled my neck forcing her tongue into my mouth. I gently nibbled her tongue.

I could feel her body temperature rising. She took my hand and placed it on her breast. Tenderly I massaged her breast searching for her nipple. She sat up and removed her bra. Her shirt unbuttoned gave me access to her nipples, they were erect and hard, I gently sucked them.

Her hands were pulling my head into her bosom. I alternated between nipples when she began, very quietly, to moan. I lifted my head and looking at her I said, "Catriona you don't have to do this. It would probably be best if I go. I don't want you waking-up in the morning feeling full of guilt." She came to her senses pulling her shirt closed.

Sitting up she smiled, "I am sorry I didn't mean to upset you."

"You haven't I loved every moment and I would love to take your naked body into my arms but I don't want to leave you feeling remorseful," I quietly replied.

"You wouldn't, I am old enough to make my own decisions and I know I want you," she quickly replied.

I leaned forward and kissed her. Catriona responded with ardent passion. My hands rediscovered her breasts. I removed her shirt and forcing her to stand I unzipped her jeans slipping my hand in to press against her vagina. She pushed her vagina against my hand. After a moment she reached for my hand leading me to the stairs and up into her bedroom. Her finger was on her lips signalling quiet.

She closed the curtains enveloping the room in darkness. I could just make outline of her body as she stripped her clothes off. I followed quickly disrobing and climbing into bed. She rolled into my arms.

I could feel her shyness and uncertainty. I tenderly stroked her hair, her very long hair that reminded me so much of Ruth. I softly touched her using my finger tips to travel the contours of her body.

Catriona was running her hand over my chest and stomach. I sensed she wanted to feel lower but was restraining, waiting until I moved to further explore, waiting for me to take the lead.

I tenderly touched her vagina gently running my fingers around her labia lips. She unconsciously opened her legs. I carefully pushed her onto her back and positioned myself to suck and lick her vagina. Her legs lifted.

As my tongue darted into the entrance of her moist vagina she stifled a squeal. With both hands she was pushing my head down and responding to my pressure by forcing her hips up to meet my tongue.

She whispered "Please now, Richard I need you now." I moved above her. She felt for fully erect Jolly Roger her hands gripped him and she gasped. Her legs opened wider as she guided him into her vagina. Whispering she said "Gently Richard, it has been a long time."

She lifted her legs high and I gradually very, very gradually eased Jolly Roger into Catriona's vagina. Although she was wet Jolly Roger was finding entry difficult. She asked me to stop and hold still.

Catriona quietly whispered "Try again but gentle please, very gentle." I eased forward a fraction feeling her tense. I stopped and withdrew. She threw herself into my arms and cried for forgiveness. I gentle hugged Catriona whispering not to worry and I understood. "You are so big, my vagina felt as if it was tearing. Oh Richard what shall we do?" she pleaded "We cuddle and hug and kiss that is what we do and if you want to we try once more but only once more."

I tenderly caressed Catriona's soft body. I asked if I could put the light on to look at her beauty. She was very reticent but succumbed to my request. I jumped from the bed and switched on the light. Catriona was holding the sheets to hide her nudity I smiled and gently pulled the bed covers away from her. She was highly embarrassed, which I couldn't comprehend.

I leaned over and kissed her nipples and ran my tongue over her tummy. I began in a reassuring voice to explain her beauty. I started to kiss her toes telling her they were perfectly sized and that her feet were dainty and attractive. I gently held her ankle describing how it elegantly tapered.

I ran my tongue over both her legs not leaving any part untouched. I said how slim and graceful they were, delicate to touch. I described her body musk as sexy and demanding. Her tummy and hips I eloquently defined to be explicitly curved to express her loveliness.

I returned to her thighs and tenderly opened her legs running my tongue between her mid-thigh to her vagina, flicking my tongue inside for a brief moment before my tongue continued on its journey down the inside of her opposite thigh.

Catriona began to writhe.

Encouraged I returned to her vagina and manoeuvred my tongue onto her very small clitoris. I tickled the clitoris swirling my tongue around and around. She began to moan holding her hand over her mouth. I could feel her begin an orgasm her clitoris reacting sending gently tremors through her loins. Suddenly she grasped my head and forced her thighs against my head. A delightful little squeal broke free from her lips.

Catriona forced me to rise above and re-enter her vagina. I positioned myself ready when she jumped off the bed and out of the door. She was back in a trice. She passed me a plastic bottle of baby cream.

I squeezed a handful and smeared it liberally over my penis and her vagina, tenderly easing the cream inside. Catriona was reacting to the movement of my fingers, I continued gentle manipulations. She clamped her thighs hard onto my hand and murmured a very quiet "Ohhhhhh".

I moved above her and guided my penis towards her vagina. Her legs opened and I began to push. Jolly Roger slowly entered. Gradually I pushed, her vagina giving way, until deep inside. Catriona lifted her hips, lowered and pushed upwards hard. She emitted a gasp and moaned "Agh." She whispered, "Richard it's so deep." Her legs started to shake vibrating against my sides.

She was lost, her body not knowing how to react, one minute she was driving her hips up, and then she was twisting from side to side. Suddenly she was saying, "Oh no, oh no." Her legs were wide. I could feel the mixture of her body juices and the cream squishing from her vagina.

I began to drive harder. Her legs lifted and her arms pulled on my shoulders. Her head began to thrash. She urgently squealed trying to speak. I slowed listening to her. I interpreted she didn't want me not to come inside her.

I reactivated my drives into her. She tensed and yelled trying hard to stifle her cries. I pulled Jolly Roger out in the nick of time my sperm shot out in a long stream across her thighs and on her tummy.

Catriona kissed me and laughed she kept saying, "Incredible, incredible, I feel wonderful, wonderful, oh so wonderful." Her thighs and tummy were thick with my sperm; she started rubbing the sperm all over her body, over her breasts and on her tummy and up to her throat. She licked her fingers, which sent a shiver down my spine. Catriona couldn't stop laughing. She began to rub her sperm covered body against me. She forced her tongue into my mouth, nibbling at my lips.

Catriona was in ecstasy, and in a very frolicsome mood. Her son, for a few moments forgotten, she, for once wanted to savour her own pleasure and she did. Eventually she began to calm, her hand covered her mouth. Her eyes were shining bright and she had a smile a mile wide.

Jumping from the bed her nakedness no longer an embarrassment she placed her finger on my lips, opened the bedroom door and pulled me across the landing into the bathroom. We showered together albeit it wasn't easy with Catriona holding on to me but we managed.

We carried the towels into the bedroom where we dried. She pushed me onto the bed and started to kiss and lick Jolly Roger. He jumped smartly to attention. She forced her mouth over the end and sucked. How she sucked, an expert.

Jolly Roger's head was all that gained entry into her mouth. However, she had, using her hands expertly, perfected a wringing motion, which combined with her soft and tender mouth constantly sucking, swiftly brought Jolly Roger to a state of climax.

I warned her but she didn't care I exploded, she gagged forcing the sperm to dribble out of her mouth down her chin and on to her breasts. Catriona was enjoying, she was alive and feeling free. She started giggling and laughing falling across me and rolling her body all over me and the bed.

To this day I do believe the release she had when we made love freed her from a torment she held deep inside. Perhaps a torment caused by her husband leaving her, which left her feeling guilty because inside she blamed herself. I am convinced the sex freed her from anguish or suffering, languishing deep inside for far too long.

We returned to the bathroom and showered once more. In the bedroom Catriona was all smiles. She kept touching, running her hands over my body, seeking out and feeling my muscles. She kissed me all over, not once but many times. Finally she lay still nestled into my arms.

She started talking rapidly wanting desperately to bear her soul. "Shamus, my darling husband left me for a girl of eighteen. I know her, her mother a friend of my mother. She's pretty but not overly intelligent. She also has a reputation for being too forward with boys. He is a hotel manager. He received a promotion without informing me and moved south, Lincoln I think, to manage a larger hotel taking her with him. I haven't heard from him since. That happened seventeen months ago. If it wasn't for my parents I would have been evicted. They until I could find the money paid my mortgage. I now have three jobs and mother looks after Fergus for me. I will not give up this house and my solicitor is positive I will not have to as long as I pay the mortgage because his absence will in time allow me full ownership. Although the solicitor did say my husband could turn up and demand his fifty percent, all of which I find confusing."

I had to admit I found it confusing, although I didn't say so, I did think that as long as his name is on the deeds, legally he owned his share of the house.

Very quietly she whispered, her tone reflecting guilt, "Richard could you please go home. I would prefer Fergus didn't find you here in the morning." I accepted her request and started to dress. She said, "Please come again tomorrow, we can have lunch. I'll cook."

Father was shaking me smiling and saying, "It's eleven don't you have any plans for today, if not lunch is on me."

"Father thanks but a certain young lady is cooking for me." He guessed Catriona. Swiftly I showered, shaved (I hate shaving) and of course dressed and sped over to Catriona.

As I emerged from the car, she opened the door, hands on hips wearing a sexy little yellow mini-skirt and green blouse. I noticed she wasn't wearing tights.

As I neared the door Fergus rushed into my legs. I lifted and swung him high in the air he shrieked. Back in my arms I pretended to drop him enforcing shrieks and giggles. I held him by his ankle his head inches from the floor. He pulled this way and that trying to climb my leg. I lifted him and gave him a big old hug. His little arms went round my neck, giggling he rubbed his nose against mine.

Grabbing his ball he held my hand and dragged me through the house and into the garden. He wanted to play football. I picked the ball up and tucking it under my arm I tried to play rugby with him. He kicked my shin accusing me of cheating, so we played football.

Catriona feeling left out came into the garden, it became two versus one. Catriona jumped on my back, which initiated a charge round the garden with her hanging on for dear life. We were all laughing and shouting.

I dipped down and grabbed Fergus under my right arm and charged faster. Catriona slipped off landing on her bottom her legs akimbo I ran over and dropped Fergus onto her. They rolled in the damp grass, mother and son pretend wrestling. Catriona was so immersed in the fun she was oblivious to the expanse of white panties and thigh she was displaying, the dark hair protecting her vagina exhibiting a delightful shadow.

I gripped her hand pulling her to her feet. She automatically fell into my arms and kissed me hard. She suddenly remembered Fergus turning to swoop down and lift him up into her arms and kiss him to.

Catriona suggested lemonade, which encouraged a cheer from Fergus. Catriona made a dash for the house I caught her and threw her high, she was as light as a feather dropping into my arms, laughing and screeching she wriggled free.

Fergus thinking he was missing out wanted to be an aeroplane. I grabbed his arm and leg and swung him round and round. His mother looking young and very happy smiled direct into my eyes. She pursed her lips blowing me a kiss.

Catriona poured the lemonade and gave Fergus a miniature bar of chocolate. He parked himself on the floor and had his own private picnic Catriona took the opportunity to lovingly kiss me whispering "I want you now."

She laughed out loud saying, "I will just have to wait." For lunch she had prepared roast chicken, roast potatoes, Yorkshire pudding, broccoli and carrots with thick gravy. I carved the chicken.

I chopped Fergus's chicken and vegetables into manageable bite-size mouthfuls leaving him to tuck in. For a toddler he was good hardly making a mess. I remembered the mess, during in breakfast, Jessica's son, James made throwing his food everywhere except into his mouth.

Fergus was made comfortable in his special armchair watching cartoons on television until he dozed off. Meanwhile I helped Catriona wash-up. Checking Fergus was sound asleep Catriona guided me upstairs. She pulled her panties down and produced a tube of K-Y jelly, which she passed to me.

She also passed me a packet of condoms saying she would be on the pill by the time we next met. I tenderly pushed her onto her back and massaged the jelly into her vagina and onto my penis. While I massaged she looked into my eyes, smiling.

I pulled her to the edge of the bed giving her a condom to fit over Jolly Roger. Jolly Roger unaccustomed as he was to wearing an overcoat allowed Catriona to complete her administrations before he gently tested her vagina for easy entry.

Satisfied I turned her onto her knees and drove Jolly Roger deep into her. I wasn't holding back. She shrieked then laughed and stage whispered "Oh Richard, push as deep as you can"

I held onto her hips and pulled Catriona hard towards me driving forward with every pull. She moaned and squealed. I needed to take my pleasure and I did pumping in and out as far as I could. The harder I rammed the harder I pulled Catriona onto me.

She pulled a bed cover into her mouth. I rammed faster and faster until I was ready to explode, I stopped for a second to feel my sperm move along the shaft and then I rammed the final drive home and sighed with pleasure holding Catriona hard against me.

She didn't climax but she did love the feel of me inside her getting pleasure knowing I had climaxed. We cuddled for a while before swiftly cleaning ourselves and washing the condom down the loo.

We descended the stairs to catch Fergus fighting to climb out of his chair. I lifted him and he punched me on the forehead. He started crying. My forehead was too tough for his little fist. In an attempt to quieten his hysterics I said we would go to a park.

We loaded into the car and drove to Chester le Street to visit one of his favourite parks. Catriona made herself comfortable sitting on a bench to watch her lover and her son play on the rides, and play chase, and generally fool around. Catriona was very happy and I was pleased for her.

233

It was a very tired little boy we put to bed just before eight. I read for a while but he quickly closed his eyes and slept. Catriona and I made ourselves comfortable on the settee talking about Fergus and his mother's dreams for his education. She wanted so much for him to have private tuition. However, she realised she probably wouldn't earn sufficient money to see her dream come true.

Catriona wanted to know exactly what my work entailed. I emphasised a tough work environment where I could spend six months or more travelling. I exaggerated a wee bit with regards the travelling in the hope it would deter her from seeking a long-term relationship, which I certainly didn't want.

Catriona, later in the bedroom, disrobed the few clothes she was wearing without the concern she had displayed the evening before. She was quite happy to let me admire her body. She rushed to the bathroom and rushed back telling me it was my turn and to hurry up. Using her toothbrush I was thinking how tight she had been and hoped to experience a similar feeling, which, as to be expected, had Jolly Roger standing firm.

Jolly Roger inched passed the bedroom door followed by his master albeit I was never quite sure who ruled whom.

Catriona waiting pounced on me putting my neck in an arm-hold. She wrestled me onto the bed and sat astride guiding Jolly Roger minus condom into her wet and creamy vagina. He went straight in all the way. She jumped up and down whispering and chuckling, "This is the best ride of all better than any roller-coaster I know."

Whether it was because I would be leaving to head south at midnight or whether she wanted to show me she cared, I don't know but she threw all caution to the wind. I didn't I made sure I wore a condom both times we made love. I showered and dressed before she came down stairs with me.

She gave me a flask of coffee and a Tupperware box with sandwiches and biscuits neatly packed inside. We sat on the settee cuddling and whispering, Catriona demanding to know when I would return to the north east. My answer revolved around forthcoming overseas trips and workload. She wasn't too pleased I couldn't give a precise date. At the door she held onto me making me promise to return the first weekend I had free.

The drive south proved traffic free and the weather held I made good time arriving at the flat just after five-forty. There were seven messages on the answering machine of which two were from Catriona. One from an irate mother, one from Carol wanting to know why I didn't answer her calls, one from Gertie inviting me to a show-business do, someone selling double glazing and the last, the important one from Charlotte, Christine's sister, verbally slating me off for upsetting her sister.

I forced my tired body under the shower, washed down, shaved and dressed for work. I drove down towards the docks heading for Sid's Café to enjoy a full breakfast. A couple of the guys were in following an all-nighter. I joined them and listened to a few gripes and a couple of new jokes. The guy's jokes were always good but buggered if I could remember them. For someone proud of his retentive memory I was a poor excuse when it came to jokes.

I was first in the office busy working, hearing but ignoring the background noise of people arriving for work. Janet, my girl Friday served a mug of coffee and plonked a two foot pile of documents and mail, and paperwork on my desk. I grimaced, she smiled and I said, "Thanks Janet, so nice to see you and such lovely gifts."

It was nearly eleven-thirty when I finished reading, making notes, dictating to Janet necessary responses and signed off leave requests and other mundane paperwork. I walked to Christine's office, shooed out one of her team, and closed the door saying, "We need to talk".

I was totally ignored she carried on doing whatever she was doing. "Okay, I'll talk and you listen." Still no response. I tried again. "Charlotte called me." Christine's head shot up her gorgeous red hair bobbling around her shoulders.

She didn't speak just looked at me with her beautiful light blue eyes. She was emotionless. I thought right, "cards on the table". "Christine I am very fond of you and you know I am. However, we are not a courting couple we are two close friends who on occasion enjoy each other's company. I have never lied to you or made any promises."

I might as well be talking to the wall but I had started and I was going to finish. "Nonetheless, as I sit here looking into your lovely eyes I will make a promise to you."

I smiled without any glimmer of a response, I leaned forward in the chair and whispered "Christine my promise is this, *"On the first of September I will ask you to be my steady girlfriend. I hope you and I will become a couple, lovers and I also hope we will look to the future, together."* She stood up and ordered me out of her office, tail between my legs I departed.

In my office I wrote a letter addressed to Christine:

Dearest Christine,
6th August 1973
I do not proffer any apology for upsetting you with my promise.
Today is 6th August 1973 in exactly twenty-five days on the 1st September 1973 I will fulfil my promise.

The reason for the delay is personal and relative to other people. In other words I am obliged to put my house in order, which I will do within the given period.

Meanwhile please be aware that I am very fond of you and have been for a long time. However, I resisted becoming too close for several reasons, which one day I will explain. Until that day comes I ask you to trust in my commitment to reveal all, which sounds pretentious I know. I promise you, second promise today I am not in the least bit pretentious when it comes to you. I care too much.

I will fulfil my promise.

Love

Richard

I read it through two or three times until satisfied. I placed it and envelope and walked from the office to a nearby post office purchased a stamp and posted the letter.

CHAPTER 24 – Twenty Five Days

Perchance on the evening of the "letter-day" I received a call from Carol. She explained she was going to visit her parents for a few days before flying off to Athens with two girlfriends for a holiday prior to going-up to university. She asked me to take her out to dinner. I was pleased to have the honour and told her so.

I collected her early at five-thirty from her soon to be ex-flat and whizzed her to a hotel in Brockenhurst where I had booked a room. I had heard the food and wine was excellent. In the boot of the car I loaded a case filled with a pair of jeans and a blouse, panties and tights I had purchased. I hoped they would fit her and clean work clothes for myself, plus washing gear and two tooth brushes.

On arrival I escorted Carol into the bar. She looked fantastic as she always did. I seated her at a table kissed her cheek and ordered a bottle of champagne. A sommelier came to the table to discuss champagne. I chose a 1966 Bollinger R.D. I excused myself to spend a penny. I rushed to reception and checked in leaving my car keys and a pound to have the case transferred to the room.

When I returned the sommelier was patiently waiting for me. I tasted the champagne and nodded my approval. I toasted Carol's holiday and her upcoming return to education. She was in a bubbly mood pleased to have made the decision to return to studying. We remembered the first night we had met, the times we made love and the numerous dinners we had shared. The Maître D' came to greet us and advise the table was ready.

The sommelier delivered the final two glasses of champagne remaining behind the waiter as we selected from the menu. Carol asked me to choose for her. I selected crab cakes flavoured with ginger and coriander, I also ordered flavoursome lamb chops, cooked in chopped fresh mint, garlic cloves, ground cumin and cayenne pepper served with potato croquettes and roasted vegetables. I chose six oysters and a lamb shank for myself.

The sommelier replaced the waiter. I asked for his recommendation. With the starters he recommended a glass of Château Caronne Sainte-Gemme. For the main course he described Chateau Lafite Rothschild as the ideal accompaniment. After conferring with Carol, I confirmed his recommendations.

I could tell Carol was excited by her trip to Athens, which she explained would be a holiday packed with tours to visit ancient civilisation sites and follow Greece's history through the centuries. Not exactly my cup of tea, although I assured her it would be both fun and interesting.

She made a point of asking how Maybury's shining star was doing and if he had risen any higher. She also wanted to know and pushed hard to get a truthful answer, how many women I had slept with during the past months.

I explained that the shining star remained stagnate at the moment but I did take the opportunity to elaborate the work we had astonishingly completed inside nineteen weeks including all my overseas travel.

Regarding women I had slept with, I told her that since I last had the pleasure of her in my bed I had only bedded one girl, an old friend. I emphasised that only the old friend had actually shared "my" bed. Not satisfied she demanded a definitive number. I told her I didn't know perhaps six, maybe ten or more.

Carol was in stitches, for some strange reason the number of conquests I bedded always fascinated her. She asked about the old friend, which when I gave Gertie's name she was once more in stitches. I also limited my liaison with Gertie to one night, which I remonstrated robustly was for old time's sake.

The hotel's restaurant lived up to its reputation. The cuisine, food and wine were exemplary. We absolutely enjoyed a fabulously prepared and cooked meal and the accompanying wines. For a while until we finished the bottle of wine the sommelier, I noticed hovered, waiting or possibly hoping for a digestif order, which he received when I ordered two Irish Coffees with double shots of whiskey.

Carol casually mentioned my comment regarding the old friend and making love for old time's sake. I was alert. "Richard, I want you to make love to me for one last time. I want it to be tender and memorable because I know we will not meet again. And I will tell you this you are the only guy I have, somewhat, been close to falling in love with, thank God I didn't, you would have broken my heart." I chose this moment to inform her I had provisionally booked a room at the hotel, adding I had packed a change of clothes, washing gear including a toothbrush.

Carol yelped, "Richard you are irredeemable there isn't another man on this planet remotely in your class. You are shameless, conceited, and pig-headed but yet, you are also absolutely gorgeous and you are a bloody bastard. You have, you bastard, once more talked my panties off, so what are we waiting for let's go."

Hand in hand we walked the stairs to the first floor. I located the room opened the door and chaperoned Carol in. She turned putting her arms round my neck saying, "Don't forget, loving and memorable. I am not a conquest, I am a very close friend saying goodbye."

I opened the case so she could inspect my purchases. After checking the sizes she seemed satisfied. Taking the washing gear she skipped to the bathroom giggling. I undressed to my boxers waiting to use the bathroom.

She walked out naked and I was immediately struck by her breath-taking beauty, a beauty I had always admired, but now she had filled out slightly presenting a slightly more voluptuous Carol and it suited her, suited her very much. She looked radiant and she knew it.

I rushed to the bathroom with an erect Jolly Roger leading the way. Carol flicked him as I passed. I expected to find her in bed but she was sitting in an armchair. She stood walked to meet me took my face in her hands and tenderly kissed my eyes and lips.

She whispered very quietly, "Love me Richard show me how much you can love, show me you have loved me." Her right leg twisted round my calf. I kissed her lips, her nose, her eyes, and nibbled her ears. I nibbled one side of her neck, and then the other. I felt her leg stiffen. I lifted her and very gently placed her on the bed.

I held her hands and kissed her, I nibbled Carol. I tickled her, brushing my lips gently across her breasts and tummy and thrilled her with my tongue. I only had one thing on my mind, pleasure Carol any which way I could. She was a beautiful gorgeous woman I wanted her to know she was beautiful and she was sexy and she was wanton. I explored every inch of her gorgeous body with lips, tongue and teeth.

I nuzzled and stroked, caressed and kissed. Jolly Roger was desperate dribbling from his meatus but nothing on this earth would deter me from what Carol had asked. I was so tender, so very tender. Twice I assaulted her clitoris bringing her to climax. She climaxed the moment I entered the first time. She was so wet Jolly Roger just went all the way with nil resistance.

He tenderly moved in and out of her always keeping pace with Carol's movements meeting her when she drove and slowing when she slowed. He held onto his sperm waiting until the lady demanded it, when she did he blasted into her. He didn't wilt he stayed on call, alert and ready.

After the first love-making we cuddled and dozed for a while. I recommenced my tender assault on Carol's body intent on making the second loving more spectacular. I re-explored and re-explored until she was pleading for me to enter her vagina. I did with a rush, withdrawing to drive in once more. I opened her legs, I lifted them high. I turned her body. I took her from behind I took her on her side. I lifted her onto the arm chair and moved her to sit astride me. I loved her as much as I had ever loved a woman before.

Throughout the night she squealed and moaned, sighed and screamed, cried and shrieked. I did everything I could think of, whether taught or learnt I did it to her, doing my utmost to ensure she was climaxing. I forced spasm after spasm through her body until she was trembling with such force I had to hold her tightly. Three times Jolly Roger exploded filling her with my sperm, yet she wanted more. I wasn't certain I could keep up with her demands. She whispered over and over, "Love me Richard, love me."

Inside Carol for the fourth time she was demanding hard action. She wanted me drive and pummel, ram and shove. She wanted hard, hard and hard. I gave her everything I had time and time again ramming and pummelling, pounding and driving. Sweat was leaking from every pore and yet I kept pounding answering her demands. Without warning she started to wail, to howl to yell. I couldn't control her. Carol was swinging her arms, kicking her legs and yelling for more. I had no more. With what little strength I had left I gave it all to Carol, merging all my remaining energy in one last effort to give her whatever she was missing, whatever her body was screaming for.

Abruptly she stopped, she was panting and licking her lips I poured her water. The room silent I could hear people outside; there came a knock on the door. I opened the door showing my face. The duty hotel manager demanded to know what all the yelling was. I did my best to explain a nightmare. He wanted to see Carol. I beckoned her to the door. She showed herself persisting she was fine. We both apologised.

I closed the door and she started kissing me, saying "I knew if anyone could do it you could and you bloody well did you absolute bastard, you took me to where I have only read about. You took me there and it was heaven for five whole minutes or however long it lasted, heaven, fabulous, fabulous heaven." Carol left me standing in the centre of the room climbed into bed, closed her eyes and fell asleep before I could say "Jack Robinson" I smiled to myself thinking whatever I had done I had obviously made a great job of it.

It was gone ten when I telephoned the office apologising to Pete for being late blaming a gang of mad friends who had descended on me and drank me into oblivion. He laughed and said, "It happens, take the day off."

I aroused Carol from her sleep. She sat up. "Did I dream it or did you?" Still confused I said, "Did what?"

"Take me there?" she demanded. "If you are referring to "to where you have only read about" or "heaven for however long heaven lasted" then yes I did. However, I expect an explanation."

First Carol laughed then she stood on the bed and threw herself at me. I managed to catch and hold onto her. "What is this all about Carol?" I asked.

"Sex Richard, pure unadulterated sex. I keep reading of women who have multi climaxes expounding of the most amazing feelings they experience and the wonders they feel inside. I decided if it was out there for me then you were the only guy I know who could find it. So my gorgeous Richard you did and I love you for it. It was utterly amazing but

240

oh so short, it doesn't last long enough. Although I must admit I am still tingling between my legs." I smiled, pleased for Carol and pleased for myself.

We checked out under scrutiny with smirks hitting us from every corner. I decided to stop off in Lyndhurst for breakfast. After breakfast I cruised back to Southampton. Besides chattering on about sex and a quick comment about the car the journey was straight forward. I escorted Carol to her door, declined a coffee and enjoyed one last hug before we kissed and said our goodbyes. I wished her every happiness and success with her studies. She kissed me once more saying, "After they made you they broke the mould."

I thought tomorrow will be the eighth, which leaves me twenty three days to see Catriona once more and bed Sam and my birthday.

Arriving home I found several cards balanced on the hall radiator. There was one from Irene and Ken demanding a visit; one from Uncle Don and also one from Joe. Two from mother, one with a letter advising me to settle down. Father enclosed a cheque for fifty pounds. Gertie invited me to share her bed and Jessica and Simon demanded a visit. Hugo simply said "another year, time you sorted yourself out. Don't forget wedding practice."

I took the nightmare drive to Whickham three weekends on the trot. The first weekend I searched for Sam. I heard Tina mention once or twice that she often frequented a pub called The Rose, Shamrock and Thistle. Saturday lunchtime I went in search and found her. When I walked in she was with two other females. She introduced them gave me half an hour to have a beer before taken me off to another pub where we had lunch and a bottle of wine.

She reaffirmed her last words, which were along the lines of "I'll be here," and she was. Within the hour we were in bed. She wanted to try me out and I obviously wanted to try her.

Naked, Sam was tall, slim and well-designed. There was nothing big or small just an exquisitely designed woman. Initially she was slow and deliberate, wanting to feel and touch and explore. What we did was in slow-motion, every moment had to be savoured, to be taken to its zenith.

Thereafter she demanded the driving and the pummelling and the pounding to enrich her climaxes and to enforce orgasm after orgasm. I had met women who when their juices were flowing it is reminisce of a tap being opened, with Sam it was the waters of a dam bursting, flooding the world.

Within minutes she would be demanding an encore. There wasn't anything she wouldn't try albeit I did draw the line when she wanted to tie me to the bed and give her free rein to pleasure the senses I know I have and the senses I didn't know I had. I did consider her proposition for all of half a second before deciding I was a coward. The thought of being tied and left to the mercy of a woman, especially one I hardly knew, was not at the top of my wish list. In many ways, when it came down to sex, she and Gertie were very similar.

She absolutely adored Jolly Roger, she treated him like a long lost brother, forever kissing him, holding him and sucking him. I know he loved every touch, every caress, and every feel of her lips and the depth of her throat. Quite simply he was being spoilt rotten and I loved it.

There are times when with a woman there is no need to caress or cuddle, there is no need to talk only time to satisfy and be satisfied. There are no rules, no expectations only sex, hedonistic sex, both contestants scrabbling for pleasure. Both are seeking that extra sensuality and consistently drive their bodies in search of gratification living through self-indulgence, mercenary and commanding, exacting every last drop of the partner and every ounce of sweat, glorifying in their lost world of uninhibited sex.

Whether being in bed, on the floor, over a table across a chair, wherever, that was sex with Sam. Her philosophy through Saturday afternoon and into the night, and on through Sunday was simple, I give, and you take. If I want, you give.

It was a very exhausted but oh so sexually contented young man who climbed into his car around ten o'clock Sunday evening to drive to Southampton. North of Northampton my eyes were closing compelling me to stop at a garage and catch forty-winks. Rejuvenated I arrived home in time to catch a couple of hours before going into work. I must have looked dreadful for virtually everyone in the office thought I was going down with flu or I had caught an incurable disease.

I was home by six-fifteen and in bed by seven, waking up at six. I tried a gentle jog for half an hour, showered and in the office back on top of the world by seven-thirty. Tuesday, through to Thursday I put the hours in ensuring that no one could complain if I left at five on Friday. I had called Catriona during the afternoon to let her know I would pop round mid-morning on Saturday. I managed to make Whickham by eleven, which pleased me. I went straight to bed.

In the morning I was given the third degree by Tina. From her observations she had gathered when talking to Catriona that she was about to marry me and Sam, stressing the point Sam was her friend, had not stopped talking about me all week. I acted dumb and stupid not given anything away. I mentioned I had dated both but there were no promises no long-term agreements beyond I would, on occasion, when in Whickham, date them.

Tina, dissatisfied with my responses, recruited father to give me a verbal going-over. I listened to father, rebuked his comments, which led to

242

a row and him calling me a narcissistic, obnoxious and pampered arsehole who wasn't too big for a good hiding. I wanted peace so I said this weekend I would end any rumours and the thoughts by either women of any long-term future. I apologised if I had caused upset, adding I would give it a few weeks before I returned and that I would visit mother, which I knew would satisfy father.

As promised I arrived mid-morning at Catriona's house. The minute I walked in the door she tugged me upstairs stripped of and started to undress me, or rather speed-up my progress. Apparently Fergus had gone out with his grandparents for the day. They wouldn't be home until tea-time.

Pulling my boxers down I said, "Hello Richard, nice to see you," would have been quite welcoming, followed by "would you like a cup of tea, coffee perhaps," would have really been welcoming. However, let's get undressed go to bed and make love is the best welcome of all." Catriona laughed grabbed Jolly Roger and pulled me onto the bed.

She said, "I've thrown the condoms, I am on the pill. A particular man hasn't made love to me for ages and I am desperate for that particular man to go about his business, make up for lost time and thrill his lady." Oh, oh I heard "his lady" careful Richard, I reasoned. However at this moment I had a woman gripping my penis, a very delicate position to be in. I smiled and put my arms around Catriona she released Jolly Roger and cuddled me.

Catriona and I made love tenderly, softly and gently. We kissed and copulated, and had sexual intercourse. It was wondrous. We sucked and we licked and we kissed and we cuddled. We didn't talk often, only the odd endearment, we were too busy enjoying each other, making love continuously.

I was able to stay inside her lovely wet vagina without moving for long periods, thrilled by the feel and the warmth. When we did move it was always slowly gradually building to a crescendo, slowing and starting over again. The feelings I experienced were deep and loving and immensely pleasurable. I lost count of how many times I actually ejaculated but each time it was fresh and lasting.

When grandparents and Fergus arrived home just before five we were playing draughts on the kitchen table, a master-stroke thought up by Catriona. When they noticed the draughts they presented a level of pleasantness.

However, there wasn't a display of affection or any sign that they were pleased for Catriona, or that she may be happy or even Fergus was happy for that matter. I think they were a wee bit miffed when Fergus saw me and charged at me demanding to be lifted and once more rubbed noses with me.

Her mother, Grace, did give me some searching looks, which when I caught her I gave off one of my bright smiles. Unfortunately her look showed disinterest and a low level of distrust. I felt like an unwanted guest. In fact I said, "I'd better be going," intending to disappear for an hour or so until Catriona's mum and dad had gone. My decision, to leave, upset Fergus, which encouraged his grandparents to say goodbye.

Fergus and I were playing cars and garages on the floor of the living room when the door bell sounded. I heard a man's voice followed by the closing of the kitchen door. I presumed it was Catriona's father, Donald, having been pressurised by Grace, returning to give Catriona some fatherly advice regarding dastardly young men who drive around in sports cars taking advantage of hapless young women.

The decibel level of the voices oscillated up and down. I was about to go and check what was going on when Catriona came through, she smiled at me saying, "Little bit of a family crisis. Could you wait here for a while?" She lifted Fergus, who yelled holding onto my shirt collar, and returned to the kitchen. I tidied the car and garage putting the toys away in Fergus' brightly coloured toy box.

I could hear childish laughter and the man's voice. I decided I would allow ten minutes then I would go and find out what the family crisis was all about. I actually waited fifteen minutes before I entered the kitchen. I knew in an instance that the man was Catriona's wayward husband.

Fergus was sitting on his knee. I said "You must be Shamus, I am Richard" he pushed Fergus into his mother's arms and stood. Catriona' expression was one of shock horror. He was probably three inches shorter than me and lean. I thought if shove comes to push this guy isn't going to be easy. He smiled saying, "I understand you have been keeping Catriona company and spoiling Fergus."

I wasn't sure what had been said during my enforced isolation or how to respond to his insinuation. I thought for a second seeking a neutral response before saying, "Yes I have. I met Catriona at the pub where she works. We have had lunch and dinner together with Fergus, and we have also been to the fun fair and played in the park."

"Yes, so I have heard. Catriona's mother telephoned my mother who called me." He had a very faint Irish accent.

I glanced at Catriona, her eyes were pleading, but I didn't know what for. We were walking on egg shells and not wanting to cause upset I said, "Are you here for the weekend?"

"Yes and every weekend hereafter," he replied taking a step towards me.

I thought, Catriona, "speak now or I walk away".

She stayed silent. "If that's right it's time I wasn't here." I walked over to Catriona and Fergus. I lifted Fergus from Catriona's arms pushed him above my head. I said, "Bye champ, look after your mother." I pecked Catriona's cheek proffered a general good-night and walked out of the kitchen followed by Shamus. At the front door I turned to him and harshly whispered, "You lay a finger on either of them and I'll be back, got it." I opened the door and walked to my car. He stood watching me.

I checked the time before deciding to find a telephone kiosk. I called Debbie. When she answered I said, "I need company are you free for a couple of hours, we could have a beer somewhere." She didn't answer immediately. Eventually she said, "There is a small pub two streets back from my street. It's called the "The Swordsman" I will be there at eight thirty." I thanked her and hung-up.

I arrived at the pub a little after eight. I ordered a pint of heavy, the local bitter and retired to a table close to a corner. The pub, for a Saturday was quiet. My mind was racing as I contemplated the recent situation, particularly I was thinking of Fergus, hoping Shamus would be a good father. I rightly or wrongly dismissed Catriona, she was given the chance to speak up choosing to hold her tongue, and hence as far as I was concerned she had made her bed now she had to lie in it.

However, Shamus's return to the matrimonial home was perfect timing, saving unpleasantness, which would have erupted when I made my well-rehearsed excuse explaining to Catriona I would be travelling overseas for a few months unable to see her for a while.

My mind moved onto Sam, who I also had to break from. However, when I considered she and me, I realised there wasn't anything to break. Her interest was wild sex, which she could find anywhere. I decided to call her. It slowly began to dawn on me that I had fulfilled my obligations, putting my house in order, leaving the way clear for Christine. However, I now had to convince Christine.

Debbie looking fantastic walked in. I immediately went to meet her. I kissed her cheek and ordered her requested vodka and pineapple juice. Sitting close to the fire she said "So Richard why the sadness? Been breaking more hearts have you?" I reached for hand saying, "Debbie I haven't broken any hearts I swear. I am simply calling on good friends to say goodbye and hope that they will remain my friends, no expectations, no demands, just goodbye. I am going to change my way of life."

"My God," she gasped. "You are going to change, I doubt it. If it's a woman she had better be damn good and I mean damn good, if she is to have any chance of holding onto you. Or have you found religion, no that's not on the cards, it has to be a woman."

I said, "I don't want to talk about me, or you. I called because I consider you a friend, a good friend who I have had fun with and I hope you have had fun with me."

She laughed, "Yes Richard we have had fun but you have also hurt me, as no doubt you have dozens of women while you have been seeking to complete your quest for stability. Actually, I am absolutely certain you have been a bastard, but because you are a loveable rogue you have skipped through life unharmed, taking women here and there leaving a trail of broken hearts. However, if you have changed and you do manage to stay true to one woman she will be a very lucky woman because one thing is for sure, and, even after considering your indiscretions, you do care about people, especially women."

I downed my beer and went to the bar to order refills. I needed a respite to think. Returning to the table I said, "Debbie, if I hurt you I am very sorry. And if as you say I have left a trail of broken hearts, it was never my intent. I did not force, nor did I lie, of course, along the way, there would have been the odd "white lie" but they were excuses not designed to cause pain. The women I have been with I have loved, whether for one night or for several weeks the women were loved."

Debbie laughed. "I know, Richard, I was one of those women and if you said to me this minute come on we are going to bed I wouldn't argue, and that is because of who you are, you have something most men do not have. You have feeling and passion and you care, that is why you are so bloody special."

"Enough, enough," I said. "For Christ's sake let's change the subject." She laughed once more. "Yes let's change the subject and the best place to do that is in bed. So dear Richard you get one last opportunity to ravish and pleasure me, are you up for it?"

"Stop playing games Debbie, I called you because as I said before you are a friend and I wanted to enjoy your company," I retorted.

"Richard, grow up. I wanted you for me, you were not available. However, here I am, a sad woman offering you my body and you want to bloody well talk, what the bloody hell will we talk about. We don't exactly have any history. We didn't go to school or college together. We didn't live in the same street. You breezed into my life, yes I made the first approach but since then it has been bed and bed, and oh yes bed. So what is there to talk about, the only history we have is bed so do you want to or not?"

We returned to Debbie's flat and made love for the very last time. The love making was tender, but ceaseless. We made love, slept and made love once more and on through the night until Sunday lunchtime when I kissed her goodbye. She cried on my shoulder hoping I would find happiness with whoever the woman was. I wished her happiness and peace of mind, which made her laugh and cry.

I went home to father's house said good bye and set off for Southampton and Christine. Later that day when re-fuelling I called Sam and told her I wouldn't see her again, she sounded quite unperturbed, which made me feel better.

Chapter 25 – Courting and Falling in Love with Christine

Monday was a bank-holiday, which I used to spring clean my flat, wash a huge pile of washing and listen to music. Worried about Christine, especially the constant cold shoulder I decided to write another letter and hand deliver:

Dearest Christine,

I hope you are well.

I have thought of you constantly these past days and weeks. I have missed your presence and the chats we had and most of all I have missed your smile and your voice.

However, I am writing to let you know that my house is now in order. All loose ends have been tidied and I am now ready to reiterate my promise.

The 1st September is next Saturday. When I hope you will meet with me and give me the time to talk to you face to face. If you agree the only question is where. I propose the following solutions, which are 1) Subject to the weather we walk and talk. 2) If Charlotte is out we meet at your flat. 3) You are most welcome to come to my flat.

I hope and pray you will give your consent to the meeting.

Love

Richard

I sealed the letter writing on the envelope "Private and Confidential"; "Delivered by Hand" and of course Christine's name. I jogged to her flat and popped the envelope through the letter box.

I jogged home. The telephone was ringing; answering I said, "Hello" and repeated my number. I heard her voice and my heart beat faster. "Richard, Christine, we'll talk now. Where is your flat?" I said I would meet her. I met her at the end of my street. My heart was racing. I smiled and fell in beside her as she set off in the direction I had come from.

I opened the door she walked in and sat down.

I offered tea, coffee, water, or beer. She said, "I'll have a beer" I poured two glasses of beer. Christine said, "I am listening."

I sat next her and took her glass. I held both her hands saying, "Christine I am extremely fond of you. You are constantly in my mind. I have pained these past weeks and I am very sorry I upset you. However, I ask you to become my one and only girlfriend, to spend as much time as possible with me, you and me together. I ask you to holiday with me, to get to know me and to become my lover. I promise you I will not be unfaithful and will only be with you."

Her expression didn't change. Christine said, "Very commendable Richard, but what about me. All I have heard is about you." She mimicked my voice, "Holiday with me. Get to know me, become my lover. Your so-called commitment is all about you."

"Christine I swear to you I have only one wish, which is you and I are together. You are very special and I care for you very much and," I hesitated, "I don't know what else to say."

Christine smiled. "So the great Richard Chambers, the Lothario, the seducer is lost for words."

Meekly I said, "I am not great, nor am I a Lothario, not any more. I have ceased forthwith if, and only if, you become my girlfriend, my sweetheart."

She laughed "So to protect the world's female population I have to become your lover." I nodded and I smiled, "I suppose, that is if you will have me as your boyfriend."

"I will but if you ever let me down God help you," she retorted. I went to put my arms around her. She repelled me. "Saturday is the 1st September you have until then to re-consider." She stood and walked from the flat. I chased after her. "Saturday Richard, Saturday until then nothing changes."

I could have cried, instead I walked to the pub and had a couple of beers returning home to shower. It took a while to fall asleep but when I did I dreamt of Christine. I loved the dream.

Saturday morning, I headed for the docks. I had seen a flower market somewhere but couldn't remember exactly where. After asking people I located it purchasing three dozen red roses from one supplier and a second three dozen from another. I drove to Christine's flat unloaded the roses and a card I picked-up at the newsagents, a drawing of a boy and girl holding hands walking into the sunset and wrote "I hope this will be us". I pressed the bell and clambered to the landing above.

I heard the door open and then Christine's laughter she called "I know you are here Richard, you dope your precious car is still parked outside" I descended the stairs watching Christine who was still smiling. She said "Come here you idiot" Her arms went round my neck and she kissed me, really kissed me.

My heart went crazy. She let me go saying "Help me carry the roses, they will have to go in the bath, we only have two vases." I carried the flowers. Charlotte said "So lover boy you have sorted yourself out, about time" the two sisters laughed and both hugged me.

The following week I was so excited full of smiles and cheerfulness. Pete called me into his office "Are you okay?" he asked. "You're not cracking are you?"

"No, no Pete, I am just very happy." I replied.

"Why?" he queried.

"It's a long story and one day I will share it with you but not just yet," I quietly replied. He was satisfied.

Later I asked Christine to come to my office. We quickly kissed before I said, "There are an awful lot of people I would like you to meet and I want you to meet them sooner than later plus we have a wedding to attend on the fifteenth."

"Who's wedding?" she asked.

I explained my friendship with Hugo, affording him his full title. I talked of his relationship and love for Miriam adding I would be the best man and due tomorrow, Saturday, to attend for the practice run and I wanted her to come with me. She smiled and agreed she would come with me.

Friday evening, Christine and I dined at a small trattoria close to the Bargate. I told her I had called Hugo to inform him I was bringing a breathtakingly beautiful girl with me. To which he had laughed, asking separate or sharing. I told him separate. Christine laughed saying, "No the time is about right we should become lovers. Call him and demand we share." I went to the small desk and asked for the use of their telephone. Hugo said, "I thought you were losing your touch, no problem, one room it is."

I collected Christine and a bloody great big case at eight. I asked what was in the case "Choices" she replied "A girl has to be prepared for every eventuality and I haven't had the pleasure of meeting Royalty before."

The drive to Hugo's father's estate, north of London took the best part of two hours. We pulled into a small drive with a lodge to the right and two very large decorative closed gates in front. A middle-aged guy came out asked my name, disappeared, returning to open the gates. I drove the half-mile to the main house remembering the days Hugo and I had visited when at school and college.

Sitting in the car Christine was gawping, I quietly said, "Close your mouth." She said, "I have seen pictures but this is something else. It is huge." I held her hand saying, "From memory it has fifty bedrooms including ten or more staterooms." She indicated the huge turrets wanting to know what they were for. "They're decorative; the bigger they are the more influential the owner," I explained.

I said, "Come on people are waiting." The same butler, slightly stooped, from those previous years stood at the top of the huge stairs. We ascended and he said, "Welcome back Master Richard." I thanked him and handed the car keys over.

Hugo came out, Miriam following, to greet us. We went through our habitual hugging, back slapping and hand-shaking watched by a bemused Christine. Miriam smiling welcomed Christine. I hugged Miriam who looked splendid, cool, distinct from the days she lived in jeans and sweaters. I whispered, "Don't let him change you too much." She pushed me away and laughed saying, "Fat chance."

Hugo said, "Too late for breakfast but if you are hungry I'll ask cook to rustle something together." I looked at Christine she nodded, "Coffee and toast would suit." I said adding, "We haven't eaten since last evening." Miriam was leading Christine towards the kitchens. Hugo and I followed. Of course he wanted to know everything about the "English Rose".

We seated at a huge solid oak table set in an alcove I vividly recalled from years before. Hugo went through to the kitchen, I waited at the door. Miriam and Christine were sat at the table talking I overheard Miriam ask, "Is he tamed yet?" Christine's response was, "It's taken a while but yes he's tamed." I heard their carefree laughter. I was happy, very happy.

The practice was set for midday when we would meet both sets of parents, the estate chaplain, the page boys, bridesmaids and others. We walked to the chapel, the weather was perfect. Hugo remarked he hoped next week would be similar.

His parents, Lady Alicia and Lord Crispin were waiting; Lady Alicia hugged me, Lord Crispin shook hands. He said, "No too much expose Richard, I know you two and what you involved yourselves in." He smiled. Lady Alicia hugged me once more and said "Take no notice Richard, you go ahead and shame Hugo." Christine was introduced, Lady Alicia said, "What a beautiful English rose you are Christine." Christine blushed.

I was reacquainted with Hugo's' two younger brothers, Edward and Nathaniel. Nathaniel, who with Josephine eloped when they were seventeen, to be married over the Blacksmith's Anvil, Greta Green was glad to see me. I had dived into the lake, when he was about thirteen or fourteen, to pull him clear of some weeds. Josephine hugged me saying how pleased she was to see me again.

I wasn't so popular with Edward the youngest because I had once tanned his backside for stealing. Hugo was aware but the secret as far as I knew remained with us three and the shop owner. It was I who suggested the punishment to protect the family from any embarrassment. Although the incident seemed forgotten when he shook my hand and grasped my shoulder.

We were introduced to a dozen or so people including two little boys, Hugo's nephews, Nathanial and Josephine's twin sons, Rupert and Roscoe.

We practiced for hours, seven attempts before Lady Alicia was satisfied. The chaplain was chastised and heavily criticised by Hugo's mother. By the seventh and thankfully final run-through he was performing like a stage celebrity. The evening was put over for a huge feast. Fortunately smart dress but not necessarily a tie was the order for the evening.

Christine and I were shown to our room. Poor Christine looked and touched stunned by the room's magnificence. It consisted of a huge bedroom with a four posted bed, a second smaller bedroom, a living room, study, bathroom and lady's dressing room. When the footman had departed she explored the rooms. She dragged me to the bathroom indicating the huge bath with pressurised jets and a walk in shower, bidet and toilet.

We unpacked our clothes, my holdall and Christine's huge case. We played about until we were wrestling on the bed. We started to kiss. The kissing became passionate. Christine pushed me away. She said "No rushing Richard. If we are to make love we will, but in our own time not a quickie to satisfy your urges" She rolled on her back laughing. I fell by her side and hugged her.

Leisurely we bathed, separately. We talked of splendour and of owning a mansion. We kissed and touched and tenderly expressed togetherness. Dressed we made our way down to the library where we were congregating for drinks. We said hello to the people we had practiced with stopping to talk to Edward and Nathaniel. A waitress took our orders. I elected to try a dry martini and Christine selected pineapple juice.

Josephine and a girl introduced as Miranda joined the company. Edward and Nathaniel for Christine's interest regaled their stories albeit Edward did not admit to the thievery only that he had been a naughty boy.

Josephine remembered me and Hugo wrestling in the mud over a rugby ball, laughing gaily, recalling how silly we had looked. I asked after their sons and what their interests were. We learnt they were inseparable and absolute terrors but so much alive.

Edward and Miranda had only recently begun courting. Her father, a well-known and outspoken protagonist against the decimalisation of British coinage, was also a Lord and close friend of Lord Crispin.

Hugo and Miriam, Miriam looking stunning, entered. Hugo came across to our little gathering while Miriam went to her bridesmaid friends, who were slightly isolated, which I hadn't noticed.

I decided to break away and join Miriam. I apologised to the ladies for leaving them to the own devises. Miriam said "This is Richard who as you all know is Hugo's best man, he's mine too" and hugged me to prove her point. Continuing she said "In case you have forgotten this is Claire, Dawn and Elizabeth, not Liz, Lizzy or Beth but plain old Elizabeth." I kissed each of their hands. "Now Richard let's hear all about Christine" said Miriam. I looked at the ladies and said "I don't think so, not right now, but I will, in due course." They politely laughed.

Miriam not to be diverted said, "Okay then tell us something about Hugo that I can use to blackmail him with." This time they laughed impolitely. "Miriam," I pleaded, "I am the best man how can I reveal his debauched past, his drinking problems and the bankruptcy issues he has. Be fair Miriam."

A punch to a fraction above the nether region was her response as well as her fabulous laughter, which brought Hugo running. "What's he been saying?" he asked with a huge smile. Miriam winked at me and touched her nose. Hugo, who couldn't care less about his past being made public, roared his infectious laugh, which encouraged the three ladies, who were perhaps a wee bit uptight, to relax.

Lady Alicia and Lord Crispin with Miriam's parents and other guests made their long awaited entry. I had no idea how old Lady Alicia was but at that moment she looked very young and very vibrant. She was tall for a woman, definitely elegant and very graceful.

She announced, "Crispy and I, Miriam's parents and our friends had drinks in our room leaving you youngsters to relax. We will go through for dinner." Where appropriate male and female paired together and the singles tailed towards the end. I felt Christine's excitement as she studied the room thrilled to be given access to the home of a member of the aristocracy.

Before we were separated Christine whispered, "How many more friends from similar backgrounds do we have to meet." Inwardly I smiled answering, "A few."

I didn't count but I estimated a good thirty people were sitting down to dinner. The table was beautifully decorated as was the dining room with its huge ornate mirrors and extra-large furniture. There were probably eight members of staff lining the room's perimeter.

The best man status seated me on Hugo's right at his end of the table. His mother sat opposite me. Lord Crispin had Sir Reginald Arkwright the industrialist to his right and Miriam to his left. Christine I was happy to see sat between Edward and Nathaniel.

The dinner was served, all eight courses. The wine plentiful and the room vibrated with conversation and laughter, and the odd giggle. Although there were eight courses the meal appeared to flash by albeit we were sat at the table for three hours. I expected Lord Crispin to call the males for cigars and cognac but thankfully he didn't.

A warm evening encouraged use of the terrace. Hugo, Miriam, Christine and I were sat together with digestifs and a footman close by. Miriam laughing regaled incidences about Hugo and his clumsiness. Her reminiscing reminded that he always had been a clumsy oaf, which I remarked on. However, Miriam wanted to know all about Christine. Hugo and I left them to it while he and I went for a walk.

We talked rugby where he remained at the top of his game. He mentioned he had played against Ben and James, and Craig a few times.

Where after the game they recalled college games and often discussed me and some of the girls. He asked if I would return to rugby, I said I would.

He knew that I had to pack in due to pressure of work but he expressed his keenness to see me playing once more. I was probably a great deal keener than he. We discussed the wedding and whether I had organised my morning suit, which he would pay for. I ignored his offer.

When we turned at the lake and headed back he told me he thought Christine beautiful, her carriage as he put it was sublime. Christine being pulled along by two horses swiftly flashed through my mind.

He asked if I had given up on chasing Sophie's replacement and now I had Christine would I give up womanising. I told him most probably and for the moment Christine was the only girl in my life, which I hoped would continue. I expressed that although we had been courting on and off for quite a while we had not maintained a regular relationship, emphasising we had just started out on our journey.

We re-joined the girls who were both smiling happily. Miriam said, "Richard the evergreen romantic, you'll never change. Six dozen roses indeed."

Hugo said, "What?" Miriam repeated Christine's story.

Hugo crashed his great paw onto my back and roared causing everyone to ask what was so funny. Within minutes the whole company were fully aware of the six dozen roses and why. I went red with both embarrassment and slight irritation.

Christine stood and hugged me, which raised a cheer. She whispered, "Sorry." I smiled and said all was fine. She said, "Bedtime." Miriam overheard and said, "Goodnight, breakfast finishes at ten."

I hugged Miriam whispering, "He doesn't deserve you."

She said, "I know."

Hugo once more slapped my back. "Goodnight old boy see you in the morning." We called goodnight to the remainder of the guests and departed.

In the bedroom, correction the stateroom, I invited Christine to use the bathroom first. She walked out in a recently purchased baby blue nightie, looking very beautiful. She had brushed her long red hair, which fell loosely over her shoulders. Her smile of innocence captivated me. I loved her loveliness.

I undressed to my boxers and used the bathroom. I brushed my teeth thoroughly and gargled with mouthwash. I returned to the room and stood looking down at Christine. Her eyes were closed. I leaned over her and kissed her forehead. She was pretending to be asleep.

Her arms shot high and encompassed my neck in a solid hold. I pulled myself upright and Christine moved with me. She was giggling. Her upper body hanging onto my neck and her legs, her long slim legs were kicking.

I moved my arms under her body and lifted her upwards, twisting her to the left until I was holding her, her head resting on my shoulder and my hands firmly holding her bottom. She gave a little squeal. She turned her head towards me and we kissed.

Her tongue was probing my mouth. I forced my tongue against hers before relenting. I sucked her tongue. She deftly, ever so deftly opened her legs allowing my fingers access to her vagina. She moved her bottom to the right so my left hand would slip further under her right buttock. One finger slipped inside a moist vagina.

Her grip around my neck tightened forcing her lips against mine kissing me feverishly. She said, "Put me down Richard, I'm a big girl and I know what happens next." I leaned over the bed and dropped her. She shrieked and jumped up. Standing on the bed she threw her arms round my neck once more.

She said, "Do you know how many dates we have had?"

I said, "No, but every one of them was wonderful." She nibbled my cheek. "You are impossible."

"I am, why?" I asked

"Because by the fifth date, maybe the sixth I was yours for the taking. Then suddenly after no less than seventeen dates stolen during your rare appearances in Southampton you decide to entertain a floosy in your flat for a whole week."

Recalling the morning I told her I asked her how she guessed it was a woman. "Because, you big idiot if it had been a guy you would have mentioned a name and probably introduced me."

I apologised, which she accepted saying, "Why?"

"Difficult to explain but I knew if I hadn't she would have haunted me forever. She was, I suppose is, a long-time friend. That week was the first and only time. It will not happen again."

Christine dismissed the discussion; she continued, "In five months we averaged three dates a month that is why you are impossible."

"We're together now?" I said with a warm smile.

I tenderly eased the baby blue nightie over her head. She shook her hair loose. I looked at her body, amazed, beautiful white porcelain, her exquisite breasts standing proud with the most astonishingly sexy pink, very pink nipples.

I ran my hands over her body, it was cool and enticing. I followed the contours of her waist, her hips and her long slim elegant legs to the shapeliest ankles and on to her graceful feet.

She didn't move, permitting me to explore her gorgeous body visually and by touch. I hadn't experienced such a pure white body before. I found the whole experience very erotic. I kissed and nibbled her nipples. Her fingers were running through my hair.

Carefully I laid her on to the bed. I kept looking at her unable to take my eyes away. Her delightful red hair guarding her vagina excited me. I kissed and sucked her red hairs running them through my teeth. I ran my tongue the length of her body stopping to tenderly kiss her lips. I ran my tongue back following the same path. I flicked her vagina with my tongue. She pulled my head up and sat up to kiss me. Her hands were stroking my back.

I was in heaven this girl excited me, excited me very much. She looked and felt virginal. She had a young, pure, and innocent quality, very sensual. I didn't want to soil her with sex. I only sought to delight her with the tenderest loving.

I once more ran my hands, mouth and tongue over her body only applying the gentleness, kindness, and most affectionate of touches. I sensed her desire. I could smell her arousal, her sexual desire and I could feel the heat rising from her body, but yet I didn't want to sully her with my passion. It was incredible. I was close to climaxing. I was in no man's land unsure of what to do.

Christine resolved my dilemma by removing my boxers. Jolly Roger shocked her. She looked then held him. She ran her hand down his shaft. She leaned forward and kissed his head. Laying back she pulled me over to her. Christine guided Jolly Roger towards her vagina. Her legs were open and her legs bent at the knees.

I started to gradually push inside her. Christine's vagina, albeit moist, was extremely small. I very carefully pushed forward gently not wanting to hurt her.

Her legs opened further and moved higher. I slipped further into her warm vagina. A little squeal escaped her lips. She was pushing up to meet me. Her tightness excited me, but I remained very tender, very gentle easing into her with care. In an instant Jolly Roger lost control, I lost control and whoosh I ejaculated. Christine murmured and smiled.

I remained inside Christine continuing to tenderly ease into her, Jolly Roger supporting my intention remained erect. She began to pull at my shoulders her hips were urgently demanding deeper penetration. I pushed all the way home. Christine cried out.

Her legs encircled my waist, she used her upper body strength combined with the strength of her legs to gain more purchase to drive her hips hard towards my thrust. We were locked as one rocking back and forth forcing a synchronised movement of my penis driving in and withdrawing and driving in once more.

Christine increased the tempo, her resolve becoming more demanding. I reciprocated her drives experiencing thrill after thrill, a tingling sensation was rushing through Jolly Roger, completely out of control I once more ejaculated. Christine could feel my sperm she wriggled her hips and shrieked. I could feel her quivering.

Her legs lifted and began kicking in mid-air. Her legs dropped and she drove her hips upwards loosening a long moan from her throat. For a trice she lay still before reaching up to wrap her arms around my neck and pull herself towards me. She whispered "Richard I feel wonderful, absolutely wonderful" She let go flopping onto the bed.

I eased my weight clear of her body and lay on my side looking at her. I was stunned, not since my very early days had I lost control so easily. Yes on occasion it had happened but not twice within minutes. What did she have that excited me so much? I was in a stupor completely bewitched by Christine.

I tenderly enclosed my arms around her and gently eased her in against my body. I could smell her sex, her sweet body odour and felt disoriented even perturbed; I was completely under her influence.

I tenderly pushed her on to her back drawing in her odour pushing my nose close to her breasts and her tummy inhaling a wonderful aroma. I ran my tongue towards her vagina, I had a desperate need to smell and look at her vagina. I very gently eased her labia lips apart studying the pinkest, sexiest vagina I had ever seen. It was beautiful. "Richard what on earth are you doing" cried Christine. I didn't know I was enthralled and I was captivated. I leaned forward and very softly kissed her vagina.

Once more I very carefully pulled Christine into my arms. I kissed her head and her hair I continued to inhale her aroma. I nuzzled her neck and nibbled her ears. I couldn't stop touching her my hands were exploring her body. I caressed and tenderly stroked her.

Completely absorbed, enchanted and delighted, totally immersed in Christine I could feel nerve ends tingling driving me insane. I had never experienced such purity, such wondrous beauty.

Christine moved away from me and stared into my eyes. "What is wrong?" she asked. I locked my eyes onto hers. I said "Nothing is wrong I promise you nothing is wrong. I am" I stuttered "I don't know what I am."

I stuttered again like a lovelorn teenager, "I am overwhelmed by your beauty and by your innocence and your sexiness, and by the beauty of your body, your beautiful breasts, your legs, tummy and hips. I am utterly lost in the aroma emitting from your body. Christine I am mesmerised by you, nay fascinated. I love your body and your whiteness, your pink nipples, your red hair. I find it all so expressive, so sensual. I cannot really explain what I am feeling because I am wholly confused."

I think I confused Christine; her look changed from concern to quizzical. Her faint eyebrows lifted, her light blue eyes sparkled and my heart raced. I had to take control. I had to pull myself together.

She said "Richard what are you babbling about. I wasn't a virgin. You didn't hurt me, in fact quite the opposite. You inspect me as if I was an alien from another planet and you shower me with flattering compliments. What on earth has got into you?" "Christine" I said a tad too harshly "I don't know." I changed my mind saying "Yes I do, you have got into me and I love the feeling. I absolutely adore the feeling."

Christine's expression switched from concern to quizzical, to confused and back again. I confused myself. Exasperated she lay on her side with her back to me. I snuggled into her back and cuddled her. She pushed my arms away saying, "Go to sleep Richard."

Neither of us went to sleep. I could feel Christine's alertness to my fidgeting. I felt her watch me when I climbed from the bed to look from the patio doors. I pulled the curtains to the side and watched moon beams shimmering across the lake. Carefully and quietly I slid the patio door open and naked walked onto the balcony. The slight breeze warmed my body. I looked to see if I could be overseen, I couldn't, the balcony unobservable.

I felt Christine kiss my shoulder. Her hands went round my waist and she cuddled my back. I reached behind me to feel her. She was warm and soft. We didn't move both savouring the moment. She kissed me again saying, "Come back to bed Richard and talk to me." I obeyed her bidding, quietly closing the patio door and closing the curtain.

She turned the lights off and snuggled into my arms. I held her tight not wanting to let go. I knew I was falling in love and I loved the moment, the wondrous feeling I was experiencing. I didn't talk and Christine didn't push me. Secure in my arms my body warming her she eventually fell asleep.

I awoke early the sun was filtering through the slight gaps to the side of the curtains, beams of light shone left and right of the bed. I watched the dust mites dancing. Christine sensing my awareness reached for me I leaned over her and kissed her passionately. Half-awake she momentarily held me back before placing her arms around my neck and returning my passion.

Within seconds I was entering her, once more being careful, aware of her tightness, but there was no need Jolly Roger slid all the way in and pushed hard. Christine moaned and said, "Push hard Richard, love me." I couldn't drive too hard I considered her too delicate, a fragile rose, an English rose. I found a rhythm, which I maintained thrusting just hard enough. Christine quietly moaned with the odd squeal and sigh mixing with her moans. Still maintaining a rhythm I increased the tempo and began to drive harder. Christine's moaning increased in volume. I felt my sperm begin to bubble. I searched frantically for something to control my imminent ejaculation. Too late I exploded and I yelled. Christine's arms grasped by neck, her teeth nibbled my arm, I drove and I as I rammed into her. I cried out. Christine cried out. I was feeling wonderful, so bloody wonderful.

Christine used the bathroom. I heard the shower. I switched on the radio on the bedside table. I was listening to beautiful songs I could not understand. My eyes watched the bathroom door waiting for Christine to exit. I was impatient to see her nakedness.

The door opened I jumped from the bed and lifted her onto it. I climbed up next to her. We were standing on the bed. Christine's' expression was one of bewilderment. I took her my arms and swayed to the music, the singing. Her face lit-up and a glorious smile brightened her features, her light blue eyes were sparkling and the sun, now high in the sky, was bouncing sunbeams off her red hair. I was ecstatic.

We kissed very passionately. Christine said, "Do you know how long I have waited for you, waited for this moment. No, you do not have a clue do you? You are blind, dense and a man, which makes you worse than useless." She laughed. "Forget what I said about fifth or sixth dates you could have made love to me in your office the first time we met. That is how long I have waited. All the time you were flying around the world I was laying in my bed fretting, yes fretting."

She gaily laughed and she kissed me and kissed me, and we fell onto the bed. We made love tenderly, very tenderly I hardly moved inside her, the feel that we were connected, was all we needed. Christine moaned and her muscles tightened. I felt her juices, the most I had felt from her, start to flow as she gently climaxed. She held on to me tightly waiting for me, I followed, my sperm spurting into her and washing the insides of her vagina. We embraced strongly, we sighed together and then we laughed. We were both immensely happy.

A knock on the door, which Christine responded to, forced us from the bed. We showered, I shaved and we dressed. Christine chose a mauve blouse with polka dots and a knee length grey skirt and light tanned tights. She looked lovely, her loveliness lighting up the room.

However, it was the lingerie I watched her put on, which very nearly sparked another assault by Jolly Roger. The skimpy beige panties and half bra with light grey decorative frills expressed her gorgeous curvy shape emphasising the wonder of her porcelain body. I loved watching her.

We found those who had not departed sitting on the terrace. Hugo jokingly asked if we slept okay and if the bed was to our liking. Miriam clipped him round the ear. We were obviously too late for breakfast.

Hugo said "Richard pop down and see cook she asked after you earlier" I took Christine's hand and we walked off to the kitchens. Cook as Hugo called her was Mrs Wainwright who had been with the family for donkey's years. She was a lovely warm lady who I remembered with a constant smile with her hair out of control and always working, she never seemed to stop.

She saw me and smiling said "You took your time have you forgotten me?" I went forward and hugged her "Never Mrs Double-U, never. I am sorry the whole weekend has been, rush here and rush there. Please forgive me." "So who is the beautiful young lady?" she asked

Christine moved forward I said, "Mrs Double-U, I have the pleasure of introducing my girlfriend, Christine." Mrs Double-U enveloped Christine in her big arms and kissed both her cheeks.

She said to Christine, "You know this boy is so full of goodness when he lost dear Sophie he broke, didn't you? For long months and years he was broken, weren't you?" Christine turned to look at me. I smiled.

"Run along. I'll bring you up some breakfast. Tea or coffee? Go on up to the table." We sat at the huge table. Christine looked at me her expression was saying loud and clear, "Explain".

"Christine," I began. "Do you remember the first letter where I said I would reveal all. Well Sophie is a major part of reveal all. Unless you insist I would prefer to be given the opportunity to tell all, my whole life, of which Sophie played a very large part, in privacy together where we cannot be interrupted." Christine considered my request. She smiled and said, "Tonight in your bed in your flat."

Mrs Double-U served bacon and scrambled eggs, tomatoes and mushrooms and great pot of coffee plus several slices of buttered toast. I asked her to sit with us, which she did. We talked and laughed as she recalled Hugo and me and the trouble we were always in. And she emphasised, laughing, how the staff all loved the pair of us. We finished our breakfast and hugged her I said, "I'll see you next week," she nodded.

We said goodbye and thank you to Hugo. I reminded him we were meeting in Richmond Thursday evening for his "stag-night". Miriam invited Christine to join her and friends. They were going into London for the evening. Christine happily accepted the invite. We called farewell to the remaining six or seven guests adding here's to next weekend. Before leaving I asked for Christine and me to be remembered to his family.

We sought out Jackson, the butler to reclaim the car keys. Jackson a staid character who once slapped the back of my head for some misdemeanour I couldn't recall was polishing brass in the entrance hall. He was in his green cover-all.

I asked how he was and told him he didn't look a day older. I rubbed the back of my head and he smiled saying, "You remember Master Richard."

I said, "I remember," and laughed. He informed us that the luggage was loaded and passed me the car keys adding Jenkins had taken the car to the garage to check water, oil and fill with petrol. I thanked him.

Chapter 26 – Christine and my Misgivings

In the car Christine was bubbling over. She had enjoyed the weekend and especially our love-making. She expounded what wonderful friends I had. She wished she had known me when I was a carefree teenager and sometime troublesome youth.

She wanted me to explain what the signal between Jackson and me meant. I told her he had given me a smack once but couldn't recall why. She chatted brightly exclaiming how big and splendid the mansion was and how she had been overawed. She couldn't get over dinner it was her first eight course one. I said in a mock accent, "Stick with me kid and I'll show you more."

I pulled up at her flat fought the stairs getting her case to the first floor. Charlotte had left a note saying she wouldn't be home until late and not to wait up. We unpacked and stowed Christine's myriad of clothes. She delved under her bed and pulled out a small case. Put her work clothes and washing kit in and the blue nightie. We drove to my flat.

In the flat I showed Christine my room. She tut-tutted and made the bed. I put the immersion on and searched for a romantic album. I found Scheherazade, which I had stolen from father. I would play it when we were in bed.

I checked the answering machine, eleven messages. I decided to let Christine listen to them to prove I had nothing to hide. I put the kettle on. Christine came into the kitchen and put her arms round me nuzzling my neck. I said, "I have eleven messages, which I want you to hear. I have no idea what they will say but I want you know I do not have any secrets, not anymore, those days are long gone."

She followed me into the living room. I switched on the machine:

Message one – Mother demanding a telephone call

Message two – Father demanding the same

Message three – Carol saying thank you for a lovely farewell and how much she had enjoyed Athens

Message four – Ken asking if I had forgotten him and Irene

Message five – Gertie, saying what a great fuck I was and when could we do it again

Message six – Mother again

Message seven – Debbie wishing me and my new lady best wishes

Message eight – Catriona apologising but saying she would always remember me

Message nine – Mother once more

Message ten – Pete saying I was needed in Belfast Monday and to pack a bag

Message eleven – Hugo saying that he and Miriam thought I had a gorgeous woman and not to let her get away

I went to the kitchen to make the tea. When I come back Christine said, "I think you had better ring your parents. I rang mother first. I promised I would visit her the weekend after next explaining I was best man at a friend's wedding the coming weekend. This earned a lecture on settling down. Father was jovial and asked if I was okay. Catriona had explained to him privately what had happened but she seemed happier.

I sat down saying, "In a fortnight you will meet my mother and Grandma Jean and the week after you will meet Father and Tina his live-in girlfriend."

She said, "Right let me work this out. For the past three weeks you have toured the country saying goodbye to girls and bedding them in the process and also telling them of my existence."

"Something like that," I answered. "And the lady who said you was a great fuck, who is she?"

"You don't want to know," I replied.

Christine put her arms round my shoulder and pulled me down across her lap and twisted my ear. "Who is she? Don't bother, she was the week's love-in wasn't she?" I nodded she gave the ear an extra twist and let me up. "Richard Chambers it is over, do you hear me it's over. I am your girlfriend there will be no dalliances when you are travelling. If there are I will know and we are dead, dead in the water. Do you hear me, do you understand?"

I put my arms round her and made another promise saying, "Christine I don't know how long you and I will be together, I hope and pray forever. However, I do promise I will not go to bed or have any type of sex with another woman for as long as we remain as one."

She said, "Good, we understand each other. Your next task is to explain the very complicated past you have lived, including why you turned down the opportunity to train with England." I looked at her. "Miriam told me."

I said, "I need something stronger than tea. I'm popping round to the off-license. Do you want anything while I'm out?"

"Only you to come back to me," she retorted with a beautiful loving smile.

I returned with two bottles, one white and one red plus a bag of Maltesers, which I had often noticed on her desk. Christine had washed the tea-mugs and searched and discovered the wine glasses. The white was warm so we opted for red. I sat by her side asking where she wanted to start. She suggested from when I first met Hugo.

I have no idea for how long I talked. However, I commenced where she asked, up at school with Hugo right up until where we were now. I explained my mother and father and my relationship with them. I described my time at college, the rugby, Sally, the early day girls and Ruth, and Ruth and the Cotswolds. Most of all I talked about my love for Sophie and the wonderful four years we had together. I described how friends had stood by me through the near fifteen months I grieved, including the celibacy during that time.

I told her how Sophie's death had changed me and I became a predator searching out women for sex. I also, with difficulty explained how I loved them, each and every one of them. Not a deep intense love but I did love each one. I told her how, if my feelings became too strong, I would walk away. I mentioned Carol, Melissa, Debbie, Margaret and Catriona as special friends. The explanation included Jessica and Simon and little James who I kept in contact with, and Irene and Ken, Sophie's parents and her Uncles Don and Joe.

I told her I was much too fond of her to allow myself to get close and hurt her. I emphasised how difficult it had been to keep her at arm's length while wanting to wrap her in my arms.

Finally I said, "I have trod a very bad path. I have unfairly treated women and I have constantly taken advantage of them, but I again point out I did feel for them and I did have a love for them. When you Christine entered into my life, I knew if I wanted to keep you I had to change, so I did. I woke up to my responsibilities and changed. But I couldn't complete the change until I had finalised unfinished business, which included Gertie and Debbie, and Catriona and Carol, particularly Carol. I am so very sorry for hurting you and I will always suffer for causing you pain."

Christine was openly weeping her arms wrapped round my neck. She said, "Sophie was very special wasn't she? You were very upset when you spoke of your love for her. God Richard you are the most unusual man and you love women as a species, you absolutely adore them." She smiled and hugged me tighter "I will have to put up with you looking and flirting which I can live with and I will live with, providing you do not touch."

Christine said, "What's next?"

I pulled her tight saying, "When we have toured the country introducing you to people we will go on a long holiday and when we return we will go and see Mr Maybury and tell him we are breaking company policy by being together." Christine laughed and hugged me saying, "Richard Chambers you are inveterate." I thought, where have I heard that before and smiled to myself.

Chapter 25 – Miriam and Hugo, and Mmmm, the Stag Night

The first person we told was Charlotte. Charlotte hugged me called me a prat and commenced to give me a lecture explaining if I ever hurt her big sister she would hunt me down and cut my balls off. There wasn't much I could say to that. However, Christine enjoyed every minute. We followed up by a telephone call to Hong Kong to inform Sadie and James, Christine's auntie and uncle and also her guardians.

The coming weekend was the wedding. I had three fittings for the morning suit before I was satisfied. We searched high and low until Christine was satisfied with her choice of outfit for the day, hat and all.

Thursday morning I told Doug that Christine and I were a couple. He was overjoyed. He drove down from head office and popped in to Christine's office congratulating her for humanising me. He also told Christine he would sort out any issues with company policy. Lunchtime we set off for Richmond.

We checked in at the hotel and telephoned both Miriam and Hugo. Miriam slipped away from her office and came to the hotel. Hugo couldn't get free until four. While Miriam and Christine were in the lounge I, with fingers crossed, telephoned the other hotels and guest houses making sure my very discreet arrangements were in place and the revellers had arrived.

I had superstitiously booked an upstairs room above a bar opposite the underground station for an evening meal and some entertainment. Ben, James, Craig, Danny were all in town with their wives and girlfriends. I invited them to the hotel for a beer and to wait for Hugo. Joss and Guy two other of our old friends hadn't arrived. I left messages for them. Edward and Nathaniel were staying in our hotel but they hadn't arrived either. My last call was to the agency arranging the entertainment. Everything, they assured me, was ready to go.

The lads and their ladies arrived; it was a very joyous moment. I introduced the bride and my lady. Miriam was the perfect host gathering the ladies together while the guys stood at the bar and started reminiscing. Edward, Nathaniel, Miranda and Josephine arrived, more introductions. Not long after Joss and Guy with their ladies turned up quickly followed by the bridesmaids and three other friends of Miriam.

The girls, radiating expressive beauty, and sounding very happy, enjoyed a cocktail before Miriam signalled the concierge. Thirty minutes later we were ushering sixteen gorgeous sexy ladies into four cars courtesy of one of Hugo's businesses. The four burley drivers would also act as chaperones. The ladies set off for London's bright lights.

Hugo arrived in time to wave to the girls as their chauffeured cars departed the hotel. His giant frame with arms wide stood in the centre of the bar welcoming his family and friends. I hadn't realised before but Edward and Nathaniel were not quite Hugo's size although they were big lads.

Hugo as always called for champagne, bottles of fizz were demanded. We had two hours before dinner I hoped they wouldn't all get silly and overdo the alcohol. I think experience constrained the imbibing keeping everyone on the straight and narrow. The only exception, Hugo who was determined to have the time of his life and if that meant getting legless, then so be it.

We were noisy customers as we remembered the many times we had sat in the Leopard drinking and trying to pull girls. Fresher girls were the favourite topic being described as ripe and ready for picking. Rugby tours were also remembered especially the weekend we won the UAU cup.

When it was time to head off, we ganged together and walked to the venue. Eleven huge men obviously with a beer under their belts must have spread nervousness and perhaps a little awe as we worked our way through Richmond.

The venue when they saw us went into panic mode. The owner called my name. I introduced myself and we shook hands. His eyes were roaming the guys he said "Please sir no trouble" I assured him we would be noisy and we would sing but trouble absolutely not.

He was half-convinced. He directed one of his staff to escort us to the room. I looked at the pub's customers they were curiously looking us over, noticing the odd plummy accent wondering who the heck we were.

The room was perfect. It had the requested stage a well-stocked bar and a very large table, and plenty of staff, all male. I had requested no females. I shouted, "No preferences, no table plan, sit where you sit."

However for the moment the bar was the targeted area. Orders were issued swiftly. The staff handled the requests admirably. I lifted my pint and called for attention. Tongue in cheek I said, "Okay this is how it works, no trouble, be as noisy and sing as loud as you want, get legless, dance naked but I emphasise no trouble."

In a more serious tone I continued, "We are NOT here to celebrate Hugo's marriage to the delightful Miriam, we are here to give Hugo a send-off and to make sure he remembers, on occasion, he was once a free man." Above a loud cheer, I shouted, "Here's to Hugo." A raucous response started proceedings, the beers were gulped and the bar staff were refilling.

The musicians, a guitarist, saxophonist and a drummer arrived, pulled the stage curtains back, one fell to the floor, winning an instant cheer, and took charge of their instruments.

Initially the musicians played background music allowing the gathering to get into the mood. I purposefully stayed away from any particular group playing the host with the most, or is it the hostess with the mostest, whatever. My sole intent was to manage my alcohol intake and the evening. I did join in listening to jokes and told one or two rather badly.

However, I was happy to sit behind the scenes and watch and listen. I found it remarkable how many of the guys had married and some had children. And Joss, my age, was already waiting for a divorce; the girl with him, Tonia, he explained, was a makeshift date, as he put it, for the weekend.

Long forgotten stories emerged by the bucket full. Special emphasis was on sex, rugby, bloody tutors and exams, and embarrassing moments. The get together was proving to be a success purely by putting old friends back in contact, which I found very pleasing. For a brief moment I did think of sixteen gorgeous girls being let loose in London, whom in the main were virtual strangers.

I received a message that they were waiting to serve dinner. I shouted above the bedlam saying "Take your seats for dinner." After the rush for seats the waiters started serving the three course meal with unlimited wine. The lights dimmed and soft music started. A naked girl walked onto the stage.

Whistling, cheering, comments and you name it were shouted from the table. She introduced Vince the Mincer, a homosexual comedian to loud jeers. He was excellent, his jokes were downright disgusting but he had the guys' belly-laughing.

The dinner proved to be a waste of money, interest centred on alcohol, debauchery and singing. In fact the food, instigated by Ben was being flicked around the table. I asked the staff to clear the table and cancelled the dessert.

Vince the mincer continued unabated for twenty minutes, causing uproar. He received tumultuous applause and ringing shouts for an encore. The naked girl reappeared causing Hugo to make a dash for the stage. Fortunately he tripped over someone's legs, which again caused uproar. She introduced Connie from Blackpool.

I thought long way to come to take off your clothes. She with the aid of a cucumber stripped to taped music and sucked on her cucumber. The obvious shouts from the table demanded she did something else with it, but she didn't until the very last moment, just before the stage lights went out when she inserted it an inch or two into her vagina. Hugo shouted "Peanuts! Show her yours King Dick", which started the singing of "Dinah, Dinah show us your leg".

The musicians returned and the singing and the drinking really started. Song after song was belted out Hugo was in his element. In fact all present were in their element singing with boundless enthusiasm. When I studied their faces my mind flashed back to our college days, the rugby training and rugby games, the boozy nights and for one brief moment, I heard Ruth's voice leading the singing.

Craig climbed up onto the table, the musicians immediately changed to playing recognisable strip-tease music. Ben and Edward jumped on the table. The three of them started to strip trying, very hard, but completely useless, to be sexy. The three show girls came out and joined in the fun.

The naked one now wearing a frock was lifted onto the table and danced sexily, which had our guys copying her moves. It was hilarious to watch. Edward raced ahead and was down to his underpants when the girl slid her hand down the front and squeezed his "John Thomas". He grabbed her, kissed her to raucous laughter and lifted her high. We all cheered.

The musicians, perhaps not wanting to be influential in causing an orgy changed tack again and started playing "On the first day of rugby". The guys returned to their youth, back in the college bar singing after a good win. More songs followed and then we were gate crashed by four girls, well actually they were more thirty something women who had heard the noisy fun and decided to take a peep. They were pulled into the room.

Two were lifted onto the table and stripper music was once more being played. There was no doubt the musicians were on the ball. The two women realising they were the centre of attraction played their part moving their bodies sensually. First one pulled her skirt up to reveal her blue panties, followed by the second who was wearing black.

Hugo's stag-night friends wanted more. The woman wearing blue panties and obviously influenced by the combination of alcohol and a throng of good-looking guys slowly removed her tights and went to remove her panties but fortunately had enough sense to keep them on.

However, she did a good job of teasing earning a riotous cheer. The four women were plied with alcohol and their glasses constantly re-filled and loved the attention they were getting from the guys. I hid in the shadows ready to halt proceedings if they went too far.

The show-girls had disappeared backstage. The naked one reappeared introducing Helena. Helena started her routine to taped music, strip music from Gypsy. She was a very sexy lady and also a contortionist, which excited the audience. Her tease albeit a tad automatic did encourage wild yelling, her final pose caused uproar as she manoeuvred into the bridge position her wide open legs facing her audience. Danny shouted, "The Mersey Tunnel" which brought howls of laughter and good humoured cheering.

Vince the Mincer returned, who catching the mood rolled off a string of jokes around sex and gang-bangs and sex and more sex. His humour, although appalling, did have everyone boisterously laughing, none more than James who was heading towards convulsions recollecting a fresher girl he had once dated a few times who would, to entertain him, pose in similar positions to the contortionist stripper.

The three of the four women whose names I forget were half-sozzled and becoming quite amorous. The fourth, despite all the noise, was sleep in one of two easy chairs. One of the women wanted to strip, which, with the help of our little band, was easily arranged.

The band played sultry sexy music and she, having being positioned at the front of the table did her utmost to present a sexy strip. The strip wasn't a problem but the sexy bit proved beyond her alcoholic condition. I stepped in when she was sitting on the stage, down to bra and nickers, massaging her vagina.

I pulled her to one side told her to get dressed and advised it would be best if her and her friends departed, or I couldn't be held responsible for the actions of my friends. Through her befuddled state and after looking at Hugo's leering wedding guests, she dressed quickly, gathered her three friends and departed.

I was booed and soaked with beer after beer being splashed over me. I smelled like a brewery. From being the great guy who had organised a terrific stag-night I was the villain of the piece.

Throughout the evening the three guys working the bar were excellent in ensuring the glasses were full at all times. Connie and Helena performed a double act that included a great deal of very intimate contact forcing three of us to hold Guy down. The musicians returned, but not for long. Three songs on and the guys were calling for action on stage.

The show girls' last performance commenced. The naked girl came on stage, this time she was dressed as a nurse, which aroused interest. The taped music started and she began to seductively strip. When down to her panties Helena came on stage and began running her hands over the girl. They were French kissing and there was no secret what their hands were doing. Moments later Connie with her cucumber joined the fray.

The two bigger girls swiftly removed the normally nurse's panties and forced her into a chair. Connie went to work with the cucumber. It was slightly erotic and certainly lewd. She removed the cucumber and Helena commenced cunnilingus. Everything was going on, the cucumber was changing vaginas rapidly and lips were following until all three went into pretend climaxes, which encouraged raucous and rambunctious cheering.

The three girls, we learnt from Vince the Mincer were available, at a price, for more intimate relationships should any of the guys be seeking private entertainment. I thanked him and declined his kind offer.

The finale over, the singing started. All the favourites were resonating around the room. In particular, "If I was the marrying kind" and "Why was he born so beautiful." There was time for one more toast, which became ten, before we were asked to leave. A very cheerful bunch of guys staggered out of the venue. On the pavement there was more singing until a police car stopped and told us to be quiet unless we fancied a night in the cells and a meeting with the local magistrate.

It was time to disperse. Hugs and handshakes and lots of merriment witnessed Hugo's stag-night come to an end. The guys dispersed, hoping to find their accommodation leaving Edward, Nathaniel and I to manoeuvre a very happy, very heavy and booming Hugo back to his flat. We struggled to carry, push and urge Hugo up the hill, find his door keys and throw him on his bed. We left him snoring away with a big smile.

Back in the hotel I was surprised to find the girls hadn't returned. Grateful I had limited my alcohol intake I stripped my beer-sodden clothes off, showered and went to bed leaving the clothes in a bath full of soapy water. I vaguely remember Christine kissing me.

I woke at nine-thirty. I looked at my English rose, deciding to leave her to sleep and went down for breakfast. Edward and Nathaniel were just finishing. I joined them and I was informed the girls didn't arrive back until three in the morning. Edward had undressed an inebriated Miranda and put her to bed. From his questioning, all he good work out was that they ended up in a nightclub on Leicester Square.

We laughed over the stag-night, which they agreed was a great night. As for the show girls they couldn't come to terms with the way they performed so lewdly in front of complete strangers, nor could they understand how they willingly interchanged a cucumber, albeit they did think it both funny and erotic. They thought Vince the Mincer very crude but also hilarious deciding they couldn't reveal to their respective ladies the goings on of the evening, I agreed.

The arrangement for Friday was lunch at our hotel for one followed by a convoy drive to Hugo's father's estate. One o'clock came and went with only a handful of the wedding party assembled. Hugo and Miriam finally managed to surface to ring-round apologising for their absence.

However, when I explained they were not alone in their absence they decided to delay the departure until five o'clock. My English rose was still fast asleep at one-thirty, however, the hotel had indicated I would need to pay for an extra night if we didn't vacate. I decided to pay as did Edward and Nathaniel.

I was sitting in an easy chair watching Christine's rhythmic breathing when she jumped and dashed into the bathroom. After a few minutes she emerged noticing me, she run across the room settled her gorgeous wonderful sexy body into my lap and started jabbering on about the fantastic evening they had enjoyed in London.

The cars delivered the sixteen girls to a wine bar off St James's Street where they had two drinks before moving onto a restaurant on Piccadilly Circus called the Criterion. Their table was situated centrally on a raised section to the rear of the restaurant. Christine giggled explaining the looks they were given when they walked through the diners referring to the walk-through as a beauty pageant. She enthused she hadn't, in the past, been in the company of so many beautiful women.

The whole evening, wherever they went, she explained, they were stared at, whistled at, heard lewd comments and had men flocking to chat them up. She was glad the drivers had stayed with them and controlled any over-eager flirtations. She considered the whole evening to be surreal.

After the restaurant the drivers escorted the girls to a very smart wine-bar where they had champagne and brandy cocktails. Laughing, she described one over-flirtatious guy bothering Josephine receiving a good slap and a cocktail poured over his head before one of the drivers pulled him clear. Christine said that on reflection they should have worn dowdy clothes to lessen the many approaches by lecherous males.

After the wine bar they were once more escorted by their minders to a nightclub with a massive queue. However the girls were waved in and directed to a VIP lounge. The lounge had a splattering of television celebrities and well known footballers. Although there was plenty of alcohol available the girls with the exception of Miranda and Tonia tended to drink little. They danced a great deal, which she had thoroughly enjoyed and they talked and talked.

Christine expounded her liking for Miriam and Josephine and Dawn, one of the bridesmaids. The drivers rounded them up just before two to congregate in the VIP lounge to toast Miriam with champagne. After which they were escorted to and sorted into the cars and the drivers delivered them safely to their respective accommodation. All-in all she said the evening was fun and she had enjoyed herself greatly.

Christine decided she needed to soak in a hot bath to rid her of the evening's odours. However, she wanted to know why a plastic bag held my damp clothes. I explained as per custom being the best man can be a very wet job, especially when ten guys decide to pour their beer over you. "Oh my poor Richard," then she laughed saying she wished she had been there.

I ordered a selection of sandwiches and two pots of tea from room service and packed the majority of our clothes.

She walked out of the bathroom rubbing her hair dry. Her loveliness refreshed the room. She was as near perfect as any woman could be. I loved her gorgeous red hair, the little triangle of red hair where her superbly shaped long legs merged into her body. As she dried her hair her breasts bobbed up and down. I was enchanted by her pink nipples. The taper from her curvaceous hips to her slim waist and her most delightful bottom, every miniscule part of her excited me.

270

While we were eating the sandwiches she asked how the stag-night had gone. I expounded the singing and the fun, told of the drunken female gate crashers, mentioned the strippers and described, without going into detail, the lewdness of the comedian. I expressed the excess alcohol that was consumed, the police warning and the hard work getting Hugo back to his flat and onto his bed.

Christine said, "It sounds like it was a drunken sex orgy to me."

"Which it was and what it was intended to be," I said laughing. I added, "There wasn't anything sedate or puritanical that I can guarantee, and nor was it an orgy. It was a group of old pals gathering to enjoy one of Hugo's final nights of freedom."

Christine smiled saying, "Yes, I suppose Miriam's night had the same connotations."

By five o'clock a very irate hotel manager was demanding we leave his hotel, in particular he was keen to empty his car park where there were nine cars waiting for Hugo to arrive to lead his wedding guest convoy. I was trapped in a parking space when the car horns started blasting signalling Hugo's delayed arrival. The cars pulled out behind his Jaguar and commenced the journey north of London to his father's estate.

Chapter 28 – Miriam and Hugo, the Wedding

Christine and I were assigned the same room, which pleased Christine. We unpacked the clothes and dressed casually to join the gang in the main hall for a buffet Mrs Double-U had prepared, and what a buffet. There were oodles of food, which I knew was very much needed and welcomed with enthusiasm. Although there was wine and beer available most of the assembly were content with water and fruit juices, and fizzy drinks.

Hugo was in evidence but no sign of Miriam. I pointed this out to Christine and she laughed at me. "You are so naïve sometimes Richard, bride and groom will not see each other again until Miriam starts her walk down the aisle." In the back of my mind I had heard this before. Nonetheless I asked why. "Because, Richard it is considered bad luck."

Somehow the gang split in half, the females at one end of the baronial hall and the males the other. We were all aware the wedding was timed for eleven and we had to be in the chapel by ten forty-five. Although it was only nine o'clock in the evening we began to disperse. I was keen to rehearse my speech, which Christine had assisted me with.

Early next morning I was banging on Hugo's door. No answer. I went to search for him. I toured the mansion, which takes some doing. Out of frustration I asked Jackson the butler. He smiled, "Have you tried Miss Miriam's room."

He gave me directions. I banged on Miriam's door. I heard Miriam, "Yes who is it?" "The man supposedly looking after the groom," I replied. Hugo's voice: "Is the coast clear?" We made a mad dash for his room.

I dragged him down to breakfast, bathed him and dressed him. Satisfied he would be a good boy I dashed to my room to bathe and dress. When I arrived back at his room he was asleep in a chair. I said, "What the hell were you doing in Miriam's room?" He laughed "Enjoying one last night as a single man."

On the way to the chapel I couldn't help but notice the number of cars. I thought the whole of Herefordshire must have been invited. We passed gatherings all along the route. Outside the chapel there were huge speakers rigged to relay the ceremonies words, hymns and songs to those unfortunates standing outside. I asked him how many guests. He didn't have a clue.

In the chapel I was introduced to dozens of people, most of who washed over my head. However, Mrs Webster I remembered purely for her tears. Hugo hugged her and promised to look after her little girl. The evening before, Mr and Mrs Webster had enjoyed a private dinner with Hugo's parents in their apartment.

I manoeuvred Hugo onto the small dais. I remembered the ring. I had passed it to Christine for safe keeping. In a panic I turned to be greeted by my beautiful lady. And she was beautiful, spectacular in her loveliness. She handed me the ring and I kissed her whispering for the first time "I love you". She looked at me wondering if she had heard me properly. I said, "Yes that is what I said." She smiled the most brilliant and most delightful smile.

There was a sudden fanfare. Hugo and I turned to look towards the most beautiful bride stood with her father and Hugo's nephews. The small choir started to sing:

We've only just begun to live,
White lace and promises
A kiss for luck and we're on our way.
We've just begun.

Before the rising sun we fly,
So many roads to choose
We start out walking and learn to run.
And yes, We've just begun.

Sharing horizons that are new to us,
Watching the signs along the way,
Talking it over just the two of us,
Working together day to day
Together.

And when the evening comes we smile,
So much of life ahead
We'll find a place where there's room to grow,
And yes, We've just begun.

The beautiful Miriam advanced down the aisle. A murmur, appreciating her beauty and her loveliness spread through the congregation. Her father handed her over to Hugo. I noticed a tear in Hugo's eye. I winked at him, he smiled.

The ceremony was a wee bit long. I don't know who chose the third hymn, whoever knew little of Hugo's college days, the hymn "Hosanna, loud hosanna" suddenly encouraged several strong male voices to replace "Hosanna, loud hosanna" with "Hannah, oh Hannah". I inwardly smiled and wished I could see Hugo's face.

The ceremony over a long winding trail of wedding guests headed toward the Baronial Hall. From the chapel entrance all the way to the main house confetti and rice and flowers were thrown with gay abandon towards the smiling Mr and Mrs Hugo Theobald Garton-Maugham.

I rushed ahead with Christine to clear any last minute obstacles of which there were none. I looked into the Baronial Hall, it was magnificent. Thinking we were only in there enjoying a buffet a few hours previously, I was truly amazed by its transformation.

Liveried staff, many liveried staff stood ready to seat the guests and provide refreshments. Christine had been given a seat next to me, which pleased me no-end. The time taken for all the guests to be shown or directed to tables took an eternity. Champagne corks were popping consistently.

The reception kicked off when the Master Of Ceremonies splendidly attired introduced himself and welcomed everyone. He introduced the wedding party and announced with great enthusiasm and applause, the bride and groom's arrival into the wedding reception.

The chaplain gave Grace, followed by the entree being served.

The Master Of Ceremonies proposed The Loyal Toast

The Main Course was served

Dessert and coffee was served

The Master Of Ceremonies introduced Mr Charles Webster, the father of the bride. He proposed a toast to the Bride and Groom.

The Master Of Ceremonies introduced Hugo who simply said "I am a very happy man and I have the most wonderful person in the world by my side. However, I would like you to raise your glasses and toast three beautiful Bridesmaids who have spread light and cheer." He waited a moment before saying, "As for any other words I leave that to my best man, and I if I may I would like to mention he is has been my best friend since school, King Dick," and abruptly sat down.

The Master Of Ceremonies introduced me and I started talking:

My Lords, Ladies, Ladies and Gentlemen & Boys and Girls! Wow that's part one of the speech over.

We are here to celebrate the marriage of The Honourable Hugo Theobald Garton-Maugham and the very gorgeous and delightful Miriam "Oh my God! What the hell am I doing here?" Webster!

Firstly, I'd like to express my delight at being here at what really is the wedding of the year and to comment on just how ravishingly beautiful the bridesmaids, and some of the men, look this afternoon! It's fantastic to be back in the beautiful village of……, where are we? – oh yes the wonderful home of Lady Alicia and Lord Crispin – and now, it seems, their beautiful home has been high-jacked by riff-raff and I refer to the noisy table over to my right.

I was often here as a schoolboy and student and the special relationship between Hugo and me is really tangible and has lasted years. However by the time I finish this speech that may change.

I also have to tell you that being asked to be Best Man for such an occasion is a great honour – bloody inconvenient – but a great honour nevertheless!

Apparently my main duties here today were to get Hugo to the church, on time, smart and sober. Miraculously it would appear that I have been a resounding success.

I know a lot of people have come a long way for this momentous occasion, which only goes to underline the friendships that these two great people have formed with you, the congregation. This is especially poignant as it's a mixed marriage – he's a business man, and Miriam is a human being!

I must say, all of us were a little surprised when the announcement was made as we were all convinced that Hugo would marry one of his father's businesses....And not just any old business but one of the larger ones which he's spent many a night with over the past few years!

So, let's just re-visit who this mysterious Hugo character actually is:

I don't mind admitting that this speech has caused me one or two problems…… As most of you will be able to verify there's a fair amount of material out there, very little of which is vaguely appropriate on such a lovely day as today, so much so that I considered performing speech A to audience A and speech B, to audience B.

I have instead decided, Hugo's mother will be delighted to hear, to make one speech and err on the side of caution as opposed to utter embarrassment. Well mostly.

Hugo was born 10th April 1947. I did try to link this date with some impressive world event ...but there isn't one.

So moving swiftly on...

He achieved immediate notoriety by being declared 'Baby of the Week' weighing in at 10lbs 2ozs. Initially however he was labelled a non-thriver but he soon developed a love of food and blossomed into the giant he is today.

It all began with Hugo at a young age moving to a school in Cumbria where he met his chief childhood partners in crime, of which there were many! In fact this was the only recorded moment in history where a Hugo became Bright in Mind and Spirit! In case you are not aware Bright in Mind and Spirit is the meaning of Hugo, which Lady Alicia, I am sure, was mindful of at the time of his Christening.

Misjudgement – is what Hugo suffered from in the early days. Like the time when he constructed 'Death-slide' in one of his parent's barns and leapt off the second floor clutching his rope with lanky arms and legs flailing desperately. Before crashing to the barn floor with a wail of fear and confusion……because the rope was too long!

Or, like the time he painstakingly constructed a beautifully crafted dog kennel and after hours of meticulous carpentry realised that the dog wouldn't fit through the cat-flap sized front door!

He did also develop an interest in the opposite sex.......... Being the experienced lothario he was at the age of 13 I remember him explaining to me one night the relative ease with which he could slip into the girl's school under the cover of darkness, for what purpose I do not know..... In fact he was going that very night and off he went......... An hour or so later a more subdued Hugo returned, having been rumbled by the house master to reveal six bright red slipper marks across his bare behind.

Hugo was a star sportsman. For a time he was uncertain which way to go because he shined at cricket, rugby and swimming. But in the end, it was rugby that claimed his allegiance, and not only for the shared experience of communal showers after the game. It was the togetherness of tackles on the field of play that swung it!

I spoke with many of Hugo's work colleagues in order to compile this speech, once the initial laughter had subsided about what a difficult task I had a number of traits begin to emerge. He is, apparently, so I was told, quick witted, honest, loyal and generous. Hmmm.

Generous....As anyone who drinks with Hugo regularly will be able to tell you, his pockets are very deep. In fact, he prefers to play a game of spoof.....For those of you that don't know the game Hugo will be happy to take some money off you later.

Although, I do, remember an instance, where his generosity was illustrated. September 1972, I had managed to wrangle 2 corporate tickets for the England v All Blacks game at Twickenham, the opening autumn game, tickets were changing hands for about £500 a go.

I had arranged the full package including a room in a Richmond hotel to collapse into after the night's merriment, even a lovely breakfast the next day. I invited Hugo as my guest and he was over the moon.

Meanwhile on the Friday, we embarked on a night of beers. Over the course of the evening we fell in with some Kiwi lads some of whom didn't have tickets, who he teased relentlessly because he had a ticket. A great deal of beer was consumed. Hugo for some unfathomable reason decided to push it too far...... he decided to announce, "Alright then you Kiwis, to show what a good sport we Brits are I will toss this coin. If you win you can go to the rugby in my place." The Kiwis won and one of them received his ticket. The next day at breakfast Hugo was speechless. Honest, loyal, generous and a perhaps a little silly.

Yes, Hugo is an adventurer! Not afraid to take a great leap into the unknown whether it's desperately clinging onto a dinghy with his feet whilst spread-eagled in a futile attempt to cling on to a bridge over the icy waters of the Thames as he did after a particularly tough rugby game or jacking-in everything to join his father on a conquest for global domination in the business world. In fact, like me, Hugo is working on his second million. We gave up on our first!

He's a man of hidden talents though – as soon as we find one we'll let you know! Luckily he's completely bi-lingual; he speaks both English and English almost fluently! But in all seriousness, Hugo is a genius – to call Hugo a business man is like calling Michelangelo a decorator! He really is the best.

Looking at the fine man Hugo has clearly become, sitting beside the wonderful Miriam, I realise what a fantastic choice he's made – I really admire his taste – which is more than I can say for Miriam's!

Some of you will know that Hugo first met Miriam through a mutual "friend" whilst she was helping with a business launch venture. As he sat huddled round an office with colleagues who were trying to get a glimpse of what this sexy-voiced female looked like, little did they know that good old Hugo knew rather more than he was letting on! Because it seemed that these two had already become Hugo and Miriam and, frighteningly a beautiful relationship was already in the making.

So, Hugo and Miriam, a special romance that emerged when "business man" Hugo persuaded "human-being" Miriam into his life and many things started to happen. I give you a romantic synopsis of the story – it all stems back to a specialist period:

Some years ago, Hugo's private activities away from his business activities actioned a move towards a girl, who became a girlfriend leaving his many drinking mates, which he had used for years without any trouble. However, he envisaged conflicts between the two and the only solution was to try and keep girlfriend secret. To make matters worse, his girlfriend is incompatible with several of Hugo's business activities such as "Lads Night Out", "Rugby" and "Client Entertainment".

Eventually Hugo tried to run girlfriend and drinking mates at the same time only to discover that when these two detected each other they caused severe damage to his morale. Hugo in desperation eventually opted to upgrade girlfriend to fiancée, only to discover he was trapped and had to upgrade further to Wife, at great expense.

So now they are married and off to sunny Hawaii in a few days for their honeymoon – God knows how Hugo's going to hold his stomach in for 10 days!

However, we, in particular me, because I know what a superb person Miriam is, know Hugo is indeed a very lucky man. He has upgraded Miriam to wife and he will, I believe, never regret his, and Miriam's decision, to join together on this magnificent day.

On yes, a final note, based on the fact that Miriam has had a sign made which hangs over their front door which reads 'Views expressed by the husband are not necessarily those of the management' I would therefore, strongly advise Hugo to follow the age-old moniker "If you want to keep love flowing, from the loving cup – when you're wrong, admit it, when you're right, SHUT UP!.

A toast to Miriam and Hugo!

The Master Of Ceremonies introduced Miriam's father. He gave a moving speech of how he and Miriam's mother had watched their bright intelligent child turn her back on school and the opportunity of college to search for an elusive future in advertising. Finally she did see the light and return to college, but only after she had met Hugo and he persuaded her to study once more. Although Miriam had expressly insisted he shouldn't mention certain factors. He would like to say he so very pleased to see she had finally given up jeans and sweaters and now dressed like a young woman, the beautiful young woman she is.

He toasted Lady Alicia and Lord Crispin.

The Master Of Ceremonies introduced Lord Crispin. He lived up to his name; his speech was crisp, to the point and very business-like. He declared how he and his wife adored Miriam and that both agreed she had brought order and stability into Hugo's life, which pleased his parents because one day he would rule the Crispin dynasty. He expressed eloquently how pleased he was now that Miriam would become part of the family. He briefly mentioned me by saying he was grateful I had not embarrassed his son and that he was fully aware I had many secrets. He encapsulated Miriam's parents welcoming them into the family and for their enthusiastic love for their daughter, which they had now passed to their new son-in-law. His last words, with a smile, we now wait, hopefully not too long for the patter of tiny feet.

He toasted Miriam, and yes he really meant what he said, which was, "Friends and family I ask you to be upstanding for the very beautiful and the very practical and very intelligent Miriam, who I am very proud to call my daughter-in law. Miriam.

The Master Of Ceremonies re-introduced me to read messages:

Statistics show that marriage is one of the reasons of divorce! So, don't get married! Oops too late. Just kidding, have a great life together, which we are sure you will. Best wishes and our love, Susie and Graham (happily married twelve years)

The Wedding ceremony is the celebration of love. You will know because we know you two will forever be together, we love you both. Mary and Tod

Your wedding day will last for twenty four hours and your love after marriage will last for a hundred years. Good luck and God Bless Kirsty and Clive

Congratulations Miriam and Hugo for your successful marriage! Now act as the jailer for each other. Be good and enjoy, we are. Love Karen and Ian

You two had two different personal worlds of your own. After today, both of you will have your own world! Love and enjoy your married life, it can't be beaten. Love "The Office Crew"

The Master Of Ceremonies thanked everyone, and announced the cutting of the cake.

Thereafter it was celebration time. However, firstly Miriam had to force Hugo to get up onto his two left feet. They danced, Hugo obviously having had lessons, to "Dream A Little Dream" by the Mamas & the Papas. Christine pulled me onto the floor, which was the signal for parents then all the guests. Christine whispered in my ear "And I love you, very much."

Hugo and I spent a good half hour conversing. We were left alone to reinforce our wonderful friendship and also to reminisce a little over school and college days and the fun and trouble we had and endured. We promised each other the earth, hugged and kissed cheeks, both cheeks. We returned to our women.

Chapter 29 – Christine, Family and Amazing Friends, and Promotion

Back at work on the Monday after Miriam and Hugo's wedding, I received a call summoning me to head office, startled to learn I would be replacing Pete. Doug explained that Pete's health was deteriorating quite quickly and he and his wife Marjorie wanted to visit their son in Australia to meet their daughter-in-law and two grandchildren.

Doug further explained that Pete suffered from advanced diabetes, which required constant treatment. However, he had decided he would rather enjoy life and not lay and suffer in a hospital bed.

After the meeting with Doug I returned to the office to seek out Pete. While I was searching, Christine found me and told me he had ceased working Friday, news to her and all the office. I called Doug he said, "Oh shit, sorry, I forgot to mention that. I am sorry." I asked, "What exactly did Pete do besides managing me and my teams?"

He said, "Come and see me after lunch," and hung-up.

After lunch Doug presented Mr Maybury's official letter informing me of my new position and a my new salary plus an improved pension scheme and the added responsibility, which included three crews, one based in Liverpool consisting of a manger, two supervising engineers and fourteen engineers of varying skills. The other based in Immingham consisted of a similar set-up, plus a small team in Falmouth, news to me, consisting of six guys. However, Doug emphasised he would like to set-up one or possibly two overseas teams, the feasibility of which he would like investigated and appropriate reports and recommendations issued.

The rest of the week flew by. Sitting in the office late Thursday night submerged in paper, Christine called. When I answered she said, "Do you know what time it is? I looked at my watch, nine-fifty." I replied, "Sorry sweetheart have I missed something?"

Christine's crystal clear laugh tinkled down the telephone receiver. "Only me, I am lying here exactly as you like, naked and warm." I laughed.

"I'm on my way don't move." She laughingly replied, "Where are you going, you don't know where I am."

"Okay my lovely lady where are you?" I laughingly asked.

"In your bed of course," she replied and hung-up.

I was home in a jiffy, in the shower and in bed cuddling my lovely lady, the best place in the world. We made love, tender love enjoying being together, connected as man and woman. Nestled in my arms Christine reminded me we were in Lytham the coming weekend to visit my mother. I had completely forgotten.

In the morning we packed and sped to the office. I drove and Christine still keeping up the pretence, until Doug gave the go-ahead, we were only work colleagues who on occasion met for a drink after work, travelled in on public transport. Although I knew that most if not all realised we were a couple.

Christine left the office at four saying to her team she had check with head office regarding the upcoming annual pay-rises. I had departed earlier leaving the office for some obscure reason. I sat in the car parked just to the left of the dockyard gates. She jumped in the car and we headed north.

Mother and Grandma Jean were waiting with supper, when we arrived shortly before ten. I had called ahead giving an estimated arrival time. Unlike Sophie, or any other girls mother had had the pleasure of meeting she took to Christine like a duck takes to water.

Mother immediately decided upon meeting Christine we were the perfect match. Mother didn't have to say anything, although I knew she would, the message in bright neon letters reverberated all over her face. After supper of cold meats, cheeses and accompaniments and a most welcome pot of tea we were shown to the guest room.

In bed Christine declared how lovely and warm she thought my mother and how sweet Grandma Jean was. I didn't bother to explain my mother had decided to ready her for slaughter, to be sacrificed to her son. We slept soundly being woken with tea mid-morning. Before I realised what happened, mother and Christine had disappeared.

I found myself alone with Grandma, chief bay-sitter, which would mean at least two hundred games of gin-rummy. Sometimes I could kill my mother. Grandma, after mentioning that Christine would be perfect, stressing Christine typified the sort of girl I should settle down with, concentrated on taking all my money at five pence a game.

Christine and mother arrived home at five. They were laden with parcels and shopping bags. One of mother's favourite pastimes just happened to be shopping, not for her but for others.

Christine, in our room expressed her embarrassment explaining how mother had virtually forced her to try on dresses and skirts, coats and jackets, blouses and shirts, and even sexy lingerie. I fell about on the bed laughing.

Christine jumped astride me, kissing me saying "Your mother thinks we are getting married" I sat up holding onto Christine so she didn't fall. "What did she say exactly?" I demanded. "How happy she is, looking forward to the wedding" I carefully moved Christine to one side and leaped down the stairs.

Before I could say a word mother said "I know, I know I'm jumping the gun. You are my son I can read you like a book. It's in your eyes, in your movements. I think they call it body language these days. You want this girl, which means you will marry her. I know and you know so let's stop the pretence shall we."

I sat down deflated and defeated realising my mother, once more had seen right through me. Mother sat on the arm of the chair and hugged me. "Richard, for once you have got it right and I am not saying Sophie wasn't right, but my God Richard how many have there been since Sophie, too many to count." I caught Christine out of the corner of my eye. I eased off the chair saying "What did you hear?" "All of it" she whispered.

We retired to the dining table leaving Grandma watching television. I took a white wine from the wine cooler, opened it and poured three glasses. I also poured a brandy for Grandma and took it to her.

Christine said "Richard do you love me?" I answered "You know I do." Mother interrupted saying "You see this is the girl for you and no mistake" I said "Mother" irritated "For once be quiet" Christine unperturbed said "Tell me, tell me now" I looked at her she looked sad. I held her hand. I looked first at mother then focused my eyes firmly on Christine's eyes and I said "Christine Clarke I love you, my heart is yours"

Two wine glasses spilt their contents as two women mother and girlfriend threw their arms round my neck. Both women told me they loved me. I told them I loved them also.

Mother telephoned father. Father wanted to talk. He simply said "Do it and do it right, no more philandering. I'll take Tina for dinner to celebrate" and he was gone. That was my father, a good man but unemotional and short on words in affairs of the heart.

Mother now in charge wanted to arrange this, and do that and so on and so on. I said quietly "Mother as much as I love you please leave Christine and I to decide what happens next" Mother smiled, left the dining room and closed the door. I looked at Christine, she smiled. I kissed her head, before collecting a tea towel from the kitchen and wiping the spilt wine.

I pulled Christine into my arms and with a happy smile, because I felt happy I said "You do know my mother has just sacrificed you to her son and that you are stuck with her son until doomsday."

She too smiled happily "I couldn't care less I am being sacrificed to the man I love and that my darling man suits me down to the ground." We kissed for a long, long time a very loving and caring kiss.

After the kiss I smiled "Once you have had the pleasure of my father and Tina and half a dozen other people, we should take that long holiday, how about Hong Kong to introduce me to your aunt and uncle." Christine, tears streaming down her cheeks said "Richard I love you, I love you with my heart, my body and my soul"

The Monday after visiting mother I sat in my office contemplating Maybury and the future. My empire wouldn't stop growing, similarly Christine's responsibilities were extending at a rapid rate, she now had a staff of eleven and she too had received handsome pay rises and additional perks.

I re-arranged the week before we would be visiting father to investigate the Liverpool, Immingham and Falmouth operations and to meet my new teams. I chose Falmouth for the first visit, deciding to leave at four, Tuesday morning. An early start would enable five or six hours with the team before driving home. I would be home by eight at the latest, a long day but I considered the effort worth it.

Christine's team put together documents representing the changes, which included the new organisational structure, an explanation of what support would be available from both Millbrook and Head offices. She also included senior management biographies all contained within an attractively designed welcoming pack, which to my ignorant eyes looked very futuristic. Christine and her team also prepared similar documents for the Liverpool and Immingham teams.

We were lying in bed Monday evening talking when an idea hit me. I said "How about I shoot to Liverpool Thursday morning, leaving Southampton at six, which means I'll be with the team at ten in the morning. I will spend the day with them, stay overnight in Liverpool before setting off for Hull Friday morning. I could be in Hull easily by ten, earlier if necessary.

In the meantime, on Friday, my very sexy maiden you make your way to Kings Cross, London and catch a train to Hull, where I'll meet you, and then we can then drive together to Whickham. I'll have the luggage in the car so all you have to carry is you. What do you think?" "Absolutely brilliant" she cried out and fell on me wanting Jolly Roger before sleep claimed us.

Making love with Christine was such a wonderful and beautiful encounter, it lasted forever. The problem, when to stop, I couldn't, the experience, so astonishingly breath-taking, I didn't want to stop.

I have no idea when we actually went to sleep only that the alarm clock penetrated my dead sleep long before I was ready. Nevertheless, I forced myself from the warmth of Christine, prepared myself and started driving.

The early start gave me clear roads as far as Oakhampton, thereafter the traffic began to build. Nevertheless I made the Maybury offices for eight sitting in my car waiting until eight fifteen when Gus Bradbury the manager pulled up. We had met once or twice before.

When he saw me climb out of the car, he looked at his watch. He strode over to shake my hand saying "Bloody hell you're the first governor to visit here in donkey's years" He made a mug of coffee and we chatted until eight-thirty, start time, when I addressed the team.

Through the day I interviewed each of the team and inspected work regimes, maintenance schedules and work practices finishing with the stores and spare parts procurement processes. I made a point of visiting where they were working. Before I left I pre-warned Gus to expect change and I would be back soon.

The drive back proved to be an effing nightmare. It took hours delaying my return home until nine-thirty. Christine, when I unlocked the flat door rushed to me, demanding to know why I was so late and asking if I had ever heard of a magical device called a telephone.

Smiling I said, "Darling if I had stopped to telephone I would still be an hour away." She made a mug of desperately-needed tea and served a stew she had made. I ate the supper, told her how much I loved her, showered, went to bed and closed my eyes.

Wednesday morning Christine received a call from her boss, Gareth Holdsworth, he wanted to see her. He explained to her the change in company policy regarding relationship liaisons. When he had finished he shook her hand saying, "You are at liberty to promulgate what ninety percent of the workforce already know, that is if you want to."

Christine laughed and thanked him and called me explaining the new policy. Doug called asking when he would receive his customary bribe for arranging the company policy re-write. I said, "I owe you and I will not forget."

Wednesday morning I cursed, I couldn't reconcile either Liverpool or Immingham's financial reports. I called accounts in. They talked mumbo-jumbo for twenty minutes before I called a halt. I said, "Answer one simple question, are they losing money, because from my understanding from the figures you have provided, they are." More mumbo-jumbo before I asked who was aware of the situation.

It appeared the buck stopped with Pete and because accounts are reported verbally to the board unless specific questions are asked the board were none the wiser, albeit each board member is issued with a copy. I immediately requested a board meeting. I received confirmation for the following Tuesday.

Doug called me and asked what I was up to. He swore and cursed me for not advising him before I requested the meeting. I apologised stating if any board member was aware it would have been him. He laughed saying, "Do you know what board members do all day?" A rhetorical question he answered, "They talk and talk, very little action."

Thursday morning, weary, I climbed into the car and headed for Liverpool. Liverpool went much the same as Falmouth except I pulled the manager, Stuart Laird and asked him to explain financial reporting. He ashamedly admitted he didn't know leaving it to a clerk in the office, which after he asked if they were correct he signed off. I very nearly sacked him on the spot but there would have been all kinds of ructions so I counted to ten instead. I sent for the clerk.

A young girl no more than twenty introduced herself. I asked her where she had been trained in accountancy practices. She hadn't, she used a calculator to add columns and that was her accounting methodology. I telephoned head office insisting upon a qualified accountant in Liverpool to reconcile the last twelve months' figures.

I called Doug to make sure the demand would be adhered to. During the conversation he advised the board meeting I requested would be delayed until robust information became available, making it clear they expected chapter and verse.

I found overnight accommodation at an out of town Motel. I telephoned Christine and we talked as young lovers do for a while. I managed, after umpteen attempts to identify she would arrive in Hull at three o'clock. In the morning at seven-thirty I hit the road for Hull.

I followed a similar routine and once more discussed with the manager, Terry Hamley the accounting principles he used. He actually prepared them himself and had a reasonable idea of what he was doing, but as before he hadn't been trained. Hence I demanded another accountant for Immingham.

I arrived at Hull station in plenty of time to meet Christine. She spotted me waiting, sprung from the carriage and yelled, "Richard." I rushed to meet her. Christine's yell and the consequent embrace and kissing accrued several smiles and the odd stare. We ran to the car like two young lovers, happy to be together and free of any encumbrances.

The journey proved to be surprisingly swift. Father's house was empty. I took Christine to my room and showed her the facilities followed by a tour of the house.

Checking the time I said, "Why don't we look around we can drive out to Tynemouth and Whitley Bay." Christine, fed-up with car travel declined, preferring a cup of tea. She asked about Tina and how long she and father had been together. I described a friendly relationship, which seemed to work admitting I wasn't too involved.

I did, however, explain the love-hate relationship between mother and father and how they were constantly conversing on the telephone. I further described how they had worked very hard to build their own businesses. Adding that I believed they had allowed work to replace personal happiness.

Father arrived home. He introduced himself to Christine and told her I wasn't worthy of her or her beauty. Christine and he chatted amiably for quite some time mostly I hate to say, about me. She informed him of my recent promotion and all the travel I had to do. He was pleased to hear of my work success referring to himself as a bloody good teacher.

He explained his plans for the evening which included meeting Tina at Newcastle station explaining that her mother had been ill subsequently

Tina travelled home to Edinburgh. After meeting Tina he had arranged dinner in a good restaurant.

We waited on the south-bound platform for the Edinburgh to London train. I watched the two diesel engines with their long trail of carriages coasting towards the station coming to a halt three minutes early. People alighted from the long train, those without heavy luggage rushed towards the ticket barrier hoping to secure taxis for their onward journeys.

Those with heavy or several cases searched for trolleys. Meanwhile replacing the passenger exodus were south-bound passengers, some assisted by porters, boarding, checking seat numbers and preparing for their journey.

However, Tina didn't appear. Father and I split-up searching the carriages. I heard a kafuffle ahead; a uniformed railway man struggled with a case before assisting Tina, who, without any doubt, was blotto, drunk as a skunk screaming obscenities.

I heard father curse as we ran to take charge of Tina. Father called to me to grab her luggage and he lifted Tina into his arms. She slavered all over father. I noted his grimace and look of disgust. I called to Christine to go and hide.

After a hold-up at the ticket barrier searching for Tina's ticket we made our way to father's car. He literally threw Tina in the back seat and shouted at her to shut-up. I placed her luggage in the boot.

Father apologised and taking thirty pounds from his wallet he told me to take Christine out on the town. He opened the car door, turned to me and said, "She's been hitting the booze heavily for a while. I am sorry, please apologise to Christine for me."

I turned and headed towards the station entrance. Christine her face a picture of concern took my arm and lightly kissed me on the cheek. I put on my best smile and apologised for her embarrassment and for Tina's behaviour. I also passed on father's apology.

Cheerfully I said, "I have orders to take you out on the town. Father gave me thirty pounds and said go. So my English rose that is exactly what we are going to do, we are going out on the town. We crossed the busy thoroughfare in front of the station and walked leisurely towards Newcastle Town centre.

Walking I started to hum a tune, which for some reason had materialised in my head. Christine recognised the tune and started to sing softly:

Once in every lifetime,
Comes a love like this,
Oh I need you, you need me,
Oh my darling can't you see.
Darling we're the Young Ones.

We both laughed and continued, in harmony, to hum.

Christine squeezed my arm saying, "You and I haven't, what's that silly expression, oh yes painted the town red, perhaps it is about time we did."

I smiled saying, "Great idea, albeit I only know of a couple of bars and one club."

Christine her cool beauty blossoming said, "Okay we will start with the bars and then we'll go to the club." Kissing her cheek I murmured my agreement.

"But first I have to remember where the bars are." Once more with Christine holding onto me tightly we laughed. I wanted to lift and swing her around shouting, "I love you, I love you."

We didn't find either of the bars so we settled on "Custer's Last Stand", a wine and cocktail bar. We entered through the jazzy entrance received a once over by a bouncer passed through double doors to be greeted by a hundred or so revellers, who by their attire, mostly men and women in business suits and some ladies wearing smart work dresses, were ending the working week with well-earned refreshments.

The bar's ambience, a mixture of rhythm and blues music and cheerful conversation, gave off a pleasing feel. We managed to find space at the far end of a very long bar tendered by seven or more staff.

Two menus appeared. Christine studied one until her finger came to rest on a Tangerine Sorbet Champagne Float, which I ordered to join my Dirty Dry Martini with three olives. The guy serving was super-efficient, delivering our drinks within minutes. I tasted Christine's cocktail, which I found delightful. She tried my Martini and wrinkled her nose. Both happy and smiling, holding hands we toasted our love and our future.

A chap with a group of guys offered Christine his stool. I watched him, his eyes travelling her lovely slim legs as I helped her to settle. He winked at me and I winked back. Christine nuzzled my neck while her hand held forth an empty glass.

I re-ordered for her only knowing from experience the effect a couple Martinis could have. Christine wanted to talk, especially regarding our living arrangements. She said "Richard the ad hoc way we live our lives is not conducive" I raised my eyebrows "Conducive to what" I asked. "Look, you are often travelling, when you are, I stay in my flat with Charlotte. When you arrive home I am in your flat waiting for you. At weekends I am forever moving clothes from one to the other. Anyway your flat is small and dark." I had to laugh.

Jokingly I said, "Okay, we move Charlotte into my flat and I move in with you." Christine did contemplate the suggestion before retorting, "Don't be silly why would Charlotte move out into your flat when she has much more room, a bedroom twice the size of yours, furniture that doesn't look like it was picked-up from a second hand shop and me as a flat mate."

"Okay, what do you suggest?" I asked.

"I'll think about it," she answered, subject terminated.

Christine was certainly enjoying the Tangerine Sorbet Champagne Floats as passed yet another empty glass. This time I refilled my glass. Her next subject, careers, specifically were we both destined to work for Maybury until we retired.

I said, "Actually that is a good point because UK and European shipping is gradually transferring to the near and far east, which means we either set-up teams overseas, which I believe will be pointless because of labour costs or the company diversifies and, or seeks an innovative approach."

Christine smiled, "Do you know I realised you were thinking things through a few days ago when you commented on the uselessness of Doug's proposal to set-up overseas teams. You will not let the grass grow under your feet, that I am most assured of."

"Does this club serve food?" asked Christine.

"It does, and very good food too," I answered, not sure whether it did or not. I based my answer on father's regular patronage. I said, "It's not far we can walk it in a few minutes, on the way I'll phone father to ensure we can gain entry." I telephoned father, asked after Tina to which he grunted and swore. I elicited his assistance to gain entry into the Mighty Quinn.

The Mighty Quinn is a very up-market club, its splendour much in evidence when we arrived at the reception desk. I gave my name. I was surprised by the number of people in the club so early. However, most were enjoying dinner, a positive sign.

A skimpily-dressed young lady escorted us to a booth, on the raised area where I had celebrated New Year with father, Melissa and Tina, and where father had been sitting when he received the mysterious note from Debbie. I thanked the girl.

The sommelier wandered over. "Good evening Mr Chambers, no Mr Chambers senior this evening?" he queried. I shook my head, he said, "There is a bottle of champagne on ice waiting for you or would you prefer a cocktail to start." I smiled.

"No, I think the champagne would be fine. However, we are hungry and would like to eat." He raised his hand and a waitress appeared with two menus.

We ordered a selection of seven starters to share. The sommelier served the champagne. He ensured we were satisfied before leaving to attend to other tables. Christine remarked on the club and how aesthetically it was presented. She also commented on the close attention provided by the staff, which she thought rare in Southampton.

In response I teased her about her clubbing habits, asking how she had become so familiar with Southampton's nightlife. She airily waved her hand, smiling she said "You know, us girls on the hunt, we have to try all clubs looking for the right man" I tut-tutted, "Christine Clarke I considered you to be the studious type not interested in the frivolities of life." She gave up and kissed me. Then I heard the voice.

"Richard, yet another beautiful woman, is there no end to your harem?" I looked up. "Hello Debbie, how are you? Allow me to introduce Christine my girlfriend." Debbie ignoring the introduction seated herself next to Christine. "Girlfriend, that's a new one, have you run out of numbers?"

Before I could answer Christine jumped in and how "Listen lady whoever you are. Yes I am Richard's girlfriend and I have been for a while. If you are one of his conquests from the past, well good luck to you and I hope you enjoyed him because you are not going to get another chance. And oh yes instead of trying to annoy me why don't you go and play with your make-up bag, your face needs some serious attention, now if you don't mind my boyfriend and I would like to be left in peace." Debbie's face dropped but she didn't move.

Unexpectedly Debbie apologised to Christine for being a bitch and for being unnecessarily sarcastic. She then apologised to me asking forgiveness. Christine relented, her soft side, or perhaps her personnel experience took over. She signalled for another glass, which the waitress rapidly delivered, pouring the champagne. I looked on, dumbfounded.

Debbie looking at Christine but speaking to me said, "Is Christine the girl you told me about?" I nodded answering, "Yes, Christine is that girl." Her gaze moved to me.

"I thought so when you walked in, your arm very protective and you were very attentive."

She turned to Christine. "He's a good bloke, very upfront, not many around, just the odd one. You have my best wishes for the future." She lifted her glass sipped the champagne saying, "I'll take this with me and leave you in peace."

Christine turned to me. "For goodness' sake Richard, how many are there? Are they spread across the country, the world?" I sighed, relieved to be saved by a flurry of waiters serving our ordered food.

When they had gone she said, "Well." Humbly I answered, "Christine they have all gone. I closed the door on my past life the day I wrote you the letter. However, I couldn't leave people unknowing. I considered the girls I had been dating, deciding I had a responsibility to each one. I visited them and explained I had a girlfriend and I wouldn't be seeing them again, and that's it darling I promise."

Christine considered my response, looked hard at me before saying, "It had better be or my boy I will castrate you. One wrong step and you'll wake up in hospital a bloody eunuch." My hand dropped to my nether region and Christine laughed. "Feeling the knife?"

Christine's cheerful and loving mood returned. We savoured the food, both realising we were quite hungry, we sipped the champagne and held hands. Christine remarked how good the food tasted once more referring to the poor standards offered by Southampton clubs.

I smiled and holding both her hands kissed her on the lips, whispering, "I have no intention of becoming a eunuch so my beautiful girl I most definitely will not put a foot wrong, you have my word."

Through the evening we danced and affected, what we were, two young people in love. Towards the end of the evening Debbie came over to say goodnight and offered her hand to Christine. When she had departed Christine said, "Actually she is a very nice lady who my lothario, is still in love with you and may yet still be holding a candle."

I asked for the bill to be informed it had been taken care of. I left five pounds on the table. There wasn't a taxi available so we walked for a while clasped together, our arms holding tight the one we each loved. The evening's chill, which we were not dressed for, descended. We speeded up reaching Grey's Monument where we managed to flag a taxi.

Entering father's house we found a bedraggled Tina sitting in the kitchen with a vodka bottle. She slurred hello and staggered to her feet to hug Christine. I stepped in and guided her back into the chair.

I asked Christine to go to our room. I found father at the dining room table with documents and work drawings scattered haphazardly. He was writing in a large book, obviously making notes. He asked whether we had enjoyed the evening. I affirmed we had and thanked him. I indicated the kitchen with my head. He shrugged saying, "Go to bed, we'll talk tomorrow."

In bed with Christine we whispered our concern regarding the predicament we were in. We were marooned in an unhappy household oblivious to why Tina had decided to hit the bottle. We cuddled and kissed both knowing there wouldn't be love that evening.

Although we hadn't made it to bed until past two in the morning we were both awake at seven. We sneaked out of bed like naughty children, showered and dressed warmly and tip-toed down the stairs. Father lay asleep in an armchair his documents scattered on the floor before him. I scribbled a hasty note explaining we would be out until six in the evening.

I closed the door with the key limiting any noise. We jumped in the car laughing; we were two naughty children. I quietly pulled away, stopping further down the road to check the atlas.

Once I had studied it I remembered the Bonneville ride deciding to follow a similar route and see what happens. I explained my intention to Christine, she would have been happy if I had decided to drive to Timbuctoo. I said, "First stop is breakfast or maybe an early lunch, you decide."

We drove to Tynemouth, where we braved the breeze to walk the castle and long harbour wall. We laughed and hugged all the way stopping to kiss at regular intervals. We raced each other and of course because I am gentleman, I lost.

We bypassed Whitley Bay and Blyth following signs to Newbiggin-by-the-sea, we stopped once more to walk to the bay and look out to sea. Not overly impressed we pressed further north towards Amble. In Amble we parked by a marina and walked following a river until we spotted another castle, Warkworth Castle.

We were cheerful and jumping about playing tag, the only people, except a man and his dog, in the world. We gave him a very cheery "Good morning." He responded with a great smile. We followed the river, which encircled a pretty town before retracing our steps, arm in arm, back to the car.

A swift check of the atlas and we were heading for Alnmouth. We were having terrific fun laughing and throwing comments around, both loving and complimentary, and cheeky. I located a car-park by the beach, we clambered down and chased along the sand.

I lifted Christine, threatening to throw her in the sea. All giggles, she shrieked like a school girl, slapping my shoulders shouting all kinds of verbal threats. We raced back up the dunes to the car.

Next stop, Alnwick, which we both agreed was an exemplar town. We toured the streets looking in shop windows, studying the wonderful buildings and also seeking a café for we were both starving. We found an ideal café overlooking cobblestone parking and an ancient horse trough. I did like the brownstone buildings as did Christine. However, we both agreed, as pretty Northumberland was, it could be cold and breezy.

In the café we enjoyed huge sausage rolls with lashings of English mustard and mugs of hot tea. Alnwick Castle and the Fusiliers Museum of Northumberland was our next stop, the family home of the Duke of Northumberland, which to our minds was very beautiful. The history, which I enjoyed, depicting battles and chivalry was enlightening. We walked the grounds hand in hand, intertwining fingers, kissing and cuddling, very much in love.

Nonetheless, we decided to continue our exploration of Northumberland leaving Alnwick for Craster. We didn't stay long in Craster, stopping a few minutes to soak in the quietness and look at the small picturesque harbour. We noticed a sign for another castle, this time Dunstanburgh Castle. However, we were castled-out deciding instead to head for Berwick-on-Tweed.

Berwick-on-Tweed, after Alnwick proved disappointing. Nonetheless we parked and walked alongside the River Tweed, the famous Salmon

River and ventured down Pier Road to a bay but otherwise we were done with Berwick.

Heading south out of Berwick I said "Study the atlas and choose a town or village where we can enjoy an early dinner. At the next telephone kiosk I'll telephone and let father know what we are doing."

"Okay Christopher," replied Christine.

"Christopher?" I queried.

Christine, a very happy lady, said, "Christopher Columbus, the explorer, dummy." My only response was "ha, ha".

Christine selected Hexham for our dinner destination. I had a rough idea how to locate the town, head towards Newcastle and turn right following signs to Hexham, I hoped. I drove steady keeping well within the speed limit, therefore when a police car, blue lights flashing appeared in the rear view mirror I pulled over both surprised and confused.

They were very friendly, asking if we were in a hurry. I immediately countered with there was no way I had been speeding. They laughed, the younger one said, "Hope you don't mind we wanted to look your car over, don't see many of the Saint's cars around here." I smiled saying, "Feel free" I opened the bonnet and boot to assist in their "look over".

Their curiosity satisfied we arrived at the Lamb, recommended by the policemen, thirty minutes before opening, courtesy of a police car escort complete with flashing blue light and, at times, hitting over one hundred miles an hour.

They waved goodbye leaving an ashen-faced Christine with a queasy smile saying, "Richard Chambers never again, you scared me half to death."

"Oh come on Christine, it was fun," I retorted.

"Fun, you call that fun! You're as mad as they are." Eventually she did manage to smile admitting it was quite fun but bloody scary.

To kill the half-hour we wandered around Hexham, which we discovered was full of quaint lanes and attractive stone houses, especially Hallgate and the Old Goal albeit the main street was a wee bit shabby.

In the Lamb we mentioned the police sergeant's name. Our welcome from the landlady went from non-committal to committal. All smiles we were shown to a table passed two menus and presented with a glass of sherry each.

While Christine was reading the menu I took her hand saying, "Do you know how much I love you?" Expecting a silly response she shook her head and pulled her hand away.

I smiled and said, "Imagine a forest full of fir trees. Have you?"

"Yes Richard I am imagining a forest," she retorted.

"Is it a forest full of fir trees?"

"Yes Richard," she smiled thinking I was a playing game.

"Can you see thousands of fir trees?" I asked.

"Yes Richard I can see thousands." Her smile signalling where is this going?

"Right have you any idea how many pine needles there are on each fir tree?" I queried. "Richard, I have absolutely no idea, nor am I interested," her smile widening.

"You should have," I said.

"Why?"

"Because, my darling Christine, every single pine needle is a message from telling you I love you. So, the forest full of thousands of fir trees, each tree with thousands upon thousands of pine needles is me telling you how much I love you."

She clapped her hands and laughed out loud. "You stupid man, I know you love me, I feel it always." She leaned across the table and kissed me full on the lips.

The landlady standing by the table obviously overheard, smiling she said, "You are a very romantic young man, I hope you don't change. Have you decided?"

Christine chose lamb chops with trimmings whilst I opted for a fillet steak, medium rare with fried onions and whatever else comes up.

As she turned I said, "Excuse me do you have a wine list please"

"Excuse me, please, where did you find him hinny? Is there any like him left over?"

She returned with a wine list. "What, for goodness sake, is a hinny?" whispered Christine. "It's a term of endearment, I think it means sweet or honey or something like that" I replied

I called to the landlady "Excuse me could we have two glasses of Cotes de Rhone please?" She was all smiles enjoying my pleasant mannerisms.

The policemen were correct the food proved excellent as was the wine, which we thoroughly appreciated. We thanked the landlady and started the journey we were dreading, the return to father's house.

As I drove towards Whickham I said, "We'll leave about mid-morning and go home." Christine holding her hand over mine, which was gripping the gear stick, squeezed. She said, "I think you should see how the land lies first. We are here to visit your father yet we have hardly seen him. Play it my ear Richard."

Father was waiting. He immediately apologised to Christine explaining Tina was on her way back to Edinburgh. He asked what we had been doing. Christine full of pleasure described our tour of Northumberland expressing the fun we had. She laughed when she related the story of the police car, finishing with the pub and dinner. Father asked if he and I could be excused saying, "Family issues".

He indicated I should sit he said, "Tina is not coming back. I will forward her belongings in the next few days. I have given a month's notice of this house and I will be move out by next weekend, including changing the locks.

I am moving to Matlock." Startled I said, "Matlock, Derbyshire?"

He smiled. "Is there another one?"

"When did you organise all this, today?" I asked.

"Goodness no, it has been on the cards for a few weeks."

He explained how R J Construction constantly received new contracts extending the work consequently they were rapidly heading towards Derbyshire. He explained the pipework they were installing was destined to terminate at a gas station in a place called Ambergate, not far from Matlock, hence his decision to move.

He said, "I have rented a farm in a village called Whatstandwell."

"A farm, what are you going to do with a farm?" I queried.

"I need storage for pipes, equipment, plant and tools." he answered.

"Am I at liberty to explain to Christine and you should let mother know," I stated.

He nodded, "Of course, by all means tell Christine. Your mother knows I talked with her an hour ago. She is of the opinion you are going to marry Christine, she is Miss Right." He smiled. "Is she?"

"I think so. Sophie has caused heartache for far too long, Christine has been a breath of fresh air and yes I have fallen in love with her." I replied.

"Good," he said. "Next time you visit I will make sure it's a good visit and Christine has a pleasant time. Right, I'm off. I am meeting some men in Harrogate then on to Matlock. Unfortunately work is pressure, which I am sure you have learnt by now. I am pleased you are doing well. I know your mother is inordinately proud and the way Christine was blowing your trumpet I am sure she is too."

Father and I returned to Christine, smiling she said, "What's the crisis?" Father laughed saying, "I am sorry, I have to leave, business. However, Richard will explain. Christine it has been a pleasure and you will do me a great favour and his mother too, if you keep this lovable rogue under control." Christine smiled and hugged father.

After he had gone I clarified for Christine what the family issues revolved around and what was happening. She said, "My God Richard no wonder you are so wary of, or have been, women. Your life story can wait but my darling you will provide chapter and verse and I will do likewise. I will tell you when, which I hope will not be long." She stood and hugged me kissing for a long time.

We went to bed to make glorious fantastic love for hour after hour, that's how it was with Christine, once started there was no way it could stop, she was so romantic, sexy, loving and so demanding and I loved her very, very much. In the early hours, just before my lovely lady closed her eyes she said, "Home is a lovely word."

I forced myself from the bed, showered, shaved (I am going to grow a beard) and dressed. I made tea and woke my beautiful English rose with a kiss. She jumped grabbed me and ordered me back into bed.

We managed to get away by eleven-thirty. Christine before I had reached the A1, the Great North Road, was asleep.

I pulled in outside Christine's flat at six o'clock completely knackered. "Why here?" she asked. "Because, darling we both need a good night's sleep and we both know together that will not happen." She kissed me. I carried her case into her flat and onto her bed. We hugged and kissed saying goodnight.

The following morning, in my office I reset my calendar to Monday 24th September, wondering where the year had gone, so much had happened. Despite a good ten hour sleep I hadn't fully recovered. I thought, "it is holiday time". I asked Janet, my girl Friday to check out the weather in Hong Kong for October and November and also check airlines and flights.

I had a session with Doug later to discuss the three satellite operations, which I couldn't see the point until we had reconciled figures from the finance department. I called him and he agreed. However he would like to discuss other issues. I asked what issues, to which he said, "Nought to do with you, just two heads are better than one."

I asked Christine to come to my office. I said, "Next weekend Minehead, the following weekend Hove then I thought end of October, Hong Kong. What do you think?" "I think" she said, "My man is, as always on the ball. When will you confirm so I can let Aunty Sadie know, and what about Charlotte she should come too."

I thought for a moment saying, "Good idea, yes Charlotte should be with us." She pecked my cheek and exited. I called Jessica to confirm we would be down the coming weekend. She sounded very excited.

Christine and I, excepting in the office didn't meet up until Wednesday evening. I kept busy working fourteen, fifteen hour days, putting together a re-structuring plan to discuss with Doug first and the board after. The company needed direction.

Yes, we still had plenty of work but not as much as previous years yet we were still carrying a full complement. I had to get my message across re diversification and innovation.

We had a light supper, a couple of glasses of wine and retired to bed. Christine came to bed with her pyjama bottoms on, which meant menstrual cycle, which for once I was quite happy about.

I told her the Hong Kong flight was fourteen / fifteen hours, which of course she already knew. I told her the cost of the flights. She whistled. I said in stern voice "Christine that was very unladylike. They are first class seats"

"My darling we are not Hugo, we don't have that kind of money" she replied. "I have and that is what we are going to do. My lady and her sister are first class so they travel first class."

I booked flights for 20th October returning 3rd November. I called Doug and advised Christine and I would be taken well-earned leave between the dates. He laughed "Honeymoon?" "No, confidentially I am going to meet Christine's guardians who are also her aunty and uncle. She was orphaned at fourteen." He said "Jesus, I didn't know." "No problem, just keep it under your hat." I quietly responded.

Thursday, I worked until midnight determined to complete the report prior to our trip to Minehead, but I knew, feeling whacked, I wouldn't finish until midway through the following week.

I went home, surprised to find a naked and warm Christine in my bed. She awakened when I inadvertently switched on the bedroom light. I quickly showered and joined her in bed. For what seemed the first time in ages, we made slow leisurely love, exploring each other with deep love and affection. There was absolutely no doubt I was desperately in love with Christine.

The weekend in Minehead proved to be a great time. Fortunately the weather was kind and also fortunately I had forced Christine into buying proper walking clothes and boots. We walked for miles with two dear friends and of course little James, who surprisingly remembered me.

Jessica, which pleased me tremendously thought Christine an angel and openly said so, which had James calling Christine "angel" for the whole weekend.

Simon and I spent a couple hours supping a couple of beers discussing his relationship with Graham and Jessica senior, Jessica's parents. The handover of farm responsibilities was going well and at the same time he slowly ran down his farm tenancy having decided to throw in the towel.

I asked if wedding bells were in the offering. He thought so but not until summer 1974. He was adamant he had to prove to Jessica's parents he would make a worthy husband. I didn't say so, but I figured if they were entrusting him with their farm, they would willingly entrust him with their daughter's hand.

Unbeknown to Simon, Jessica had already cornered me to try and persuade him to decide upon a spring wedding. So I waffled for ages telling how Jessica had always dreamt of a spring wedding, I also mentioned farming seasons, a guess. He rubbed his chin saying "You might have something there. I think I had better re-consider." I laughed out loud, and he joined in. Two weeks later I received a telephone call from

Jessica telling me I was her best friend and a diamond. They planned to wed spring 2014.

Jessica and Christine, during the walks, talked for hours leaving Simon and I to keep James occupied and entertained, which was quite good fun. James adored the countryside consistently asking questions about plants and trees, birds and animals and yet to be named wild animals were also high on his list of questions.

He had a thing about size demanding explanations why cows were larger than pigs, and dogs larger than cats. However, picture books of the animals that roamed Africa and India were very useful.

I reengaged with Jessica senior and Graham who welcomed Christine into their home with open arms. The two Jessica's thought Christine divine and were dazzled by her English beauty, referring to Christine's red hair, porcelain colouring and freckles albeit the freckles, which I had tried to count on numerous occasions, were quite mild. After a sumptuous tea in the huge kitchen in the main farm house we said our goodbyes and started the three hour drive back to Southampton.

During the drive Christine raised the subject of accommodation once more and the inconvenience of my work hours, and the added inconvenience of living in two homes that were a mere few hundred yards apart.

I listened as I always did before mentioning her comment the last time we discussed the subject, she was going to think about it and find the solution. I said, "Christine unless you have a plan we are where we are. I can't move in with you for obvious reasons and my flat is too small, beyond those two points I do not have an answer." We both knew there was an answer but neither would commit, not just yet anyway.

The following week, similar to the previous, I worked non-stop. Christine disowned me and Charlotte called to thank me for the flights to Hong Kong and also mentioned Christine was miserable because "lover boy" is always working. I laughed with her joyous laughter.

Friday morning, my report very professionally prepared by Janet, all three hundred and sixty pages of it was issued to Doug. On receipt he telephoned me and called me a thousand unmentionable names saying he would read over the weekend and we would talk the following week.

I wasn't looking forward to Hove. I called to confirm our visit and also asked if we could meet with uncle Don. We left mid-morning Saturday.

I had forgotten just how busy the Bear would be Saturday lunchtime. We were overwhelmed by the welcome. Hand-shakes and hugs, and back-slapping, my poor old arm ached by the time I reached Irene and Ken, and Joe. Josie and Gwynne rushed round from the bar to hug and kiss me.

When I fell into Irene's arms and hugged and kissed her, not wanting to let go, I felt her tears streaming down her cheeks. Ken took one of my hands and shook it gently easing me away from Irene. He said, "So Mr Ship Repairer and international traveller, what news do you bring Hove."

I watched, from the corner of my eye as Irene rescued Christine from the melee. I smiled at Ken, "All in good time," and moved to hug Joe. He had a tear. Poor Christine didn't know what the hell was going on especially when a pub full of strangers had started hugging and welcoming her.

We were ushered upstairs to the living room, a living room full of photographs of Sophie, Sophie and me, and the large one of me on my knee in the Richmond hotel proposing. I had forgotten the photographs, which I had insisted Irene and Ken must have. I looked pleadingly at Christine. She smiled and nodded her head signalling everything was fine. Irene fussing put the kettle on and produced cakes and tarts. I thought typical of the lady always practical, as was her daughter.

Irene paid particular attention to Christine making her feel welcome. Ken wanted to know everything there was to know about work and travel. Joe, the inscrutable Joe smiled and shook his head, smiled some more and nodded. I hadn't realised but my last visit was pre the complex period of international work. I apologised supplicating work and more work.

Ken, Joe and I talked for an hour discussing everything from the Bear and the customers to Muscat, to the Azores and all points west. Ken was impressed with my rapid acceleration through the ranks to General Manager and the fact I had only just passed twenty-six. He kept on laughing saying he always knew I had balls. Then he said, "Sophie would have been so proud."

I heard Irene say, "Richard, haven't you done well. Christine has been telling me what you have achieved in such a short time from re-organising the stores and procurement to organising men working all over the world, how exciting." I went to Irene's side. She held my face "Dear Richard" and kissed my cheeks.

Irene suddenly said, "Now then, we have heard all about Richard, now let's hear Christine's story." I told Christine's story including our courtship and our new found love. I didn't hold back on anything. I expounded the great job she was doing and also how much I relied on her personally and work-wise.

When I had finished Irene clasped her hands together and said, "I think it's just as well we are going to the Sapphire tonight, we need a diversion." The Sapphire, news to me but I was glad I wanted to see Sophie's Uncle Don.

Pushed out by Irene, Ken, Joe and I went down to the bar. Irene wanted to talk to Christine. I asked Christine if she was okay being left with Irene, she smiled and nodded. In the bar the beers were lined up and I did my best. However, lack of rugby, both training and playing had impacted on my beer drinking capability.

After the initial three pints I apologised and declined any further servings. I still remembered how to clean the bar after closing time, a closing time, which took forty minutes to eject the last hanger-on's.

The bar cleaning helped to alleviate the alcohol intake; therefore by the time we returned upstairs I was back to normal. Christine and Irene were in the kitchen with Josie and Gwynne serving the late lunch. With our plates of thick slices of beef, mashed potatoes and vegetables we all went downstairs where Joe had prepared tables.

Clustered round the table regenerated long forgotten lunches and dinners, and in particular one Christmas lunch, all of which were now, thanks to Christine and her obvious acceptance and understanding of my past, very happy memories, tinged with sadness. As usual dear Ken wanted to make toast after toast.

First he toasted Christine welcoming her into the family. Second was a rather elaborate toast about true love, which was directed at Christine and me. And the third was to Sophie, although he didn't mention her by name, he simply said, "to a missed but not forgotten daughter".

We teamed together to wash the dishes, clean the bar once more before, at last, Christine and I were given some privacy.

We were shown into Sophie's old room. However, the room had been completely redecorated in bright colours as had the bathroom across the passage. All traces of Sophie had been removed, which I presumed had been an action enforced by Irene. Ken was too sentimental to have instigated such radical change.

Lying on the bed holding hands Christine said, "Sophie was a very beautiful girl." I stayed quiet. "Do you miss her?" she asked.

"I did for a long, long time but not now," I replied.

"Will she be a ghost in your memory?" Christine queried.

"No, not anymore," I whispered.

We lay in silence for some time. Christine continued, "Jessica thinks I should meet Gertie." I said, "I don't think that's a good idea."

Christine said, "I'll meet her at Jessica's wedding but I would rather meet her before." Irritated I retorted, "Christine you are a big girl, if you want to do that, then fine meet Gertie"

Christine then said "You are a strange man, all these people they adore you. Wherever we go people adore you. When we walked in downstairs and they lifted and cheered you I have never seen such a welcome." Once more I didn't respond.

Christine determined said "Richard I know everything there is to know. First Jessica and now Irene have both explained how you and Sophie loved each other, and how you changed after her death, how morose and cold you became. Now they are happy for you, for us, pleased you have reverted to the old Richard, and yes they are actually pleased you have met me and we are a couple. Richard, damn you, you cannot shut me out. If we are the future, then damn well talk to me."

"Christine, I couldn't talk about it, I couldn't talk about Sophie. I died inside, my heart ached, and I changed. You, thank God, have changed me once more. I am human." I laughed, "Well I hope I am, human I mean."

"You see that wasn't so bad was it?" she said.

I said, "I walked into the Bear, I met Sophie, and within days we were in love. Through the summer we became inseparable. For four years we remained inseparable, we lived and loved. If you must know, four wonderful glorious years, and she died. She died in a crappy road accident ninety minutes from where I waited. I waited for her at Jessica's. We were meeting with Jessica and Simon, Hugo and Miriam, and Gertie and Sylvie and Ryan, and many more to celebrate Jessica and Simon's engagement. We were two weeks away from our wedding day, a day I was looking forward to so much. When Sophie died, my life ended with hers. I became intolerable for fifteen months and yes I was morose and cold. After being morose and cold I became contemptible. I was contemptible when I met you, but you were different, I couldn't bring myself to treat you as a one off, a casual affair, so I kept you at arm's length. You, thankfully, saw beyond the façade. You became fond of me and we were dating. You, my lovely lady thankfully, stopped me being intolerable and stopped me being the contemptible person I had become and, mercifully, I fell in love once more, with a woman I have come to love and adore, satisfied?"

"Yes my love," she said as she pulled me into her arms. "Yes I am satisfied, and you will be too. I needed to hear, albeit not quite so succinctly, from you and you my darling, whether you wanted to or not, had to talk to me, to break free to share the hurt and the pain. There was a barrier that needed to be smashed aside, and my Richard we have just done that, smashed it aside." I hugged Christine and kissed her.

Christine asked the significance of Uncle Don and the Sapphire Club and who were Sylvie and Ryan we were lunching with the next day. I explained Uncle Don was Ken's brother and the break-up of their business relationship, and his special relationship with Sophie and especially how long it took for him to accept me as a suitable suitor.

I reminisced over the Sapphire and previously when it was the Blue Indigo and the Green Parrot way back when. I recalled how, he, Ken and father financed the wedding and among other things an amazing New Year party. As I was talking, I realised Christine had broken the spell I was indeed free, one hundred and ten per cent free. I pulled Christine into my arms so fiercely she winced and cried out. I kissed her hard and ardently wanting her to feel my love, to know she was the only woman for me and always would be.

I explained Sylvie and Sophie's incident with her ex-boss and the policeman who had intervened. I expounded Sophie's success at work, the demand for her to attend conferences and functions to orate. The Greek night was mentioned and the mad-cap dancing and the earlier celebratory promotion presentation when she invited all her work colleagues to our wedding. I rambled on how Sylvie and Ryan became part of the Hugo, Miriam, Richard, Sophie, and Jessica and Simon, and Gertie gang. I was in full flow my mind zooming in on memories long blacked-out, I was truly free.

When I finished talking and we were lying touching fingers Christine said, "Richard, make gentle love to me, very gentle." I locked the door and undressed Christine kissing and caressing her very sensual body. Christine helped me to disrobe. We touched and cuddled, stroked and kissed. I gently laid Christine beneath and very, very gradually pushed my penis into her warm, very pink vagina. She sighed, saying, "I love you Richard. I really, really love you."

For an immeasurable length of time we made love tenderly, loving together, feeling wonderful little sensations vibrating through our bodies, blissfully thrilling in the magic of our love. I whispered, "Christine, my lovely, lovely lady I am adrift in heaven."

Christine responded by driving her hips hard towards me. I could feel my sperm begin to squirt into her. I whispered "I'm coming; I'm coming" Christine moaned, "Ohhh." We held each other so very tight feeling our love juices flow to marry together, to bond us in love, very deeply in love.

Nestling in each other's arms we dozed, dreaming, remembering and knowing we were one. We were Christine Clarke and Richard Chambers, maybe one day soon we will become Mr and Mrs Chambers or even Mr and Mrs Clarke-Chambers.

I was roused from sleep by Ken's voice advising a car would be outside in forty-five minutes. We erupted from the bed, I called "Okay" and we kissed running hands over bodies. Christine pushed me away and pulled on a bath robe hanging behind the door saying "I bag the bathroom first"

When I returned from the bathroom I was instantly mesmerised by Christine's loveliness. She was wearing a dark blue cocktail dress, which my mother had chosen, the dress was mid-thigh emphasising her long slim and graceful legs.

The dress highlighted the shape and lift of her delightful breasts, which in turn accentuated her slim waist and curvaceous hips. The delightful dress with her gorgeous red hair and light blue eyes, and her sensual lips radiated heavenly splendour. For a moment I just stared, no I ogled, running my eyes from top to toe and back again. She smiled and ordered me to hurry up and get ready.

Christine and I (I had to shave) were ready with a few minutes to spare. I thanked, tongue in cheek, Ken for the generous time he afforded us to dress. Irene, her eyes slightly damp remembering the beauty of her daughter, praised Christine's beauty and of course the Bear's infamous wolf whistling started.

I as I always used to, bowed getting as I always had jeers and boos. Smiles and laughter and Christine's blushing made the moment precious. Ken, dear Ken laughed. I kissed Josie and Gwynne goodnight and winked at Joe.

Don had dispatched a car. We were dining in the restaurant extension at nine. The bouncers, either pre-warned, or they recognised the similarity between Ken and Don spoke into a walkie-talkie. Before we had climbed from the car Don waited to greet us. He hugged Irene who hugged him, the family feud long over and now discarded. He and Ken hugged.

He looked at me and shouted, "Come here," and he squeezed me so hard I thought my ribs were going to splinter from the force of his embrace. He whispered "You certainly know how to pick them" and laughed. He kissed Christine's hand saying "You my dear are poetry in motion, a delight for my tired old eyes."

He waved his arms "Come on, come on its party time" Walking through the doors I asked after his Christine. "She is in Cyprus something to do with her work, you know her advertising malarkey."

The club, as ever, was packed with revellers, party people floor to roof, the sound deafening. Christine squealed her hips swaying, my girl wanted to dance. I took her clutch-bag and passed it to Irene for safe keeping. I winked at Don shouting "Excuse us for a while" he winked back and gestured with his hand towards the dance floor.

Christine found space and we danced. I watched her amazing body as it quivered from the slight shake of her head, the twist of her upper-body, the sway of her hips and the gracefulness of her legs.

Christine was an astonishing sight, her body, when she danced, was so fluid. We gyrated, or rather I did and Christine danced. We were laughing, touching and stealing kisses and shouting our love. The over-packed floor was bouncing, we were being bumped but we didn't care we were simply having fun.

The music mood slowed and we fell into each other's arms and moved slowly amidst other loving couples. We kissed passionately and we never stopped telling each other of our love. Christine ground her pelvis into mine and I pressed a hardening Jolly Roger into her private region.

She was laughing and hugging and kissing the happiest I had seen her for a while. We smooched and smooched until the music, song after song began to increase tempo. We kissed fervently once more before climbing the stairs to the VIP lounge.

Irene, Ken and Don were seated at Don's private table accompanied with two ice-buckets, one with champagne and the other white wine. We joined their company. "Well?" asked Don "What do you think?" He had obviously forgotten Sophie and I had attended shortly after the extension and refurbishment works. "Fantastic," I called back.

He continued, "Me and your dad talk every now and again, he's visiting soon, once he has settled in Derbyshire, some village with a weird name."

"Whatstandwell," I stated.

"That's it, have you been there?"

"No not yet," I replied. He turned his attention to Christine, asking her questions about our relationship.

Meanwhile I was talking with Irene and Ken. Ken asked what my future plans were. I said "For the moment I will remain where I am, the money is good and I have a free-hand, which is also good." I explained my thoughts regarding the future of the company with regards my views on diversification and innovation. He was, surprisingly, very interested asking pertinent questions.

Irene wanted to talk about Christine. She mentioned the similarity in height and body shape with Sophie. She also considered there were similarities between Christine's red and Sophie's auburn hair. Smiling she asked if I had a preference although I did point out my mother had auburn hair.

Irene pushed to know if we were serious and would we marry saying she hoped we would. As we talked I began to realise Irene was looking upon Christine as a substitute for Sophie. The more we talked the more she looked at Christine, imagining, I presumed it was Sophie she was observing. I held her hand.

A young girl whispered in Don's ear. He indicated our table was ready. We trailed through the bar taking a short-cut to the restaurant. The restaurant was full. Glancing at the diners I recognised money. He had achieved his goal, which was to embrace the higher society of Newhaven and surrounding areas, which was confirmed by the greetings he received as we threaded between the tables.

Dinner arrived, the first platter, an array of Tapas accompanied with a bottle of Rioja. The consumption of both Tapas and wine thoroughly savoured. Don permitted a break for tummies to settle before the second platter of fish, some in batter some grilled in butter and some in sauce, accompanied with a bottle of Chablis.

The food and wine were perfect, in fact delicious. How we managed to eat so much I don't know. The ambience and friendship around the table felt warm and the company were splendid. My darling Christine was being treated like a queen. I looked at my friends, my friends who in reality were and extended family.

I realised, the dinner was a means of welcoming Christine into the bosom of their family. Her face, all through dinner, was a picture to behold; she radiated happiness, her natural charisma infectious.

It had to come, a bottle of Richard Hennessey appeared with the appropriate balloons, once filled, Ken, my good friend Ken, toasted Christine and my future and Sophie's memory. The toast although solemn carried with it much warmth.

Around one in the morning Christine suggested we danced once more, mainly she said to rid the extra weight we had accumulated during dinner. On the dance floor we kept to the perimeter dancing close. I shouted we wouldn't reduce weight smooching. Shouting back she made it clear she didn't care as long as we were close. I had the feeling Christine was desperate to converse; however, the thunderous decibels amplified from the DJ's turntables squashed any chance.

So instead we kissed. Holding tight we barely moved rocking and swaying to the music. We stayed locked together through to the evening's last smooches oblivious of the hundreds of clubbers doing their thing. We wearily made our way back to the VIP lounge.

In the car-park we embraced and thanked Uncle Don for a great evening. I had just helped Christine into the car when he called, "Don't forget my invite." Christine pushed herself above the car door calling back, "We won't," and blew him a kiss, which he smacked onto his cheek and roared with laughter.

During the journey we expressed our gratitude to Irene and Ken for a fabulous welcome into their home and for the evening. Ken said, "Family is for family, you're family." Irene nodded her agreement. I cuddled Christine with one arm and held Irene's hand with my free hand, which she squeezed at frequent intervals.

I lay in bed with Christine fast asleep in my arms, thinking of our upcoming trip to Hong Kong to meet her aunty and uncle. Although I wasn't overly concerned, I did feel apprehensive. What if they disliked me or decided I wasn't right for Christine. All these stupid thoughts were swirling in my head. Finally I slept.

Irene knocked calling tea and bacon sandwiches would be ready in twenty minutes. Christine still asleep hearing the knock, opened her eyes, asked the time, gave me a big kiss and said she loved me, and climbed out of bed. I watched, thinking Don was right "poetry in motion".

We showered quickly dressed casually in jeans and shirts with sweaters, the sweaters just in case they were needed. Irene and Ken were in the living room, Irene sewing a button on Ken's shirt while he caught up on sport results. Irene asked what time we would be leaving. Checking my watch, it was eleven.

I answered saying, "We are meeting Sylvie and Ryan at one o'clock at the hotel they have booked for lunch. So, I suppose if we depart twelve forty-five we'll be fine." Fortunately Irene hadn't made the bacon sandwiches, conscious we would be lunching quite soon we cried off, settling for tea, which Christine and I made.

The packing was outstanding, which I swiftly attended to before we said goodbye. The farewell proved to be very emotional especially when Irene hugged Christine, she didn't want to let go. Ken and Irene came down stairs with us. After popping into the bar to say good bye to Josie, Gwynne and Joe and the regulars, and amidst shouts of hurry back, we exited the Bear. I loaded the car helped Christine in and pulled away waving goodbye to Irene and Ken and half a dozen regulars standing on the pub's steps.

Christine, as I manoeuvred onto the Kingsway joining the traffic flow, said, "Richard you have amazing friends, wherever we go they open their arms and their hearts for you. It must be a wonderful feeling to know you have such good friends." "It is my darling and they are now your friends who will always welcome you," I replied.

She hugged my arm. I looked at her and said, "I love you Christine Clarke and don't you ever forget it."

After parking we were five minutes late. Sylvie and Ryan were waiting astride stools at the bar. I embraced Sylvie and lightly kissed her on the lips. Ryan and I shook hands and hugged. I felt good. Christine was quickly introduced receiving similar treatment.

Sylvie advised she had pre-ordered a shellfish platter for lunch remarking she hoped Christine liked oysters, and prawns, and crab and lobster adding she was excused the whelks and cockles. Christine confirmed she indeed enjoyed shellfish. We would be sitting down at one-forty-five, causing concern with the staff, which they had managed to overcome.

Ryan was pouring white wine when I was staggered to see Nancy, an ex-work colleague of Sandra making a bee-line for me. "Hello Richard, long-time no see. How are you, you look well." I felt Christine's eyes boring into the back of my head. "Hello Nancy, I'm fine, how about you?" Nancy proffered her cheek for a peck, cornered I had to oblige. I introduced Christine as my girlfriend; Christine received a good looking over, and Sylvie and Ryan as dear friends.

Nancy said, "Just saying hello, we don't see you in Brighton very often. Do you still live in Hove?" I answered, trying to keep everything low key. I did mention Christine and I shared a flat in Southampton, which caused Nancy's eyebrows to lift.

She kissed my cheek saying "I'm still with Titus so if you're in town give me a ring" and flounced off. I held Christine back. Christine displaying an exaggerated sweet smile said, "Another one?" If I denied I would be suspected of lying so I nodded.

Sylvie laughed breaking the tension, saying, "Christine, if you are his girl, whom Richard has assured me, you are, you have no need to worry, this guy is as straight as they come. I could tell you stories of girls galore trying to get in his trousers, but Christine, he did not waver, Sophie was his girl and no other girl was going to have him, isn't that right Richard?"

I nodded and added, "Christine, Sylvie has known me a long time and Ryan has also." She looped her arm through mine and lifted her glass saying, "Sylvie, Ryan, it is a pleasure to meet you." We chinked glasses the unwanted interruption brushed aside.

We stood at the bar joshing and recounting incidents. Of course the Greek night and my dancing and the five girls with me raised lots of laughter. Sylvie brilliantly demonstrated albeit with exaggerated emphasis the steps and hand clapping I had displayed, she insisted I join her as together we attempted to reproduce the energetic kicks the Greek waiters taught me, subsequently we both ended-up laying on the floor clasped together laughing.

Christine, watching the impromptu demonstration had tears streaming down her cheeks caused by her happiness and laughter.

Ryan demonstrated, or rather tried to demonstrate his version of Cossacks, squatting and kicking out his legs. He was hilarious. It was at this stage a manger appeared and asked, very politely, that we behave. Sylvie shooed him away, promising we would quieten down.

The Maître D' came leading the way to the table. We ordered a second bottle of wine, however Ryan and I refrained leaving Christine and Sylvie to giggle all through the shellfish and the wine. Ryan, while the girls were busy, explained he and Sylvie had agreed to marry sometime in 2014, probably in the spring.

I was so pleased I hugged him. Sylvie noticed and said, "You've told him haven't you?" Ryan admitted he had. Christine asked what was going on. I looked at Sylvie "Alright, Ryan and I getting married, the stupid man hasn't a clue what he is letting himself in for" And snorted.

Christine was so pleased for them both any observer would have thought they were old friends. She left the table to hug Ryan returning to embrace Sylvie. Ryan did top our half empty glasses up so Christine could call a toast, which she did most eloquently referring to her two old friends. Sylvie was in stitches.

Following the demolition of the shellfish platter I had two black coffees before we set-off on our two hour drive to Southampton. Meanwhile

Christine and Sylvie emptied the wine bottle. Both were tiddly and couldn't stop giggling. Ryan and I looked on with amusement.

Eventually, with Sylvie and Ryan accompanying us I steered Christine to the car. We had our second emotional farewell of the day. With Christine waving wildly and blowing kisses I pulled out of the car park and set course for Southampton, a drive I knew intimately. Christine was soon asleep. To keep me company I quietly played a Deep Purple album.

I delivered Christine to Charlotte who laughed and dragged her sister into the flat I followed kissed both girls goodbye and went home. Tomorrow, Monday would be the 8th October, twelve days before flying to Hong Kong.

Monday I spent all day closeted with Doug going over my proposal. He was certainly impressed congratulating my forethought. He invited me to attend the next board meeting, which was programmed for the 18th October. In the meantime he would copy the document and issue under "for your eyes only" signed agreements. He didn't want the proposal to become public knowledge.

Christine and I didn't see each other until Wednesday evening when, with Charlotte we went out for Chinese. The dinner arranged to finalise travelling plans gave the girls the opportunity to describe Hong Kong and the bright lights, the ferries and the famous Peak.

Christine and I were booked into a hotel, Christine had insisted, and Charlotte would stay with Sadie and James. They were looking forward to seeing their relatives and in particular their baby brother, Charles. Christine came home with me.

We made wonderful love. We talked of happiness and the excitement of our holiday. We remembered the past weeks, Lytham, Whickham, Minehead and Hove and all the people. Christine was so happy, so very happy.

In the morning Christine awoke in an extremely sexual mood wanting to make love. We would be late for work but we dismissed the thought and investigated our love, touching and feeling, kissing each other to reach explosive climaxes. We held on and thrilled in the joy we produced for each other.

We must have awakened early because we were not late for work. Now we were official under the new company policy we were free to arrive and leave together albeit such a luxury was rare.

Chapter 30 – Crisis Time

The finance department having completed the reconciliation exercise issued their findings, which didn't make for happy reading. On Thursday, Doug and I, and the accountant responsible for the reconciliation, poured over the figures.

The problem, I thought obvious, we were over manned, business development non-existent plus the accounts had been mismanaged adding salt to the wound.

I decided to hit Liverpool and Immingham with unexpected visits on Monday and Tuesday the following week. Doug asked, nay pleaded with me to keep my cool.

Over the weekend we shopped for travel essentials and the girls purchased new outfits. I went wild and purchased new boxer shorts and a couple of pairs of trousers. The girl's flat looked like a disaster area. Clothes were hanging, lying strewn and piled everywhere. One glance and I said goodbye. The laughed me out of the door stressing strongly that I didn't understand the finer points of women. I accepted their light-hearted criticism.

Sunday we had a roast lunch at a pub. I told Christine I would be away leaving early Monday, returning late Tuesday night. I explained the situation and the reason for my visit. Quite rightly, she said, "I should be with you to deal with personnel and union issues."

After lunch I called Doug at home. He wholeheartedly agreed annoyed we hadn't considered the option. As an afterthought he said, "No sexy clothes, business suit, okay?" "Of course," I replied.

It was hard work but I succeeded in getting Christine up, washed and suitably attired and in the car with her luggage by five-thirty, a whole half hour later than my intent. The drive to Liverpool went quite fast. Keeping my eyes peeled for the police I gunned it most of the way. At one stage, without realising, I hovered on the ton-ten mark.

Unsurprisingly Christine slept until I stopped at a café for breakfast. I jokingly asked, "What is it with you and cars, all you do is sleep."

She smiled, "It's a good job I haven't bought a car then isn't it?" My ears pricked up. "Do you have a license?" "Yes both Charlotte and I have licenses," She laughingly replied.

I left it there; I didn't want to hear whatever was in her head. However, Christine being Christine said, "We did think about purchasing a small run-around, a Mini perhaps but decided public transport was adequate. We also recognised we would end up fighting over who should have and who shouldn't have use of it."

The breakfast as they normally are in trucker's café's was first class. We both had the works, bacon, eggs, fried bread, tomatoes, beans and steaming mugs of tea.

The drive into the docks because of rush-hour took ages. We didn't reach the office and workshops until ten. The minute I pulled up I leapt from the car and entered the workshop. Not knowing what to expect I was aghast to find two guys crashed on work benches oblivious to the world. I looked for and found a hefty metal bar and clanged it very loudly onto a metal waste bin.

One fell off the workbench, the second guy barely moved. I closed in on him. I could smell the alcohol at two yards. I stormed out, Christine standing by the car signalled calm down. I located Stuart Laird, the manager, with his feet on his desk reading a bloody newspaper. He jumped up. I yelled "Right get over to the workshop send the two guys home especially the drunk, then come back here and show me today's work routines." He looked at me agog. "NOW," I shouted.

He rushed out, Christine rushed in. She quickly checked the offices. Turning to me she said, "Richard, for God's sake calm down. There are ways of doing this, get it wrong and we could have labour issues, particularly union issues."

I garbled about blokes sleeping on workbenches, one being drunk and the manager with his feet up reading the paper. There was a knock on the door. Still annoyed I shouted, "Wait" Christine grabbed my shoulders saying, "I handle this now calm down." She went to the door and ushered the manager in. He stood shamefaced looking at her.

I hadn't seen Christine in action when dealing with labour, she was good, damn good. She left the manager standing, her back to him she moved papers around on his desk. Turning to look at him she said "I am Christine Clarke, head of personnel for Mr Chamber's division. You are, I assume, Stuart Laird, the manager, an employee for the past eleven years with Maybury." He nodded replying, "Yes Madam." I very nearly laughed; instead I moved from his sight and leaned against the wall.

Christine very deliberately sat in his chair. "Why were two men sleeping in the workshop?" He said he didn't know they were. She nodded saying, "Okay, did you, this morning undertake a roll-call, in accordance with company policy and also because of the demands of Health and Safety, when working in dangerous environments."

"Yes" he answered. In a moderate voice she asked him for the work register. He blustered.

Christine firmly said, "Mr Laird I repeat my question, did you undertake a roll-call this morning." He shook his head.

"Mr Laird, the failure to do so is a sacking offence. You do realise that don't you." He murmured, "Yes."

Christine continued, "Mr Laird please show me the work register." He went to a filing cabinet and pulled a file. He passed it to Christine. She scrolled through the file. After several minutes she looked up. "Mr Laird in the past two months you have managed seven, only seven roll-calls."

She paused for effect. Resuming she said, "Mr Laird I am going to compose a letter suspending you until further notice, which Mr Chambers will sign. We will continue to pay you for one month. Do you understand?"

The guy cracked pleading for his job, for his family. He listed several excuses with regards the men ignored his instruction and he couldn't get support, which he asked for on many occasions, from head-office.

He rushed to the filing cabinet, scrambling about he produced a second file, which he passed to Christine. Christine studied the file before once more looking at the guy she said, "Mr Laird please wait outside we will call you back shortly"

He exited and Christine called me over she said, "In the last eleven months our Mr Laird has written to Peter Jackson no less than five times requesting both personnel and management support."

I said, "Oh shit, what the fuck." I was swiftly rebuked and I apologised.

Christine said, "We can still suspend him, which under normal circumstance would be my recommendation, but with Hong Kong looming it is better to have a manger than not, plus he will pull his socks up following today's exposure. The decision is yours."

Under my breath, in my head I cursed and blasphemed. Nevertheless, I understood what Christine insinuated. I bit my tongue and said, "Fine, we know he is weak, and we know he hasn't the balls for the job. Therefore we transfer one of Jimmy's team to take control. Jimmy, when you contact him to explain the situation, will select the right man. I want whoever Jimmy recommends here tonight, and I don't care if he flies, the man gets here tonight, okay?"

I thought for a moment taking onboard Christine's words. "Now Mr Laird, he is told in no uncertain terms where he stands and in all probability he will lose his job. In return for leniency he writes a complete breakdown of events for the past twelve months. That's it. Ask no quarter, give no quarter."

Christine looked at me. For the first time she was witnessing the business man, the man who delivers and doesn't accept failure. She smiled, "If that is how it is, then fine, that is what we do." She opened the door and called Mr Laird in.

She read him the riot act adding he had a very short period to pull himself together. Exclaiming that by the following morning he would have support. Also she told him to expect contact sometime during the day. In the meantime he should go home and be thankful that Mr Chambers chose not to sign his suspension letter.

As Stuart Laird turned to exit I said, "Before you go I want every Maybury man, excluding the two you sent home, here within one hour and I also want, as I originally requested all work routines for today. In fact I want work regimes for the last two months. You are able to do that I assume." The man now defeated not knowing his future said, "Yes Mr Chambers."

Christine called Jimmy following her explanation she said "Okay, this is the number," she read out the office telephone number and said, "I'll wait for your call."

Five minutes after Laird had walked from the office, a knock on the door from an adjoining office revealed the young girl I had met on my previous visit. She entered carrying seven files, not one of them was thicker than an orange peel. Christine took the files from her and instructed the girl to sit.

In a kindly tone Christine asked the girl her name. In a clear voice she replied "Rebecca". I pulled a chair close sitting to face her. In a soft voice I said, "Rebecca, you appear to be central to all operations. Perhaps you would be kind enough to explain exactly how the Maybury operation works."

As an afterthought I added, "By the way, Christine is on your side, she is your personnel manager here to support you. I am the General Manager and this business is now my responsibility."

She smiled. "I collate paper work, file it and answer the phone."

I smiled in return. "Do you remember a couple of weeks ago when you explained your involvement in accounting?"

"Yes, but a man from head office came and took all my paperwork away," she quietly responded.

I indicated the files now in Christine's charge asking if one of them contained the work regime file. Rebecca selected a green folder. I opened the folder and started to scan through the eight pages.

Very quickly I realised Liverpool did not have enough work for six engineers, never mind a manager, two supervisors and the fourteen engineers we carried. I closed the file and asked the girl to describe how new work was identified and secured. She didn't know except that one of the supervisors, Allen Peters tended to win most of the work.

Scratching my head, feeling Christine looking at me, I internally condemned my inaptitude to investigate further during the previous visit. I asked Rebecca to explain the work regimes and sales charts I had been presented with during that ill-fated visit. I learnt Laird and the Labour Supervisor, Des Barnes prepared the documents based on information taken from late 1960's archived files.

Christine intervened asking Rebecca to describe a normal day's work. It was a good question, which detailed a rota system whereas the engineers were divided into three groups working one week on, two weeks off.

Rebecca added if there was sufficient work the rota had been designed to cover work output. Christine gently asked who had devised the system, Des Barnes who also managed Laird, appeared to be the culprit. I was looking forward to meeting Mr Barnes.

Christine persisted, asking question after question and taking copious notes. Satisfied with her studious investigation she explained to Rebecca that she was not in any trouble. She asked for and was given Rebecca's contact details before advising her to go home until contacted, adding she would remain on full pay.

Rebecca's exit coincided with a knock on the door. Christine called "Enter". A solid looking guy walked in introducing himself, Allen Peters. He walked over to Christine asking "Are you the personnel manager?" Christine confirmed she was.

He handed two sheets of paper to her. He turned to me and said, "You must be Richard Chambers, the new boss. I have heard of you."

"Really," I retorted.

"Yea I heard you don't take prisoners, but you are fair and respectful."

"Is that right and where did you hear all this?" I queried.

"Word gets around, you know what its like," he confidently responded.

Christine waving the two sheets of paper signalled I should read them. Two more letters to Peter Jackson, the latest one explaining, albeit briefly, there was goings-on he should be aware of and he, Peter Jackson should visit Liverpool to see for himself. I thought Doug isn't going to like this, his right-hand man of many years being proved incompetent, inefficient and by the sound of things down right lazy.

I said, "Take a seat, Allen and describe to Miss Clarke what the hell has been going on." He explained in detail, while Christine took notes, how Des Barnes ran the show. By the time he finished his graphic description of how Maybury's Liverpool operation worked we had enough evidence to dismiss the whole workforce including, despite his letters to Jackson, him, and he knew exactly where he stood.

He stood to leave saying the five guys on-site were in the workshop. "Allen," I said, "Who are the good guys, are there any?" He sat back in the chair. After a few moments he said, "Rebecca, Johnny Dobson, Scouse Callaghan and the Italian, Alfredo De Luca who we call Alfie, and maybe Taffy Thomas." I asked if any those named were in the workshop. "Alfie and Scouse." he replied. "Okay, you stay here with Christine, this won't take long."

I entered the workshop looked at the crew stood waiting. I shook my head saying, "It's over. Which of you are Alfie and Scouse?" They raised their arms. "Go over to the office, the rest of you go home until further notice, we will be in touch. And one of you may want to call your union representative." I followed Alfie and Scouse to the office.

In the office I banished the three guys into an adjacent office. I turned to Christine saying "Contact the union and explain what is occurring, try and fix a meeting."

I walked into the adjacent office. I said, "Allen can you contact the other blokes whose name you gave me and ask them to come in" He nodded leaving to enter Rebecca's little domain. I heard Rebecca's voice. "What do you want Allen?"

I followed and asked Rebecca why she was still here she replied, "Sorry Mr Chambers but I thought Miss Clarke and you might need help to find things and if you want typing or telephone calls." Her voice trailed off.

"Smart girl Rebecca and thank you, help Allen then pop and ask Miss Clarke if you can type her notes."

Rebecca swiftly located the requested information. Allen Peters made the calls to the two men, when he had finished, he said, "They should be here within the hour." I nodded. I returned to Christine who stood behind Rebecca typing the notes.

Christine smiling for the first time said "We are meeting Maybury's shop steward and a local union rep at the Mountain Hill Motel, Bootle at six this evening. The local rep called, he's Scottish and very rude." I laughed and winked saying "Terrific just what we needed, a stroppy Jock." I said to Rebecca "Do you know where we can find an interpreter?" Christine said "Ignore Mr Chambers Rebecca he is trying, but failing, to be funny"

The telephone trilled and Christine answered "Hello Jimmy, yes, yes, that's fine, okay. Spike MacDonald" she looked at me. I nodded. Christine resumed talking to Jimmy "Barrow-in- Furness, three hours, fine. Give him this number and we will direct him in. Thanks Jimmy."

Christine asked "Do you know him?" "No but I have heard his name, Jimmy speaks highly of him, one of his supervising engineers." I replied.

Christine and Rebecca continued working on the notes to prepare presentable documentation for the meeting with the union representatives.

I telephoned Doug. He listened in silence while I explained the situation. When I had finished he abruptly said, "I'll call you back" and hung-up. In the meantime the blokes Allen had called arrived. I asked Christine to join me in the workshop. As we walked over I said "If I go off track or say something or sound like I may say something incorrect jump in and, oh yes I love you"

I told them to make themselves comfortable. "Okay this is where we're at," I started, "You are as of now, and until further notice, Maybury's Liverpool engineering crew. A supervising engineer called Spike

MacDonald, his Christian name is Trevor, will arrive from Barrow in about two hours' time. He will take responsibility for the immediate future as acting manager."

Allen Peters asked what was happening to the rest of the Liverpool men. "They will receive letters, hand delivered, this evening, suspending them until a full inquiry is completed."

He pointed out we would have the unions breathing down our necks. I informed him we were meeting them at six, mentioning the Motel. He shook his head saying, "Home turf, the motel is their unofficial office, and don't take your car." I asked why. "Because Mr Chambers, when you come out your wheels will be missing and you will have an iron pole shoved through the roof and for good measure probably an axe in the bonnet." I looked at Christine, she shrugged.

I looked at Allen. "What do you suggest?" He also shrugged. He asked who we were meeting. Christine answered. "Too late you've agreed the meeting, they won't change now."

I was thinking when he added, "Barnes with a couple of his cronies will be in the bar itching to get at you so watch your back."

I said, "Effing terrific I am now going to be facing a bunch of scousers wanting to tear me apart, this will be fun." I laughed saying, "It's ages since I had a good scrap."

Allen Peters suggested I called Tony Slattery the union's regional branch secretary. He further explained who Slattery was and his position also mentioning that the guy was four square.

Allen tracked down his number and Christine telephoned him. Once more she described the turn of events. Listening to Christine's side of the conversation he obviously asked many questions. Time moved on until she replaced the receiver. She said, "He'll be at the meeting however, he has suggested you and I meet him at four-thirty in a wine bar on Bootle High Street called," she looked at her notes, "The Merry Widow."

I looked at my watch. I looked towards Christine. "Christine sweetheart," I stopped mid-sentence. A smile appeared on Christine's face. Allen Peters burst out laughing, his motley crew joined in. He said, "It's alright Mr Chambers, its common knowledge you're walking out with Miss Clarke."

"As I was about to say, before being boisterously interrupted, Christine SWEETHEART will you work with Rebecca and sort through the suspended men's files for addresses and also compose appropriate letters. Also SWEETHEART could you track down a professional courier service who can deliver the letters tonight. Thank you SWEETHEART."

The remnants of the Liverpool team were laughing their socks off, as was Christine before she sweetly said, "Yes darling, right away darling", which encouraged more raucous laughter.

Spike MacDonald arrived at two-thirty. He and I went for a walk. I described the unsavoury state of affairs asking if he was up for the challenge. He asked relevant questions, his final question centred on the guys I had kept back.

My answer was, "I don't know, I have known them for a few hours but Peters, the supervisor did try and warn head office of the problems, but was ignored. He also advised that the guys he selected were the best of a poor bunch so I have put a certain amount of trust in him. But Spike you will be the arbitrator, the judge over the next few weeks."

I asked where he lived and if he had any family issues that needed resolving, which he didn't. He was single and he would telephone his parents. I also told him I would arrange to increase his pay in line with his responsibilities and also pay expenses to cover living allowance. All expenses were claimable including accommodation to work travel costs.

Returning from the walk I introduced him to Allen Peters and the others. I said, "Christine and I have a meeting with the branch secretary of the union so we have to shoot. Allen will show you the ropes. I will be here first thing in the morning, see you all then."

I rushed over to the office Christine and Rebecca were sealing the suspension letter envelopes. Christine said, "I've PP the letters and Rebecca is going to wait for the courier company," she looked at her watch. "They should be here within next half-hour." I asked Rebecca for directions to Bootle High Street, which thankfully was close by.

In the car Christine was all smiles, she said, "Mr Chambers, are you walking out with me?" "Well Miss Clarke, it would appear so." We both laughed. Christine had taken copies of her notes, which I needed to read before any meetings took place. We found "The Merry Widow" which looked in darkness. I parked the car, checked the time and read the notes twice over. "Great job Christine, accurate and to the point, well done"

We walked back along the High Street and stood outside the wine bar. After a few minutes the door opened a voice asked "Chambers" I responded. Christine and I were shown in. A dapper little guy stood to meet us, following introductions, which included his assistant Mrs Donnelly, he said "What is all this about?" Christine gave an explanation. She then passed each a copy of her notes and advised they should be read.

The guy who had opened the door asked if we wanted a drink. Slattery said, "My son, his bar." We both settled for water. Slattery addressed Christine, "How correct is this?"

Pondering the question she responded, "The information was provided by two employees without any provocation. The manager himself, a certain Mr Laird, although I have not included his remarks, was also forthright."

"Why haven't you included his comment?" Mrs Donnelly asked. "We made the decision to exclude his remarks because he became extremely emotional and he began to blabber somewhat. Therefore we decided in his best interests to re-interview him when he is more cognisant." They both nodded.

An in depth discussion ensued for a considerable time. Comment, question, what action and finally the question I had been expecting: "Do you intend to close down the work or do you intend to re-build?"

Without hesitation I explained the immediate action. I looked him in the eyes and said "If the work is here, and it is tangible then we re-build. However, it will take three or four months to determine if the company has a future in Liverpool." Again he addressed Christine "Would proper redundancy packages be available fully paid up?" Christine answered, "Without doubt, Maybury is a fair employer and although the company has been hoodwinked for months, probably years it will honour its commitments."

He gathered together his paperwork, looked at his watch saying "We had better get a move on. I suggest you leave your car here and travel with us." I was pleased to agree. In his car I said, "What's the verdict?" He smiled in the rear view mirror. "Liverpool is rife with unemployment, best to save some jobs, don't you think?" I nodded my agreement.

The meeting in the Motel was loud, angry and extremely uncomfortable. I felt Christine's hand on my arm several times, she, knowing that for tuppence, I would have hit the Scotsman into next week.

In the end after a great deal of swearing and blaspheme the Scotsman accepted the branch secretary's argument. Slattery, throughout, remained calm but very authoritive. He was a first class negotiator. Mrs Donnelly wasn't too bad either regularly clarifying issues, the pair made a good team, worthy adversaries. I considered we were fortunate to have their support and not going head-to-head against Mr Slattery and Mrs Donnelly.

The Scotsman and his two cohorts stormed out of the motel. I caught sight of three guys who I assumed to be Barnes and his cronies exiting a door, which I presumed was the door into the bar. They scooted behind following the union representatives into the car-park. Slattery lifting his bulky briefcase quietly said "A good bottle of wine, what say you Miss Clarke?" Miss Clarke thought Slattery's proposal was spot-on.

Walking from Slattery's car to the "Merry Widow" Christine whispered, "Where, my knight in shining armour, will we be sleeping tonight?"

"Probably a bench on Lime Street station," I answered with a big smile relieved the awkwardness of the day was over.

When we walked in to the wine-bar it was busy, an evening crowd fortifying themselves before moving on to clubs and discos. Slattery's son led the way to the table, decorated with a huge "reserved" sign, we had vacated some three hours earlier.

The glasses filled Slattery looking at Christine said, "Mr Chambers, you owe Miss Clarke here a huge thank you. She was obviously controlling a young man who had lost patience with words and was looking for action." He turned to look at me, continuing he said, "They identified you as the weak link. If you had struck out in retaliation to their baiting all would have been lost. Well done Miss Clarke, I raise my glass to you."

Upon hearing Slattery's words Mrs Donnelly proceeded to lecture me saying "You are rather young to be a General Manager, which is probably why diplomacy is an obvious deficiency, requiring attention, in your character. I am not saying discipline is not needed, of course it is, but I am saying the power of words, will, more often than not, and in the majority of situations, win the day"

I wholeheartedly agreed with her admitting I did need to adopt a higher level of patience. However, I did gain kudos when I said "Observing you Mrs Donnelly, Mr Slattery and of course Miss Clarke, three erstwhile colleagues this evening, I identified words will confuse, they will encourage, and they will cause despair, an invaluable lesson."

Christine squeezed my leg. Mrs Donnelly looking at me with an appealing smile asked, "Are you and Miss Clarke courting?" Christine and I looked at each other and in unison nodded. Mrs Donnelly laughed and Mr Slattery smiled a fatherly smile saying, "Good luck to you."

We proffered sincere apologies explaining we had to find a hotel. I emphasised most firmly my gratitude for their help and for resolving a very unpleasant situation. We went in search of the Adelphi Hotel, highly recommended by Mr Slattery.

In the hotel room, with Christine's assistance, I unwearyingly prepared a report depicting the whole day's programme of events ready for Rebecca to type and post to Doug. Christine proof read the document corrected parts and rearranged the time-log. When she was satisfied I called room service and ordered food, we both plumped for fish and chips.

The following morning, after breakfast we reached the offices in good time to stand in the autumnal sunshine with Spike as he welcomed his recently acquired workforce. He excused himself and shepherded his team into the workshop. Christine and I retired to the office both curious and anxious. A telephone trilled and was answered, we realised Rebecca had turned in to work.

Christine went through to welcome Rebecca and pass her the typing work we had prepared the previous evening. I popped in to her office and wished her a cheery good morning.

However, my mind was focused on Spike and how he would handle the challenge we had tasked him, and the future of Maybury in Liverpool. I checked the time deciding Doug was in work I telephoned him. I provided a brief synopsis of the evening's occurrences adding we would be posting a full report for his attention.

Watching from the office window I was pleased to observe engineers, smiling and jesting, tools and equipment on trolleys, disperse to attend to work matters. Spike trotted to the office. He said, "Everything is fine. Allen Peters is going to introduce clients and dockyard personnel he thinks I should meet, which will take until lunch. The guys have been allotted tasks, worksheets and set regimes so they will be busy all day. Later today, Allen, Rebecca and I will check and re-check all paperwork, outstanding works and get some order in place. I'll post a written report as soon as I have collated all the facts."

Inwardly I was over the moon thinking "good man" and well done Jimmy. Outwardly I said, "Excellent Spike, Christine and I are moving onto Immingham. I proffered my hand. We shook hands. I said "Thank you for your assistance, especially the swiftness in reading and understanding the situation. And for introducing discipline and direction."

He looked slightly embarrassed. I said, "All yours, I'll pop up and say hello in two or three weeks." He turned and trotted to his car. I waved my thanks to Allen Peters, giving the "thumbs-up" sign.

Back in the office I spent half an hour tracking Jimmy until he, having received one of the many messages I had left, called me. He was in Barrow with two engineers who would replace Spike. They had driven north last night. I expressed my gratitude to Jimmy and his choice of Spike, further expressing how impressionable the young man had grasped the mettle. We ended the call.

I considered myself blessed to have the likes of Rebecca, Spike, Jimmy, even Allen Peters and his guys supporting me and therefore the company. We read through Rebecca's typed report. We thanked her and departed for Immingham knowing we wouldn't be back in Southampton until late Wednesday.

In the car I asked Christine to arrange Spike's improved remuneration package outlining my agreement with him. I also asked her to arrange a ten per cent pay rise for Rebecca.

When we arrived in Immingham a nervous manager, Terry Hamley waited in his office, an office submerged in cigarette smoke. Christine coughed and I said to Terry let's walk. Outside I introduced Christine.

The three of us set off. I said "The bush telegraph is obviously in good working order." He answered, "Yes I heard and I have given my operation some thought. I could probably change a few things." For a while, him waiting for a response, so he could verbalise his thoughts, we walked in silence. Christine breaking the quiet said, "Such as?"

Without hesitation he listed a dozen changes he would like to introduce. The changes ranged from altering work practices, to improved procurement procedures and store control, to reducing his team by three engineers, and volunteering to attend a course on bookkeeping. Christine following his commitment closer than I, asked, "Do you have a prepared programme, particularly one which demonstrates action, cost and output?"

As soon as Christine asked her question she caught the man with his trousers down. He, not having a programme, had obviously thrown caution to the wind to curry favour. Christine's next question was the killer "Why wait until today, specifically today, before presenting your proposals, could it be you've heard what happened in Liverpool, which we know you have. Perhaps, correct me if I am wrong, working for Maybury is a cushy number, for which you have been handsomely paid. A case of "don't rock the boat", don't you think Mr Hamley."

Hamley, for a moment was stunned. He stopped walking looking at Christine then at me. He addressed me. "Mr Chambers, the work has gradually dried-up through no fault of mine. We have lacked support from head office for quite some time. I failed, foolishly to present an argument, convinced I wouldn't be listened to."

He turned to Christine continuing his tirade. "And yes, Miss Clarke you are absolutely right, I didn't want to "rock the boat" and I will tell you why. Immingham and Liverpool have become forgotten outposts of the great Maybury enterprise. Mr Chambers here was flying and no one could touch him and yes fair play to him. In the meantime we were ignored brushed under the carpet."

I said, "Terry, return to the office and collate two lists. List one should provide positive information for consideration. List two should include the downside of Immingham's operation. We will go and have lunch and return to discuss your two lists. Is that reasonable?"

"Yes Mr Chambers."

After he had departed I said to Christine "What do you think?" She didn't respond immediately preferring to dwell on the circumstances. "Unfortunately, he is doubtlessly correct in his summation, which leaves not only Peter Jackson exposed but more worrying will Doug Robertson be exposed, if so there will be an instant threat against you. Doug will probably unload some of the blame onto Peter, but he will not be able to unload it all. Richard you are going to need to be ultra-careful."

We found a café, neither being hungry, we ordered mugs of tea. Sitting to the rear of the café I said, "Let's re-cap we have two businesses losing buckets full of money, both of which were managed by Doug and Peter. Whether Doug left the management to Peter prior to his board appointment is a moot point. However, whichever way we approach the fallout and fallout there will be, you and me, need to be both diligent and vigilant."

Collecting my thoughts I continued, "If not we will be screwed, probably by Doug, to protect his own backside. Personally, I am for full exposure. Yes, by all means give Doug the satisfaction of receiving all the relevant information first. By all means give him time to make pertinent decisions. However, we ready ourselves to issue all documents to the board. The problem we have is ensuring a third party has sight of the report and witnesses its issue to Doug."

My gorgeous lovely Christine had the answer. "Simple, I have my Dictaphone with me. I will read the Liverpool report. Similarly I will do likewise, once we have prepared it, with the Immingham report. I will post the cassettes to Amy, my supervisor, instructing her that the documents are highly confidential and for her eyes only. I will ask her to type and file in a secure place, probably the personnel file cabinet, which is permanently under lock and key. When the Immingham report is typed I will ask her to take a copy and issue to Doug. In fact I will ask Amy to issue both reports to him at the same time. The process is correct and in accordance with company policy."

"Fantastic," I shouted. Christine's eyes reminded me we were in a café. In a low voice I said "My brilliant lovely lady you are marvellous. I now know why, I really fell in love with you, because you are clever, witty and intelligent, and brimming over with common-sense. I love the simplicity" In return I received a wonderful loving smile with a hint of "pretty smart eh?" in her eyes.

We returned to meet with Terry Hamley. He was locked in deep discussion with his administrator. We left them alone. I said, "We should find accommodation for the night." I informed the manager we would be back within the hour adding I hoped he would be ready.

We reserved a room in a Hotel depositing our luggage we once more returned to meet with Terry Hamley. Terry waited with Lilly his administrator. We crowded into his small office. Christine closed the door. He presented the two requested lists. I decided we would review the downside list first. There appeared to be four major concerns, first, all work pricing was undertaken by Peter's team, now my team using southern rates, which weren't competitive in Immingham.

Secondly support for the past three years from head office, particularly business development had virtually ceased. At this stage he produced a document he issued to Peter Jackson and Doug, February 1972 outlining business development issues.

His third issue dealt with training for engineers to bring them up to speed with new technology. I thought that a good point and worthy of further investigation for all teams.

The fourth issue raised explained that he couldn't work with the local union due to his lack of negotiating skills, which he either needed training for or head office support. He produced a second document, a recent request to Peter Jackson for personnel management support. I asked Christine if she was aware, which she wasn't.

I said, "Why didn't you catch a train and visit head office demanding support?" He gave me an old-fashioned look, which spoke volumes. He was convinced a visit would not have accomplished anything.

He believed head office had little interest in Immingham. He said "I have lost my three best engineers to the competition. When I telephoned Peter he said, "There is no shortage of engineers in Immingham, replace them."

"I tell you this, the man had no idea." He bit his lip wishing he hadn't made his last comment. Christine said, "Your comment will not be recorded," and he smiled at her.

I asked Christine to spare a minute. We retired to an outer office not to discuss his issues but to give rise that we were. The discussion would come later when we prepared the report. Returning I said "Okay, what is on your positive list?" The list uncompromising covered seven positive outcomes if certain changes were instigated. I said, "Terry this is very comprehensive. I think the best way forward is for you to take each heading and explain the end product."

With Lilly's help he presented sound argument complimented with action plans plus an outline programme of events. His presentation proved positive and confident. Christine, when he had finished, his brow glistening from his enthusiasm, in a quiet voice asked if he had presented any of his points to Peter, Doug or any other senior management. He shook his head saying, "I did request on three occasions for senior management attendance to discuss Immingham's future, although I received affirmed responses no one turned up until Mr Chambers a couple of weeks ago."

Christine queried why he didn't present his ideas to me. He answered, "Mr Chambers was on a flying visit, he scanned whatever I showed him. His only interest at the time seemed to be finance. Not once did he ask if I had any comment on how to enhance business or improve work outputs." I thought Richard, "you aren't as clever as you think you are", the man had a very fair point.

In sport, attack is the best form of defence, so I attacked saying "Ridiculous Terry you only had to give me one or two reasons why Immingham was losing money and I would have been all ears. Instead you made excuses, which didn't wash with me. I consider myself to be a reasonable chap and if given good cause I listen. Listening is how one learns, don't you agree?"

Not having a clue what part of my statement he was agreeing to, he agreed. I immediately, in a kind manner, attacked once more. "You should have been demanding, insistent and if necessary shouted at me. Trust me I would have listened."

He smiled saying "Now I have met you properly I can see that, next time I will shout and elicit Lilly and a couple of the engineers to tie you down, physically I mean."

"Good," I said. "Do that, however from here on in you will become sick of the sight of me." We all smiled.

We excused ourselves to return to the hotel to discuss his options and ideas and also to prepare a report for Amy to type. As we left I said "Terry, Lilly we will see you in the morning for an hour or so before we head south."

We checked with the hotel's reception the time last post was collected. I checked my watch we had three hours to complete the report and get Christine's Dictaphone cassettes it in the post so Amy would receive it with first post. We managed it by the skin of our teeth. I sped to the main post office, doubled the required stamp value and posted the package. I crossed my fingers.

When I returned to the room Christine was in the bath. I stripped off and climbed in with her. I kissed her and praised her for her competence, her intelligence and her wondrous beauty. She laughed saying "Forget the wondrous beauty until you finish with the praising after which Mr Chambers I might, just might let you have a good look and maybe, just maybe let you touch." I splashed water over her, which she returned with profit.

We dried each other and climbed into bed. I explored Christine's exquisite body stroking and caressing, and kissing every inch of it. She lay still forcing herself not to react to my tenderness allowing me full access to her beauty. I marvelled in her loveliness. So perfect, so astonishingly beautiful I could never tire of her allure, of her exquisiteness.

Christine by now breathing quite hard and obviously excited lifted her twitching legs and said "Richard for goodness sake make love to me, you're torturing me." I entered Christine with a whoosh as Jolly Roger pushed air from her wet, wet vagina. She squealed with delight and lifted her legs higher. I pushed hard into her. She quivered and released her so sexy sigh, which excited me so much.

I speeded up and began to drive harder until Christine was pulling my hair whispering "Harder darling, harder." I used my strength to drive deeper and harder. Her legs were touching the wall above the bed and she was holding onto them. Her head lifted from the bed to try and bite me but couldn't reach. Her hands left her legs and reached for my upper body. She levered herself up and dug her teeth into my arm. Then she screamed, God did she scream, the sound reverberated around the room and beyond. I called "Christine my darling, oh my darling" I released my sperm deep into her, splattering the walls of her vagina.

The sensations were amazing, my body rippled as I felt the spasms following ejaculation flowing. I whispered "You are some woman every time is incredible." Christine laughingly said, "Some woman? Who are you referring to? Some woman indeed, you had better rephrase." As I rolled clear I responded, "The, I mean the, the only, the one, the love of my life, the only woman in my life. The only woman I want in my life." We were both laughing and cuddling. I started repeating myself. Christine bit my ear saying "Shut up you idiot I accept the rephrasing." We kissed demonstrating with passion the love we felt.

Christine asked if I was hungry "Only for you" I replied Christine holding her legs at right angle to her body retorted, "You can have me any old time but restaurants open and close at set times so my man are you hungry or not. Speak now or forever keep your peace." I laughed and pushed her over, falling she said, "Shower, food, wine and love. What do you say? "I say love, food, wine and more love." I dived for her she evaded and run into the bathroom locking the door.

We walked down the road to an Indian restaurant the girl on reception recommended. She actually curled her lip up when I asked what the hotel's food was like. We ordered five dishes to share, and forsook the wine for cold beer. Strolling back to the hotel we realised that in a couple of days we would be aboard an aeroplane destined for Hong Kong. We were both excited and very eager for the next few days to pass swiftly.

The following morning we spent an hour and a half with Terry, his two supervisors, who he was keen for us to meet, and Lilly. During the discussion he promised he would prepare a workable programme of events.

He emphasised he had, just, enough work to keep his team fully employed but he did warn us that from time to time there wasn't sufficient work for half his engineers.

I responded saying "Think about time and motion and how you are able to work into your programme of events, shift work perhaps" "Or" I added "you may have to look at reducing the team by three or more." He agreed.

Before departing Christine checked with Amy and I called Doug. After our respective calls Christine confirmed Amy had received the cassettes. I affirmed Christine that I had told Doug he should receive the Immingham report sometime today. He, which I found surprising, hadn't asked how or where from. We said our goodbyes to Immingham promising I would be back in two or three weeks.

We made Southampton in good time. We pulled outside the office going straight to Christine's group, to see Amy. We learnt she was at head office. Christine said, "Delivering the reports I assume." I asked one of her team. They confirmed she had been typing all morning and had left with two envelopes. We entered Christine's office, closing the door I said, "We wait for the fireworks."

Amy returned to the office. We called her into Christine's office. We asked if there was any show of surprise or comment when she delivered the reports. She smiled explaining Mr Robertson wanted to know where the documents had come from. I told him, his expression changed into a wolfish grin. He said "Richard Chambers, you smart bastard" I thought although it was Christine's brilliant idea, I'll willingly take the blame. I returned to my office. The effing in-tray was nearly touching the ceiling. "Bollocks" I said out loud. I rolled up my sleeves and got stuck in.

Christine ventured to my office at six-thirty. She knocked, as she always did and waited for my call of "Enter".

"Heard anything?" she asked. "Not a dickey-bird, if I had I would have let you know," I replied. She said, "Yes I know. Anyway Mr Chambers this girl wants to go home."

"Well Miss Clarke, if the girl, the only girl of my life wants to go home then that is where she will go," I smilingly responded.

In a quiet voice she said, "I'll pop in and say hello to Charlotte but I want to be with you tonight" I smiled back, "That you will. However, don't make a habit of it." She whispered, "I love you." Bang the door burst open.

Doug was framed standing looking at both of us and said, "Ah the love birds. Good trip?"

I answered, "I think so, and we resolved some pretty delicate issues and also dealt with the tough ones as well. It wasn't a picnic but it's now done. I will be visiting both operations immediately after our return from holiday." "So" he said "Whose bright idea was it to follow company policy, yours Christine"

Before Christine could respond I said "No actually it was mine. I was reading the company policy guide and discovered I hadn't been following procedure so I corrected the situation."

He grunted and took the seat opposite me. He said to Christine, "Leave us please Christine".

He looked at me. "You know if these reports are seen by the board, in particular Gareth and Mr Maybury, my arse will be on the line." I considered my response.

"Yes Doug I do, but you are the only one who has a copy. I decided if you had access you could tidy up loose ends before it is issued." His fingers were beating on the desk. "You intend to issue?"

"Doug, I don't have a choice, I would be remiss in my responsibilities if I didn't." I retorted.

His fingers still drumming on the desk he said "How long before you issue?" "The Wednesday after I return from leave" I replied "Good man" he retorted "I'll prepare a memo for you to send to me with copies to all board members. Is that acceptable?" "Yes Doug, but subject to the content of the memo" I responded.

"What is your overall view Richard" he asked "You either took your eye off the ball or you piled too much responsibility onto Peter. "Or" I added "You had lost interest because the revenue compared to the rest of the division was so minute you didn't think it worth worrying about."

Looking at me once more he said, "I saw your ability the first time I met you, and you haven't let me down. You've been good for me and good for Maybury, but my old son don't get too clever."

Very quietly I said, "Is that a threat Doug." He heard the menace in my voice.

He smiled. "No, Richard it is not. It is a warning that there are one or two senior managers who would whip the rug out from under you at the first opportunity and I am the one keeping the rug firmly fixed to the ground."

I was getting annoyed saying, "No Doug, that was a threat. I know damn well it was a threat. If you cocked-up then admit you did. You can easily spread the blame across two inept managers, an ill Peter Jackson and you can include the board because they didn't pay attention to the monthly management accounts. No Doug, give your position some thought and yes I will support you, but do not, don't you dare dump it on my doorstep."

He stood saying, "I'll write the memo tonight ready for you in the morning and for the record I was not threatening you." He held out his hand I shook it thinking "poison chalice". I followed him out of the office to find Christine and go home.

Christine looking very worried jumped from her chair to embrace me when I walked into her. She of cause and quite rightly wanted to know what had occurred between Doug and I.

I talked through the whole scenario, she said, "Richard tread lightly, you are not infallible." I smiled. "Thank you for waiting darling and I know I am not infallible, nor am I a walkover. Anyway let's get you home. Did you call Charlotte?" Christine confirmed she had.

The following morning Doug waited for me in my office. He handed the memo he had prepared over, I read it:

Dear Mr Robertson,
  Reference: Liverpool and Immingham Operations
  Further to a recent discovery, of unacceptable financial losses, at the above two operations, and due to the operations being transferred into my division, it was decided necessary to further investigate. I with Miss

Christine Clarke representing personnel visited both sites. The detection of mismanagement and fraud was evident in Liverpool.

A resolution for Liverpool, with the help of the regional union branch secretary and particularly Miss Clarke was accomplished. The resolution was reached by temporarily transferring a supervisor from an existing Maybury team to manage the remnants of the Liverpool operation. Ten local Maybury personnel were suspended pending further investigation. One supervisor, four engineers and an administrator were retained.

The former manager, the retained supervisor and the administrator provided robust evidence pertaining to fraud and serious over-manning. Subsequently following a series of meetings with union officials, site staff and with assistance from the retained supervisor and the administrator, official letters advising of suspension were issued, delivered by hand and acceptance signatures received, to each of the ten employees under investigation.

In the meantime the transferred supervisor appointed as acting manager is ensuring all work commitments are honoured. He will issue a report before the end of this week.

Immingham does not appear to have a fraudulent situation. It does however have an over-manning issue and a serious lack of work. The manager, under strenuous questioning, revealed specific aspects, which are having or have had a negative impact on the work operations of Immingham. The manager with assistance is constructing a workable programme of events. He has been allocated two weeks to prepare the programme.

Meanwhile, following our meetings regarding the issues at both operational sites, I trust, during my leave period, you will provide support and manage the specific phases highlighted in the two reports I issued to you Wednesday 24th October 1973. Upon arrival at my holiday destination I will provide contact details for your attention.

It is my intention, upon return from leave to request a board meeting to discuss the ramifications of the disturbing elements unearthed during the operational visits.

Yours sincerely
Richard Chambers
General Manager
Maybury Marine National & International Ship Repairs

Distribution:
Maybury Board Members
Miss Christine Clarke, Personnel Manager

I read the memo twice before saying, "I would like to run this past Christine for her comment." Doug agreed. I called Christine to my office. She read the memo. She considered it bland and slightly ambiguous but was satisfied the memo would provide an element of protection. Plus, she thought it would satisfy the board that action had been taken and was on-going. I signed the memo passing it to Christine for distribution. Doug accepted Christine managing distribution.

The rest of Thursday disappeared in a flurry of tasks to ensure my desk would be clear before the weekend; I held individual and group meetings with the senior managers of the division. I didn't quite complete the paperwork but I felt confident it would be up-to-date prior to commencing my leave. I issued several memos regarding various subjects. I composed two letters, one for Spike Macdonald copying Jimmy and Doug. The second for Terry Hamley copying Doug.

Friday, after completing all paperwork I visited head office to meet with Doug. Christine was ceasing work and handing over to Amy at lunchtime. Doug, in a mon ami mood, had me on edge. However, he did his best to allay any concerns I may have while on holiday. He reiterated he wasn't threatening me.

He also emphasised without providing any relevant information, which annoyed me, he would be working on a long term scheme based on the report I issued on diversification and innovation, which he would pass onto the board. The board, he advised would review the report and meet with me upon my return from leave.

The scheme he stated would support my report and benefit Maybury. He stressed he intended to reveal the scheme at a follow-up board meeting, which would invariably be called after the first meeting to debate my document.

I departed head office at two and went to my flat, ostensibly to pack.

Chapter 31 – Hong Kong and Proposal

The airline, because we were first class travellers would send a car to collect Charlotte, Christine and me and deliver us to the airport. The downside, the car would be arriving at Christine's flat at four in the morning. I was busy packing before taking my case to Christine's flat where I would stay the night when Carol called.

She was in town for a long weekend and would like to meet for dinner. I explained I would be leaving for Hong Kong, she assumed for work reasons. I didn't want to rush out, meet Carol and enter into an explanation regarding Christine, deciding an explanation could wait until a convenient time.

She suggested coming to the flat. I fibbed, saying I would be leaving for the airport within the hour due to the unearthly time of the flight. We did discuss her biology course, which she loved. Carol adamantly expressed that if I hadn't nagged her she wouldn't have re-enrolled for which she would be eternally thankful.

After deliberating my work and the excessive travel she quietly said "I miss you. I should have pre-warned you I would be in Southampton. I only came home to see you and you, you bugger, fly off abroad. How am I going to ensnare you if you are not where I want you when I want you?" Laughingly I retorted, "That sounds a wee bit one-sided. I hear nothing for weeks and suddenly you are calling me."

She too laughed. "Of course, a woman's prerogative." We said good bye with a promise from Carol she would warn of future home visits.

My case packed I delivered it to Christine's flat before driving the car to the office where I had arranged safe parking. I walked back to Christine's flat, a good twenty minute walk. When I arrived Charlotte rushed out to buy pizza for the evening's meal.

Three very excited young people, chomping on pizza, expounded the fabulous fortnight they were about to enjoy, Charlotte and Christine more so than I because they would be catching-up with family.

I jumped from bed sharp at three in the morning responding to an alarm clock, which Christine was oblivious to. I kissed her and bit her nipple, subsequently Christine, after kissing me back and biting my shoulder forced her body to vacate the bed. Christine banged on Charlotte's door until she received an "Alright, alright, I'm up" response.

Meanwhile I made the bed. I waited forty minutes until Christine and Charlotte completed their ablutions, leaving minutes for me to shower, shave, clean the bathroom and dress before lugging four cases down the stairs.

I was halfway up the staircase after depositing the final case when two excited and two gorgeous red-headed girls rushed towards me trying to whisper, but failing, to inform me the car waited.

I stopped them and went through the routine check of passports, tickets, money and personal luggage. Upon receiving visible confirmation I moved aside to let them complete their rush. I trailed behind and helped the driver load the cases, which ended with Christine and me sharing the car's rear seat with a case.

Once at the airport the driver and I loaded a trolley, which he took charge of assuring me it would be on the aeroplane, and following his directions headed to check-in. We enjoyed a glass of champagne and nibbles before finally boarding.

The flight, especially being a long flight, took as to be expected forever to reach Hong Kong. I slept, read and watched a movie. The two girls made me change seats a dozen times to accommodate either them sitting together or Christine, or Charlotte an me together. Finally I gazed out of the aeroplane's port-hole watching the mountains, Hong Kong apartment blocks, the very small runway and Hong Kong's harbour pass by as we descended into Kai Tak airport.

Passport control and luggage retrieval was handled efficiently and we headed landside. I was busy manoeuvring the overburden trolley when I heard the shrieks and two girls charged towards their aunty, uncle and brother. James and Charles after Christine had indicated me came over. Similar to Christine and Charlotte they were both tall. Charles, also with red hair, looked like he worked out where James was much leaner. We shook hands and I was welcomed to Hong Kong.

Charles took charge of the trolley. Sadie came to meet me and following a hug said "So you're the chap who has stolen my niece's heart, I can see why." Christine smiling called "Aunty" to signify Sadie shouldn't be so overt.

I noticed my name being held high by a uniformed chauffeur who had been dispatched by the hotel to meet Christine and me. Charlotte would go with her guardians and brother. One of the cases shared Christine and Charlotte's belongings. However, Sadie took charge saying, "You two go and check-in. We'll take Charlotte and settle her in and meet you at the hotel in, say two hours. We'll bring Christine's things with us, okay?" Following further hugs from Sadie we separated.

Checking-in at the hotel completed we were shown to our room, which overlooked the harbour. Christine obviously in a great mood, very happy was pointing out landmarks, Victoria Peak and the direction of Repulse and Deep Water Bays, Kowloon and several places she wanted to take me.

We both showered, together, which of course instigated Jolly Roger entering into Christine, which as she always did, welcomed him willingly.

329

Under the warm spray we coupled together. Behind Christine I bent my knees and pushed upwards into her beautiful appreciative vagina. Her wet red hair was washing across my face and my hands held her hips firm as I drove up and up. I felt my sperm begin its charge along Jolly Roger's shaft and explode inside Christine, but continued driving until Christine cried out and clamped her thighs, digging her nails into my thigh. Her body relaxed and she turned her face aglow and kissed me, the warm water continuing to tingle our bodies.

We received a call from reception advising Christine's family arrival they would be waiting in a bar on the first floor. We dashed out and descended to the first floor we exited our lift as they did likewise. Charles handed me a half filled case, which I delivered to our room.

Charles and I sat talking education, engineering, rugby and cricket while the two girls, Sadie and James talked of the lives the girls were building in UK.

I liked Charles straight off he was on the ball, particularly with the economic issues in the UK. He hadn't decided which educational route to pursue. He had only just turned eighteen deciding to delay his university enrolment until 1974. He peppered me with engineering questions asking what my thoughts were on a career in engineering and which engineering speciality he should consider. He wanted to know why I had chosen marine engineering and whether I had considered other branches of engineering, giving examples such as aerospace, automobile and construction.

He was crackers when it came to cricket and way beyond crackers when it came to rugby. He absolutely loved the game, which pleased me, his enthusiasm reminded me to re-connect with training and work myself back into fitness and selection availability with my club.

Apparently in one of Christine's letters there was mention I declined opportunities to train with England, which baffled him. Nonetheless he had determined I must be quite a good player. Pushing for answers to several rugby questions he also discovered the name of the club I had captained, which enthralled him.

He asked if I would join him at his club based in Happy Valley for a session or two while in Hong Kong, which I said I would be honoured to. I knew Hong Kong had a serious rugby fraternity and it would be interesting to chat with a few.

We were starting to discuss cricket however James came over saying it was late, and Christine and me needed to catch-up on beauty sleep and that tomorrow was another day.

Upstairs in our room Christine interrogated me wanting to know what Charles and I had been discussing. She expressed her pleasure that our conversation had been both instructive and constructive. She asked what I thought of her baby brother. I was truthful saying I found him intuitive, aware and that he came across as very settled young man who would do well.

Christine queried whether I would employ him if he remained in England on completion of his education. I answered truthfully saying I thought him too bright for marine engineering adding he would be wise to look at other professions. She considered my response before agreeing with my assumption.

Christine said, "Am I your lovely lady?"

"You most definitely are," I responded.

"Then make love to me, love me Richard and never stop loving me."

I held Christine close in my arms gently kissing her head. My hands roamed over her body, I began to undress her. I slowly unfastened the buttons to her blouse, removed her skirt and slowly pulled her tights off. I lifted and stood her on the bed. She laughed "Not again. How many times are you going to inspect the merchandise?"

I placed my hands on her bottom and pulled her close inhaling her scent and kissed her tummy. I croakily whispered "I could never become tired of inspecting you, there is an allure, a special charisma, which will always entice me to appreciate your beauty. I cannot explain I just love to look at you."

I turned her kissing her hips and her bottom through her scanty panties. I ran my tongue down the backs of her thighs. Christine shivered. I slowly, very slowly removed her panties kissing her legs every inch of the way. She lifted one foot, which I held holding onto her with the other hand and sucked her toes. She slapped my head "How could you."

"You are too wondrous, you have a natural aroma, that's how." Lifting her right foot I repeated the action, her hand was stroking my hair.

I pulled her vagina onto my mouth and kissed her Mon Venus. I held her bottom tightly and pushed my tongue into the top of her vagina. I turned her again removing her bra, freeing her breasts and their beautiful pink nipples. I sucked her nipples. I lowered Christine onto the bed. She smilingly said "Are you keeping your clothes on?"

My clothes were discarded. I opened her legs and using my tongue with the utmost tenderness I massaged her clitoris forcing her to arch her body and demand I entered her. She guided Jolly Roger home. He was pleased rushing all the way into her. Christine held onto my neck. We kissed. I nibbled her nipples. She whispered "I am in love" I feigned deafness.

I withdrew and tenderly turned her over and entered her from behind. Christine gasped and pushed back "Oh that is so lovely" she cried. I moved in and out of her gaining momentum and gaining depth. She shrilled a whistling sound through her half closed lips. The tempo of our love increased and increased. I could feel sensations racing over my body.

Christine's body was quivering uncontrollably, she cried out "Oh my God Richard, what am I feeling, oh my God something is happening" she was pushing back as hard as she could I grabbed her hips and dove hard into her.

Her shrill was constant. The beginning of a series of spasms raced through her body. Christine was lost in multi orgasms, she had lost control of her body, contractions and seizures had taken control. She was panting, crying out and finally I sensed an orgasm so powerful she grabbed her stomach. I felt her vagina grip with such power I cried out. Her legs were shaking her body was struggling to hold position. Her beautiful porcelain body rippled and I exploded, I exploded so penetratingly that I was shocked. I hadn't experienced such a feeling before. It felt as if my penis had exploded shattering into a thousand pieces.

Electricity was causing astonishing pulses to run from the tip of my penis into my loins. I bit my tongue and gripped Christine's hips and with staggering strength I lifted her clear of the bed holding her fixed to my penis as it discharged and discharged. I dropped Christine on the bed she fell and rolled onto her back. I was watching her juices and my sperm spilling from her very open and very pink vagina. I collapsed onto the floor.

I rested my head on the bed and looked at Christine she was in a trance, panting. I reached and touched her taking a hand I very hoarsely whispered "What happened, what the hell happened?" She had the biggest smile. Her eyes were radiant her cheeks were flushed red, but her breathing was still a problem. I started whispering breathing exercises telling her to listen. The whole situation was surreal. With a huge effort I pulled myself onto the bed and cradled her head. I urgently whispered asking if she felt alright. I heard a little voice say "I'm okay, I'm fine." I relaxed.

We were in the tightest of tightest embraces. I kept saying over and over again, "I love you Christine, I love you Christine." She put her hand over my mouth and kissed my nose and my eyes. I heard her say, "Stop it Richard, I know you love me and I love you, I love you with all my being, now stop it."

Very quietly my voice dry I uttered, "Christine darling did you feel what I sensed. Did you explode inside, did your inners rip apart, and were you experiencing electricity and tingling throughout your body."

She looked at me and smiled. "I felt it all and yes all those things happened and more. I felt your love explode inside my heart and I understood how much you loved me. Whatever happened, whatever those sensations pulsating between you and me were they signalled your freedom, from what I don't know, and I don't want to know. You were released from whatever has been plaguing your inner soul, to love and to be in love. You were liberated to love me and that was all I am asking for, all I ever wanted."

I was so light-headed, very happy, the past finally extinguished, ousted from my troubled mind. Sally, Ruth, Sophie, Debbie, Carol, Melissa and many, many others, all wonderful women, who had haunted me year after year were extinct. I now had a clean sheet of paper, the new start I had sought and craved for. I could look to the future planning for a life with Christine, our life. Somehow, God knows how, I had won the most beautiful woman to walk this earth and I loved her intensely.

We lay on our backs, our fingers intertwined. The resultant silence charged with love, our love. There were no words needed. We didn't need action, the sensations we experienced making love were still with us pulsing through our touch, through our fingers. Our hearts were throbbing. We could both sense the phenomena that enveloped us.

Christine stirred rolling onto her side her hand stroking my chest, twirling my hairs in her fingers. Her voice thick with emotion she whispered, "I am in love, very much in love and I am loved. I can feel love radiating from every pore in my body. In the same way I feel your love sweeping through and over me, warming my heart."

Her light blue eyes slightly moist, were shining, huskily she murmured, "My poor heart is beating a hundred beats a second. I am breathless."

Sleep had bypassed us, our body clocks out of sync. We lay tightly clasped in each other's arms, touching and kissing, our bodies subjected to little tremors. Christine leaned over and passionately kissed me, her lips explored my face, "Richard I need you to love me. I need you by my side today and tomorrow, and the next day and every day thereafter. At this moment, I need to feel you inside once more propelling your love into me. I need to feel and know your seed is within me. I need to know I will bear and nurture our children."

Christine gently manoeuvred my body above and my penis into her vagina. She released a long pleasing sigh. Her arms enfolded my body into hers whispering "My love, my Richard we have discovered a love so immense and so special nobody will understand. From this day on we will be in love and we will love."

The touching and kissing and joining as one continued into the morning. We embraced, loved and adored each other, unable to extricate, to draw apart. We slept through the day only awakening once when the lady cleaner entered and withdrew holding the "Do Not Disturb" sign.

I felt the gentlest of kisses brushing across my lips opening my eyes I looked in the loveliest blue eyes and the prettiest nose encrusted with faint freckles one would ever hope to see, I whispered, "Hello you gorgeous creature I love you." Christine smiling radiantly replied, "I love you too and it's dark." I laughed. "Terrific, I love you and dark in the same sentence, something incongruous is going on." She laughed and I watched her beautiful breasts jiggle. I pulled her over to nibble her nipples one after the other.

Christine jumped up saying, "Get showered and you need a shave, we are due at Sadie and James's flat twenty minutes ago. Did you disconnect the telephone? There was a message pushed under the door. Don't worry, your secretary called passing on your apologies." She smiled.

We arrived at the apartment situated way up Victoria Peak one hour twenty minutes late full of apologies. Sadie and James were fine. Charles and Charlotte were visiting old friends. Christine and Sadie disappeared into the kitchen.

James started to ask about the UK, England in particular admitting there were times he missed the home country. I cut across him saying, "James I am not sure how this works." He looked at me quizzically. "Do I ask you both or just you?"

James said, "Richard you are not making sense." I apologised and said, "I would like to propose to Christine but I think I need to ask you, or Sadie and you for your blessing."

He called, "Sadie love, come here a minute please." Sadie exited the kitchen on her own. James quickly explained what I had said. Sadie hugged by head against her stomach saying "Ask ahead, she is waiting for you to"

I whispered urgently, "I want it to be romantic." They both smiled James asked if I had a ring, which of course I didn't. Sadie said, "Leave it to James and me we'll arrange something by tomorrow evening." I thanked them.

Throughout the fish supper and white wine Christine continually asked why everyone was smiling and what was she missing? Somehow we managed to divert her questioning.

The next morning, under cover of visiting the hotel's gym, as arranged I met with James in the hotel's foyer. His and Sadie's' plan was to hire one of Hong Kong's quintessential Junks for an evening cruise to an island. I would propose on the island. During the day Sadie would select a temporary ring to be replaced the following day. She would also purchase a card I would write suitable words in including the ring is temporary until we chose the one Christine wanted. We agreed the timing and it was up to me to suggest the Junk cruise.

After the gym where I punished myself I returned to the room saturated in sweat. Christine none the wiser for the activated plans told me I stunk and to shower. I walked from the shower saying I had noticed an advert for Junk trips and I thought it would be a good idea for she and I to take one this evening. I added it would be quite romantic. She neither agreed nor disagreed. So I telephoned the concierge and arranged one with a picnic and wine, which I changed to champagne. Christine looked at me as if I was mad. I was I was madly in love with her.

We joined James, Sadie and Charlotte and Charles for lunch during which time the temporary ring and a small card were passed into my possession. Charlotte regaled happily how much fun her and Charles were having, especially re-connecting with old friends reminding Christine she also had friends.

They were going to a disco in the evening, where Charlotte would meet one of her school day boyfriends. She was quite excited. Christine described me as a madman arranging junk cruisers and picnic, which of course both Sadie and James said, "How romantic."

In the afternoon we retired to bed, not to make love but to readjust our body clocks albeit we did, make love. However, we did sleep for three hours. While Christine was in the bathroom I wrote the card:

"Love is precious and my proposal is the first step towards our marriage, which will be filled with passion, love, and happiness. My proposal is meant as a celebration of our love, the love of you and me preparing to make a lifelong commitment to our love."

PS *"My Darling the ring is temporary, tomorrow we will select YOUR ring."*

Love and fir tree forests full of love and more love, Richard

Dressed and ready we hailed a taxi leaving the concierge to explain where the junk would be located. A slight Chinese man came over to meet the taxi, we walked the dock until we the man indicated his junk. I helped Christine aboard. The skipper skilfully navigated into the harbour. He was heading for a beach on Round Island. Christine searched the shoreline pointing out landmarks and particular suburbs of Hong Kong. The junk travelled swiftly towards our destination, its engine chuntering, the skipper soon indicated the island.

He shepherd the junk close in. I carried the picnic basket ashore before returning to piggy-back Christine. Christine laughing expressed time and time again she thought I had lost my mind. The skipper pulled away pointing to his watch and holding up two fingers, which I presumed a signal that he would be back in two hours.

Christine moved along the beach, which at best couldn't have been sixty metres long until she identified a rocky outcrop to be used as the picnic table. "Richard, why are we here? We are on an island, in the middle of the sea with bright lights shining from all directions to eat a picnic, why. If you wanted romance we could have played soft music and ordered dinner in the room. Or alternatively there are a dozen or more romantic restaurants, or we could have gone to bed and made love" I smiled saying "Christine this is my first time in Hong Kong, please humour me for an hour or so."

We laid the food on the near flat rock and I opened the champagne. Christine was not in an eating mood so I thought, this is it. I said, "Christine," and she looked at me. I dropped on to one knee and her hands went to her mouth, I said:

"Christine, when I think of the future, I imagine you and I together walking on deserted beaches like this one, I am holding your hand and hearing you talk, we are always side-by-side. I imagine you and I intertwined, bonded firmly together, our love strengthening as the years pass by, nurturing and cherishing our children, until once more we are alone to love and enjoy who we are, and to be with each other day after day. Christine will you please do me the honour of becoming my wife so my imaginations will come true."

Christine her hands over her mouth just stood and looked at me, tears were streaming down her cheeks. I stood and opened my arms and she collapsed. I caught her and held her tight.

Openly weeping her tears uncontrollable she smiled through the tears. She said, "You idiot man of cause I will marry you. I will marry you now, this minute. I am married to you. My heart is yours and has been for a long time."

Her arms encircled my neck and she kissed me, a lingering loving kiss expressing her feelings and her love. Laughing she said, "You still haven't told me why we are on this island." She jumped at me and I swung her around and around and Christine screamed with joy and happiness.

I gave her the temporary ring and the card. The ring went onto the appropriate finger the card was read and read, she said, "I don't need another ring, this one, the one Aunty Sadie has loaned you will be perfect." She noticed my look. "Of course it belongs to Aunty Sadie I have seen her wear it a hundred times."

Her laughter was loud and gay. "I understand, you actually asked for my hand, and they suggested the junk and the island, how wonderful, you are such a gentleman." She walked into my arms and we kissed once more. We packed the untouched picnic and waited for the junk.

The junk arrived, during which time we hadn't said a great deal. We had held hands and cuddled and kissed and we watched the twinkling lights in the distance, and aeroplanes fly overhead, and boats and ships pass our island.

We were at peace with the island and the little beach, we were together, very content, and euphoric with our commitment to be with each other, in love and loved. We boarded the junk cuddled close together on the wooden seat and steamed back to the rickety jetty. We gave the skipper the contents of picnic basket and the untouched, albeit opened bottle of champagne. His toothless grin was all the thanks we wanted.

At the end of the jetty we crossed an open space to reach the road where the original taxi had dropped us off passing an array of cafes used by local people. Christine suddenly sat at one of the empty tables pulling me to sit with her. In broken Cantonese she ordered green tea, with her cup in her hand she looked into my eyes, blue on blue and toasted our love.

In the taxi back to the hotel I rested my arm over Christine's shoulders and she nestled into my chest.

Once in our room we embraced holding on for dear life. Christine said, "You do know you have just asked me to marry you and I said yes, don't you." I feigned shock horror blaming the lack of sleep.

She clung onto me saying, "There is no escape you are stuck with me for the next hundred years."

I retorted, "Is that all I was hoping longer." Christine kissed me before saying, "Who do we tell first?" I replied suggesting Sadie and James, and Charlotte and Charles.

We both spoke to them as we received their hearty congratulations. Christine asked Sadie if she could keep the ring offering to replace it. I am not sure what deal they struck but I do know a deal was reached. I thanked both Sadie and James for their wonderful support. And as to expected, I received a lecture from Charlotte regarding the responsibilities of a good husband.

The time in England was mid-afternoon. I telephoned mother and Grandma Jean. Mother as normal went over the top threatening to fly to Hong Kong to celebrate with us. Curiously I received a similar lecture from Grandma Jean as I did from Charlotte with regular comparisons with my late Granddad. Christine and mother talked for ages. In the end I said "Say goodbye, this will be costing the earth"

I didn't have a new number for father so I couldn't ring him. Instead I rang Hugo who was ecstatic for us both. Miriam and Christine then entered in to a long discussion with me pointing at my watch and getting waved away by Christine. I decided enough was enough and that it wouldn't take long for the jungle telegraph to transmit the message once we were home.

Christine was now in wedding mode, demanding when. I said, pick a date and that will be our special loving day. Her next demand was where? I realised I didn't know Christine's birthday, which was the 5th April. I suggested her birthday; she dismissed my suggestion for several reasons, none more so than she didn't want to celebrate both on the same day because she would lose one celebration per annum. She delved into her handbag for her diary after careful studying she selected 4th July 1974.

Suddenly with the date chosen there were three hundred and one things to do. I listened but did not comment. However, I was forced into a debate on where. I said, "Greta Green sounds good to me," which gained me a nip on the arm. Christine determined the "where" issue would be resolved

337

later. The next important question was who and how many guests. I said, "I am going to have a shower and go to bed."

Christine after writing copious names down on paper finally gave up and went into the bathroom returning naked and beautiful and exquisite. I reached out for her pulling her into my arms. Our love making tender and exceptional we stayed connected not wanting to separate. There wasn't an urgency to climax or seek wonderful sensations only the need to remain meshed together experiencing our tremendous love.

We did talk but only to remind each other how much we were in love and how fabulous we felt and to reiterate our happiness and joy of being in harmony and in agreement we were destined to live our lives as one.

The rest of our Hong Kong holiday rapidly passed by, the days became inseparable. Charlotte and Charles were always out meeting friends or partying or attending discos. Christine wandered off for a day to enjoy afternoon tea with all her old friends. Sadie and James carried on with their busy lives and Christine and I were lost in our love. We did of course socialise.

Christine and Sadie arranged a luncheon attended by forty plus friends to announce our engagement and upcoming marriage. I went rugby training three times where I realised I had much work to do once we were home, training with the club.

We dined with a group, which included business colleagues from James's work, an evening full of laughter. Stories emerged of gambling trips to Macau and camping weekends in the New Territories. Weekend sailing, both under sail and motor were regaled particularly the fishing experiences.

The last evening before flying back to London we all dined at Peak Café, a treat from Sadie and James. Although the evening very pleasant it was tinged with sadness knowing the following day would be farewell to Hong Kong and specifically farewell to Christine and Charlotte's family.

Christine made sure Sadie diarised the 4th July ensuring James and Charles also diarised the date. We all thanked Sadie, Charles and James for being perfect hosts and I reiterated my thanks for helping plan my proposal to Christine. It was three sad people who boarded the London bound flight.

Chapter 32 – The Clarke-Chambers Cloud and Maybury

Christine's forethought to book the holiday until the 6th November offered respite for three very tired people who arrived at Christine and Charlotte's flat at five on Sunday morning. The luggage, left untouched, sat piled in the small hall as we prepared and went to bed.

Charlotte the first to recover called through Christine's door mid-afternoon that the kettle had boiled and black tea or coffee was available in the kitchen. We struggled out of bed to meet Charlotte in the kitchen.

Walking into the kitchen and seeing Charlotte, for a brief moment, I could have been looking at Christine. I hadn't realised how similar in mannerisms, looks and even their choice of clothes were. Their height and slim bodies, and the lift of their breasts were all identical. If I didn't know there was two years between them I would have sworn they were twins.

Charlotte, dressed, and Christine and I utterly dishevelled, planned the day ahead, which would be unpacking, and sorting items for the laundry or dry cleaning. I proposed we should eat out at the Trattoria or the Duke of Wellington, their choice.

Tuesday morning we boarded a bus heading towards the office, when I realised I had not contacted the office to provide contact details as I had committed to, prior to the holiday. I said to Christine, "In five minutes we will know the good, or the bad, or even the damn right ugly. We will know whether we have been shafted."

Christine smiled and said, "If they have shafted us, as you so descriptively put it, it will be their loss, so my darling I think not. They wouldn't because they know the loss would be too high. And what if you joined a competitor, and we both know there are a couple of companies out there who would snap you up, what then? No my lovely man we have not been shafted."

When we entered the office the welcome was warm. Amy, making a cup of coffee, full of smiles turned to meet Christine. Jimmy and Spike were sitting in my office. We shook hands. Jimmy said, "Good holiday?"

I nodded, he followed through with, "Forget it, it was yesterday," and smiled. "Okay, first, what are you doing in Southampton, Spike?" I asked.

"Here to welcome you home, boss. However, I think we have secured, or rather Allen Peters thinks we have secured a cracker of a contract, a three year deal maintaining the whole of Jetspur Shipping's fleet, some thirty ships of varying sizes trading throughout Europe. They want to meet you pronto, like yesterday." I slapped his back. "Excellent, will today do? Where are their offices?" Jimmy answered, "E2, London."

I seated into my old office chair and asked for details. Between them they explained the deal, which on the face of it sounded very exciting.

They explained the price issued provisional based on labour, travel, equipment and test and inspections but not spares, only consumables. Spares were subject to sign off by the client. The provisional price, a whopping three-point-two million, for the first year, and, subject to inflation, the same for years two and three. A very pleased Richard Chambers expressed gratitude and thanked Spike and Jimmy for managing the situation in his absence.

I called "Enter" in response to a knock on the door. Christine entered, "Sorry to interrupt but we are both required at head office to attend an extraordinary board meeting to discuss your report, among other things."

I acknowledged her adding I would be ready in five minutes. I asked Jimmy and Spike whether the probable contract was common knowledge, it wasn't only they, Rebecca and Allen Peters were in the know. I thanked them inviting both to lunch at the Duke of Wellington agreeing to meet at one.

I collected Christine and we sped to head office. At reception we were directed to the main board room where the board waited. I knocked and we walked in. Once more the welcome was warm. We were offered refreshments and placed side by side at one end of the rosewood board table.

The five board members looked expectantly to Mr Maybury. He coughed, blew his nose before saying "If the company is to continue to prosper it needs young blood who are energetic, innovative and to some extent fearless. Therefore I advise you that I am standing down as Chairman and Gary is also standing down from Head or Personnel and Commercial." Christine and I looked at each other, then at Doug.

Resuming Mr Maybury said, "John Adams, the Head of Finance will step down in nine months. We three are shareholders and we will continue to take a keen interest in the workings of the company. Initially we will probably be pests. Nevertheless, our concern will always be in the best interests of the business, and don't forget we have some pretty good contacts." He paused to blow his nose again and I thought where is this going, what is he leading up to?

He looked directly at Christine. "Miss Clarke, I understand from your CV you studied accountancy as a conversion course during your undergraduate course, is that correct." In a clear voice Christine answered, "Yes My Maybury."

"Well then, we are, if it is acceptable to you, sending you off to college to undertake a crash, come refresher course, on accountancy, the course is one day a week, you will be a late entrant because the course has already started."

Once more in a clear voice Christine said, "May I ask why, Mr Maybury?" I watched the other board members, their faces expressed faint smiles. "Because, Miss Clarke you have been selected, subject to the result of your course and your acceptance, to become Maybury's Chief Administrative Officer to work alongside the new Chief Executive Officer, who will be, if he accepts, Mr Chambers."

I said, "Shit," Doug laughed, and the board members stood as one to congratulate us both. Re-seated we were informed that Doug would become Chairman and that Rod Young would become Chief Accountant following John Adams retirement. Adams would also manage the transfer of power from his team to Christine. Gary would be on-hand to assist in the transfer of his responsibilities. I realised the nine months grace prior to Adams's retirement had been agreed to cover Christine during her studying.

The report I had so painstakingly prepared, Gary Holdsworth said was now the responsibility of the Chairman and CEO, Messrs Robertson and Chambers. Mr Maybury closing the meeting added, "And oh yes I forgot to ask, what are the future plans for Miss Clarke and Mr Chambers?" Christine beaming from cheek to cheek said, "We plan to marry on 4th July and you are all invited." More congratulations followed. Christine and I floated out of the board room aboard the Clarke-Chambers cloud.

As our cloud floated towards the reception area Doug called us both to his office. He was grinning proffering his hand towards me before hugging Christine. "My two bright sparks who will move this company forward, and what a team you will make, no we will make, we three are Maybury's future and by golly we will do the company proud. The other point, which was overlooked during the meeting, is that you will become shareholders. Mr Maybury has already instructed a corporate lawyer to re-structure the company's shareholding." Christine reached for my hand and squeezed it.

I asked him why the sudden change. He explained Mr Maybury and Gary had been threatening retirement for years. He pointed out that Mr Maybury was seventy and Gary sixty-eight and that John Adams was sixty-six. I asked him how he had brought the change about inside two weeks adding I assumed this was his "long term scheme" he had casually mentioned in his office prior to our leave.

"Of course," he retorted. "Your report was perfect, the motivation needed to convince the board they were aging and new blood was necessary, you are the new blood. Let's face it they knew the energy required to instigate change and move forward would be too much. In fact you report gave them the opportunity to graciously step-down, all I did was present the benefits of young blood, specifically you two."

In the car Christine and I burst out laughing, we were shocked by the impact of Mr Maybury's words. We hugged and congratulated each other before beginning to realise the massive responsibility we had been burdened with. For two people so young, our aggregated ages below fifty, we had a great deal to live up to and a great deal to deliver.

Christine sobbed, "Richard we can do this can't we?"

"Christine," I whispered. "You and I can do whatever we set our minds to, we are strong, young and ambitious, and so sweetheart we will succeed, most definitely we will."

I checked the time saying to Christine, "It is not ideal but I have arranged lunch with Jimmy and Spike in the Duke of Wellington, would you like to join us?" I put my arm round her and kissed her cheek. She affirmed it would be nice to catch-up with Spike and Jimmy.

Jimmy and Spike were sat at the bar. They welcomed Christine asking after her holiday. She flashed her ring, they roared and hugged her and congratulated me. Spike said "Allen has arranged the meeting with Jetspur tomorrow at ten. He will travel down from Liverpool on the early train and we meet at their offices." Christine said, "What's this?" Spike quickly explained. Meanwhile Jimmy purchased drinks, a pint for me and white wine for Christine.

We ordered lunch and forgetting work we were four young people happy in each other's company regaling holidays past and Christine and mine in Hong Kong. Stupefied and unable to stop her I listened when she regaled my proposal, including her exasperation of being dumped on an island. I made the two of them swear the proposal story would not go any further, knowing damn well eventually it would become common knowledge.

Later in the day after I re-checked the provisional pricing and studied the proposal we would be discussing the following morning with Jetspur, I called it a day, and collected my fiancée from her office. I realised immediately, when Amy gave me a lopsided smile that the tale of my proposal had been passed onto yet another work colleague. Also while I was closeted with Jimmy and Spike, Christine had received the information with regards her refresher course, which she would commence on Thursday, six weeks behind programme.

The following morning we arrived at Jetspur's offices, Boundary Street at nine-fifty to find Allen Peters waiting in reception. We were shown into a meeting room and offered refreshments. Three guys walked in, after introductions when Allen failed to add I was the General Manager, the elder of the three said, "We are expecting the General Manager." I very nearly answered they had the CEO but bit my tongue saying, "Gentlemen I am the General Manager."

After a good looking over well aware they were considering my age. I said with a smile, "Appearances can be deceptive but I assure you I am highly qualified for the position and I am also aux fait with the demands of the post. Perhaps it would be advisable if we provide details of our experience."

The older man, Mr Burnside, said, "No need, can we proceed?"

Two hard worked hours later we exited Jetspur with the contract, subject to final legal advice and the usual clause alterations firmly in Maybury's pocket. The price was the main stumbling block. However, we had prepared for this; subsequently the figures presented had room for manoeuvre and for expected adjustments. Both sides reached agreement and shook hands. Allen and Spike would issue the revised figures the following day.

I hadn't seen the inside of my flat for nearly three weeks. However, when I entered it was warm and cosy with the pleasing aroma of what smelled like curry. Christine was on the floor surrounded with books and writing pads. She jumped up and hugged me. We happily kissed. She said, "We will have to go house-hunting, we can't live here when we are married, it's not large enough."

Christine's books were from her college days, she had busy revising readying for her first day back at college. We briefly discussed the day's events, which included the fact that our engagement was now common knowledge.

She also had interesting news-- Jimmy and Candy, Casey's daughter, were courting and also that Amy and the chief designer Terry Whitehead were dating regularly. She further explained she would be spending a great deal of time at head office with Gary Holdsworth and John Adams.

I didn't see Christine again until Friday night, albeit we did keep in touch via the telephone. She explained when we did meet that she had work to do to catch-up with her fellow students, which would take all weekend. Her tutor had supplied her with books and notes. And did she complain, by golly she did. Her main gripe the re-adjustment she had to do to re-train her brain to listen, understand and learn once more.

At a loose end Saturday, I called my rugby club to find out where the first team was playing. I drove to Portsmouth to offer my support. In the stand I re-connected with the club's selectors and head coach. After the game, which we won I also re-connected with the team I had once captained. The reunion had a good feeling; I enjoyed the comradery. I re-assured everyone I would soon be back in training. Scotty the head coach reminded me I would start at the bottom, well not quite, but probably in the third or fourth team.

The following Monday Mr Maybury's and Gary's retirements were officially promulgated. Tuesday morning Doug and my new positions were also promulgated. Christine's confirmation as Acting Chief Administrative Officer followed on Wednesday. And the gossip started, the rumours raced around the company and dozens of congratulation memos and telephone calls were received. Thursday with Christine at college Amy came to see me she wanted to know why Christine was acting. I asked her to discuss with Christine and I assured her all would be explained.

Thursday, Doug and I strategized the changes the company would have to go through during the next six months. We also considered a similar re-structuring exercise. The main issue an acceptable diversification programme, which identified markets where Maybury's expertise would fit.

Further discussion ensued regarding opening a new division geared for example commercial office, industrial plant such as sewage works and manufacturing plant engineering. I walked away with a ton of work of which a great deal would be researching appropriate operational markets.

Friday, thankfully, following two days of legal Ping-Pong, we received the appointment from Jetspur to commence the contract 1st February 2015. I called Allen Peters and congratulated him informing him he would receive commission for his good work. Jimmy and Spike, more Spike, began to prepare the ground work prior to the contract commencing. I thought good luck.

Throughout the past three or four months I had, with the exception of monthly progress and finance meetings, virtually ignored Charlie Reynolds and Martin Stevens, the other two team managers. I contacted both and invited them to lunch for a catch-up and to thank them for keeping the work rolling in and for the success of their two business units, which had been extremely lucrative. I arranged for two substantial bonus payments to be paid with their next month's salaries.

Christine and I rarely saw each other. She absorbed in catching-up, and then concentrating on her course plus the hours and days she was spending with Holdsworth and Adams, made her far too busy for her fiancée.

I found a card depicting a young couple, arms round each other's waists looking at a house, with a heart balanced on the roof, inscribed with the words "two bedrooms, living room, dining room, a kitchen and room for loving in". Inside the card I added the words "When study and / or work seem overwhelming remember you have me." I popped it through her letterbox.

Friday evening in my flat I found my fiancé waiting for me. Christine embraced me whispering she loved me, would always love me and was very sorry for being overwhelmed.

She led me to the bedroom and undressed me. She undressed and stood on the bed reaching her hand for me to join her. She dropped to her knees and with her exquisite silky soft hands and her lips she manipulated Jolly Roger ready to explode. She opened her mouth and took him deep into her throat until Jolly Roger was rock-solid. She lay down and pulled me into her and we loved, and we loved. Christine wanted hard and rough and I gave her all I had driving and ramming until she screamed and yelled and yelled. I blasted into her and Christine her body thrashing with her legs wrapped around my neck called for more. I drove on relentlessly and still she called for more. Her body began to vibrate her lips fastened onto my arm and bit deep until she cried out with joy. Her erratic spasms started and she crooned, funny wheezing noises escaping from her throat. Sated, she lay still and smiled saying, "My man loves me and his woman loves him and she will always love him."

After showering we returned to bed and made love once more this time tenderly and much more lasting, realising the orgasms we had come to expect and love. Christine wanted to be loved time and time again throughout the night and morning. The magic of our love, the beauty of her exquisite body and her pure unrivalled sexiness fed my senses keeping Jolly Roger hard at work, both he and I loving every moment.

Christine throughout went into ecstasy after ecstasy, her spasms were often uncontrollable her yelling piercing the night. We loved and we loved and we loved some more, never wanting to stop until exhaustion claimed us, intertwined we fell into a deep sleep.

It was Saturday lunchtime when the telephone awakened us. It was mother demanding what plans we had implemented for the wedding. After a few minutes I knew she would be arriving in Southampton in the next couple of days. I was trying to pacify her when Christine took the receiver from me. After Christine hung-up she informed that Mother and Grandma Jean would be with us the end of the following week. I was charged with finding a short let two bedroomed apartment.

Christine seeing my face laughed saying, "It's not the end of the world your mother is a smart lady she will soon organise and clarify many things we just don't have the time to attend to." I agreed with Christine. I also realised I hadn't told mother or father of my recent promotion, or Christine's promotion come to that. Further, where was father, he hadn't made contact, nor could I contact him.

I made a pot of tea while Christine made the bed and showered. I asked her to remain naked so I could watch her. I adored her body and her colouring, her red hair, light blue eyes, faint freckles and beautifully sculpted breasts and her wonderful pink nipples excited me. Her long slim graceful legs, perfect bottom and curvaceous hips where they flared below her slim waist portraying loveliness beyond description. Christine just thought I was a pervert and often told me so. However, we both knew my appreciation pleased her.

Christine did dress but only after I had had time to admire her English rose porcelain and statuesque beauty.

Saturday afternoon we were in the office waiting delivery of two Mercedes 280CE, our new company cars, followed by an hour of Christine driving around Southampton docks, until she was satisfied she was both competent and confident, to drive on Southampton's busy roads.

When we returned from collecting our new company cars, she explained, she would study hard tomorrow, Sunday, thereafter she would be up to speed, which would leave her with Thursday, nine until six at college plus ten to fifteen hours homework per week. Her time with Gary Holdsworth and John Adams now managed whereas she was with Gary for Wednesday mornings and with John Wednesday afternoon and Friday mornings. She suspected Gary would pull clear within a couple of weeks. We both knew John would be around until she finished her course.

Gradually I took on the full mantle of CEO. I was greatly assisted by Mr Maybury and Doug. Doug moved into My Maybury's office and I moved in to Doug's. Gary handed over his office to Christine.

With John Adams, Larry Fortune and Sharon Cummings the other two board members, Doug and I supported by Christine, thrashed out our intended re-strategizing and re-structuring plans, I could see we were flying way over Sharon's head. Sharon, head of PR and marketing had been with Maybury since its inception. Rumour had it that she had been Mr Maybury's long-time mistress, hence her position, true or not I didn't know or care.

But I did care that the board members understood the future strategy of the company. I said to her, "Sharon you looked perplexed, is there something you don't quite understand?" I watched her face I could see she had been a good-looking woman but now in her mid- to late-fifties she had lost much of her looks.

She frowned, scratched the back of her neck before asking to see Doug outside of the meeting. We waited ten minutes before Doug returned with no sign of Sharon. I lifted my eyebrows querying Doug. Doug turned to Larry and me and asked us both outside. Sharon sat in my new CEO's office.

We all entered the office, Doug said, "Sharon has verbally resigned from the board deciding she should step aside. She will formally put her resignation in writing during the course of the day."

He turned to Larry. "Larry, I have asked you here to see how you feel. I think Richard's document is beyond your grasp and I certainly know the future strategy we were discussing in the meeting was also beyond your grasp."

Larry was the company's client consultant who would meet with potential clients to consult business solutions, particularly contract terms. However as we retained a legal firm it was hard to realise his continuing use. Also much of Christine's new responsibilities included the commercial aspects of the company, which is why she worked with Gary Holdsworth.

Larry considered his situation before answering, "I would prefer to have a discussion with Mr Maybury, and perhaps it would be beneficial if Sharon, you Doug and I had a meeting with him." Doug looked at me. I nodded. "Okay Larry, Sharon I'll arrange it." They departed and Doug and I returned to the meeting.

Doug as he entered the meeting room laughed and said "And then there were four" John Adams asked what was going on. Doug described the last few minutes.

John said, "Probably for the best, we have had a good run and yes the business is entering a modification stage, which to be quite honest Sharon and Larry would not be happy with. They would find the whole mechanism incomprehensible, yes probably for the best."

The reality, which dawned on me driving home, Doug, Christine and I, we three were suddenly responsible for a twenty-five million per annum business, which we were looking to diversify and innovate to double the revenue.

I turned to Christine and said, "My sweetheart we have one hell of a job ahead of us. It will mean long hours, little love-making and tired minds and bodies, are you up for it?" "With you Richard I would swim the Atlantic" she laughingly replied. Yes I decided we could do it.

I used the following week to return to Immingham. I arrived unannounced sitting in the car-park when Terry Hamley pulled in. He parked and walked quickly over to my car. I climbed out stretching my limbs. We shook hands. I followed him to the offices. Several cars, a bicycle and a moped also arrived.

Terry and I scrutinised his programme of events. I pre-warned him I would pick as many holes as I could to test the robustness of his work. After several hours he said "It will work Mr Chambers I will live in these offices to make it work." I had cajoled, coerced and found fault at every opportunity but the man remained upbeat, very promising.

The final document, a busy spreadsheet detailed revenue, profit and loss, and cash-flow. However, the positive he had included comprehensive milestones determining precisely when the operation would move into profit.

However there remained one issue he wanted resolved before I departed to share his programme with others, total commitment, including business development and the company's management team. Otherwise he categorically stated the programme would not work and Maybury might as well close Immingham. I considered his ultimatum before saying, "Subject to a couple of points, which I will contact you on before the end of the week, consider absolute support from management."

When I arrived home there was a message from Christine, saying she would be staying in her own flat until Friday accusing me of being a distraction. I smiled. I called Allen Peters on his home number. I asked him four questions. "Allen, are you married?"

"No, divorced," he answered.

"Do you have dependents in Liverpool?"

"No, we didn't have kids and my parents live in Morecambe," he replied.

"Are you good enough to sell Maybury services across the north particularly starting in Immingham?" he hesitated for a fraction of a second. "With professional support and the ear of senior management, yes I am."

"Do you want a robust and secure future with Maybury?"

"I wouldn't mind especially now you are the big chief," he laughingly replied.

I said, "I'll be back to you before the end of the week and, Allen, good answers, especially the third and fourth."

I cornered Doug and discussed my new concept regarding business development involving Allen and a good secretary to prepare documents and handle office work plus he would be stationed centrally in the North of England, specifically with road communication to major ports and we would provide a fully expensed car.

I presented Terry Hamley's programme of events pointing out the four redundancies recommended would pay for Allen and support. His running costs would be charged against contracts secured. It took some convincing before Doug accepted Allen Peters would be the right guy.

In the evening I called Allen, I didn't dilly-dally I said straight off, "Subject to your agreement to being re-located at Maybury's cost you will be promoted to Business Development Officer, North of England. You will have complete support guaranteed by me and a good secretary to support you who will need to be recruited locally from wherever we decide is the best town or city to base you."

I could hear the stunned silence. He came back, "Mr Chambers, sorry, could you repeat please?"

I did adding, "I am looking to re-locate you to Wakefield, Morley somewhere in that area. Have a good think and I will telephone on this number around nine in the morning." I hung-up. I didn't want questions I wanted him to think for himself.

I called Allen at the pre-determined time, his only comment was, "When do I re-locate." I thanked him advising I would be in contact to arrange a meeting next Thursday. Afterwards I called Terry explaining my decision and the thinking behind it. He sounded slightly dubious. I advised him also I would arrange a meeting for Thursday.

I stopped to think about the decisions I was making on the hoof. Realising I knew the end-game it was in my head, but I wasn't, unless I had to, sharing it with colleagues. I called a meeting for Friday morning for all managers responsible for profit and loss, seven in number. I invited Doug and Christine, and John Adams. I considered the seven main characters.

Casey McLaughlin, responsible for national and international consumables, spares and stores. Over eight million per annum passed through his control.

Charlie Reynolds, revenue of five-point-five million making twenty-six percent gross.

Martin Stevens, revenue of six million making twenty-two percent gross.

Jimmy Johnson, my successor, revenue seven-point-two million making twenty two point five percent gross.

Terry Hamley, revenue one-point six million losing eleven percent.

Trevor MacDonald (Spike), revenue eight hundred thousand losing fourteen percent.

Terry Whitehead, revenue two-point-eight million making fifty percent gross.

Falmouth, under Jimmy, one-point-two million making nineteen percent gross.

To prepare for Friday I called in Rod Young. "Rod, on Friday," I began, "I have a meeting with the senior managers, which I would like you to attend. In preparation I would like appropriate spread sheets detailing revenue, material costs, labour costs and overhead costs for each team. If there are any anomalies please highlight them.

Also I would like you to go through each team's figures without pulling any punches, can you do that?"

"No problem Richard, what time Friday?" he asked.

"Eleven," I responded. I issued an agenda Wednesday night. Thursday I dashed to Immingham and met with Allen and Terry, departing when satisfied they would work competently as a team.

Friday morning, with management assembled I stood before a flip-chart I had prepared and started explaining the business where it was today and where we intended to be. I expounded it couldn't be accomplished without their one hundred and ten per cent determination, which called for each of them to improve their team outputs and manage costs more effectively. I emphasised I expected proposed efficiencies within six weeks after the meeting prepared and issued followed by one-to-one meetings.

I exclaimed business development in existing work streams and the appointment of Allen Peters and we would commence a search for an appropriate person to fulfil similar responsibilities in the south.

I explained diversification and innovation expressing that new business streams were under consideration. Adding further information would be available in due course. "Finally," I said. "Before you are several spreadsheets detailing every team's financial activities, which Rod Young will elucidate. I want you all to understand you are not Lone Rangers, we are a team and we must demonstrate closer co-operation."

Rod's in depth breakdown of each team's financial status plus his observations gained good interest. Doug nodded his head and Christine smiled at me. However John Adams visibly impressed listened and assisted Rod at every turn. The management I intended to entrust Maybury's future with enthused, firing questions at me and adding constructive comment.

I could feel the excitement in the room, fully aware these blokes hadn't previously been given a fraction of the information I now shared. Palpable recognition they could play an important role in re-structuring and expanding Maybury, very much in evidence, giving rise to open interconnectivity.

More importantly they were sharing opinions and moving closer. I witnessed the spawning of the team they had to become. Only team work would realise the ambitious objectives being set, which they realised and understood.

Later in Doug's office, he, Christine, John and I conferred expressing the success of the meeting and the obvious enthusiasm portrayed by the managers. John had overheard arrangements being made for managers to meet or confer by telephone information which would prove beneficial. I was energised my mind racing. Christine could feel my passion she gently placed her hand on my arm, which felt electric.

Chapter 33 – Wedding Plans and Things

Saturday morning Christine and I were meeting Mother and Grandma Jean at Euston Station, London at eleven. I had identified and paid two weeks in advance for a comfortably furnished apartment just off the Avenue, quiet with pleasant views over Southampton Common.

I warned Christine mother would pack sufficient luggage for a world cruise, which Christine laughed off until at Euston, she watched four large suit cases a trunk and holdall being loaded onto a trolley under mother's directions. We needed two taxis to transfer to Waterloo, where I found a porter and arranged with him to load the luggage into the goods carriage of the Southampton train.

In Southampton we once more required two taxis. I paid the drivers to assist with moving the luggage to the apartment. Mother and Grandma were pleased with the apartment, which was a relief. I was dispatched to the nearest off-license to purchase a half-bottle of brandy, Grandma's daily medicine and six bottles of wine, three red and three white for mother's consumption.

When I returned Christine and mother were still unpacking. It was late into the afternoon before the last garment was stowed. Christine laughed, staggered by all the clothes they had packed. However, mother as expected wanted to talk weddings just as we had throughout the train journey from Waterloo.

She did ask if I had spoken to father. I explained I couldn't contact him. She mused over this because she hadn't heard from him either. Usually she stated he would call every ten or so days.

Mother decided father had found Tina's replacement, hence his lack of communication. I told mother we wouldn't be available tomorrow, Sunday due to house-hunting. Christine gave me a questionable look, but kept quiet. Once more, mother dispatched me, this time in search of a take-away meal.

I returned with Chinese for two explaining Charlotte had cooked. Christine glanced towards me with yet another questionable look. We departed agreeing to dine with mother and grandma Monday evening.

In the car Christine accused me of being ill-mannered stating quite clearly that mother had noticed. "Christine," I said a tad too loudly, "Mother will encamp in Southampton until she is fully satisfied the wedding is properly planned, the guest list complete with invitations, the church and vicar are booked and the reception including entertainment is in place."

Modulating my voice I continued, "Thereafter she will arrange the reception Master of Ceremonies, the decoration, the menu and goodness knows what else, and then she will return to Lytham and not one minute before."

I reached across and held Christine's hand, "Oh and I forget she'll insist upon taking you shopping for your bride's dress, recommend colour schemes for the bridesmaid's dresses, help you choose your trousseau, trust me I know my mother."

Christine burst out laughing saying "Great isn't it we can sit back and let your mother get on with it" Smiling, I replied, "I'm afraid not, she'll be on the telephone day and night, and for goodness sake do not divulge your address otherwise she'll be on your doorstep dragging you off to see this and that" "Scary" responded Christine.

Laughing I said "It's simple, mother has, when it comes to her little boy, a heart so big it is overpowering and because she has fallen for you she will at full pelt do all she can to please you also. We, my darling, are the puppets. We will be manipulated, manoeuvred and directed until the whole wedding thing is in writing and in triplicate" Christine put her head in her hands and cried out "Bugger, bugger and bugger".

During Monday Christine, Jimmy and I were interviewing a business development officer candidate to fulfil a similar role as Allen Peters in the south when Janet, my girl Friday apologised calling me out. My father was on the telephone demanding to talk to me. I had the call transferred to Christine's extension, closing the door I lifted the receiver saying, "Hello stranger, how is Derbyshire?" The call finished I sat and contemplated the conversation.

Firstly he wanted Christine and I to meet with him in Hove in a fortnight's time when he would be visiting Irene, Ken and Don, secondly Dulcie had left Chas and now lived with father, a woman half his age, thirdly after I informed him of the marriage, he would visit Southampton pre-Christmas to celebrate, fourthly he would like Christine and I to welcome Dulcie as part of the family when we meet her in Hove. There was something else, the flat, something about the flat, whatever he had said had slipped my mind. I decided it couldn't have been important.

In the early hours of Tuesday morning I was sleep with Christine lying in my arms when I shot upright knocking Christine, yelling, "Christine father has given us the monies for the flat, all we have to do is sell it. Christine, Christine did you hear me? Christine."

"Yes, darling I heard you, and so did half of Southampton."

I remembered the conversation. "He said we could use it as a deposit for our matrimonial home, how could I forget, I am cracking."

"Richard, it is halfway through the night and I have a progress exam tomorrow so please go back to sleep, we will discuss tomorrow, or is it this evening," sighed Christine.

352

Obviously I couldn't sleep too busy buying a house, a beautiful house for a beautiful lady. Where to purchase? My mind searched Southampton and suburbs, the New Forest, out towards Romsey and the villages off the A27 towards Fareham.

The alarm clock awakened me. Following routine I made tea for Christine and coffee for me, and toast, or prepared cereal, or boiled eggs while Christine readied herself.

Together we enjoyed breakfast discussing the value of the flat and how much we could afford per month for a mortgage. We realised our combined salaries were very impressive and finding a mortgage wouldn't be a problem. Christine alluded to information she wasn't prepared to share, not just yet.

Christine cleared the breakfast things away while I showered and shaved (I still hate shaving) and dressed for work. Sitting enjoying a second cup of coffee Christine decided to declare the information she was holding back. She explained that she, Charlotte and Charles were part of a trust set-up by her deceased parents and continued by Sadie and James; however, she had no idea of its value. All she knew was that the trust did not activate until either an offspring realised twenty-five years of age or if marriage preceded the age, subject to the trustees' agreement, available.

We agreed to register the flat for sale and commence searching for a house.

We met with father and Dulcie in Hove, dined with Irene and Ken and visited Don at the Sapphire club. Both Christine and I driving home Sunday afternoon agreed the weekend flashed by, probably the result of too much alcohol and over-eating. Nevertheless, Dulcie seemed pleasant enough and much more attractive than I recalled.

Irene and Ken were terrific as were the Bear's customers including the wolf-whistles for Christine, and Don was Don, albeit father and he spent a great deal of time whispering, suggesting something was afoot.

Chapter 34 – Christmas 1973 & New Year 1974

Friday, 21st December and the company would shut down, except for emergency works until 3rd January 1974. With the onset of the changes and the renewed energy flowing through the company, and Christine's studying coupled with her work responsibilities, wedding arrangements and my constant travelling, the weeks had dissipated without trace.

Mother and grandma stayed on in Southampton deciding to take Charlotte, her boyfriend, Christine and I for Christmas Lunch at the Polygon Hotel. However, before then father arrived on the 21st, alone. He took mother, grandma, Christine, Charlotte and me out to dinner, which turned out to be very profitable for Christine and I. Mother hearing father's intention to pass the sale price of the flat to Christine and I, mother stated she would match the sale price, and then blow me down if grandma didn't add another thousand pounds. Christine and I were knocked for six and extremely grateful.

Mother and father's relationship was remarkable it was very obvious they still cared deeply for each other but for one reason or another they could not live together. Their situation was always a phenomenon I could not come to terms with. Christine did remark how close they were, asking for an explanation, I told her I couldn't, I didn't understand either.

Christmas 1973 is best forgotten. Christmas Eve night as we were dressing for dinner at the Dolphin Hotel I received a call from Martin Stevens, two of his engineers had answered an emergency call to a freighter, which had lost steering off Canvey Island in the Thames estuary.

They boarded the flag of convenience ship to discover the rudder system had rotted. One of the engineers crawling along the main shaft slipped, grabbing for safety a heavy rusted cage collapsed onto him, trapping him in the bilge water. I explained to Christine, kissed her and set-off for Thames Haven where there would be a fast boat waiting for me.

During my drive Martin had mobilised a small team with lifting kit and appropriate tools he also organised medical support. A custom's launch ferried me to the ship. I clambered down to the bilge area to find Martin and three of his men. They had managed to feed a breathing tube to the engineer, Micky French, who, although obviously in pain remained lucid and cheerful.

When he saw me he shouted, "Hey lads, here comes the Christmas bonus." We worked carefully not to cause him any further pain of body damage. Once the cage was clear and he could be moved we called the medical team in.

He was rushed to hospital where the doctors were more concerned with the bilge water he had swallowed as opposed to his physical injuries. He had a broken wrist and a compound fracture of his right ankle plus light bruising and cuts.

During the rescue I arranged for taxis to collect his parents and sister and his girlfriend. Once the doctors transferred him into a private room, which Maybury would bear the cost of, his family overwhelmed him. Seeing me stood at the nurse station, he winked.

I sent the Maybury chaps home wishing them Merry Christmas and a promise of a little extra in their next wage packets. Martin and I hung about for a couple of hours satisfying ourselves he would be alright. We went over to say our farewells. He asked about the freighter. I assured a second team were working on the rudder system.

I insisted Martin went home to his family and returned to the freighter, its condition a disgrace. By the time I arrived the relief engineers were wrapping-up their work completed, the system back in working order. We were shuttled ashore. I thanked them promising a similar little extra in their wage packets.

Exhausted I drove home watching the sun through my rear view mirror, what there was of it, rise above the horizon. I drove steadily the journey taking three and a half hours. The opposite journey had only taken two hours. Christine lay asleep in father's old chair with a blanket to keep the chill off. For a brief moment I remembered Sophie in a similar situation.

I put the kettle on, made tea and wakened her with an oily smelling kiss. I said, "Merry Christmas my lovely lady. I love you." Smelly or not, Christine's arms wrapped round my neck. "Oh my Richard, Merry Christmas and I love you too, love, love you." After I relayed the happenings of the night Christine proposed we cancel Christmas lunch but I was against the idea. I pointed out Mother and Grandma would be awfully disappointed.

Christine before ushering me into the bathroom firmly stated we couldn't open our presents until we were home after lunch. In the shower Christine scrubbed and scrubbed to rid the smell from my body.

Clean and fresh I rolled into bed, Christine lie alongside me and cuddled until I dozed off.

She awakened me at twelve-fifteen. She was dressed ready to go. She looked stunning in a light blue dress that flared from her slim waist, the dress's colour matching her eyes, her cascading hair fell shoulder length framing the wondrous beauty of her delightful features. God I loved this woman. I reached out and pulled her towards the bed, she slapped my wrists. "Behave, Richard Chambers and get ready or we will be late."

We collected Charlotte and Brian, her boyfriend managing to arrive at the hotel first. We gave mother's name and were shown to the table. I ordered aperitifs, four champagne cocktails. Grandma entered, striding towards the table signalled a waiter. "My boy a large brandy, house will do, and a small jug of hot water," Mother trailing behind touched the waiter's arm, "Bring me a sweet sherry, thank you dear."

The hotel's traditional Christmas lunch of roast turkey and stuffing with all the trimmings followed by Christmas pudding with cream proved to be jolly good. The ambience, once the crack-cracking of the crackers, and the many families occupying several tables had donned their Christmas hats became extremely cheerful. We toasted each other, our engagement and the upcoming wedding, which I was reliably informed, and confirmed by Christine now fully organised. All we had to do was turn up.

Christine explained the emergency call-out and remonstrated I hadn't slept so we needed to get me home to catch-up or I would be useless for the rest of the Christmas break. Mother showed concern and agreed we had to go. We said our good byes and departed.

As we exited Christine remembered mother and Grandma's Christmas presents, which delayed our departure. Christine had chosen well, I noticed how pleased both my relatives were. Mother adored her Pearl Necklace and the gold Wishbone ring Grandma held to her bosom while she expressed how she loved it.

The Christmas presents were all stacked under the Christmas tree at Christine and Charlotte's flat following Christine's decision to decorate and provide a tree complete with twinkly lights. She also decided my flat too small. Once in the flat I opened a good red wine and we sat on the floor close to the tree waiting for Charlotte to exit the loo. Christine took charge; I genuinely think woman in general believe men are incapable of giving and receiving presents.

The first present I opened was about eighteen inches high, and heavy. It was a statue of a rugby player who looked suspiciously like me. The statue even had number seven on the shirt. I adored it but at the same time I felt guilty because I still had not returned to training therefore I wasn't being selected. I silently promised myself as I kissed my thanks to Charlotte, I would definitely return in the New Year.

I asked how they had managed to portray such a good looking fellow on a statue. Charlotte explained a complicated process which included photographs stolen (borrowed) from my office desk draw where I kept my scrap books.

Christine and I, having noticed Brian's attraction for gold, gave him a chunky gold bracelet sending him into spasms of delight. Christine presented Charlotte with a large gold key, a replica of the flat key with an appropriate inscription which read *"She's got the key of the door, never been twenty one before"*, which had two connotations, the first being Charlotte would be twenty-one soon after the New Year and it wouldn't be long before Christine vacated the flat.

Brian gave Charlotte a beautifully crafted brooch, earing, bracelet and necklace set in white gold. It must have cost him a fortune. Charlotte threw herself at Brian yelling, "Tell them." Brian described how he and Charlotte had been courting for nearly a year, consequently he had asked her, taking into account their ages, that if they continued steady for a further six months she would become officially engaged to him. Not actually a proposal but a young man covering his backside. Christine hugged Brian and I hugged Charlotte.

After thinking for a moment Christine said, "What exactly is it, it is not engagement, Brian hasn't proposed, what exactly is the arrangement called?" Brian answered, he was smiling "We are engaged to become engaged." We all laughed.

Charlotte gave Brian a Tag Heuer watch, a solid stainless steel monster, with date and day mechanisms, depth regulator and stop watch, and even a little alarm buzzer. In the box was a small card saying "No more excuses" Apparently Brian was a very poor time manager.

Christine handed me a wrapped box, which I carefully opened. Inside were six pair of boxers and six pair of socks. "My darling, perfect, thank you, you have saved me a trip to Marks and Sparks." We all laughed.

Christine selected the present from me. She opened to find twenty-four caret gold charm bracelet, which told our love story to date. The first charm represented where we met. I used a charm depicting the famous Southampton Bargate. The second charm a gorgeous lady representing Christine, the third a rugby player, me. The fourth a ship, the business we both worked in. The fifth, a girl and boy embracing, represented Christine and me. The sixth, a ring signifying our engagement, and the seventh portrayed Hong Kong's famous skyline. After my explanation I said there would be additions as the years rolled by.

However, Christine had me spread-eagled on the floor sitting across my chest planting kisses all over my face. Amidst the attack I heard Charlotte say to Brian, "See that, that's love, watch and remember."

Christine climbed off me and disappeared into her bedroom. She returned with an envelope, which she passed to me. Inside was a cheque for seven thousand, eight hundred pounds. I looked at her blankly.

She sat next to me and put her arms around me saying, "That is half of my inheritance towards our house. The other half will be used to furnish it. That is if we ever go searching." I held Christine very tight, we would move into the most amazing house, which we would furnish with loving care.

There were many smaller presents, which were opened as we went along but the ones mentioned were the important ones.

For New Year we managed to gain access to one of Southampton's premier clubs, if not the premier one. Mr Maybury pulled some strings to arrange a super table where we four were joined by Jimmy and Candy, and Amy and Terry.

The evening was terrific, specifically the head-line entertainment, a female songstress I appreciated. The evening proved to be a huge success, the owner came to our table and chatted, offering free membership based on the fact he had heard Christine and I were now very much in the driving seat steering Maybury into the future. We all accepted, why not.

During the evening we danced and danced exchanging partners until I became fed up of not having my lovely lady in my arms. I said, "Enough, until we are kicked out the only lady I am dancing with from now on, is my fiancé." We held close and whispered and kissed and expounded we were the luckiest people in the world. We had our love, an amazing career, terrific friends, and astonishing relatives who had combined to give two young lovers the greatest start in life they could ever wish or dream of.

Christine and I returned to my flat. When we entered I turned to Christine saying, "This is a dull, boring cruddy little flat, a flat I once loved; now I want out. I want and need you and I together, living as Mr and Mrs Clarke-Chambers." Christine looked at me, asking if Clarke-Chambers would be our married name. "Christine," I said. "My darling, if we are marrying then our names should marry, don't you think?"

In the early hours of the first day of 1974 I quietly climbed from the bed and composed my thoughts, which I reaffirmed as a letter, needless to say the thoughts and therefore the letter were based on my love for Christine:

My Dearest Darling Christine,

Today is the 1ˢᵗ January 1974, a mere six months until the 4ᵗʰ July 1974 when you my darling, and I, will marry, united together.

You, my lovely lady, are the light of my life, a light, which brightens my existence and dulls all around me. It is an extraordinary light given into my possession, for you, and for you alone.

The light is my love for you. It is pure and good and cannot be sullied. It is a singular love, which imprisons, for which I am indebted.

It is a love which encircles my body entrapping me within a network of tangled threads. It enchants me to such an extent I am overawed. It penetrates my heart, it runs through my veins and it anesthetises my soul.

I am saturated by my emotions, my love for you. I experience astonishing feelings, yet all I can offer in return, is to hold you Christine, hold you close and hold you forevermore, and articulate my love, a weak return for the powerful feelings reverberating through my heart.

I love you
Richard

I scribed the words many times until satisfied with the standard of my hand-writing and the significance of my words. It was important for Christine to welcome in the New Year, safe in the knowledge I will love, honour and protect her, come what may. I left the sheet of paper whole not wanting to crease my words. I climbed softly into bed reaching a hand to touch Christine, to feel her life within and to know she was by my side.

The letter, quadrupled in size, hangs in our entrance hall at home. Christine found a calligraphist who reproduced the letter in gold leaf gilding set upon a dark maroon background. It does look good but it is also romantic.

When men who are not bosom buddies read it they give me a sideways glance. However, when Hugo, for example first read it he waggled his thumb to signify I was under thumb.

Ladies tend to ah, and sigh, and say phrases such as, "my goodness did Richard write this" or "no, not Richard surely", which of course Christine loved. Her typical response would be "of course, why not?" or "Richard is a romantic, his love is in his heart", the second being her favourite.

Chapter 35 – Our House and the Hen / Stag Night

We, after Christine had decided and I agreed, put in an offer for a substantial property with an acre of land, located in a village north of Southampton. We still live in the house today. It is an early nineteenth century two storey property, which today following extensive renovation works consists of a galleried first floor leading to five bedrooms, two with en suite bathrooms and a family bathroom.

The deeds for our dream house were registered two weeks before the wedding. Within a week Christine had priced a new kitchen, new bathrooms throughout and arranged re-wiring and re-plumbing works. The second week she finalised a new central heating system.

She appointed Casey and Jimmy to manage the works. Casey for procurement and best prices and Jimmy for the actual physical works. The works were completed the first week of July. The only furniture came from my flat, which went in storage following the flat's sale.

The large down payment for the house came from the sale of the flat, mother's commitment, Grandma Jean's one thousand, Christine's seven thousand-plus inheritance, the sale of my sporty car and five thousand from the residue of my twenty thousand pound bonus.

We could have purchased outright, however we were advised to take out a mortgage for taxation purposes. Christine and I amalgamated her inheritance residue and all my savings. The greater proportion of those monies paid for all the work Christine organised.

The ground floor has a magnificent sixty square yard living room, a super-sized dining room, a massive kitchen containing a walk-in pantry. Adjacent to the kitchen is a utility room with an external door, which opens onto a covered walkway leading to the double garage. Near to the door leading to the rear garden is a cloakroom.

The most important room in the house is Christine and Richard's den with a single patio door, which opens onto a small granite patio. It has a small, but rarely used bar, an old-fashioned three piece but comfortable suite, and a television to watch rugby games uninterrupted. The den also includes an expensive music system and computer.

There are occasions when we may open a bottle of wine or indulge in a cognac. The den came into existence, we think, because when on a whim we purchased the bar, we had no idea where to position it. Hence it was stored in the den until we decided.

Overtime the bar moved from one corner of the room to another until one day it stopped moving coming to rest to the right of the patio door. During the early heady days when we were building Maybury, Christine and I would spend hours in the room conversing business strategies planning the expansion and success of the company.

Afterwards, exhausted and ready for bed, sitting on the old settee from my flat, we both enjoyed a cognac and soda to ease the anxiety of work.

The old settee was replaced, and Christine decorated the room fitting it out for our comfort and our needs. We continue to utilise the room where we mostly talk, which we do a great deal of, read and listen to music, quite often holding hands or cuddled together.

When the children were born we habitually closed the door keeping it for our exclusive use. Richard, our eldest, when he was nine or ten, produced a sign that read *"Mum and Dad's Watering Hole"*, which prompted Christine to re-produce professionally. The den was designated as our room, which as far as the family were concerned it was off-limits.

Externally, Christine after fighting the local planners and utilising Charlotte's contacts converted two outbuildings into accommodation for domestic helpers. Mr and Mrs Hopkins took up residency when Christine was five months pregnant with our first child.

In July Christine was informed she had passed her course with flying colours. Her title of Acting Chief Administrative Officer immediately lost the word "acting" and the information promulgated company wide.

Late in July after our wedding, Christine appointed an interior design company owned and managed by two ladies, Jackie and Rachel. On Thursday 5th September we moved from the living room where we had lived utilising the flat's furniture into a sumptuously decorated and furnished home, our home. Saturday 7th September saw me wave goodbye with the exception of the settee, to my old flat's furniture, before rushing off to play the first rugby game of the season.

The months leading to the wedding were hectic, very hectic. Work, due to new business strategies, demanded a complete overhaul of work methodologies and systems, during which time we tip-toed into the world of Information Technology to learn a new language, which still baffles me, albeit Christine is a whizz.

The wedding, largely organised by mother, turned out to be a glorious sunny day. The ceremony attended by seventy people and the reception, which doubled the attendance to one hundred and fifty souls, went off without a hitch. Hugo, my best man was brilliant, only dropping me in the mire three times, three times I had to explain to Christine what Hugo referred to, or for one particular comment, who.

Sadie, James and Charles arrived from Hong Kong, father without Dulcie, and of course mother and grandma were all present dressed in their finery. James gave Christine away, Charlotte with Jessica, Miriam, and believe it or not, Gertie, Sylvie, Amy and Candy were all Maids of Honour. Their orange blossom gowns were splendid and as Hugo pointed out they all looked incredibly sexy.

Irene, Ken and Don, and Gwynne and Josie and five of the Bear's regulars attended leaving Joe assisted with temporary staff to run the Bear. Deborah, June and Helen with their partners, Ryan, Sylvie's partner now husband, and Gordon Wilson, Sophie's ex-boss with his wife also attended.

Mr Maybury, all the old board and their partners, Doug and his family, my seven senior managers and their families all turned up. Christine's teams at both offices were all present and Brian, Charlotte's man and some other people who were friends of Charlotte and Christine before I arrived on the scene also attended. Further guests included many members of my rugby club.

Finally, the college gang, the ones who attended Hugo's wedding landed in Southampton, with their partners on the Thursday before the big day. I wasn't sure but I was under the impression Christine with her twenty strong contingent had reserved a private room at the club where we celebrated New Year. I could just imagine the clubbers faces when an array of beautiful females descended to the dance floor.

The evening Hugo had organised for that Thursday was a sombre occasion for all of two hours as we were seated for a formal dinner complete with speeches and awards. We too were closeted in a private room high above a particular hotel's dining rooms.

I received "Wally of the Year 1974" award, a beautifully crafted penis, which sits on the bar at home. However, with the onslaught of children it was in storage on my office desk for several years. Ben and James were joint recipients of the "Leopard "Holy Cow- Tits" Award" for repeating time and time again, "holy cow look at the tits on that," every time a well-endowed fresher or indeed any other female similarly blessed entered the Leopard.

Speeches and awards over I came to realise just how romantic my best friend, Hugo was, with tremendous passion he read a poem;

> The first primrose of springtime
> I found and picked for you
> and when I find another one
> then you shall have it too.
>
> Waves rushed foaming to the shore,
> the tide went in and out
> and while I chased the breakers
> it was you I thought about.
>
> I climbed high to a mountain top,
> a valley did I see,

I hoped that you were in it
and looking back at me.

Resting in the forest
beneath a tall green tree
I closed my eyes pretending
that you were there with me.

Rain came pounding on the ground
the wind came roaring through
and though it was ridiculous
I watched the trail for you.

A burning mountain sunset
was brief, but still I knew
that you were somewhere watching it
and thinking of me too.

A silver moon rose in the east,
its brightness shone so new –
I kissed each velvet moonbeam
hoping they'd all dance to you.

I was very touched; however, I was astonished to see how my rowdy drunken rugby playing friends of many years were also taken by the poem. After Hugo finished, a hush settled on the room. Eventually Hugo with a huge grin shouted, "It's time for dancing, follow me."

We clambered down the stairs to board a coach. The coach after a few minutes halted outside the club where I had thought Christine and her friends were dining. We entered into an empty club, the bar manned by five staff and a DJ playing soft music.

Perplexed we turned to Hugo, who with the aid of two staff, ushered us into a large banqueting room. We were asked to keep the noise down. Waiters armed with champagne flutes and bottles of cold champagne rushed here and there serving drinks. The tune of Sweet Chariot began rippling through the speakers. Quietness forgotten, excited voices reacted to the tune with the words of the fabled song reverberating off the four walls of the banqueting room.

The door to the room was flung open standing in the doorway were Miriam and Christine with Gertie standing behind. Miriam's voice silenced the room. "Hugo, what are you playing at? Why is the club empty? And why are you here?"

The three girls were bustled into the room followed by the rest of the hen-night ladies. Some were smiling, some looked irritated and some looked nonplussed. Christine, hands on hips, had a brilliant smile exuding from her beautiful face, Miriam's delightful features also transposed into a wondrous smile. "Okay you great big monster what have you arranged?" All the ladies were now smiling happy to be with their menfolk.

Hugo looked to Ryan. Ryan put to fingers to his mouth and let-rip a tremendous shrill whistle. A band in the main club area started playing. I immediately recognised the music, the band, now a firm favourite of Christine and Charlotte, regularly topped the charts, and was riding high with a second Platinum album. Charlotte half screeched and half shouted, "Oh my God it's Cloud Sixty-Nine." I looked to Hugo he smiled and winked. I felt great I took my darling wife-to-be and led the way to the dance floor.

I held Christine close, too close and told her how much I loved her and how fortunate I was to be marrying her. I expounded the amazing friends we had and yes, the odd tear did roll down my cheek in memory of Sophie but they were more significantly for my Christine, my delightful, beautiful Christine who I loved with all my heart.

Chapter 36 – The Wedding

The church packed every guest crammed into the Church of St Joseph-on-the-Green to hear an incredible array of songs, hymns and wedding sermons and of course our vows. The Reverend Denbigh T. Flowers proved to be an inspired choice by mother. He was vociferous in every sense of the word. He smiled all the way through and cracked one-line joke after another.

The congregation were treated to a one-man show cabaret. And when Hugo dropped the ring he dropped onto his hands and knees quickly snaffled the ring, not admitting he had it until there were half a dozen of us searching high and low, with darling Christine fit to burst with laughter, having spotted the Reverend's indiscretion.

However, it was my bride, my Christine who outshone everyone, who stole the show, for she looked magnificent in her virginal gown, she wore a trumpet gown, whatever that may be, but I can say the gown fitted close to her body emphasising her perfect curvaceous figure, until it gradually flared from her hip to the ground.

If Christine had been wearing wings I would have assumed I was marrying an angel, in fact I was marrying an angel, my angel. I wore my favourite jeans and a T-shirt emblazoned with a huge picture of Christine, which really annoyed Christine (just kidding).

Trailing behind Christine there followed a mile-long train under the astute control of James, Jessica's son, nearing six and Gillian, a niece of Candy.

The Guard of Honour, and I am at a loss how they managed it, were dressed in rugby kit. My only thought is that we took so long to sign the register and traverse the aisle receiving hugs and kisses that they, probably the perpetrators of the hugging and kissing, found time to change. As she passed Hugo, Christine hugged and kissed him pulling the hairs of his leg.

The whole day a wonderful experience, joyous and magical although mother did overdo the reception detail, which went on evermore until father stood and shouted, "Boys and girls, ladies and gentlemen can we please cut to the chase and get on with the partying." He received very warm applause and a dirty look from mother who soon forgave him.

The Bride and Groom were directed to the floor to dance signalling the "party starts here". We danced, holding very tight, to "You Needed Me" by Anne Murray;

I cried a tear, you wiped it dry
I was confused, you cleared my mind
I sold my soul, you bought it back for me
And held me up and gave me dignity
Somehow you needed me

You gave me strength to stand alone again
To face the world out on my own again
You put me high upon a pedestal
So high that I could almost see eternity
You needed me, you needed me

And I can't believe it's you I can't believe it's true
I needed you and you were there
And I'll never leave, why should I leave, I'd be a fool
'Cause I finally found someone who really cares

You held my hand when it was cold
When I was lost, you took me home
You gave me hope when I was at the end
And turned my lies back into truth again
You even called me friend

You gave me strength to stand alone again
To face the world out on my own again
You put me high upon a pedestal
So high that I could almost see eternity
You needed me, you needed me
You needed me, you needed me

I couldn't help but notice that both my parents had tears in their eyes. Christine also noticed, she whispered *"I will love and care for you. I will be your mother, and your father, and your best friend and I will be your love and your lover. You will need for nothing else in this world because I will give you all of me."*

Tears streamed down my cheeks. My mother noticed as did Miriam they pulled respectively father and Hugo onto the floor welcoming all our guests to begin the celebration for Christine and my very special day.

We danced and danced, and laughed and laughed, we cried out with joy and we celebrated our love. One hundred and fifty wonderful friends and family rejoiced and revelled sharing our marvellous magical day.

The time came for Christine and I to depart to locate the hotel Hugo had arranged for three nights as Mr and Mrs Clarke-Chambers. The send-off with fireworks and a candle-lit drive, and the Mercedes, daubed with slogans towing a converted perambulator with huge wheels, containing two deeply in love passengers slowly traversed the drive.

Five miles down the road we could smell fish cooking. I stopped opened the bonnet to find two fish wrapped in foil fixed to the engine block. We thanked Hugo for supper.

Our guests did party until the wee hours of Sunday morning, when we heard days later, new romances began the rocky climb towards love. Happy couples confirmed their love for each other. New friends were made and Gertie ended up with a guy, called Guy, the lead guitarist of the band, Red Destiny who provided the entertainment. Two years later, autumn 1976 we attended their wedding in Roehampton.

The hotel Hugo arranged, a 17th century inn nestling close to the Solent in the New Forest was enchanting, we loved it. Mr Humorous himself had registered Christine and me as Lord and Lady Maybury. Whether it was the false title or not we were treated remarkably well, I suppose as if we were royalty. The three nights and days were wondrous never to be forgotten. However, we were due back at work on the Tuesday, to wait until 1975 before we actually honeymooned.

Chapter 37 - Maybury

Weeks and months passed witnessing Maybury spread its wings moving into new operational fields. The transition albeit swift, especially considering how exceptionally demanding the re-organisation programme had been, had its moments, but we with magnificent support from the whole management team, middle management, supervisors and engineers, who worked round the clock grappled on towards the goal.

There were mistakes, plenty of them, but we were not deterred we all knew where we had to get to and by golly we were going to get there come rain or shine. Christine and her teams re-structured, re-financed and super-efficiently commercialised the company from top to bottom and back up to the top.

Martin Stevens, Jimmy Johnson and Charlie Reynolds, and a newly recruited senior manager, Steve Lancing, experienced in industrial and manufacturing engineering formed an Operations Board chaired by yours truly. Quite unexpectedly the industrial and manufacturing engineering business blossomed, securing project management and engineering consultancy contracts nationwide. This success instigated the transfer of Jimmy into that side of the business and the promotion of Spike MacDonald.

Allan Peters re-located to Morley, rented a house, converting the small front room into an office for him and his secretary, Raquel. He worked wonders securing work as far afield as Glasgow, Barrow-in-Furness and Tyne and Wear.

Liverpool under Spike took on the works in Barrow-in-Furness and supported Terry Hamley with work in Glasgow. Terry's programme of change certainly turned the tide in Immingham, where orders in excess of two million pounds were secured. With Spike's promotion later in the year we accepted his recommendation that Johnny Dobson should replace him.

The appointed business development officer for the south did not fulfil the company's expectation. He was, therefore, released. Allen Peters, off his own bat, took up the challenge quickly securing two good sized contracts, one in Falmouth and the other across the Solent in Fawley.

Following his success, he requested a meeting with Christine where he presented a business plan but he would require an assistant. Christine based on his plan commenced a search. She recruited Peter Jackson alias PJ, who was a perfect fit for Allen.

In 1975 we recruited two more business development officers, both experienced in industrial and manufacturing engineering who also reported to Allen. Allen re-titled to Head of Business Development joined the Operations Board.

The challenge I set before senior management regarding efficiencies uncovered an array of cost saving exercises, which according to Rod Young in finance would recoup one and a half million pounds during a one year period. I have to say I was pleased with progress. The company became quicker and slicker by the day.

In 1980 Maybury secured its target of fifty million pounds revenue, realising seven percent net profit. The big-boys targeted Maybury; they wanted some of the action, subsequently in 1982 we sold out to a group. Doug retired, Christine took on the role of Chairman and I remained CEO.

In 1988 a larger group purchased our group. Christine and I after, driving the company to a revenue exceeding seventy million managed the transition ensuring there wouldn't be any redundancies. We worked hard to ensure the managers and teams who had sweated tears were looked after. In fact in the twelve month transition period we added another seven million to the top line, which helped significantly when we cashed in our shares, which made us quite well-off. We departed becoming unemployed July 1989.

Chapter 38 - Children

Christine, throughout the rapid expansion and success of Maybury gave birth to four children. She worked and never complained. She would work until a couple of weeks prior to the expected birth. A month after birth, she was back in harness, baby, then baby and toddlers in tow. She hi-jacked the office next-door to hers and converted it into a nursery. To provide assistance, Doug insisted that Maybury employ a nanny. Sharon Lawrence joined the company and went on to stay with Christine and the family until 1995, leaving on her own accord one week after Charles's, our youngest, fifteenth birthday.

Christine managed her workload and responsibilities ably assisted by her team, never muttering a complaint or becoming irritable with tiredness, well not in the office. Every night we dedicated time to the children and weekends, no matter what, we gave all to the children. We were a very, and still are, happy loving family.

The children arrived in rapid succession. Richard first born in 1977, he is a lawyer based in Winchester, married to Judith, who is also a lawyer and they have two sons, Richard and James.

In 1979 out popped Charlotte and Christine, both now married. Charlotte after a career in advertising married Christopher, who is something to do with Foreign Affairs in the Middle East. They have one girl, Christine and a boy, Charles.

Christine, who is still active in accountancy, her chosen career, married the Reverend Simon Roberts who administers his Christian beliefs in a multi-village parish in Wiltshire. They have a son, Michael.

Charles popped into the world in 1980, a mere twelve months after Christine and Charlotte. Three days after Christine disclosed her pregnancy, I caught a train to London, where I had a vasectomy.

Charles remains single and resides in Australia. He is a Regional Manager for a Pharmaceutical Company. However, he always graces us with his presence for Christmas and New Year, which translates into him honouring Christmas lunch and for the rest of the time he borrows one of the family cars, and thereafter we see very little of him.

We now act as surrogate parents, from time-to-time, for our seven grandchildren and the threat of more to come, which I complain bitterly about.

Chapter 39 – The Penultimate, Odds and Ends

Christine after the birth of Charles became a gym addict. Yoga, Pilates and Squash, and working out two or three times a week on gym machinery. We both joined a squash club playing two nights a week.

Today she is sixty-four looking forty. She had a face lift and a neck lift and does the Botox thing every so often, and unbeknown to me she sneaked off for a breast lift, the other great help, which she swears by was her decision to visit a specialist HRT doctor in London, who she consults with annually. She remains beautiful and continues to be sexually demanding (thank goodness for Cialis).

I returned to rugby managing to make a return to the first team for the final four games of the 1975 season. In September at the beginning of the 75/76 season I was rewarded for my training determination and hopefully for my skill and game-reading abilities, regaining the captaincy of the first team. I also gained two permanent supporters, Charlotte and Christine and later a horde of children including Charlotte and Brian's offspring.

The acre of land with the house became a habitat for animals of all shapes and sizes. Today it is inhabited by three goats, two pygmy pigs, an old donkey Charlotte rescued, and all are well past their prime. We also have chickens, and four cats and two dogs. On cold days the cats take over the house and the dogs only have limited access to the kitchen and utility room.

July 1989, being unemployed with four boisterous children and a nanny, we took two cars; mine towing a caravan and toured France, Spain and Portugal for six fabulous weeks. The caravan supplemented by a tent extension just managed to house the family.

We commenced our journey in Boulogne and after travelling south to Cannes we hugged the coast through France, into Spain. Keeping to the coast we traversed Spain into Portugal before cutting across Northern Spain back into France and north back to Boulogne.

The whole six weeks were directed at children pursuits, swimming, sailing, beaches, amusement parks, water parks, zoos and safari parks. We travelled five thousand miles and spent nearly a hundred hours driving. We lived off fresh food and good wines.

The children, today, still remember the holiday.

After we had dumped them off at their school, a boarding establishment, Christine and I enjoyed two weeks in the South of France making love, drinking great wine and eating superb French food. I, today, remember the love-making.

Although we were under no pressure to return to work we decided we would metamorphose, all too soon, into old people if we didn't work. Hence on the 9th May 1990 Clarke Chambers & Associates came to life.

Two partners and a girl Friday, set-up an office in Southampton, to start all over again, to build a business.

The first eighteen months were tough going during which time we lost money. Nevertheless we persevered working every hour available. Christine, a whizz with fangled-dangled computers, produced the most amazing presentations, and I, who could talk the hind-legs off a donkey, together began to win work. I will admit some well-placed contacts in a certain group, of which Maybury was a subsidiary, helped tremendously.

Once we had a half-decent portfolio with case-studies the company took off. We worked and worked, Tracy our girl Friday was magic, between the three of us we realised half a million pounds in revenue by early 1993. Thereafter, we recruited clever go-getters proffering shares in the company based on individual success.

Today, we employ twenty-one boys and girls, Christine's name for them. They all have shares in the UK based company and consequently work their socks off. The company went international in July 2004 opening an office in Dubai, followed by a second one in Qatar, which opened 2007. A third was opened in Shanghai in 2011.

The UK-based company's revenue equates to eleven million pounds per annum supplemented by another five million pounds from the international operations. The difficulty setting-up in Dubai, Qatar and Shanghai was identifying suitable sponsor companies. Nonetheless we have been extremely lucky partnering good local people.

Christine is sixty-four and I am sixty-seven, we have been married a tad over forty years, which is a long, long time to be in love, very much in love. Not as long as some, nevertheless a healthy period. We still kiss and hug, dance in our own little world, manage the odd game of squash and Christine keeps attending Yoga classes and utilising gym machinery.

Together we have agreed to work a further three years until I hit seventy. After which we are going to bed to make love and more love. I haven't told Christine.

Audrey Hepburn once said *"The beauty of a woman is not in a facial mode but the true beauty in a woman is reflected in her soul. It is the caring that she lovingly gives the passion that she shows. The beauty of a woman grows with the passing years."*

Miss Hepburn couldn't have stated truer words.

Chapter 40 – Remembering & "The End"

Many people enter into our lives and leave. The reasons they enter and leave are numerous and we don't always understand. We hear stories, but do we really understand.

Christine is absolutely certain, most definite she would not have married anyone else but me. She will swear on the Bible she knew she was going to marry me the first day we met.

Christine doesn't know how, but is adamant she realised I would become her man when I said during our very first meeting "Do I get to buy my personnel supervisor dinner?"

On the other hand I am secure in the knowledge, I would have worked like crazy, to climb the hill and plant Ruth and Richard's flag, and we would have married.

Sophie I would have definitely married, we had conquered our hill. We were deeply in love.

Christine, God Bless her is the ultimate lady, our marriage has been blissfully happy and we have been extraordinary fortunate in love and life. The wonder of her love and her beauty exhilarate me, and I will be forever grateful to whoever steered Christine into my arms.

I love Christine a million times and more today than I did on the day we married, and by God I loved her then. I have been truly blessed by knowing and loving Christine, and spending the majority of my life with her.

Our children and multitude of grandchildren represent and celebrate our life together. Either individually or collectively they also remind Christine and I of our fantastic friends and family:

Grandma Jean lived to the ripe old age of ninety-nine, still compos mentis, for which she thanked her medicinal brandy. She would have lived on but while attempting a high kick a rib snapped and pierced her lung.

Grandma Chambers was seventy-eight dying in Middlesex hospital, London. I remember vividly, when visiting her, how she thought I was father instructing me to go and prepare the pony and trap for Granddad Chambers.

My wonderful mother died 30th July, 1981, aged sixty-five from alcoholic poisoning. I cried and cried, my heart broken, for she was a magnificent mother, a very warm and caring lady.

Richard Chambers Senior, my workaholic, loving father managed to realise ninety-two dying in Winchester hospital May 2011. He, as always, had a girl-friend half his age. He was a tough man who lived life to the full and I loved him dearly.

Tina died in Glasgow. Dulcie, after five years, packed her bags and walked out on father.

Sophie died 23rd July 1971 in a road accident. Her death caused much heartbreak and much grieving. I loved her dearly and will never forget Sophie. For four years she was my one and only love. Now and again I still remember the happy times we shared.

Sadie, Christine and Charlotte's aunty, come guardian, passed away in 2011. She caught a nasty cold in the winter which she couldn't shake. She died in her sleep aged eighty-eight. She too was a wonderful caring lady.

James, Sadie's husband, I think more from a broken heart, died in his favourite chair Easter 2012. He, a generous and kind man, wasn't always with us mentally but he never forgot Sadie.

Charlotte and Brian married following a six month trial engagement, which paved the way for Brian's proposal and an eighteen month official engagement. They married on a beach in the Caribbean. Thirty-five guests arrived from the UK and three from Hong Kong to celebrate their special day. Today they own and manage a successful recruitment agency with several offices dotted throughout the UK. Their three children, Darren, Samantha and Ian all live and work overseas.

Charles, Christine and Charlotte's baby brother, after Sadie and James returned to the UK, remained in Hong Kong becoming a successful lawyer specialising in shipping. He married Angela, a beautiful Eurasian girl. They have one son, James.

Irene and Ken sold the Bear and retired to Cyprus. They both died within weeks of each other during autumn 2002. Ken suffered several heart attacks before the one that took his life, and Irene never forgetting Sophie died from a broken heart giving up on the pain she lived with after losing Sophie and then Ken. Irene and Ken were both eighty-three.

Uncle Don died unexpectedly whilst meeting his wife, Christine at Gatwick airport also from a heart attack. He was sixty-nine.

Joe, Irene's brother, now ninety-seven resides in an old folk's home in Brighton. Unfortunately, we are not regular visitors, although we do manage two sometimes three times a year, which includes the anniversary of Sophie's death, his very special niece. The other times are if we are visiting Sylvie and Ryan and their daughter Gracie.

Jessica and Simon married spring 1974. The wedding was a quiet affair, although the Wednesday evening before the wedding, Jessica, Miriam, Gertie, Sylvie and Christine did liven-up Minehead, ending-up in Butlins holiday camp. Leaving Hugo, Ryan, Simon and I to share a few bottles of wine and play poker while babysitting James.

Jessica and Simon produced two more offspring, Gertrude and Sophie. Simon unfortunately died March 2014, suffering from cancer. James, Jessica's first born, manages the farm ably assisted by Jessica.

Gertie fell in love with Guy, a guitarist with Red Destiny, whose real name was Mike Gregory. They married, lived together for two years separated and divorced. Gertie became a music producer, magazine column writer and a constant traveller, seeking the next band to rule the pop industry, another Beatles, Oasis, or similar. She still resides in London living in a very large apartment in Fitzrovia.

Gertie, Jessica, Miriam, Sylvie and Christine, over the years, regularly meet in London for a weekend shopping, sometimes to see a show or to enjoy dinner, or both, and always to talk. They, together, are always a bundle of fun.

Hugo's parents Lord Crispin and Lady Alicia passed away 2000 and 2002 respectively. Hugo is now Lord Crispin. He and I, Christine and Miriam, remain great friends. Miriam and Hugo have three children, two boys and a girl, Hugo, of course, Sebastian and Marian.

Our combined seven children became great friends and remain so today.

Mr Maybury, Gary Holdsworth, John Adams, Larry Fortune and Sharon Cummings the instigators and founders of Maybury all passed away. Many of Maybury's old guard attended their funerals paying respect to the people who provided their careers.

I am afraid I lost contact with Josie and Gwynne.

Johnny McGrath, father's long suffering business partner returned to Clifden, Galway, Eire with Teresa, his wife. Their brood have or are in the process of colonising Derbyshire. They have several companies all prefixed with McGrath, in Haulage, Coaches, Courier Services, Taxis, Warehousing and Car distribution / dealers.

Father's regular lads with the exception of Wexford and Jerry returned to Eire. Jerry died in Southampton and Wexford remains with his wife and children in the Whickham area.

Doug, after retiring died walking to his local newsagents to purchase the Sunday papers. He was sixty-eight. Christine and I were very upset. Although we didn't always see eye-to-eye he was a great friend and supporter of us both.

I attempted twice to track down Sally, my "puppy love" and the girl who was compassionate and understanding during my adolescent years. The first time was after Ruth walked out and the second following Sophie's death. I wasn't successful albeit I did learn she had become a Mid-wife serving a countryside community in Devon and married.

Carol, now a professor, married a professor. We still have the occasional meeting, which Christine and Carol's husband attend. However, she and her husband are rarely in the UK.

I did hear Sandra made it to Madison Avenue fulfilling her dream before opening an advertising agency in Sydney, Australia.

Debbie married an architect. Unfortunately I am lacking in further information.

Melissa disappeared off the map. I did call round once or twice as I promised I would when visiting mother, but her parents were vague regarding her whereabouts. Their loving daughter informed them one Saturday morning she was off to explore the world. The last they heard she was teaching English in the Mekong Valley, Vietnam.

Suzy and Cheryl, especially Cheryl remains within my memory bank.

James (ex-rugby and college) retired to Malta, following a successful career as the head of a large European corporation. We meet with Hugo periodically to thrash over old times.

Ben (ex-rugby and college) lives in Canada and is, or was a Professor of Mathematics. We rarely meet, I think three times in the past forty years.

Martin Stevens and Charlie Reynolds received handsome pay-offs and both retired. Charlie retired to Spain and Martin to Suffolk.

Allen Peters went from strength to strength and now resides permanently in Yorkshire near Malton. He married Raquel his secretary and they have two children. Allen is semi-retired, a substantial shareholder in freight shipping company.

Jimmy Johnson until taking early retirement served on the board of the larger group of which Maybury is a subsidiary. He managed Maybury with Trevor "Spike" MacDonald as his number two. Jimmy married Candy. We meet them and their two children, both boys, Danny and Jimmy three or four times a year.

Terry Hamley did well, becoming a senior manager, overall in charge for both Liverpool and Immingham and all north of England contracts, albeit he died 1999 following a short illness.

Oh yes, Maybury pressed charges against Des Barnes and Stuart Laird. Des Barnes received a twelve-month sentence and Stuart Laird received a stern warning from the court.

Amy and Terry Whitehead married and live happily in Almeria, Spain. They didn't have children due to a medical condition Amy suffers from.

There were hundreds more, Casey for example, and Mr Maybury, even Jock Inglis, other women, Catriona and Sam, they all passed through my wondrous life and I recall the instances, not all, but most.

And then there was Ruth, I understand from the following letter, which after it found its way to me via a hotel reception, I shared with Christine, made her decision and I was glad to read she lives happily and has her own children.

My Dearest Richard,

A few hours ago I touched you for the first time in over twenty years. I followed you into Harrods. I was waiting for a girlfriend when I saw you alight from a taxi. I walked behind you watching you walk remembering how tall and proud you always were. Nothing has changed-- you remain tall and proud. I continued to follow, watching your every move. You were hurrying. I guessed you were meeting your wife or a lady-friend. Close behind I followed you into the food hall. I heard a lady's voice call, "Richard over here." It was your mother.

I wanted to touch you so I purposefully bumped into you, mumbled an apology and moved away. I found a vantage point to watch you and your mother. She was looking great, not aged at all since I had met her that weekend in Freckleton. I stood there watching, my feelings in turmoil. I knew I still loved you and I was deeply regretting the day I walked out of your life, out of our lives.

I waited and waited for over an hour, watching you and your mother, waiting for you to finish your lunch, finally you did. I once more followed you as you and your mother wandered around the store. I watched as your mother tried on shoes. I watched when she purchased a handbag. I was desperate to walk over and kiss you, hold you and tell you I still loved you. I knew I wouldn't but I did want to so much.

You looked at your watch several times before saying something to your mother. You hugged her, how I wished that was me. She pecked your cheek and you headed for the door. I followed keeping ten or more yards distant. When you boarded a taxi at the rank I jumped in the one behind. Believe it or not I told the driver to follow your taxi.

The taxi followed, I followed you. Your taxi stopped at a hotel, you alighted. I gave my taxi driver twenty pounds and chased after you. I watched you enter the hotel. I crept in trying to keep concealed. A uniformed man asked if I was alright. I laughed, not out of happiness but from fright. I pointed towards you asking the man if you were staying at the hotel. He told me you were.

I failed to meet my friend instead I rushed to write this letter as you will see I used the hotel's headed paper I begged from reception, this is the third attempt.

By now you will have noticed the enclosed photograph recognising me, I hope. The man is my husband, Gerrard, yes Jewish, and our three children. The elder boy who is thirteen is christened, after you, Richard. I love him so much, unfairly much more than Rachael and Ruth the two girls.

I re-live our short ten months together quite often. I remember the rugby, the Dramatic Society, our jogging (I still jog), our beautiful flat (ha,ha), the constant beautiful love-making and the studying, the awful non-stop studying and funnily enough when we would sit together at the little table in the kitchen reading our books and making notes.

There are other times when I remember the old gang and wonder where they are now. Who could forget the laughter and the joy we enjoyed, the friendships we had and the mischief we would get up to, such warm memories.

Most of all I remember the first night we met in the Leopard, the day I moved into the flat, the first time you made love to me and with tears, the most glorious Christmas and New Year we shared in the Cotswolds. There are many other happy wonderful memories but those four are the most prominent. Don't worry I will not come knocking on your hotel door.

I have been married for fifteen years, Gerrard is a wonderful caring man, and he loves me and the children very much. We live in Surbiton in a lovely house and the children attend private schools.

Richard I am pleased to say loves Rugby, we watch him playing regularly, which sometimes revives old memories. Gerrard is a financier in the city. His office is on Leadenhall Street. I teach history, surprise, surprise, at a girl's school in Kingston. Fortunately we are comfortably off and want for very little.

I do not love Gerrard. I am extremely fond of him and like him a great deal also, which is important. He courted me with so much ardour it was difficult for me to refuse him marriage, which I have not regretted. Our life together with the children is a happy one and in many ways I have been very lucky.

Time and again I wonder if you ever married and whether you have children. I sometimes, not too often, imagine how our lives would have been if we had climbed "the hill" and reached the summit to plant Ruth and Richard's flag. Do you remember "the hill?"

The main reason I am writing is to tell you I have never stopped loving you. I know I shouldn't and I am being selfish, nevertheless, my heart and head, my muddled head forced this letter to be written. I hope, when I left you, you found it in your heart to forgive my disappearance, which I explained in the letter, poorly I think.

Do you still have the plaque? I retain the framed photographs and newspaper.

When I recall the content of the letter I realise what a stupid, stupid headstrong idiot I had become. I cried for weeks and months, forever telling myself I had made the correct decision, knowing I hadn't, but too proud to come and beg forgiveness.

Take care Richard, I love you.

My love always, Ruth

Epilogue

Life is truly a journey of discovery, destined to confront the trials and tribulations one meets along the way. It has been a challenging journey to identify who I was, and who I became. It has been a never-ending journey, at times it was heart-breaking and there were very sad periods, very sad. However, the majority has been extremely enjoyable, bringing contentment and great happiness.

I thank, from deep within, the countless people who enriched my life. Many remained sharing the journey, and some stayed a while, and many departed, but all are affectionately remembered, for they all contributed in making my journey one of development and one of discovery.

The three ladies, Ruth, Sophie and Christine, who I loved deeply and unfettered were intelligent and innovative, beautiful and wondrous, sexy and demanding, challenging and sentimental, and were the major contributors in forging my character, my persona.

The journey continues, now in its sixty-seventh year, slowly advancing towards the final phase, readying to enjoy the final years with my adored Christine, she and I together, holding hands and remembering the wonderful life we have lovingly shared.

My absolute final comment is for my lovely lady, my English rose, my porcelain beauty, my Christine:

"I have heard it said that sex is the ultimate desire of man. I refute because the love I have for Christine far outreaches the pleasure of sex. The deep love I have for Christine transforms into adoration and worship, and when Christine looks into my eyes and smiles, the love she displays is far greater and far more pleasurable, and far more sensational than sex, for sex is an act, love is body, soul and heart." Richard Chambers

Thank you, Christine, for your love, our children and for our life together.

Acknowledgements

Writing a book is demanding, frustrating and to a lesser extent nerve-wrecking. However, with a word here and there; a push in the right direction and sound advice the book finally arrives at its destination; the market place. Subsequently, this humble writer acknowledges without hesitation the combined efforts of Sam Rennie, the production manager largely responsible for "a word here and there" and publishing the book; David Walshaw the publishing consultant who would call and rejuvenate my keyboard activity. They of course were supported by Daniel Cooke, the managing director, all of whom represent New Generation Publishing, a professional proficient publishing business I am very grateful to.